Jacques the Fatalist
and His Master

❧ ❧ ❧

DENIS DIDEROT

Jacques the Fatalist
and His Master

Translated and with Introduction and Notes

by

J. ROBERT LOY

W · W · NORTON & COMPANY
NEW YORK · LONDON

W. W. Norton & Company, Inc., 500 Fifth Avenue, New York, N.Y. 10110
W. W. Norton & Company Ltd., 37 Great Russell Street, London WC1B 3NU

Published simultaneously in Canada by
Penguin Books Canada Ltd,
2801 John Street, Markham, Ontario L3R 1B4.
Printed in the United States of America.

First published as a Norton paperback 1978.

Library of Congress Cataloging in Publication Data

Diderot, Denis, 1713–1784.
Jacques the fatalist and his master.

Translation of Jacques le fataliste et son
maître.
Reprint of the ed. published by New York
University Press, New York.
Includes bibliographical references.
I. Title.
PZ3.D5617Jac   1978   [PQ1979]   843'.5   78-13064
34567890

ISBN 0-393-00903-3

For
N. L. T.

Introduction

✣ ✣ ✣

IN 1772, FINALLY, AFTER SOME TWENTY-FIVE YEARS OF PREPARATION, headaches, heartaches, and enough hard work to discourage a lesser man, Editor Diderot saw the last volume of illustrative plates for the *Encyclopédie* off the press. It is true that during those years he had somehow found time to turn out his own work—several philosophical treatises; three plays and theories about a new kind of theater, which had already had an influence in France and Germany; several amusements; art criticism, which remains an interesting genesis of a genre; lively correspondence; and those masterpieces of the novel, *The Nun* and *Rameau's Nephew*. But now, for the first time in his adult life, a weight has been lifted from his shoulders and he is free to do all the things he has complained so bitterly he could not do before. He is rapidly approaching sixty, his reputation is secure if not so brilliant as that of a Voltaire, his financial status is solvent if not lordly, thanks to the gracious interest of Catherine II of Russia, his daughter is married and not too badly, and he has learned the important lesson (absorbed more easily and naturally by a Voltaire) that a writer in the nervous pre-Revolutionary society of the *ancien régime* must not always say what he thinks even when the silence hurts and the subterfuge strikes at the heart of personal integrity.

In the fall of 1773, yielding finally to the long-extended invitation from his good friend Catherine, Empress of all the Russias and "Semiramis of the North," he starts out on the long trek to St. Petersburg with the mixed excitement and misgiving of the intelligent man with limitless interests, who yet feels that home is home and that Paris is the world—as it has been since the day a wide-eyed student from Langres first set foot in her ageless streets. After a stopover of a few months in Holland, where he writes "two or three rather gay little works," a long but fairly pleasant trip to Russia, a stay of seven months with the Empress (who does not always coincide with his Parisian dreams of the enlightened monarch), and a miserable long return, he resumes again, wearily but happily, residence in his own rue Taranne, just around the corner from the secular tower of Saint-Germain-des-Prés. Somewhere among the papers in his desk drawer—started when, finished when, it is impossible to say, but presumably completed save for minor retouches—lies a strange masterpiece, *Jacques the Fatalist and His Master.*

The French literary world will not hear of it until 1796; Diderot has learned his lesson well. And by that time *Jacques* will already have established a reputation in Germany among such aware critics as Goethe and Schiller. For the reader acquainted with the fortunes of Diderot's offspring, this is no surprise. *The Nun* (written in 1760) will wait as long as *Jacques;* so will the *Supplement to Bougainville's Voyage* (1771). The vital philosophical work, *Conversation Between D'Alembert and Diderot,* followed by *D'Alembert's Dream* (1769), will be published first in 1830. And his unchallenged masterpiece, *Rameau's Nephew,* although published after a fashion in 1823, will appear in its authentic form only in 1891, thanks to the fortuitous find of a bibliophile as he pursued the traditional sport of *flâneurs* along the bookstalls beside the Seine. Such stories could be multiplied; the works have proved almost as elusive as the author sometimes seems. Herbert Dieckmann's happy discovery of more than fifty volumes of manuscripts in 1950 is the latest example of scholarly devotion to this Denis Diderot, whose stature continues to grow.

Jacques has had a mixed fortune in France. For too long too many critics dismissed it as a disorderly and obscene work that did little credit to Diderot's reputation. For the past forty years literary criticism has seemed to point in the opposite direction, thus accompanying a general growth of Diderot's importance in French letters. The general public's interest in *Jacques* would seem to be fairly constant if one can judge by the regularity with which new editions have appeared. Since 1946 there have been at least four. In Germany and Slavic countries the work has found a public particularly in excellent translations by Widmer (German) and Boy (Polish). In English it has appeared exactly once. In 1798 an English lord commissioned a personal translation, copies of which are extremely rare. It is certainly time for English readers to know the work; that conviction is the *raison d'être* for the present edition.

When, however, the average English reader opens *Jacques* and reads the first few pages, he is apt to feel slightly dismayed. He will rapidly suspect that he is not reading a usual novel; he will probably be disconcerted by the apparent disorder of incident and the downright disregard for the propriety of verbal tenses. Let him be reassured; his reactions are normal and part of Diderot's plan. The following introductory notes will help him perhaps to see more clearly into that plan and make him a confederate of the author, without destroying his own sense of discovery, without spoiling a string of good yarns by disclosing them prematurely.

The difficulty at the outset lies in the suspicion that this is not a usual novel. Admirers of *Jacques* have long cast about for the proper identification. It has been called novel, satire, novella, conte, *récit,* and (to borrow an invention or rejuvenation of Gide for his *Caves du Vatican*) a sotie. The terms "anti-novel" and "a-novel" lend a slight extension of comprehension, but both notions are essentially so negative that they leave us where we were before. The simplest solution is to call *Jacques* a novel and to warn the reader at the same time that it cannot be judged according to the usual rules of that genre. For Diderot has written *Jacques* to show what a novel is not, what a novel could be, and, in many ways, to suggest that all that has been called the novel before should be discounted. He is not far from wrong when he insists that the eighteenth-century stereotype of the genre is the love story. It is clear from what he weaves into his book in the way of episode that he is also aware of the historical role of adventure in the novel, from the Spanish *picaro* to his own time. His own recipe—not to be taken as entirely facetious—is an indication of the various elements he acknowledges to be part of the novel's lineage: "Take eight to ten pages of the *Roman comique* (Scarron); four chapters of *Don Quixote;* a well-chosen paragraph of Rabelais; mix all this with a reasonable quantity of *Jacques le Fataliste* and *Manon Lescaut* and change these drugs as herbs are varied by substituting others possessing somewhat the same qualities." All this, Diderot has finally decided, is at least good for the vapors, although his earlier judgment had stamped novels as merely frivolous productions. The specifics collected into his recipe reveal the following elements in his analysis of the novel: adventure and the picaresque, the voyage and a loose philosophical goal, humor (probably earthy), sentiment and romance, and, finally, whatever else he thought to have put in. These elements, then, are present in the novel before we—in retrospect—assume the complete formation of the genre to be a late eighteenth-century achievement or synthesis in both England and France.

The novel is in a strange way the theme of this strange novel. Call it, if you will, a book about the novel. But the novel is not, as I hoped to show elsewhere (*Diderot's Determined Fatalist* [New York: King's Crown, 1950]), the unique theme, and therein lies the most apparent explanation of the reader's initial confusion. For there are three major themes in this experiment in the novel: the novel itself as a genre of pseudorealistic literature; the problem of fatalism, which has determined the title; and the feasibility of outlining ethical directions in a world of relative values.

What Diderot has said above serves well as an introduction to his thinking on the novel. He does know the various elements that have seemed to contribute to the contemporary novel. He does not approve of the novel in its present form as a serious literary endeavor. Still he is no fool; France cannot return to the classical tragedies and comedies of Racine and Molière, as Diderot has already made clear in his theories (and examples) of a form, neither comedy nor tragedy, to be called "drama." Just so, he is aware that romances, boudoir tales, and so-called novels have had a tremendous vogue with the reading public. If we cannot call Diderot a democrat, we can call him a practical observer, for he is vitally concerned about the increasing number of people who read. His thinking in *Jacques* on this score—when one can see beyond the intentional moments of good-natured frivolity—would seem to center on the possibility of making of the novel an honest and worthy medium. But the problems—as he is ready to admit throughout *Jacques*—are thorny ones. First of all he meets the classic obstacle of any writer pretending to convey life as it is: the problem of literary realism (and he has certainly made clear in *Jacques* that the novel, unlike other genres perhaps, must be true and real, or seem to be). Envisaging and yet skirting widely the kind of realism that will drive the later Naturalists to confuse literary invention and mechanical documentation, he casts about for the optimum method of counterfeiting reality, of attaining the lifelike as opposed to a pure actuality, which can patently not be literature. His scorn throughout the book for what he calls the ease of fabricating the usual novel must not be overlooked, but it must not blind the reader to the fact that Diderot knows the spot he is in —mocking the novel-manufacturers for sins that he himself has no tested method of avoiding, although he recognizes them as sins. One of the novelist's first technical problems is, of course, the form of his work. Shall he narrate the incidents from the relatively safe position of the omniscient author, shall he remain utterly frank and keep us aware that all the incidents are proceeding forth from his brain, or shall he turn the initiative over completely to his characters and reproduce dialogue in what is essentially a theatrical form? In reality, Diderot does all three things, as if allowing the reader to put the author's alternatives to a test. There is the usual amount of "he said" and "she said" reported by the long-forgotten narrator; there are the frequent and sometimes (intentionally) irritating intrusions of the author recalling the unwary reader to his responsibility in this matter of fiction—and just at the point where the reader would only too gladly settle for the rest of the story at any cost; and finally there is a preponderance of pages in which the characters are identified as in a stage script and left to say their lines in complete objectivity. Which form is the privileged form? None, or rather we might say that Diderot would seem not to be sure; we (the author and his reader) are still experimenting.

There is a second classic problem. Does the novelist more rapidly reveal his characters by description, by gesture, or by dialogue? On this first score Diderot, like Jacques, has little time for long-winded verbiage about inconsequential physical backdrop and even less for usual portraiture. Yet the reader must take great care here, for at every other moment in *Jacques* the author would seem to be bogging down, precisely, in description. There are obviously several kinds of description. The padding description, the cold, subjective (although the author would claim objective) portrait must go. The "still" or "frame" (to appropriate anachronistic cinema terms) must stay, for it is this occasional halt that allows the reader to size up his (and the author's) mental creations. They are only halts, and their usual function is to freeze some revealing gesture in the act of performance. Gesture, says Diderot here and in many other places, has taught more than pages of explanation. It is at moments of such plastic freezing or grouping that the reader is most likely to call a plague on the head of the translator for having suddenly, and without justification, switched to the present tense. The present tenses and the justification are in the original. In conjunction with the gesture (which is an exceptional measure, not to be overdone) comes the more usual pattern of dialogue. If there was ever a master of dialogue, it is Diderot; his lifelong interest in theater and his contemporary reputation as an irresistible conversationalist are not fables. Here the author is immediately confronted with the problem of vocabulary and expression appropriate to the character on stage, and Diderot makes it clear that he writes with the critical eye and ear of his reader directed to his page. He is not at all sure that there can ever be a perfect realistic form; there are, however, valid techniques and bad techniques. For the rest, the questionable gap between the author's best and life as it is—this is what makes the whole interpretative attempt worth the while of both writer and reader, this is what makes possible styles and techniques, this is what makes literature.

There is, however, another and nontechnical problem of the novel that haunts Diderot. The novel must entertain, must even on occasion turn frivolous and inconsequential in the sense that not every line of every page need prove something. And yet somewhere in the total effect the novel must prove something, or at least say something of universal human value. Just so does *Don Quixote,* for all its wonderful foolery, express many grim truths; just so Rabelais, for all his frolicking verbiage, convinces the reader of the potential grandeur of man; just so does Abbé Prévost, for all his seeming delight in the physical charm of Manon, manage to state the beauty and danger of passion. Whether or not this moral function of the novel will find much consent from later critics of the genre, for Diderot it is an absolute necessity. That is why of all the novelists he mentions sympathetically there is one for whom he reserves a very special niche. This is Richardson, and the special novels are *Pamela, Grandison,* and *Clarissa.* It is difficult to understand how far Diderot's ecstatic praise for his British contemporary can go until one has read his *Praise of Richardson,* written concurrently with his planning and execution of *Rameau's Nephew* and *The Nun.* Diderot would prefer to call the works of Richardson not novels but moral dramas. Although it is possible to assume that some of the heated admiration may have cooled in the years separating the *Praise of Richardson* from *Jacques* (there is Diderot's increasing awareness of another genial talent, that of Laurence

Sterne—and of that, more hereafter), this work, with all its other madcap qualities, remains a proof that the word "novel" to Diderot suggests moral message. That everything he managed to write in the fictional field has little to do in a direct way with the works of Richardson changes the situation not at all.

Jacques's second theme is frankly philosophical and, just as frankly, far from professional philosophical competence and form. *Jacques* is literature. But the theme is one vital to understanding Diderot in general and, indeed, to understanding his concern with the realism of the novel. For if the writer is to presume to create living characters, what must he assume to be the basic motivation of their actions? Or, to put it otherwise, if one would catch the vastness of life—human and cosmic—in all its ramifications, what shall he assume to be the role of the human individual projected against the vaster plane of human variety, against the possibly unfeeling and adamant terrestrial and celestial spheres? Jacques's answer is simple: everything has been written up yonder. But Diderot is not so fond of his creation as to follow him blindly; the reader would do well to follow the creator's lead.

Basically, although the reader is warned to seek the shelter of no constant in this book, Jacques is the disciple of strict fatalism and his Master is the spokesman for the necessity of free will. Jacques's fatalism, which he pretends to trace through his captain to Spinoza, contains all the usual elements of the ancient *fatum* and fortune as well as more Christian notions of Providence and predestination. He holds that a man is what he is and could not possibly be anything other without breaking the universal laws of creation. Thus, like the Nephew in *Rameau's Nephew,* where Diderot had already come to grips with the same problem, Jacques must assume that vice and virtue are without meaning and that satisfaction and regret are worthless and bothersome terms. Yet unfortunately he has his moments of inveighing against the Great Scroll on which all has been written, and he assumes at crucial moments in his own individual existence the self-confessed heresy of wishing things could be different, of regretting past actions—in short, of being happy and unhappy. The Master, who finds his lackey's strange dogma not the least of the impertinences every master must tolerate, is nonetheless intrigued by the regularity with which the doctrine seems to work. Diderot has fairly consistently assigned to the Master characteristics of the slow, plodding, reactionary mind. Man is held to enjoy free will by the most reputable and traditional of Christian authorities, and the Master, as representative of the upper class of his Christian society, can only assume that this is what any honest man ought to believe, and leave the actual discursive proof of the status quo to others more competent than himself. And yet he is strangely dissatisfied with the ammunition he can personally bring to bear against the attraction he feels for Jacques's heresy.

There are momentary shiftings of position on the part of the two protagonists throughout the book. Diderot, who is in many ways both Jacques and the Master, just as he was in *Rameau's Nephew* both the *Lui* and the *Moi,* is not apt to allow positions to lack the basic uncertainty of existence itself. But by the time the reader falls on the important philosophical showdown at the close of the book, the positions are clear. The Master, as good traditionalist, has found his stand in Descartes and Leibnitz and the best of all possible worlds. Jacques remains the Spinozist, with an occasional cursed tendency toward inconsistency. Then comes the incident whereby Jacques proves, he believes, that the Master does things without willing them. And Jacques would seem to be victor.

But, as always in this novel in which the author insists on his role as active character, there is Diderot to be heard from. Jacques was very sure that he had arranged the final scene to prove total lack of willing, indeed unconsciousness, on the Master's part. The vital word is, of course, "arranged"; and Jacques the Fatalist, far from proving his point of absence of free will and total subservience to fatality, has introduced what he himself calls "the other force" into the affair by his arranging. His psychological action, added to his physical action, has *determined* the "accident" that befalls the unwitting Master. But, as Diderot allows us finally to gather, the determinism of that victorious gesture of Jacques's is precisely what the lackey has been calling fatalism throughout. And although in the determinist's system there is no room for unmotivated or pure free will, there is the force that was provided by Jacques's planning and arrangement of the final test between Master and lackey. Call it what one will, Diderot is here talking of moral freedom and refuting both of his pseudo selves, Jacques and the Master, who so stanchly represent fatalism and free will. The whole train of Diderot's life, the thorny history of the *Encyclopédie,* and the searching of the *philosophes* in general point incontrovertibly in that direction. There can be no unmotivated free will for Diderot despite the brain-breaking apologies concocted for it on occasion by the philosophers. Yet if all is a result of the peculiar organization of matter in the universe (as scientific method of the period would have us believe), then there is clearly little possibility of improving man's lot. But Diderot and the *Encyclopédie* pretend to do just that. Man is, then, different. The stone beaten by the stick does not react, but the man will remember the stick and perhaps change. In that "perhaps" lies the lifetime dilemma of Diderot and the explanation of *Jacques.* Never before has Diderot come so close to offering a philosophical explanation for his stand. And it is in *Jacques,* an essentially droll concoction, that he chooses to attempt such a synthesis. Traditional Christian belief for Diderot is long in the past; his violent reaction to the pure materialists such as La Mettrie and (rather recently) Helvétius has made it clear that he cannot turn completely to them with a clear conscience. What then remains? There remains the essentially tenuous solution of moral freedom and determinism (material and psychological) and the necessity for believing that man can be happier as he knows more and more of the countless heretofore hidden springs of his individual and social behavior. As Norman L. Torrey has put it in his *Spirit of Voltaire:* "Moral freedom within the determinist's system depends upon relative development of the intellectual faculties, memory, imagination, and especially knowledge; for no man can choose a good of which he is entirely ignorant. But unfortunately children, lackeys, and even kings are not always intelligent." But Jacques the Fatalist sometimes weeps, and Diderot the Determinist sometimes grows discouraged. What then remains? The answer in *Jacques* is evident if not systematic. At all times when pure materialist philosophy would seem to confuse and thwart the humanist—paradox, contradiction, inconsistency notwithstanding—the humanist must remain. And after *Jacques,* the humanist remains naturally, for the humanist can be, must be, and, in Diderot, is (in others, perhaps, will eventually be) synonymous with the materialist.

The third general theme of the book—the possibility of an unrevealed ethics—falls naturally into place here. Just before writing *Jacques,* Diderot had written one of those diverting little "tales" for which he is justly famous. Either Diderot or his sometimes difficult literary executor, Naigeon, attached to this tale about Mme de La Carlière a significant subtitle: *On the Inconsistency of Public Judgment of Our Private Actions.* Heavy as it is, it sums up rather well a thread running through all Diderot's recent tales (*Mme de La Carlière, This Is No Invented Tale, Talk Between a Father and His Children, Two Friends from Bourbonne*). This has ever been a point of continual return for him from his earliest production through the *Nephew* and *Bougainville's Voyage.* It now becomes the refrain of every episode in *Jacques,* with the possible exception of Jacques's love story.

The problem, as he had already stated it in *Rameau's Nephew,* as he returns to it again and again, is simply this: If a man is the total determined product of tendencies—physical, cosmic, and psychological—that he can never hope to know in their entirety, how shall a relativistic society set up an honest code of ethical

conduct? That there needs to be such a code Diderot never doubts
for a moment. He would have easily accepted Jacques Barzun's
conclusion in his study of a later period (*Darwin, Marx, Wagner*):
"Hence the right understanding of relativism must lead not to
greater laxity everywhere, but to greater firmness in moral intention,
greater precision in intellectual, greater subtlety in esthetic." But
if he betrays therein his "bourgeois" character, he has been frank
enough to confront this bourgeois character pitilessly and painfully
with such "monsters" as the Nephew, Jacques, and a series of unusual nonconformists ranging from the criminal to the superman.
For Diderot frankly admires the outsider, the nonconformist, the
"character." Although socially censurable, the grand criminal, somewhat like the genius (a constant concern of Diderot), is certainly
more of a man than the quiet, unthinking, unproductive, solid
citizen of his static community.

All this being true, where is the thinking man to set limits of
social behavior so as to encourage the optimum development of
varied personalities? The dangerous temptation that comes again
and again to Diderot's mind in his various fictional incarnations is
that perhaps the thinking man should set no limits at all. But even
this "head that turns on its shoulders like the weather-cock in
Langres" cannot settle for anarchy. What that head will not accept,
however, is the smug and unexamined prejudices of the ruling or
elite group. From beginning to end *Jacques* is filled with icono-
clasts: Jacques himself, Gousse, Jacques's captain, M. Le Pelletier,
and, standing above all the others, Mme de La Pommeraye. At
most points Diderot is content to let either Jacques or the Master
or the reader draw his own conclusions about these strange characters, even though he is fairly certain that the Master and the
reader will probably discount Jacques's liberal tendencies in their
assumption that these people do not belong to "our group." But
after the long and masterly story of Mme de La Pommeraye's
vengeance, Diderot can no longer remain silent. He forces his way
into the affair to suggest all the other points of view to be examined

before judgment is made. Later he will play in much the same way the devil's advocate, after he has recounted with obvious relish the somewhat salacious experiences of Jacques's initial loss of innocence.

There would seem to be, at the end of *Jacques,* still no formula for intelligent ethics. There is, however, throughout the book a continual and vital reinforcement of former ideas. Ethics are admittedly a social problem to Diderot, and societies change—indeed he is devoted to encouraging them to change intelligently in proportion to the endless process of enlightenment. There is, then, no ultimate handbook, no sacrosanct measuring device. The important consideration is that ethical judgment be levied only after exhaustive examination of what is best for the particular individual in terms of his society at his particular stage of enlightenment. Rules and regulations cannot be abandoned overnight. Nor should they clothe themselves in mythical mystery and become untouchable. The conclusion of Diderot's *Supplement to Bougainville's Voyage,* where he concentrates on problems of sexual morality familiar to the post-Freudian age, has complete validity in terms of his treatment of ethics in *Jacques:*

A.—What shall we do then? Shall we return to nature or submit to laws?

B.—We must speak against insane laws until they are reformed; while waiting, we must submit to them. Anyone who infringes a bad law by his own private authority authorizes all others to infringe the good ones. There is less inconvenience in being mad among madmen than in being wise alone.

Education, examination, consideration—these and similar words ring the changes of Diderot's whole reason for existing. Can one, however, be patient enough to remain with the madmen while awaiting the encouragement, the spiritual support, and the physical numbers of other wise men? "Almost all the questions . . . of delicate moral nature are in that position," reflects Diderot. "It is easy to laugh at them, impossible not to believe them. The heart and the head are such different organs. And why shouldn't there be circumstances in which there are no means of conciliation?" The significant question, after *Jacques* and its happy foolery, has become: And why couldn't there be a conciliation, however momentary, in rationalized jesting? It will perhaps be the only one.

The three themes that form the organization of *Jacques* in no way exhaust all that can be said about the novel. They take no account of the most obvious reason for reading it—the jolly Pantagruelian chuckle; no account of the discerning reflections—this time in the best tradition of the traditional novel—of life as it is lived in eighteenth-century France: the scenes of highroad and inn, the picture of decadence and petty crime that creeps into the Master's story of his youth in Paris, Diderot's analysis of a contemporary problem, dueling, with its Freudian overtones, and the evocative account of the master-servant relationship in France. Hegel found in this easygoing connection between Jacques and his Master a symbol for the whole eighteenth century; Marx and Engels will see there suggestions of ideal management-labor relations. Others have attempted to read incipient revolution into the quarrels of the pair. They insist too much. There is in play here, between lackey and master, not revolution but rather evolution, and it is already Jacques "who has the stuff" and the Master "who has the titles." The story of Jacques and his Master is in a sense the story of the whole *philosophe* movement. But with what fear and stealth must one proceed! The Masters are afraid of the Jacques, and the Jacques cannot but distrust the Masters when their well-meant (and perhaps somewhat insolent) attempts to help are met with fearful repression. Jacques sums up rather well this fear of fear when he remarks: "All of us, in this house, are afraid of each other—which proves we are all stupid." The basis of revolution, of timeless human tragedy is there, and it would suffice for the tone of the novel to change from Jacques's spoofing to a darker hue to understand fully Thomas Carlyle's statement about *Jacques,* that "its darkest indigo shall not affright us. . . . Wearisomely crackling wit gets silent; a grim, taciturn, dare-devil, almost Hogarthian humor rises in the back-ground. Like this there is nothing that we know of in the whole range of French literature." Like this, there is much else to talk of in this "wriggling, disjointed" novel. But the reader has his basic lines of guidance; he can read and discover for himself.

As he reads, he will be reminded of many spirits akin to Diderot: Boccaccio, Rabelais, Cervantes, and the affable dean who sired *Tristram Shandy*. Here we must hesitate long enough to encourage the laying of a ghost. Since the eighteenth century, critics have accused Diderot of robbing Laurence Sterne, probably because Diderot has confessed his borrowing of several paragraphs from *Tristram Shandy*. The actual borrowing, all things considered, reduces to a passage at the beginning of *Jacques* and a passage at the close, as if Diderot had given himself the task of writing a Sternean kind of novel within that frame. Diderot clearly admired Sterne, whom he met in Paris, and he speaks to Sophie of *Tristram Shandy* as "This book, so mad, so wise, so gay . . . the Rabelais of the English." The actual copied passages are not half so important, however, as the kindred spirit he finds in Sterne. Although Diderot has already shown great admiration for Richardson and Fielding, it is in Sterne that he finds liberation from the rational, from the classical, into the many-faceted, wriggling human existence as it is lived; liberation into the seeming confusion of Time, Personality, and Relative Attitude in a world no longer limited by classic literary canon (cf. B. H. Lehmann, "Of Time, Personality, and the Author," in *Studies in the Comic* [Berkeley, Calif., 1941]). Much more than copying needs to be pointed out in these cross-Channel eighteenth-century minds; the important reflection to be made is that they envisaged in their rollicking Pantagruelism a whole new approach to life and literature, each from the standpoint of his national and cultural background. But the study of these two men has been done, and done well, in Alice G. Fredman's *Diderot and Sterne* (New York: Columbia University Press, 1955).

What is the twentieth-century reader to think of this book, which has suffered such neglect in English-speaking countries and has elicited so much abuse from some critics and such glowing praise from other creators such as Stendhal and Goethe? Goethe it was who feasted upon *Jacques* even before it was known in France: "From six o'clock until past noon I have read *Jacques le fataliste* without interruption. I read it with the delight of the Bel of Babel enjoying an immense feast, and thank God, I was able to devour such a portion with the greatest appetite, all at once, as if I were drinking a glass of water, and yet with an indescribable voluptuousness." The modern reader need not gourmandize over *Jacques* as Goethe did. But he will probably soon recognize three remarkable qualities about the book. From the point of view of style as well as of creative technique, he must soon be aware that *Jacques* is pregnant with premonitions of modern literary aims. Stream of consciousness, surrealism, flashback, and time manipulation—it is not much of a stretch of the literary imagination to foresee them all here in Diderot, whether he was fully aware of the potential of his playful experiment or not. J-J. Mayoux, in a 1936 article ("Diderot and the Technique of Modern Literature," *Modern Language Review*, XXXI), has nicely summed up such potential:

Taken as a philosophy of things in themselves, Jacques' fatalism is negligible; taken as a philosophic analysis of appearance of things as they impress us currently, as a study in direct impressionistic portraiture of life consciously reacting against literary convention, this fatalism is one of Diderot's bold excursions toward us. Thereby he outstrips the crude logic of the novelist's construction. Unpredictable chance, Jacques' true master, is the approximation of an artist-minded philosopher or a philosophically-minded artist, to reality in the concrete; a figuration of the enormous complexity of causes coming to effect from all sides in the corner segregated by the novelist. . . .

Artistically, if not metaphysically, *esse est percipi.*

The importance of that *percipi,* to both Sterne and Diderot, is a natural consequence in their Lockean century. In the constant fertility of perception and analysis *Jacques* must have another message for the present era. In an age in which conformism rapidly threatens to become the ideal, it may encourage the reader to be himself, to explore and reflect the million uncharted corners of the physical universe and human personality. The twentieth century is in a pass to echo Jacques's words: "All is reasoned, formal, stiff, academic, and flat. Oh, divine Bacbuc! Oh, sacred gourd! Oh, divinity of Jacques! Come back to our midst!"

Finally, this foolish, rhapsodical work cannot but encourage us to consider again the humanist faith of the eighteenth century, that faith in human nature and achievement too long held as naïve and irresponsible. "To Posterity and the Being who does not die"—there is the final word of the Encyclopedists, of Diderot, and of *Jacques,* and it need not change in an age that combines atomic fission and rockets to the moon with nostalgic return to unexamined religious faith. The Jacques and the Diderots—except in those off moments that plague the flesh—would have felt no qualm as they entered the atomic age. As Lewis Carroll's White Queen has made clear, the important thing is to consider, "Consider anything, only don't cry." For *Jacques* and Diderot during those off moments have a faith that is not just a whistling in the dark, but rather an advised whistling in the dark. And for moments when even to the devoted humanist the dark seems to endure past hope, there is finally the chuckle of *Jacques.* Every age—and perhaps particularly our own—must have its renewal of Pantagruelism.

J. ROBERT LOY

Geneva, N.Y.
1958

NOTE ON THE NORTON EDITION

❧ ❧ ❧

THIS REISSUE OF *Jacques the Fatalist* HAS BEEN EMENDED TO FOLLOW the text of the critical edition of *Jacques le fataliste et son maître* by Simone Lecointre and Jean Le Galliot (Paris-Geneva, Droz, 1976) with additional corrections by Jacques Proust (*Bulletin de la Société Française du XVIIIᵉ Siècle,* Jan., 1978). Division into chapters is my own as well as a few minor preferences of readings.

J. ROBERT LOY

City University of New York
1978

Contents

Masters and servants are both tyrannical; but the masters are the more dependent of the two.

G. B. SHAW

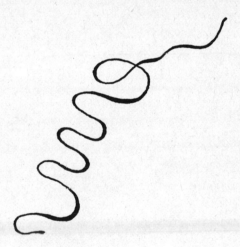

LAURENCE STERNE

Jacques the Fatalist
and His Master

❖ ❖ ❖

1

❧ ❧ ❧

HOW HAD THEY MET? BY CHANCE, LIKE EVERYONE ELSE. WHAT were their names? What does it matter to you? Whence had they come? From the nearest possible spot. Where were they going? Do we ever know where we're going? What were they saying? The master said nothing, and Jacques said that his captain said that everything that happens to us down here, good or bad, was written up yonder.

The Master. That's saying a lot.

Jacques. My captain added that every bullet that left a gun had its billet.

The Master. And he was right.

After a short pause, Jacques cried: "The devil take the tavern-keeper and his tavern!"

The Master. Why give your neighbor to the devil? It's not Christian.

Jacques. It's just that while I am getting drunk on his bad wine, I forget to take our horses to the watering trough. My father notices and becomes angry. I shrug my shoulders; he takes a stick and lays on a little heavy across my shoulders. A regiment was passing on its way to camp before Fontenoy.¹ Out of spite, I join up. We arrive and the battle is on.

The Master. And you receive the bullet with your name.

Jacques. You have guessed it—wounded in the knee. And God only knows the good and bad adventures brought on by that shot. They hold together neither more nor less than the links of a curb bit. For example, without that shot in the knee, I don't think I should ever have been in love, nor lame.

The Master. So you were in love, then?

Jacques. Was I ever!

The Master. And because of a bullet shot?

Jacques. Because of a bullet shot.

The Master. You have never told me a word about it.

Jacques. I dare say I have not.

The Master. And why not?

Jacques. Because it couldn't have been told any sooner or any later.

The Master. And the time to learn of your loves has now come?

Jacques. Who knows?

The Master. Well, in any case, start on them.

Jacques started the story of his love affairs. It was after dinner, the weather was sticky, and the master went to sleep. Night overtook them in the middle of the fields, and there they are, lost. There is the master in a terrible rage, falling on his lackey with a whip, and that poor devil saying with each blow: "That one, too, must have been written up yonder."

You see, reader, that I am well on my way, and that it is completely up to me whether I shall make you wait one year, two years, or three years for the story of Jacques's loves, by separating him from his master and having each of them go through all the vicissitudes that I please. What's to prevent my marrying off the master and making him a cuckold? Shipping Jacques off to the islands? Guiding his master to the same place? Bringing them back to France on the same ship? How easy it is to fabricate stories! But I'll let them both off with a bad night and you, with this delay.

Dawn arrived. They are back on their horses, and on their way.—And where were they going?—Now that's the second time you ask me that question and the second time that I tell you: "What's that to you?" If I get into the story of their travels, good-by to the story of Jacques's loves.—They rode on for a while in silence. When each had gotten over his peevishness a bit, the master said to his lackey: "Well, Jacques, just where were we in your love story?"

Jacques. We were, I believe, about at the rout of the enemy army. Everyone flees, is pursued, thinks of himself. I remain on the battlefield, buried under a prodigious number of dead and wounded. The next day, they threw me on a cart along with a dozen others to be taken to one of our hospitals. Ah, sir, I believe there is not a crueler wound than that on the knee.

The Master. Come now, Jacques; you exaggerate.

Jacques. No, by heaven, sir, I do not. There are in a man's knee I know not how many bones, tendons and other things whose names escape me.

A nondescript peasant was following them on horseback, riding a girl behind. He had been listening to them, cut in and said: "The gentleman is right."

They didn't know to whom this "gentleman" was addressed, but it was badly taken both by Jacques and the master. Jacques said to the prying interlocutor: "And what business is that of yours?"

"It happens to be my business; I am a surgeon—at your service —and I am going to show you."

The woman he was carrying behind said: "Doctor, let's continue on our way, and leave these gentlemen who don't want to be shown."

"No," said the doctor, "I want to show them, and I shall—I shall prove to them . . ."

And, turning about to start his demonstration, he pushes his companion, makes her lose her balance, and tumbles her to the ground, one foot caught in the flap of his coat and her skirts piled up over her head. Jacques dismounts, frees the poor soul's foot, and lowers her skirts. I don't know if he started by pulling down the skirts or by freeing the foot, but, to judge her condition from her outcries, she was seriously injured. And Jacques's master said to the doctor: "You see? That's what it is to show things!"

To which the doctor retorted: "That's what happens when you

don't want to have it shown."

Meanwhile Jacques said to the woman, either still fallen or picked up: "Console yourself, old dear, for it's neither your fault, nor the doctor's fault, nor my fault, nor the fault of my master. It's just that this day, on this road, at the present hour, it was written up yonder that the doctor would gossip, that my master and I would be surly, that you would end up with a bruise on your head, and that your backside would be shown."

What couldn't this adventure become in my hands, if I took it into my head to tease you! I should make that woman an important character—the niece of the neighboring village curate. I should stir up the peasants of that village; I should prepare all sorts of combats and love affairs, for, actually, this peasant woman was beautiful beneath her petticoats. Jacques and his master had noticed that. Love has not always awaited such an attractive situation. Why couldn't Jacques fall in love a second time? Why couldn't he be a second time the rival, and the preferred rival at that, of his master?—You mean that had already happened once?—What? more questions! Don't you want Jacques to get on with his love story? For the last time, make yourself clear: would you like him to, or wouldn't you? If you would, then let's put our peasant girl back on the horse behind her companion, let them go and we'll get back to our two voyagers. This time, it was Jacques who started the conversation and said to his master: "Now, that's just the way of the world; you who were never wounded in your life, and know nothing about a shot in the knee, you try to tell me—me with a shattered knee and limping these twenty years."

The Master. You might be right. But thanks to our impertinent doctor, here you are still on the cart with your comrades, still far from the hospital, far from recovery, and far from falling in love.

Jacques. However it please you to think of it, the pain in my knee was excessive; it became still worse from the hardness of the cart, and the rough roads; and at each bump I would let out a sharp cry.

The Master. Because it was written up yonder that you would cry out.

Jacques. Most assuredly. I was losing all my blood, and would have been a dead man if our cart, the last in line, hadn't stopped in front of a thatched cottage. There I ask to be let down. They put me on the ground. A young woman who was standing in front of the door of her cottage went into her house and came back almost immediately with a glass and a bottle of wine. I hastily downed one or two draughts. The carts in front of us got under way again. They were about to throw me back on with my comrades, when, holding for dear life to the woman's skirts and to everything around me, I protested that I would not get up there again, and that, were I to die, I liked better to do it here in this spot than two miles farther along. As I concluded those last words, I fell into a dead faint. When I came to, I found myself undressed and tucked in a bed which stood in one of the corners of the cottage. Standing about me were a peasant, the head of the house; his wife, the woman who had come to my aid; and several small children. The woman had moistened the corner of her apron in vinegar and was rubbing my nose and temples.[2]

The Master. Oh, you sorry fellow! You rascal! You wretch! I see what's coming.

Jacques. My master, I think you see nothing of the kind.

The Master. Isn't this the woman you're going to fall in love with?

Jacques. And suppose I had fallen in love with her? What about it? Are you ever your own master as to falling or not falling in love? And if you are in love, can you act as if you aren't? If that had been written up yonder, I should have already told myself all that you're preparing to say; I should have boxed my ears; I should have beat my head against the wall; I should have pulled out my hair—the result would have been more nor less and my benefactor would nonetheless have been a cuckold.

The Master. But in following your line of reasoning, there is not a single crime that you couldn't commit completely free of remorse.

Jacques. What you are objecting to there has more than once ruffled my poor head, but however that may be, I come back always to the words of my captain: "Everything either good or bad which happens to us down here in this world is written up yonder." Would you be knowing, sir, some way to erase that writing? Can I *not* be me? And being me, can I act other than myself? Can I be me and somebody else? And since the very moment I came into the world, has there been a single instant when that wasn't true? You may preach as much as you like, and your reasons may perhaps be good ones, but if it's written in me or up yonder that I shall find them bad, what would you have me do?

The Master. There's one thing I keep thinking about—and that's whether your benefactor would have been a cuckold because it was written up yonder, or whether it was written up yonder because you would make your benefactor a cuckold.

Jacques. Both were written at one and the same time, side by side. It was all written together. It's like a great scroll which unfolds little by little.

You can imagine, reader, just how far I could push this conversation on a subject about which so much has been said and written for two thousand years, without, for that, advancing the argument the slightest bit. If you are not too happy with what I do say about it, be much happier about what I leave unsaid.

While our two theologians disputed without understanding each other—which can happen so easily in theology—night came on. They were crossing a stretch of country that had always been dangerous and was all the more so now that misery and bad administration had endlessly multiplied the number of evildoers. They stopped at the most miserable of inns. Two cots were set up for them in a room, so partitioned and latticed as to be half-open on all sides. They asked for supper. They were given puddle water, black bread, and sour wine. The landlord, the landlady, their children, and the servants—everything had a sinister air about it. They heard nearby the boisterous laughter and unbridled merriment of a dozen brigands who had preceded them there and taken all the food. Jacques was rather calm; his master was far from it. He, poor fellow, paraded his worry all about him, while his lackey devoured bits of the black bread and swallowed a few glasses of the bad wine with a grimace. At this point they heard a knock at their door; it was a servant. Their insolent neighbors had forced him to bring to them, on one of the brigands' own soiled dishes, all the bones of a chicken the rogues had eaten. Jacques, indignant, takes his master's pistols.

"Where are you going?"

"Let me go."

"Where are you going, I say?"

"To teach those scoundrels a lesson."

"Do you know there are a dozen of them?"

"Were there a hundred, the number makes little difference so long as it is written up yonder that there aren't enough of them."

"The devil take you and your impertinent formula."

Jacques escapes from his master, goes into the outlaws' room, a cocked pistol in each hand. "Quick, now, get into those beds," he said, "and the first one that moves—I'll blow his brains out." Jacques's manner and tone of voice were so convincing that these rascals, who cared as much for life as any honest man, got up from the table without a word, undressed, and went to bed. The master, uncertain about the outcome, awaited his lackey in fear and trembling. Jacques came back loaded down with the clothes of the brigands, having snatched them up lest the fellows be tempted to get up again. He had blown out their light and double-locked the door. The key dangled close to one of the pistols. "And now, sir, we have only to barricade ourselves by pushing our beds against that door, and sleep peacefully." And he set about pushing the beds, relating coolly and succinctly to his master the details of his expedition.

The Master. Jacques, what a devil of a fellow you are! You believe, then . . .

Jacques. I neither believe nor disbelieve.

The Master. But if they had refused to go to bed?

Jacques. That was impossible.

The Master. And why?

Jacques. Because they didn't refuse.

The Master. If they had gotten up?

Jacques. It would have been for better or for worse.

The Master. If . . . if . . . if . . . if.

Jacques. If . . . if! If the sea boiled, there would be, as they say, a lot of cooked fish. What the devil, sir, a little while ago you believed that I was in great danger, and nothing could have been more false. Now you think you're in great danger and nothing, again, is more false, perhaps. All of us, in this house—we are afraid of each other, which proves we're all a bunch of fools.

And, while holding forth thus, there is Jacques undressed, in bed, and sound asleep. His master, finally taking his turn at a bit of black bread and a drink of the bad wine, with an ear cocked in all directions, looked on the snoring Jacques and said: "What a devil of a fellow he is." And taking his lackey for an example, he stretched out on his own pallet, where he did not sleep as well as the model. At the first glimmer of daybreak, Jacques felt a hand nudging him. It was his master who was softly calling: "Jacques, Jacques!"

Jacques. What?

The Master. It's daylight.

Jacques. That's possible.

The Master. Get up then.

Jacques. Why?

The Master. So we can get out of this place as fast as possible.

Jacques. Why?

The Master. Because we're in a bad spot here.

Jacques. How could you know that, or if we should be better off elsewhere?

The Master. Jacques?

Jacques. Good Lord! Jacques! Jacques! What sort of a devil of a fellow are you?

The Master. What sort of a devil of a fellow are you really? Jacques, my friend, I beg of you . . .

Jacques rubbed his eyes, yawned several times, stretched his arms, got up, dressed leisurely, pushed back the beds, left the room, went downstairs, walked to the stable, harnessed and saddled the horses, woke up the landlord who was still asleep, paid the bill, kept the keys of the two rooms—and our friends are on their way.

The master wanted to be off at a great trot; Jacques, at a walk, and, again, in keeping with his system. When they were rather far from their unhappy shelter, the master, hearing something jingling in Jacques's pocket, asked him what it was. Jacques answered that it was the keys to the two rooms.

The Master. And why didn't you give them back?

Jacques. Well, if they have to break down two doors—our neighbors' door to free them and ours to get at their clothes—that will give us time.

The Master. Very fine, Jacques, but why gain time?

Jacques. Why? I'm sure I don't know.

The Master. But if you wanted to gain time on them, why are you going at this slow walk?

Jacques. It's just that, not knowing what is written up yonder, we know neither what we want nor what we do; so we follow our fancy which we call reason, or our reason, which is very often but a dangerous fancy and which turns out sometimes well, sometimes badly. My captain believed that prudence is a supposition in which experience authorizes us to survey the circumstances where we find ourselves as causes of certain effects to be hoped for or feared in the future.

The Master. And you understood something out of all that?

Jacques. Certainly. Bit by bit I got around to understanding his language. "But," he used to say, "who can flatter himself that he has had enough experience? The very one who has boasted of being the most experienced—has he never been duped? And then, too, is there a man capable of appreciating the position in which he is momentarily situated? The calculation that goes on in our heads and the calculation laid down on the register up yonder are quite different calculations. Is it we who lead Destiny, or is it Destiny that leads us? How many very wisely planned projects have failed and how many more are doomed to fail? How many mad projects have succeeded, and how many will continue to succeed?" That's what my captain kept repeating to me after the capture of Bergen-op-Zoom and Port-Mahon,[3] and he added that prudence does not assure us of a good outcome, but that it consoles and excuses us for a bad one. And so the night before an encounter he slept under his tent just as if he were in garrison, and he went off to battle as to a ball. It's of him you would have said: "What a devil of a fellow!"

The Master. Could you tell me what a wise man is and what, a fool?

Jacques. Why not? A fool, a fool—let's see—a fool is an unhappy man; and therefore, a happy man is a wise one.

The Master. And what is a happy man and an unhappy man?

Jacques. Now that's easy. A happy man is one whose happiness is written up yonder; and, therefore, the man whose unhappiness is written up yonder is unhappy.

The Master. And who wrote up there your happiness and unhappiness?

Jacques. Well, who wrote the Great Scroll where all is written? A captain, friend of my own captain, would have given a tidy sum to know. My captain wouldn't have given one iota, nor would I, for what good would it do? Should I avoid for all that the hole where I am to break my neck?

The Master. Yes, I think you would.

Jacques. Well, I don't. For then one of the lines on that Great Scroll containing all truth and nothing but the truth would have to be false. Could it be written on the Scroll: "Jacques will break his neck on such and such a day," and then Jacques wouldn't break his neck? Can you conceive how that could be possible, whoever may be the author of the Great Scroll?

The Master. There are a great many things to be said on that score. . . .

As they arrived at that point in their discussion, they heard noises and shouting at some distance behind them. They turned their heads and saw a troop of men armed with long sticks and pitchforks advancing on them with great speed. You are going to think that it was the people from the inn, the lackeys, and the brigands of whom we have spoken. You are going to think that when they had broken down their doors for lack of keys that morning, the brigands imagined that our two travelers had made off with their belongings. Jacques believed as much, and muttered through clenched teeth: "A curse on the keys and on the fancy or reason which made me carry them off! A curse on prudence," etc., etc. You are going to think that this little army will fall upon Jacques and his master, that there will be a bloody action, blows of clubs exchanged, pistols shot off. It's completely up to me whether it happens or not, but then, good-by to the truth of this story, good-by to the history of Jacques's loves. Our two travelers weren't followed at all; I don't even know what went on in the inn after their departure. They continued on their way; going always without knowing where, even though they knew fairly well where they wanted to go; deceiving boredom and fatigue with silence and chatter, as is the habit of those who walk, and sometimes even of those who sit still.

It's quite evident that I'm not writing a novel for I neglect to use what no novelist would fail to use. He who takes what I am writing for the truth will be, perhaps, less in error than he who takes it for a fable.

This time, it was the master who first broke the silence and who started with the familiar refrain: "Well, Jacques, and the story of your loves?"

Jacques. I don't know any more where I was. I've been interrupted so often that I should do as well to start all over again.

The Master. No! No! Having come out of your fainting spell at the door of the cottage, you were now in a bed, and surrounded by the people who lived there.

Jacques. Ah yes, very good! The most urgent thing was to get a surgeon, and there was not one to be had for a good league about. The good man had one of his children mount a horse, and he sent him to the closest place. Meanwhile the good woman had heated some raw wine, torn up an old shirt of her husband's, and my knee was cauterized, covered with compresses and wrapped in bandages. They put a couple of grains of sugar, stolen from the ants, in a portion of the wine which had served for my knee-dressing, and I swallowed it. Then they begged me to have patience. It was late; they sat down and ate supper. Supper finished—and still the child did not return, still no surgeon. The father fell into a mood. He was a naturally gloomy fellow, and sulky with his wife. Nothing ever pleased him. Harshly, he sent his other children off to their beds. His wife sat down at a bench with her distaff. As for him, he paced back and forth, and in pacing, he tried to start a quarrel on every score. "If you had been at the mill like I told you . . ." and he finished his sentence by shaking his head in the direction of my bed.

"We'll go tomorrow."

"It's today you should have gone, just like I told you. And the rest of that straw which is still atop the barn, when are you ever going to take it up?"

"We'll get it tomorrow."

"What we have is about gone, and you would have done a lot better to take it up today, like I told you. And then that pile of barley spoiling in the granary, I'll wager you haven't even thought about turning it."

"The children did it."

"You should have done it yourself. If you had been in the granary, you wouldn't have been at the door."

Betimes there arrived first one surgeon, then a second, and then a third with the little boy of the house.

The Master. Which leaves you as well fixed for surgeons as a dog for fleas, and St. Roch for hats.[4]

Jacques. The first one was away when the little boy arrived at his house, but his wife had gotten in touch with the second, and the third one had accompanied the boy. "Well, good evening, colleagues," says the first. "Here we are then!" They had come in haste, and they were warm and thirsty. They sit down at the table from which the cloth had not yet been taken. The wife goes down to the cellar and comes back with a bottle of wine. The husband kept grumbling under his breath: "Ah, what the devil was she doing there at the door?" They drink, talk of the sicknesses in the neighborhood, start out on an enumeration of their patients. I remonstrate, and they say: "In just a minute we'll be with you." After that bottle, they ask for a second, to be added to my bill; then it's a third one, and a fourth one, likewise to be added to my bill. And with each bottle, the husband came back to his first plaint: "Ah, what the devil was she doing at that door?"

To what great advantage would any other writer have turned these three surgeons—their conversations over the fourth bottle, the multitude of their miraculous cures, the growing impatience of Jacques, the bad humor of the peasant, the remarks of our country Aesculapii over Jacques's knee and their differing opinions: one holding that Jacques was a dead man if they didn't hasten to cut off the leg, the other insisting that they had to extract the bullet and the bit of clothing which had followed it, and save the poor devil's leg! Meanwhile, you would have seen Jacques sitting on his bed, beholding his leg mournfully, bidding it fond farewells, just as we have already seen one of our generals do betwixt surgeons Dufouart and Louis.[5] The third surgeon would have stood idly by until the quarrel started between the other two, until from invective they arrived at blows.

I shall spare you all these things, which you may find in novels, in ancient comedy, and in society. When I heard the peasant cry in reference to his wife: "What the devil was she doing at the door?" I couldn't help thinking of Molière's Harpagon,[6] when he said to his son: "What was he doing in that galley?" And then I realized that it wasn't enough to be real, but that you also had to be amusing, and that this was the reason why people would keep on saying "What was he doing in that galley?" and why my peasant's expression, "What was she doing at the door?" would never become proverbial.

Jacques did not treat his master with the same taste and reserve that I show for you; he omitted not the slightest detail, even at the risk of putting his master to sleep a second time. Although he may not have been the most skilled, at least it was the most vigorous of the three surgeons who finally took over the patient.

So you ask me, aren't you going to draw forth scalpels before our eyes, cut up flesh, make blood flow, and show us a real surgical operation? In your opinion, don't you think that would show good taste? All right, all right then, we'll skip the operation; but, at least, you'll let Jacques say to his master, as he did actually: "Ah, sir, it's a terrible business to repair a broken knee!" And maybe you'll allow his master to reply as before: "Come now, Jacques; you exaggerate." But what I shall not leave unsaid for all the gold in the world, is that scarcely had the master emitted this impertinent reply to Jacques than his horse slips and falls flat, and the master's knee strikes hard against a pointed rock, and there he is crying at the top of his lungs: "Oh, I am dead! My knee is broken!"

Now even though Jacques, the best-natured kind of fellow you could want, was tenderly attached to his master, I should still like to know what went on way down deep in his soul, if not in the very first moment, at least once he was well assured that the fall would have no tragic results. I wonder if he could keep back a slight feeling of joy at this accident which would teach his master just what a knee-wound was like. One more thing, reader, and I should really like you to tell me. I wonder if maybe the master wouldn't have preferred to be wounded—even more seriously wounded—in any other spot but the knee, or if he was more sensitive to the pain than to the shame.

When the master had recovered a bit from his fall and his pain, he remounted and, spurring his horse five or six times, rode off like a flash. Jacques's mount did as much, for there was between the two animals the same intimacy as between their riders; they were two pairs of friends.

When the two horses, winded, fell back to their normal pace, Jacques said to his master: "Well, sir, and now what do you think of it?"

The Master. Of what?

Jacques. Of a knee-wound.

The Master. I agree with you completely; it is one of the worst.

Jacques. That is to say, if it's *your* knee?

The Master. No, no, no. Yours, mine, all the knees in the world.

Jacques. Oh, my master, my master, you haven't thought that out well! You must know that we never pity anyone but ourselves.

The Master. What a mad idea!

Jacques. Ah, if only I knew how to say what I know how to think! But it was written up yonder that I should have things in my head, and that the words would not come out.

Here Jacques got entangled in metaphysical speculations, very subtle and, perhaps, very true. He was trying to show his master that the word "pain" was without meaning, and that it started to mean something only when it recalled to our memory a sensation that we had already experienced. His master asked him if he had ever given birth.

"No," replied Jacques.

"And you think that the pains of labor are great?"

"Why certainly!"

"Do you pity a woman in travail?"

"Very much."

"Then sometimes you pity someone other than yourself."

"I pity all those who twist their arms, pull their hair, and cry with pain for I know from experience that you don't do that unless you're suffering. But for the particular pain of a woman in travail, I don't pity her, for I don't know what it is, thank God. However, to get back to a pain that we both know now, namely, the story of my knee, which has become yours by reason of your fall. . . .

The Master. No, Jacques; say rather the story of your loves which have become mine by reason of past disappointments.

Jacques. Well, we find me washed and a little comforted, the surgeon gone, and the peasant couple retired and in their bed. Their room was separated from mine only by some picketing on which they had stuck grey paper decorated with some colored figures. I couldn't sleep and I heard the woman saying to her husband: "Let me alone; I'm in no mood for jollity. A poor unfortunate soul dying at our very door!"

"Woman, you can talk of all that later."

"No, I tell you, I'm not going to. If you don't stop, I'm going to get up. How could I possibly enjoy that when my heart is so heavy?"

"Oh now, if you're going to make me coax you, you'll be the loser."

"I'm not trying to be coaxed; it's just that sometimes you grow so hard! That sometimes . . . that . . ."

After a short pause, the husband resumed and said: "There now, woman, admit that by misplaced compassion you have put us in a fix that it is practically impossible to get out of. It's been a bad year; we'll scarcely be able to look out for ourselves and the children. Grain is unreasonably dear. And there's no wine! It would be different if a man could get work, but the rich are cutting back, and the poor do nothing. For every day of work you get, you lose four. And nobody pays what he owes; creditors are enough to drive a man to desperation—and this is the time you choose to take in an unknown man, a stranger who will stay here as long as it pleases God, or the surgeon who most certainly will not be in a hurry to cure him, for those fellows make a sickness last as long as they can. And he hasn't a sou, yet he'll double, even triple our expenses. Now then, woman, how are you going to get rid of the fellow? Come, talk to me, woman, and make some sense."

"Who can talk sense to you?"

"You're always saying I'm moody and that I'm a grouch. Well, who wouldn't be? Who wouldn't grumble? There was still a little wine in the cellar; God only knows how fast that will go. Those doctors drank more last evening than we and the children would have drunk in a week. And the surgeon won't come for nothing. Who's going to pay him?"

"Oh yes, that's all very nicely said. And so, because we're already in misery, you make me another baby, as if we didn't have enough already."

"Oh no, not that."

"Oh yes! I'm sure I'm going to be pregnant."

"Oh, you say that every time."

"And I've never been wrong when my ear itched after; and I feel an itching there now like never before."

"Your ear doesn't know what it's talking about."

"Don't you touch me! Let my ear go! Stop, I tell you, man; are you crazy? You're going to make yourself sick!"

"No, no; that hasn't happened since Midsummer's Eve."

"You're going to keep at it, until—and then in a month you'll take it out on me as if it were my fault."

"No, no."

"And then in nine months it will be even worse."

"Oh, no, no."

"And you'll take the blame?"

"Yes, yes."

"And you'll remember? You won't say what you said all the other times?"

"Yes, yes."

And so from no, no, to yes, yes, this man holding it against his wife for having given in to a feeling of compassion.

The Master. Just the reflection I was making to myself.

Jacques. It is clear that the husband was not very consistent; but then he was young, and his wife, pretty. There are never more children made than in hard times.

The Master. Nothing multiplies like the rabble.

Jacques. One more child is nothing for them; charity feeds it. And then, too, it's the only pleasure that costs nothing. They console themselves at night, at no expense, for the calamities of the day. However, for all that, the fellow's reflections were right. Whilst I was thinking as much to myself, I felt a violent pain in my knee and I cried, "Ah, my knee!" And the husband cried, "Ah, my wife!" and the wife cried, "Ah, my husband! But—but—that man who is there!"

"Well, what about that man?"

"He must have heard us."

"And if he has?"

"I shan't be able to look at him tomorrow."

"And why not? Aren't you my wife? And am I not your husband? Does a woman have a husband and a man a wife for nothing?

"Oh, oh, owwwww."

"Well, now what?"

"My ear!"

"What about your ear?"

"It's worse than ever."

"Go to sleep; it'll go away."

"Oh, I couldn't. Aha, my ear, my ear!"

"My ear, my ear—that's very easy to say."

I shall not relate what happened between them, but the wife, after having whispered many times, in a low precipitate voice, "my ear," ended up by muttering in jerky syllables, "My eeee-ruh. Myyyy eeee-ruh." And following that last eeee-ruh, a certain something joined to the silence made me suspect that the trouble in her ear had been quieted in some way or the other, it matters not how. It made me happy. But then, think of her!

The Master. Jacques, put your hand on your heart and swear to me that it's not this woman you fell in love with.

Jacques. I swear it.

The Master. Worse luck for you.

Jacques. Worse luck or better. You seem to think that women who have an ear like hers listen better.

The Master. I think it is written up yonder.

Jacques. Well, I think it is written right afterwards that they don't listen to the same one for long, and that they are just as easily inclined to lend an ear to someone else.

The Master. That is possible.

And this sets them off into an interminable quarrel on women: one maintaining they were good, the other bad; and they were both right; one stupid, the other witty; and they were both right; one false, the other faithful; and they were both right; one that they were stingy, the other that they were generous; and they were both right; one ugly, the other beautiful; and they were both right; one gossipy, the other discreet; one frank, the other deceptive; one ignorant, the other enlightened; one virtuous, the other licentious; one mad, the other reasonable; one tall, the other small; and they were both right.

On such a dispute they could have circled the globe without stopping one minute or for that matter without agreeing, but at this point they were met by a storm that forced them to get on their way.—Where?—Where? Reader, you have a most embarrassing curiosity! And what the devil is it to you? Suppose I had said that it was toward Pointoise, or Saint-Germain or Notre-Dame de Lorette, or Santiago de Compostela, would you be any further advanced? If you insist, I shall tell you that they were traveling toward—yes, why not?—toward a tremendous castle on whose front could be read the inscription: "I belong to nobody and to everybody. You were here before coming, and you will still be here when you have left."—Did they enter this castle?—No, because either the inscription was false or they were already there before entering.—But, at least, then, they came out of it?—No, because either the inscription was false or they were still there after leaving.—And what did they do while there?—Jacques said what was written up yonder; his master said what he pleased: and they were both right.—What sort of crowd was there?—Mixed.—What did they say?—Oh, some truth and lots of lies.—Were there any witty people?—Where aren't there some? Along with some cursed questioners whom they fled like the plague. What most shocked Jacques and his master while they walked about there . . . —Oh, they walked about, then?—They did nothing else, except when they were seated or lying down.—What most shocked Jacques and the master was to find there some twenty brazen persons who had snatched up the most sumptuous rooms, where they were almost always still pinched for space; they claimed, against all common right and the true sense of the inscription, that the castle had been left to them alone as clear property. With the help of a certain number of pricks in their pay, they made another gang of *coglione* in their pay believe it; these rascals were all ready—for a little cash —to hang or assassinate the first person who would have dared contradict them. However, in the days of Jacques and his master, they sometimes dared to.—With impunity?—Well, that depends.

You are going to say that I'm joking and teasing, and that, not knowing what to do next with my travelers, I jump over into allegory, the usual resort of sterile minds. I shall sacrifice my allegory, and all the richness I might draw therefrom; I shall agree to whatever you say, if only you stop bothering me on the point of this last shelter sought by Jacques and his master—whether they got to a big city or whether they slept with women of easy virtue;

whether they passed the night with an old acquaintance who entertained them as best he could; whether they took refuge with some mendicant friars, where they were ill-fed and ill-lodged for the love of God; whether they were received into the house of an important personage, where they lacked every necessity in the midst of all that is superfluous; whether they set out next morning from a large inn where they had paid dearly for a bad supper served up in silver plate, and for a night passed between damask curtains and damp, wrinkled sheets; whether they accepted the hospitality of a country curate with the usual allowance,[7] who ran off for contributions from the barnyards of his parishioners in order to have an omelet and a chicken fricassee; or whether they intoxicated themselves on excellent wines, enjoyed great feasting and appropriate indigestion at some wealthy Bernardine abbey—for, however much all of this seems equally possible, Jacques would not have agreed. There was really possible only the thing that had been written up yonder. What is true, then, is that from whatever spot you choose to have them leave, they had not gone more than twenty paces when the master said to Jacques (after having, naturally, as was his custom, taken his pinch of snuff): "Well, Jacques! And that story of your love life?"

Instead of replying, Jacques cried: "To the devil with my love story! Now haven't I just gone off and left behind . . ."

The Master. Left what?

In answer, Jacques turned all his pockets inside out and searched everywhere hopelessly. He had left his wallet under the bolster of his bed, and had no sooner disclosed this fact to his master than the latter cried: "To the devil with your love story! I've gone and left my watch hanging on the chimney place."

Jacques didn't need to be coaxed; immediately he turned about, and returned at a leisurely gait, for he was never in a hurry, to . . .
—The great castle?—No, no; from the different spots I have enumerated above, choose whichever one best fits the present circumstances.

Meanwhile, his master kept riding ahead. But here we have the master and his lackey separated, and I don't know which one I should choose to follow. If you want to follow Jacques, be very careful, as the hunting for the watch and the wallet might become so long and complicated that he wouldn't be able to rejoin his master for a long while, and since the master is the sole confidant of his loves, good-by to Jacques's love story. If, on the other hand, you abandon him in his search for watch and wallet, and choose to keep the master company, you will be polite but very bored. You don't know that type of fellow. He has very few ideas in his head; if he happens to say something that makes sense, it's either from memory or momentary inspiration. He has two eyes like you and me, but you don't know most of the time if he is seeing through them. He doesn't sleep, but he doesn't stay awake either; he lets himself exist, that's his usual function. This automaton kept going on, turning from time to time to see if Jacques were coming; he would get off his horse and walk a bit, get back on, go about a quarter league, dismount again and sit down on the ground, the bridle of his horse under his arm and his head bent over on his hands. When he tired of that position, he would get up and look off into the distance to see if Jacques were coming. No Jacques! Then he grew impatient, and scarcely knowing if he were talking or not, said: "The scamp, the dog, the rascal! Where is he, and what is he doing? Does it take all this time to pick up a watch and wallet? I shall beat you unmercifully. Oh yes, I shall beat you; that much is certain." Then he would look for his watch in his vest pocket where it was not to be found, and that was the last straw, for he did not know what might happen to him without his watch, his snuffbox, and Jacques. These were the three big resources of that life which was spent in taking snuff, looking at the time, and questioning Jacques, and these, in all possible combinations. Deprived of the watch, he was thus reduced to the snuffbox, which he opened and closed every other second, as I do myself when I am bored. What remains in my snuffbox in the evening is in direct proportion to the amusement, or inverse proportion to the boredom, of my day. I beg you, reader, to familiarize yourself with this type of writing borrowed from geometry, for I find it very exact and shall use it often.

Well, have you had enough of the master? And since his valet is not coming to us, would you like us to go to the valet? Poor Jacques! At the very instant we are talking about him, he was crying painfully: "So it was written up yonder, then, that on one and the same day I should find myself taken into custody as a highwayman, on the point of being led away to prison, and accused of having seduced a girl!"

As he had been slowly approaching the castle—no, the place where they last slept, one of those itinerant merchants called peddlers, passes by and cries out to him: "My fine gentleman and lord, garters, belts, watch chains, snuffboxes of the latest style, rings, watch fobs. A watch, sir, a watch, a handsome gold watch, engraved, double case, like new." Jacques replies: "Well, I am looking for one, but it's not yours." And he continues on his way, still at a walk. But going along, he believed that he saw written up yonder that the watch the man had offered him was his master's watch. He retraces his steps and says to the peddler: "My friend, let's see your gold watch; I have a strange idea that it might be what I want."

"My word," said the peddler, "I shouldn't be a bit surprised, for it's lovely, very lovely, made by Julien Le Roi.[8] I have had it only for a short time; I picked it up for a song, and I'll give you a good price on it. I like the system of small profits repeated very frequently. But the way things are nowadays, a man is pretty miserable. I shan't have another windfall like this for a good three months. You seem like a gay young blade; I had rather you profited by it than another."

While talking, the merchant had placed his trunk on the ground, opened it, and drawn out the watch which Jacques recognized immediately and without the slightest astonishment for he never hurried and was seldom astonished. He looked at the watch rather intently, then said to himself: "Yes, that's it." To the peddler, he said: "Yes, you are right; it is beautiful, very beautiful and I know it's a good one." Then, slipping it into his vest pocket, he remarks to the merchant: "My friend, I thank you kindly."

"What do you mean? You thank me kindly?"

"Just that, for it's my master's watch."

"I don't know your master; this watch is mine for I have bought and paid for it."

And grabbing Jacques by the collar, he starts to take back his watch. Jacques leans over to his horse, takes one of his pistols, and pushing it against the peddler's chest, says: "Draw back, or you're a dead man." The peddler, terrified, looses his hold. Jacques gets back on his horse, and continues at a walk toward the village, saying to himself: "Well, now that the watch is recovered, let's see to the wallet." The peddler hurriedly closes his pack, swings it onto his shoulder again, and follows Jacques shouting: "Stop thief, thief, murder, help, help!" It was the harvest season; the fields were covered with workers. They all drop their forks, gather about the merchant, and ask him where the thief and murderer is.

"There, there, down there."

"What, you mean that fellow ambling toward the city gate?"

"Yes, that's him."

"Come now, you're crazy; a thief doesn't dawdle like that!"

"Well, he is one, he is one, I tell you; he just took my gold watch by force."

The people didn't know what to believe—the shouts of the peddler or the calm pace of Jacques. "In any case, my friends," added the peddler, "I am a ruined man if you don't help me; that watch is worth thirty louis if it's worth a sou. Help me, he's carry-ing off my watch, and if he starts to go faster, my watch is lost."

If Jacques was not in a position to hear this conversation, he could at least easily see the crowd, and for all that he went no less slowly. With the hope of a reward, the peddler prevailed upon the peasants to run after Jacques. Thus, a multitude of men, women and children were running and crying: "Thief, stop thief, murder!" plus the peddler following them as closely as the burden with which he was weighed down would allow, and likewise screaming: "Robber, thief, murder!"

They have gone into the city, for it is in the city that Jacques and his master had spent the night before, I just now remember. The inhabitants leave their houses, join with the peasants and peddler, all of them crying in unison: "Stop thief, robber, murder!" They catch up with Jacques all at the same time. The peddler throws himself on Jacques and the lackey lets fly a kick with his boot which turns the peddler rolling over, still crying all the while: "Rascal, wretch, varlet, give back my watch; and even if you give it back, you'll be hanged nonetheless." Jacques, keeping calm and cool, addressed the crowd, which was swelling each second, and said: "There is a magistrate of the police here; take me before him, and there I shall prove to you that I am not a cheat and that this fellow might very well be one. I took a watch from him— that is true; but this watch is my master's. I am not completely unknown in this place, for yesterday evening we arrived here, my master and I, and we spent the night at the house of Monsieur the lieutenant-general, his old friend." Now if I haven't told you before that Jacques and his master had passed by way of Conches, and that they had lodged with the lieutenant-general of that place, it's because all that hasn't occurred to me before. "Take me to the lieutenant-general's," said Jacques as he swung his feet to the ground. You could see him there at the center of the group—him, his horse, and the peddler. They walk on and stop at the lieutenant-general's door. Jacques, his horse, and the peddler enter, Jacques and the peddler grasping each other by the lapel. The crowd remains outside.

During this time, however, what was the master doing? He was napping at the side of the highroad, the lead of his horse passed under his arm. The animal was grazing the area about the sleeper as far as his halter would permit.

As soon as the lieutenant-general recognized Jacques, he cried: "So it's you, my poor Jacques. And what brings you here alone?"

"My master's watch; he left it hanging on the chimney corner, and I found it in the sack of this fellow. Also my wallet, which I left under my pillow and which will be found if you so order."

"And may that be written up yonder!" added the magistrate.

On the spot, he had his household called together, and immediately the peddler, pointing out a strange tall fellow of nasty mien, newly installed in the house, said: "There's the fellow who sold me the watch."

The magistrate, putting on an air of severity, said to the peddler and to his lackey: "You both deserve the galley: you for having sold the watch, you for having bought it." Then, to the lackey, he said: "Give back the money to this fellow, and drop your uniform on the spot." Then to the peddler: "Be quick and get out of this section, if you don't want to get strung up here for the rest of your days. Both of you are in a business which can bring only trouble. And now, Jacques, your wallet." The woman who had taken it, showed up without being called; she was a big woman, extremely well put together. "It is I who took the purse, sir," she said to her master, "but it was not at all stolen, for he gave it me."

"I gave you my wallet?"

"Yes."

"Well, it's possible, but the devil take me if I remember it."

The magistrate said to Jacques: "Come now, Jacques; let us not go deeper into this thing."

"But, sir!"

"She is pretty, and agreeable from what I can see."

"But, sir, I swear to you . . ."

"How much was there in the wallet?"

"Close to nine hundred and seventeen livres."

"Now, by heaven! Nine hundred and seventeen livres for one night; that's too much for both of you. Give me the wallet."

The big girl gave the wallet to her master, who pulled out a coin of six francs. "Here," he said, throwing it to her, "here is the price of your services; you are worth more probably, but for someone other than Jacques. I hope you'll get twice that much every day but not in my house, you understand? And you, Jacques, hurry, remount, and get back to your master."

Jacques bade farewell to the magistrate and withdrew without replying, but as he went, he said to himself: "What a shameless wench! The hussy! It was written up yonder that someone else would sleep with her, and that Jacques would pay. Come now, Jacques, cheer up; aren't you only too happy to have found your wallet and your master's watch, at such little expense?"

Jacques gets back on his horse and pushes through the crowd that had gathered at the courtyard gate of the magistrate, but since he took it ill that so many people should think him a rascal, he pretended to draw his watch from his pocket and look at the time; then he spurred his horse, who, being hardly accustomed to it, started off with all the more speed. His custom was to let the horse go at its fancy, for he found it as inconvenient to stop the animal when it galloped as to goad it when it dawdled. We think we lead Destiny, but it is always Destiny that leads us, and Destiny, for Jacques, was everything that touched or came close to him: his horse, his master, a monk, a dog, a woman, a mule, a crow. And so his horse carried him at top speed toward his master, who was dozing at the side of the road, the lead of his horse passed under his arm, as I have told you. Then the horse had been on the other end of the halter. When Jacques arrived, the halter was still in position, but the horse was no longer there. Some scoundrel had apparently slipped up on the sleeper, gently cut the lead, and led the animal off. At the noise of Jacques's horse, the master awoke and his first words were: "Come here, come right here, and about time! I'm going to . . ." At which point he was overtaken by a yard-long yawn.

"Yawn, yawn on, sir, to your heart's content," said Jacques to him, "but where is your horse?"

"My horse?"

"Yes, your horse."

The master, realizing at that very moment that someone had stolen his horse, was about to fall upon Jacques with the bridle thong when Jacques said to him: "Easy, easy, sir, I am not in a mood to be beaten today; I may take the first blow, but I swear that at the second, I shall spur my horse and leave you stranded here."

This menace from Jacques suddenly eased off the master's fury, and he said, in a calmer tone: "And how about my watch?"

"Here it is."

"And your wallet?"

"Right here."

"You took long enough."

"Not too long for all I've done. Listen well to my tale. I went off, got myself beaten, roused up all the peasants of the countryside, panicked all the inhabitants of the city, was taken for a thief, was led before the judge, and underwent two hearings; I almost had two men hung, had a lackey put out, a serving girl dismissed, and they managed to convince me that I had slept with a creature I never in my life saw before, but whom, nonetheless, I seem to have paid. And then I came back."

"And me, while I was waiting for you . . ."

"While you were waiting for me, it was written up yonder that you would fall asleep, and that your horse would be stolen. Well, sir, think no more on it! Here's one horse lost and perhaps it's written up yonder that he will be found."

"My horse, my poor horse!"

"You could go on wailing until tomorrow, but it won't change things."

"What are we to do?"

"I'll take you on in back, or, if you prefer, we'll take off our boots, put them on the saddle of my horse, and we'll continue on foot."

"My horse, my poor horse!"

They decided to continue on foot, the master wailing from time to time, "My horse, my poor horse," and Jacques embroidering on the summary of his adventures. When he came to the part about the girl, his master said: "Is it really true, Jacques? You didn't sleep with that girl?"

Jacques. No, sir.

The Master. And yet you paid her?

Jacques. Definitely.

The Master. Just once in my life I was more unfortunate than you.

Jacques. You paid after having slept?

The Master. You have guessed it.

Jacques. Won't you tell me about that?

The Master. Before getting into the story of my loves, we've got to get out of yours. Well, Jacques, on with those loves, which I shall take for the first and only ones of your life, despite your adventure with the servant of the lieutenant-general of Conches; for even had you slept with her, you wouldn't have become a lover for that. Every day we sleep with women we don't love and don't sleep with women we do love. But . . .

Jacques. Well, but . . . but what?

The Master. My horse! Jacques, my friend, don't get angry; put yourself in my horse's place. Suppose I had lost you and tell me whether you wouldn't respect me more if you heard me crying: "Jacques, my poor Jacques"?

Jacques smiled and said: "I think I had gotten to the conversation between my host and his wife the night following my first dressing. I rested a bit. The peasant and his wife got up a little later than usual."

The Master. I should think so.

Jacques. When I awoke, I opened the curtain quietly and saw my host, his wife, and the surgeon in a secret conference near the window. After what I had heard during the night, it was not hard to guess what was going on. I coughed. The surgeon said to the husband: "He's awake; neighbor, go down to the cellar; we'll have a round, it steadies the hand; afterwards I'll pull off his dressing and we'll see about the rest."

The bottle brought and emptied—for, in terms of the medical art, "have a round" equals "empty at least one bottle"—the surgeon came up to the bed and asked: "How was your night?"

"Not bad."

"Let's see your arm. Good, good, the pulse is not bad at all, there's practically no fever left. Now we must see to that knee. Come here, Mother," he said to the wife, who was standing at the foot of my bed behind the curtain, "give us a hand." She called one of her children. "It's not a child we need here; it's you. A false movement would cost a month's effort. Come closer." She approached with lowered eyes. "Take that leg, my girl; I'll take the other. Easy, easy—toward me; a little more toward me. My boy, a little turn of your body to the right—to the right, I said, and there we are."

I gripped the mattress with two hands; I gritted my teeth. Sweat poured from my face. "My boy, it's not easy."

"I can feel that."

"There you are. Mother, let loose that leg, take the pillow and bring up that chair and put the pillow on it. Too near—a little farther. Here, boy, give me your hand; hold me tight. Old girl, get in there between the wall and the bed and hold him under the arm. Excellent. I say, my good man, is there anything left in the bottle?"

"No."

"Come here and take your wife's place and have her go get another. Good, good, fill it up. You, woman, leave your husband where he is and come here next to me." She again called one of her children. "Ah, devil take it, I already told you, a child is not what we need. Get down on your knees and slip your hand under the calf of his leg. Old girl, you're shivering as if you've had a bad spell; come now, courage. The left under the lower thigh . . . there . . . above the bandage. Very good!" And so the surgical stays are cut, the bandage unrolled, the dressing removed, and my wound uncovered. The surgeon feels over and under, on the sides, and each time he touches me, he says: "The stupid ass, the dolt, and he calls himself a surgeon! That leg, a leg to be cut off. It'll last as long as the other; I'm here to tell you that. . . ."

"I'll get well?"

"I've cured lots of others."

"I'll walk again?"

"You'll walk."

"Without a limp?"

"That's something else again; what the devil, my friend, how you do go on! Haven't I saved your leg? And besides, if you limp, what does it matter? Do you like to dance?"

"Very much."

"Well, even if you walk a little less well, you'll dance all the better. Mother, the hot wine. No, the other first; one more little glass, and your dressing will be all the better for it."

He drinks; they bring the warm wine, they bathe me with it, put back the dressing, stretch me out on the bed, entreat me to sleep if I can, close the curtains, finish the open bottle, bring up another, and the conversation between the peasant, his wife, and the surgeon is resumed.

The Peasant: "Neighbor, will it take long?"

The Doctor: "Very long—to your health."

The Peasant: "But how long? A month?"

The Doctor: "A month! Make it two, three, four, who knows? The kneecap is nicked, the femur, the tibia. . . . To yours, old girl."

The Peasant: "Four months! Good Lord! Why did we have to

take him in? What the devil was she doing at that door?"

The Doctor: "To mine, for I did a good job."

The Wife: "Husband, there you are at it again. That's not what you promised me last night. But just wait, you'll soon be harping on it again."

The Peasant: "Well, just tell me then, what are we to do with this fellow? It wouldn't be so bad at that if only it weren't such a bad year!"

The Wife: "If you like, I could go see the priest."

The Peasant: "If you set one foot in that direction, I'll thrash you soundly."

The Doctor: "Why so, neighbor? My wife goes there often."

The Peasant: "That's your business."

The Doctor: "To my god-daughter! How is she these days?"

The Wife: "Very well."

The Doctor: "Come, neighbor, to our wives, yours and mine, for they are two good women."

The Peasant: "Yours is a little more clever and she wouldn't have done such a stupid . . ."

The Wife: "Well, there are always the gray sisters; I suppose we could send him there."

The Doctor: "Come now, my good woman! A man, a man in amongst the sisters! Then too, there would be a little difficulty, not much bigger than your finger. Let's drink to the sisters, they're good enough girls."

The Wife: "What difficulty is that?"

The Doctor: "Your husband doesn't want you to go to the priest, and my wife doesn't want me to go to the sisters. But, come, neighbor, one more draught, that will give us some ideas maybe. Have you questioned this man? Perhaps he is not without funds."

The Peasant: "What, a soldier?"

The Doctor: "A soldier has a father, mother, brothers, sisters, relatives, friends, someone on this earth. Have another drink, then move away and let me handle this."

2

❧ ❧ ❧

SUCH, TO THE LETTER, WAS THE CONVERSATION OF THE SURGEON,
the peasant, and his wife. But what other coloring shouldn't I have
been able to give the scene by introducing a felon amongst these
good people? Jacques would have been seen, that is, you would
have seen Jacques in the act of being torn from his bed and thrown
on the highway or into a slough.—Why not killed?—Killed, no.
For I should easily have known how to call someone to his aid;
this someone would have been a soldier of his own company; but
that would have smelled to high heaven of *Cleveland*.[9] The truth!
The truth!—The truth [you will say] is often cold, uninteresting,
and flat; for example, your latest recounting of Jacques's medical
dressing is true, but what is there interesting in it? Nothing.—I
agree.—If you must be true, it should be in the manner of Molière,
Regnard, Richardson, and Sedaine,[10] for truth has its interesting
sides, which one can catch if he has genius.—Yes, if he has genius,
but suppose he lacks it?—If he lacks that, then he ought not to
write.—And suppose that, unhappily, you were like a certain poet
whom I sent to Pondichéry?—What about this poet?—Well, this
poet . . . but, reader, if you interrupt me, and if I interrupt myself
at every turn, whatever shall become of Jacques's love story? Listen
to me and forget the story of the poet. The peasant and his wife
drew off . . . —No, no, no! The story about the poet of Pondichéry!—The doctor came up to Jacques's bed . . . —The poet
of Pondichéry, the poet of Pondichéry!!—One day, there came to
me a young poet, as happens every day . . . but, reader, what
possible connection does this have with the journey of Jacques the
Fatalist and his master?—The story of the poet of Pondichéry!—
After the usual compliments on my genius, my mind, my taste,

my good deeds, and other like remarks (of which I believe not a word even if I have been receiving them for twenty years, and, who knows, perhaps sincerely), the young poet drew a paper from his pocket. "They are verses," he tells me. "Verses?" "Yes, sir, about which I hope you will be so good as to give me your opinion." "Do you like truth?" "Yes, sir, and I demand it of you." "You shall know it directly." "What, you are stupid enough to believe that a poet comes to you looking for the truth?" "Yes." "And that you should tell it to him?" "Certainly." "Frankly and without circumspection?" "Of course, for the most cleverly contrived circumspection would be but a crude insult; faithfully interpreted, it would mean that you are a bad poet and, since I don't think you're man enough to hear the truth, an insipid fellow to boot." "And such frankness has always succeeded with you?" "Almost always." I read the verses of my young poet and then say to him: "Not only are your verses not good, but it's fairly clear to me that you will never write any good ones." "Well, then, I shall have to write bad ones, for I couldn't possibly keep myself from doing it." "Now there is a terrible curse! Consider, sir, into what ridicule you are going to fall! Neither the gods, nor men, nor the booksellers have ever forgiven mediocrity in a poet; 'tis Horace who said it."[11] "I know it." "Are you rich?" "No." "Are you poor?" "Very poor." "And you want to add to your poverty the ridicule of being a bad poet! You will have lost your whole life and you'll be old . . . old, poor, and a bad poet . . . ah, sir, what a role you choose for yourself!" "I realize that, but I'm drawn on nonetheless." [Here Jacques would have cried: "It was written up yonder."] "Have you a family?" "I have." "Who are they?" "They are jewelers." "Would they do something for you?" "Perhaps." "Well, then, see your relatives, suggest to them that they advance to you a packet of gems. Sail for Pondichéry; you will make bad poetry en route, once arrived you will make a fortune. Once your fortune is made, you can come back and write as many bad poems as you please, provided you don't have them printed, for you wouldn't want to ruin anyone."

It must have been about twelve years after I had given this advice that the young man reappeared; I didn't recognize him. "It is I, sir," he said, "the man you sent to Pondichéry. I went there and gathered together about a hundred thousand francs. I have come back and have begun again to write verses and here are some I've brought for you to see. Are they still just as bad?" "Still bad, but your fate is decided and I consent now to your continuing to write bad verses." "That's precisely what I intend to do." [12]

And the doctor approached Jacques's bed, but the latter gave him no time to speak. "I have heard everything," he said. Then, turning to his master, he added . . . he was going to add, when his master stopped him. Tired of walking, he sat down alongside the road, his head turned toward a traveler approaching them from the side, leading his horse by the bridle.

You are going to believe, reader, that this is the horse stolen from the master; and you would be wrong. That's what would happen in a novel, sooner or later, in this way or some other; however, this is not a novel; I've told you before, I think, and I repeat it. The master said to Jacques: "Do you see that man coming toward us?"

Jacques. Yes, I see him.

The Master. His horse looks like a good one.

Jacques. I was in the infantry; I wouldn't know.

The Master. Well, I was an officer in the cavalry, and I know.

Jacques. So?

The Master. And so I should like you to go propose to the man that he give us his horse; for money, naturally.

Jacques. That's rather a crazy idea, but I'll go. How much do you want to offer?

The Master. Up to a hundred écus.

Jacques, after having admonished his master not to fall asleep, goes to meet the traveler, proposes the transaction, pays him and brings back the horse. "Well, Jacques," says his master, "if you have your presentiments, you see I also have mine. This is a fine horse; a horsetrader would have sworn he was faultless, but then in the matter of horses, all men are horsetraders."

Jacques. And in what aren't they horsetraders?

The Master. You will take this horse and give me yours.

Jacques. Agreed.

So there they are, both mounted, and Jacques says: "When I left home, my father, my mother, my godfather had all given me something, each according to his limited means; and I had held in reserve five louis, of which my elder brother Jean had made me a present when he left on his unhappy trip to Lisbon." [13] Here Jacques started to cry, and his master started to point out to him that everything was written up yonder. "It is true, sir; I have told myself a hundred times; and yet, nonetheless, I can't keep from crying."

So Jacques goes on weeping and sobbing all the more, and his master takes his pinch of snuff and looks at the time. Then, putting the reins between his teeth and mopping his eyes with both hands, Jacques continued: "Out of the five louis from Jean, my enlistment money, and the presents of my family and friends, I had made an emergency fund from which not one sou had been taken. I found this little nest egg very handy. Don't you agree, my master?"

The Master. It was impossible for you to stay longer in the peasant's cottage?

Jacques. Even had I paid.

The Master. But why should your brother want to go packing off to Lisbon?

Jacques. It seems to me that you are deliberately attempting to lead me astray. With all your questions, we shall have circled the globe before getting to the end of my love story.

The Master. What does that matter, so long as you talk and

I listen? Aren't they the two important points? You are scolding me when you should be thanking me.

Jacques. My brother had gone to look for peace in Lisbon. Jean, my brother, was a witty lad; that's what led to his downfall. It would have been better for him, had he been stupid like me. But that was written up yonder. It was written that a mendicant friar of the Carmelites would come to our village to solicit eggs, wool, hemp, fruit, and wine every season, would stay at my father's house, would debauch my brother, Jean, and that Jean, my brother, would take the robe.

The Master. Your brother, Jean, was a Carmelite?

Jacques. Yes, sir, and a discalced one.[14] He was active, intelligent, clever; he was the consulting lawyer of the village. He knew how to read and write, and from early youth he took up deciphering and copying old manuscripts. He tried all occupations of the Order — porter, cellarman, gardener, sacristan, steward's aid, and banker; at the rate he was going, he would have made a fortune for all of us. He married off two of our sisters and several other girls in the village, and he married them well. He never passed through the streets that fathers, mothers, and children didn't run up to him and call: "Good day, Brother Jean; how are you today, Brother Jean?" It is certain that when he entered a house, the benediction of the Lord entered with him; and equally certain, if there was a daughter, that two months after his visit she would be married. Poor Brother Jean! Ambition lost him. The steward of the house to whom he had been given as aide was old. The monks said that my brother had formulated the plan of succeeding the old steward on his death and that toward that end, Jean had upset the whole archive room, burned old records, and drawn up new ones so that when the old fellow died, the devil himself could not have seen through the succession deeds of the community. If they needed a document, they lost a month looking for it, and then very often did not find it. The fathers uncovered Jean's trickery and his plan; they took the thing seriously, and Brother Jean, instead of becoming steward as he had flattered himself, was put on bread and water and thoroughly disciplined until he had surrendered to another brother the key to his records. Monks are implacable. When they had drawn out of Jean all the information they needed, they made him a coal carrier in the laboratory where they distill the Carmelite water. Brother Jean, up to then banker of the order and aide to the steward, now a coal man! Brother Jean was a spirited fellow; he could not stand this descent in splendor and importance, and waited only for the chance to escape such humiliation.

It was at this point that there arrived in the same monastery a young priest who was accepted as the marvel of the whole order on the bench and in the pulpit; he was called Father Angel.[15] He had beautiful eyes, a handsome face, arms and hands worthy of modeling. And so he preaches and preaches, confesses and confesses; and the old confessors are deserted by their pious ladies and the ladies become attached to Father Angel. The eves of Sundays and great feast days, the shop of Father Angel is surrounded by men and women penitents, and the older fathers wait in vain for trade in their now deserted places of business, which naturally hurt them greatly. But, sir, suppose I stopped there on Brother Jean's story and took up again my own loves; that would be perhaps gayer.

The Master. No, no. Let's have a pinch of snuff, see to the time, and continue.

Jacques. All right, since you want it that way.

But Jacques's horse was of another mind; for suddenly he takes the bit in his teeth and hurls himself into a ditch. Jacques tries in vain to squeeze his knees together and shorten the reins, but from the bottom of the ditch the obstinate animal darts out and begins to climb a small hill, where he pulls up short and where Jacques, looking about, finds himself under a gallows.

Any other than myself, reader, would not fail to garnish this gallows with its appropriate game, and to shock Jacques with a gloomy realization of his surroundings. If I told you this, you would believe it perhaps, for stranger things happen, but the thing would be nonetheless false. The gallows was empty.

Jacques gave his horse time to catch his breath; the horse of his own accord went back down the hill, came up out of the ditch, and brought Jacques back beside his master, who said to him: "Ah, my friend, what a scare you gave me. I took you for dead. But you are dreaming; what are you thinking of?"

Jacques. About what I found up there.

The Master. And what did you find?

Jacques. Gallows, a yardarm.

The Master. The devil you say! That's an ill omen; but, then, think of your doctrine. If it's written up yonder, you may do as you will, you will be nonetheless hanged, dear friend; and if it's not written up yonder, then the horse has lied. If that horse is not divinely inspired, then he's subject to crazy whims; you'll have to be careful.

After a moment's silence, Jacques rubbed his forehead and shook his ears, as you do when you want to be rid of an unhappy thought; then he continued abruptly: "The old monks held a meeting amongst themselves and resolved, at whatever price and by whatever means, to rid themselves of the young upstart who humiliated them. Do you know what they did? My master, you aren't listening."

The Master. I'm listening, I'm listening; go on.

Jacques. They got the ear of the porter, who was an old rascal like themselves. This old rascal accused the young father of having taken liberties with one of his religious ladies in the guest salon, and swore under oath that he had seen them. Perhaps it was true, perhaps it wasn't. Who knows? What is amusing, however, is that the day after the accusation the prior went on record to some doctor as being satisfied with the remedy administered to that knave of a porter for one of Venus' maladies. My master, you aren't listening to me, and I know what is distracting you; I'll wager it's that gallows.

The Master. I can't deny it.

Jacques. I catch you studying my face; do you find me a forbidding sight?

The Master. No, no.

Jacques. Which is to say, yes, yes. Well, if I frighten you, we have only to go our separate ways.

The Master. Come now, Jacques, you're out of your mind; aren't you sure of yourself?

Jacques. No, sir, I am not. And who *is* sure of himself?

The Master. Every virtuous man. Doesn't Jacques, my honest Jacques, feel horror for wrongdoing? Come, Jacques, let's finish this dispute and get on with your story.

Jacques. As a consequence of the calumny or slander of the porter, they felt justified in perpetrating a thousand deviltries, playing a thousand nasty tricks on this poor Father Angel, who seemed to be losing his mind. Then they called in a doctor whom they had corrupted, and who attested to the fact that the monk was mad and needed to breathe his native air once again. If it had been only a question of putting Father Angel away or shutting him up, it would have been easy enough. But amongst the pious ladies whose darling he was, there were several important ones to be reckoned with. They talked to these ladies about their director with hypocritical pity: "Alas, poor Father Angel! It's really too bad! He was the guiding star of our little community!"—"What has happened to him?"—To this question the brothers replied only with deep sighs, lifting their eyes to heaven. If the ladies insisted, they would lower their heads and say no more. To this mockery they would sometimes add: "O Lord! What shall become of us? And yet, sometimes he has his surprising moments, flashes of genius. Perhaps he will come around, but there is very little hope indeed. What a loss for religion!" Meanwhile the evil-doing redoubled. They stopped at nothing to bring Father Angel to the point of madness where they reported he had already arrived, and they would have succeeded if Brother Jean had not taken pity on him.

What more is there to say? One evening as we were all sleeping, we heard someone knocking on our door. We got up and opened the door to Brother Jean and Father Angel, both of them disguised. They passed the next day in our house; the day after, at dawn, they decamped. They were going away well supplied, for Jean said to me as he was leaving: "I have married off your sisters; if I had stayed on in the monastery only two more years in the position where I was, you would be one of the richest farmers in the county. But all has changed, and here is all I can do for you. Farewell, Jacques; if we run into luck, the Father and I, you shall profit by it." Then he dropped into my hand the five louis of which I have spoken, with five more for the last of the village girls that he had married off and who had just given birth to a big, bouncing boy as like Jean as two peas in a pod.

The Master (his snuffbox open and his watch back in his pocket). And what did they have to do in Lisbon?

Jacques. Look for an earthquake that couldn't happen without them—be crushed, swallowed up, burned, just as it was written up yonder.

The Master. Oh monks, those monks!

Jacques. The very best of them is not worth much.

The Master. I know that better than you.

Jacques. Did you ever have anything to do with them?

The Master. Some other time I'll tell you all that.

Jacques. But why are they so evil?

The Master. I think probably it's because they're monks. And now let's get back to your love story.

Jacques. No, sir; let's not get back.

The Master. You no longer want me to hear about it?

Jacques. Oh yes, I still want to tell it, but fate doesn't want me to. Haven't you seen how as soon as I open my mouth, the very devil steps in and some incident always comes along to cut me off. I shall not finish the story of my loves, I tell you, for it's written up yonder.

The Master. Try, my friend.

Jacques. Perhaps if you were to start the story of *your* loves, that would break the spell and then afterwards mine would go more smoothly. I have this strange idea in my head that that's how it must work; you see, sir, sometimes it seems to me that Fate talks to me.

The Master. And do you always find it worthwhile to listen?

Jacques. Why, of course. Take, for example, the day it told me your watch was on the peddler's back.

The master started to yawn; in yawning he struck the edge of his snuffbox; in hitting his snuffbox he looked off into the distance; and in looking off into the distance, he said to Jacques: "Don't you see something there to your left?"

Jacques. Yes, and I'll wager it's something that doesn't want me to continue my story, nor you to start yours.

Jacques was right. As this thing came toward them and they went toward it, the two progressions in inverse direction shortened the distance. And soon they saw a wagon draped in black, drawn by four black horses covered with black cloth which went from their heads right down to their feet. Behind, there were two lackeys in black followed by two others dressed in black, each astride a black horse caparisoned in black. On the seat of the coach was a coachman in black, his hat dangling down and encircled with a long piece of crape which extended along his left shoulder. This coachman, his head leaning to one side, let his reins float loosely and directed his horses much less than they directed him. Our two travelers arrived at the side of the funeral coach. At this instant Jacques lets out a cry, falls rather than gets off his horse, pulls his hair, rolls on the ground and cries: "My captain! My poor captain! It is he, I know it, for those are his arms." There was, as a matter of fact, a long coffin under a funeral drape on the coach, and on the drape was painted a sword with a cordon, and beside the coffin, a priest, breviary in hand, was walking along chanting. The hearse continued its way, Jacques following it in tears, his master following

Jacques, swearing, and the lackeys assuring Jacques that this was indeed his captain's funeral, for he had died in a neighboring city and they were carrying him to burial in his family grounds. Ever since this soldier had lost in death another soldier friend, a captain of the same regiment, and had thus been deprived of the satisfaction of dueling at least once a week, he had fallen into a melancholia that had finished him in two months. Jacques, after having paid his captain the appropriate tribute of praise, sorrow, and tears, excused himself to his master, got back on his horse, and they rode off in silence.

But for God's sake, author (you beg of me), where were they going?—But for God's sake, reader, I shall reply, do you ever know where you're going? Take you, for instance, do you know where you're going? Must I recall the adventure of Aesop? His master, Xantippe, told him one evening—either in winter or summer, for the Greeks bathed in all seasons—"Aesop, go to the baths; and if there aren't many people, we shall bathe." Aesop leaves. On the way he meets the Athenian patrol. "Where are you going?" "Where am I going?" replies Aesop, "I'm sure I don't know." "Ah, you don't know; then march off into prison." "Well," said Aesop, "and didn't I tell you that I didn't know where I was going? I meant to go to the baths, and here I am, going to prison." Jacques followed his master just as you follow yours; his master followed his own master just as Jacques followed him.—But who was Jacques's master's master?—Fine question! Does one ever lack a master in this world? For every one of them, Jacques's master had a hundred more, just like you. But among so many masters for Jacques's master, there must have been some who were not satisfactory, for from one day to the other he changed masters.— Well, he was human after all.—Yes, an impassioned man like yourself, reader; a curious man, like yourself, reader; a questioning man like yourself, reader; an importunate man like yourself, reader.— And why did he question?—That's a fine question! He questioned so as to learn and then repeat; just like you, reader.

Jacques's master said to Jacques: "You don't seem much disposed toward continuing your love story."

Jacques. My poor captain! He has gone away where we are all bound, where, as a matter of fact, it is strange he hasn't gone before. Ah me! Ah me! Alas!

The Master. Why, Jacques, you're crying, I do believe. "Weep then without restraint, for you weep without shame; his death freed you from that scrupulous decorum that bothered you all your life. You haven't the same reasons for hiding your grief as you have for hiding your happiness; we shall not think of drawing the same conclusions from your grief that we should draw from your joy. Grief one can pardon. And then, at this particular time, one must seem either oversensitive or thankless, and, all things considered, it is better to uncover a weakness than to let oneself be suspected of a vice. May your weeping be free so as to be less painful; violent, so as to be less lengthy. Remember, exaggerate even, what he was: his ability to penetrate the deepest matters; his measure in discussing the most delicate; his unswerving taste which attracted him to the most important; the fecundity he threw into the most sterile subjects; with what skill he defended the accused. His indulgence gave him a thousand times more wit than self-interest or pride gave to the guilty man; he was strict only with himself. Far from seeking out excuses for the petty faults he allowed to creep into him, he worked with all the ill will of an enemy to exaggerate them, and with all the cleverness of a jealous man to underrate his virtues by rigorously examining the motives that had perhaps determined his action without his knowing it. Put to your grief no other limits than time will put to it. Let us bow to the will of the universal order when we lose our friends, just as we shall when that order shall be pleased to dispose of our poor selves; let us accept without despair the verdict of fate when it condemns one of them, just as we shall do without resistance when it shall pass judgment on ourselves! The duties of burial are not the last duties of friends.

The earth which seems so upset now will resettle over the ashes of your lover, but your soul will preserve all its feeling."

Jacques. My master, that is very pretty; but what the devil has it to do here? I have lost my captain; I am heartbroken; and you reel off to me, like a parrot, some shred of a consolation speech from a man or a woman to another woman who has lost her lover.

The Master. I think it's from a woman.

Jacques. I'm more of the opinion that it comes from a man. But however that may be, man or woman, what the devil has it to do here? Do you take me for the mistress of my captain? My captain, sir, was a fine man; and I, sir, have always been a good boy.

The Master. Who is doubting it, Jacques?

Jacques. Then why the devil all this consolation of a man or woman to another woman? If I ask you often enough, maybe you'll tell me.

The Master. No, Jacques; you'll have to find that reason all by yourself.

Jacques. Were I to think about it the rest of my life, I should not guess it; I should still be at it come the Last Judgment.

The Master. Jacques, it seemed to me that you listened attentively while I was speaking.

Jacques. Could you do otherwise with something so ridiculous?

The Master. Ah, very good, Jacques.

Jacques. I was all but ready to burst out laughing at that place about the rigorous decorum which had bothered me all during the life of my captain, and from which I was freed by his death.

The Master. Very good, Jacques! I succeeded then in what I proposed. Tell me if you know a better way to go about consoling you. You were crying; if I had spoken to you about the object of your grief, what would have happened? You would have cried much more and I should have ended up by grieving you the more. I have played a good one on you, both by the stupidity of my funeral oration, and by the little spat that followed it. Agree that right now the thought of your captain is as far from you as the hearse which takes him to his last resting place. And so, I think you can take up again the story of your loves.

Jacques. I think so too. "Doctor," I said to the surgeon, "do you live far from here?"

"A good quarter of a league at least."

"Are you adequately housed?"

"Yes, fairly so."

"Could you spare one bed?"

"No."

"What! Not even if I paid, and paid well?"

"Oh, if you pay and pay well, pardon me. But, my friend, you seem hardly in a condition to pay, even less to pay well."

"That's my business. And shall I be somewhat cared for at your house?"

"Very well. I have a wife who has cared for invalids all her life, and an eldest daughter who can take on any comer, and who can pull off your dressing for you as well as I."

"How much would you charge for my board and your services?"

The surgeon said, scratching his ear: "For the lodging, food, care . . . but who's going to guarantee the payment?"

"I shall pay every day."

"Now that's what I call talking."

But, sir, I don't think you are listening.

The Master. No, it was written up yonder that you would talk this time, which won't be the last time perhaps, without being listened to.

Jacques. When you don't listen to the speaker, it's because you're thinking of nothing at all, or of something other than what is being said. Which of the two were you doing?

The Master. The last. I was thinking of what one of those lackeys who followed the hearse said to you, to the effect that your captain, by the death of his friend, had been deprived of the pleasure of dueling at least once a week. Did you understand what he meant by that?

Jacques. Of course I did.

The Master. Well, it's a puzzle for me, and you would do me a favor to explain.

Jacques. And what the devil does it matter to you?

The Master. Not much, except that when you talk you want to be listened to, don't you?

Jacques. That goes without saying.

The Master. Well then, in all sincerity I can't guarantee anything so long as that inscrutable remark knocks about my head. Rescue me from that, I beg you.

Jacques. Good enough. But promise me, at least, that you won't interrupt me.

The Master. Come what may, I promise.

Jacques. Well, it's just that my captain, a good man, a gay fellow, a deserving lad, and one of the best officers of the outfit, although a bit strange, had met and struck up a friendship with another officer of the same company, himself a good man, gay fellow, deserving lad, as good an officer but as strange a man as my captain.

Jacques was about to get into the story of his captain, when they heard a large troop of men and horses coming along behind them. It was the same lugubrious coach coming back. It was surrounded . . . —By revenue guards?—No.—By mounted constabulary?—Perhaps. Whatever it was, this hearse was preceded by a priest in cassock and surplice, with his hands bound behind his back; by the coachman in black, hands tied behind his back; and by the two lackeys in black, their hands, too, tied behind their backs. And who was surprised at that? It was Jacques who cried out: "My captain, my poor captain is not dead! God be praised!" Then Jacques turns about, spurs his horse, and flies toward the masquerading procession. He was scarcely thirty paces from it when the revenue guards, or the mounted police, take aim and shout to him: "Stop! Go back, or you're a dead man." Jacques stopped short, consulted Destiny in his head, and it seemed to him that Destiny said: "Go back!" which he did. His master said to him: "Well, Jacques, what is it?"

Jacques. By heaven, I don't know.

The Master. And why?

Jacques. That I don't know either.

The Master. You'll see; they're smugglers who filled that hearse with prohibited merchandise, and they've most likely been sold to the police by the very rascals from whom they had bought it.

Jacques. Then why this coach with my captain's arms?

The Master. Or perhaps it's a kidnapping. They have hidden in that coffin—who knows? A woman, a girl, a nun. It's not the shroud that makes the corpse.

Jacques. But why this coach with my captain's arms?

The Master. It's whatever you please; only please finish the story of your captain.

Jacques. You still want that story? But perhaps my captain is still living.

The Master. What would that have to do with it?

Jacques. I don't like to talk of the living, for from time to time you're brought to embarrassment by the good or ill you have said of them—the good that they destroy, the ill that they repair.

The Master. Be neither trite panegyrist nor bitter censor; say the thing as it is.

Jacques. That's not easy. Hasn't a man his own character, his interests, his taste and passions according to which he either exaggerates or understates? Say the thing as it is, indeed! Why that doesn't happen—perhaps not even two times a day in a whole city. And the one who listens, is he better disposed than the one who speaks? No. From which it follows that scarcely twice a day in a big city is a man understood as he has spoken.

The Master. What the devil, Jacques. Here are maxims enough to proscribe the use of the tongue and the ears, to say nothing, hear nothing, and believe nothing! However, speak on as you; me, I'll listen as me, and I'll believe whatever I'm able.

Jacques. If one says practically nothing in this world which is understood as it is said, there is something even worse, for one does practically nothing that is understood in the spirit in which it was done.

The Master. There is very probably no one head under heaven which contains as many paradoxes as yours.

Jacques. And what is wrong with that? A paradox is not always a false statement.

The Master. That's true.

Jacques. We were going through Orléans, my captain and I. All the talk in town was about an episode recently experienced by a citizen named M. Le Pelletier, a man moved by such deep compassion for those more unfortunate that, after having run through a considerable fortune by means of unreasonable charity, he had fallen into dire straits and went from door to door to find in someone else's pocket the help he was no longer able to draw from his own.

The Master. And you believe that there could be two opinions on the acts of that man?

Jacques. Not among the poor. But practically all the rich, without exception, looked on him as a sort of fool, and his family was all but ready to have him put out as a prodigal and wastrel. While we were refreshing ourselves in a tavern, a crowd of loafers had gathered about a sort of orator, a barber of the streets, so to speak, and they said to him: "You were there; tell us how it happened."

"Very gladly," said the street orator, who asked nothing better than to give a speech. "M. Aubertot, one of my clients, whose house is directly across from the Capuchin church, was standing at his door. M. Le Pelletier comes up to him and says: 'M. Aubertot, won't you give me something for my friends?' for that's what he calls the poor, you know.

'Not today, M. Le Pelletier.'

M. Le Pelletier insists: 'If you only knew for whom I'm asking your help! It's a poor woman who has just given birth, and who has not so much as a rag to wrap her child in.'

'Couldn't possibly.'

'It's a young and beautiful lady who is out of work and bread, and whom your liberality might save from a disorderly life.'

'I can't do it.'

'It's a manual laborer who had only his arms to keep him alive and who has just smashed a leg by falling from his scaffolding.'

'I couldn't do it, I tell you.'

'Come, come, M. Aubertot, let yourself be moved, and know that never will you have a chance to do a more praiseworthy deed.'

'I can't, I tell you, I can't.'

'My good, my compassionate M. Aubertot!'

'M. Le Pelletier, leave me in peace. When I want to give, I don't have to be coaxed.'

"And having said that, M. Aubertot turns his back, goes through the door and into his shop where M. Le Pelletier follows him. He follows him from the shop into the back room, and from there into his living quarters. There, M. Aubertot, at the end of his patience, what with the insistence of M. Le Pelletier, gives him a slap."

At this point, my captain gets up suddenly and says to the speaker: "And he didn't kill him?"

"No, sir; does one kill for such things?"

"A slap! A slap, by God! And what did he do then?"

"What did he do after he had taken the slap? He put on a smile and said to M. Aubertot: 'That is for me, but what about my poor . . . ?'"

At this, all the audience cried out in admiration, except my captain, who said to them: "Your M. Le Pelletier, gentlemen, is a sorry beggar, a coward, a wretch, for whom this sword would have done quick justice if I had been there, and your M. Aubertot could have counted himself lucky if he had lost only a nose and two ears."

The speaker then replied: "I see, sir, that you would not have given this insolent man the time to recognize his error, throw himself at M. Le Pelletier's feet, and give him his purse."

"No, certainly not."

"You are a soldier, sir, and M. Le Pelletier is a Christian; you have not the same feelings about a slap."

"The cheek of any man of honor is the same."

"That is not exactly the opinion of the Gospels."

"The Gospel is in my heart and in this sheath; I know no other."

Your Gospel, my master, is I know not where; mine is written up yonder. Each of us judges of good and evil in his own manner; and perhaps not two seconds in our whole life do we have the same judgment.

The Master. Yes, yes, cursed gossip, and then what?

When Jacques's master grew thus moody, Jacques would be quiet and begin to dream; very often he would break the silence only by some remark, linked up in his own mind, but as disjoined from the conversation as if one were reading a book and skipping several pages. This is precisely what happened when he said: "My dear master . . ."

The Master. Ah, you've finally found your tongue. I am happy for both of us, for I was beginning to get bored at not hearing you, and you were the same at not talking. So speak.

Jacques. My dear master, life passes in taking things for what they are not. There are blunders in love, blunders of friendship, blunders in politics, in finance, in the church, in the magistracy, in commerce, blunders of wives and husbands.

The Master. Come now, leave off your blunders, and try to realize that you make a gross one by embarking on a chapter of morality when we are concerned with a historical fact. The story of your captain?

Jacques was about to start again the story of his captain when, for the second time, his horse, launching off abruptly to the right of the highway, carries him across a long plain, a good quarter of a league's distance, and pulls up short under a gallows . . . Under a gallows! Now there's a strange streak in a horse to take his rider under a gibbet! [16] . . . "What does this mean?" asked Jacques. "Is it a forewarning of Destiny?"

The Master. My friend, have no doubt of it. Your horse is inspired, and the devil of it is that all our prognostications, inspirations, and forewarnings from above in dreams or apparitions are worth nothing. For the thing happens just the same. Dear friend, I advise you to put your conscience in good order, to arrange your little personal affairs, and to dispatch to me, as rapidly as you can, the story of your captain and of your loves, for I should be upset to lose you without having heard them. Even were you to worry more than you do, what possible good could that do? None. The verdict of your destiny, twice pronounced by your horse will be carried out. Consider now. Have you nothing to return to anyone? Confide in me your last will, and rest assured that it shall be carried out faithfully. If you have taken anything from me, I give it to you; only ask God's pardon and during the short or long time remaining for us to live together, rob me no more.

Jacques. However much I go back over my past, I find nothing there to set straight with the justice of men. I have neither killed nor robbed nor raped.

The Master. So much the worse, for I should much prefer that the crime be committed already than that it remain to be committed, and for good reasons.

Jacques. But, sir, perhaps it's for someone else's fault, and not for my own, that I am to be hanged.

The Master. That's possible.

Jacques. Perhaps it will be only after my death that I shall be hanged.

The Master. That also is possible.

Jacques. Perhaps I shan't be hanged at all.

The Master. That I doubt.

Jacques. It is perhaps written up yonder that I shall merely be present at the hanging of another, and who knows, sir, who that other is? Who knows whether he is near or far?

The Master. Mister Jacques, be hanged, since Destiny so desires, and your horse says as much. But don't be insolent! Finish with your impertinent conjecturing and then give me quickly the story of your captain.

Jacques. Don't be angry, sir; honest folk have sometimes been hanged. It's a blunder of justice.

The Master. These blunders of yours are maddening. Let's talk of something else.

Jacques, somewhat reassured by the diverse interpretations he had found for the horse's prognostication, said: "When I entered the regiment, there were two officers of about the same age, same birth, service, and merit. My captain was one of the two. The only difference between them was that one was rich and the other had nothing. My captain was the rich one. This duplication of character ought to have produced either a deep sympathy or a very strong antipathy; it produced both."

Here Jacques stopped. This happened to him several times throughout the story; each time the horse bobbed his head to right or to left. At such times, he would repeat his last sentence before continuing, as if he had the hiccoughs: "It produced both. There were days when they were the best friends in the world, and others when they were mortal enemies. The days of friendship, they sought each other out, feted one another, embraced, shared all their sorrows, pleasures, and needs; they consulted one another upon their most secret affairs, upon their domestic interests, their hopes, their fears, their plans for advancement. The next day, were they to meet, they would either pass close to each other without looking, or else they looked at each other ferociously, called each other 'sir,' exchanged harsh words, fell upon their swords and fought. If it so happened that one was wounded, the other would drop beside his companion, would weep and wring his hands with despair, accompany the other to his house, and would install himself there at the bedside until his friend was cured. One week, two weeks, a month afterward, it was all to do over again. It was clear from one incident to the next that two good men, two fine men, two sincere friends risked perishing, one at the hand of the other; and, of the two, the dead man would most certainly not have been the more pitiable. People had talked to them many times of the strangeness of their conduct. As for me, when allowed by my captain to express my opinion, I would say to him: 'But, sir, what if you should happen to kill him?' At these words he would start to cry and cover his face with his hands; he would run about the apartment like a madman. Two hours later, either he carried his friend, wounded, back to his house, or the friend performed the same service for him. Neither my remonstrances nor those of others had any effect at all. There was no other remedy but to separate them. The minister of war was informed of this singular perseverance in such opposite extremes, and my captain was named to command another post, with the express injunction that he go there immediately and not leave it. Another order limited his friend to our post. (I believe this cursed horse will drive me mad.) Scarcely had the orders arrived from the ministry when my captain, under pretext of going to thank them for the favor, left for court where he pleaded that he was rich and that his poor friend had as much right to the favors of the king, that the post they had just given him would recompense the diligence of his friend, would add to his small fortune, and that, as for himself, he would be greatly overjoyed. As the minister had no other objective save to separate the two strange men, and since generous actions are always effective, it was decreed . . . (Cursed animal, will you hold your head up straight?) it was decreed that my captain would stay with the regiment, and that his friend would proceed to take over the new post.

"Scarcely had they been separated when they felt the need of one another. They both fell into deep melancholy. My captain asked for a six-month leave to go back to his own country; but, not two miles from the camp, he sells his horse, disguises himself as a peasant, and proceeds toward the place where his friend was in command. It seems that this was a prearranged scheme between them. He arrives . . . (Well, go where you want to then! Is there still some gibbet you wish to visit? Laugh if you like, sir, for indeed it is very funny.) he arrives, but however many precautions they took to hide the satisfaction they had in seeing each other, and however careful they were to meet each other only with the outward signs of subordination expected of a peasant for a military governor, it was written up yonder that some soldiers and some officers who were by chance present at their meeting and who must have heard of their adventures would begin to have suspicions and inform the town commandant.

"This fellow, a wise man, smiled at the report but did not fail to attach to the matter the importance it merited. He put spies about the major. Their first report was that the major went out very little, and that the peasant went out not at all. It was impossible that these two men should live together for one week at a time without their strange mania overtaking them—which didn't fail to happen."

You see, reader, how obliging I am. I should need to give only a crack of the whip to the horses pulling the hearse draped in black, to bring together at the door of the next inn Jacques, his master, the revenue officers or mounted police along with the rest of the procession; to interrupt the story of Jacques's captain and to try your patience as much as I pleased. But for that I should have to lie, and I don't like lies, unless they are useful and absolutely necessary. The fact is that Jacques and his master never again saw the coach draped in black, and that Jacques, still upset about his horse's mania, continued his story: "One day, the spies reported to the town commandant that there had been a very lively dispute between the peasant and the major, that afterward they had gone out, the peasant in the lead, the major following him regretfully, and that they had gone into a banker's in the city, where they still were.

"We learned afterward that, having given up hope of ever seeing each other again, they had decided to fight in earnest, and that, sensitive to the commitments of the tenderest sort of friendship at this very moment of unbelievable ferocity, my captain, who was rich—as I told you already—(I trust, sir, that you will not condemn me to finishing my story on this queer animal), my captain, who was rich, had demanded of his friend that he accept a letter of exchange for twenty-four thousand livres, which would assure him of a living abroad in the event that my captain were killed. My captain swore he would not fight without this understanding; the other replied to this offer saying: 'Do you think, my friend, that if I were to kill you, I should long survive you?'

"They came out of the banker's, and were walking toward the gates of the city when they found themselves surrounded by the commanding officer of the town and several subordinate officers. However much this seemed to be a chance meeting, our two friends, or our two enemies as it please you to call them, were not fooled. The peasant let his identity be known. They went to spend the night in a remote house. The next day, at the blush of dawn, my captain, having embraced his friend several times, left him, never to see him again. Scarcely had he arrived in his home country when he died."

The Master. And who told you he died?

Jacques. And what of this coffin? This coach with his arms? My poor captain is dead; there can be no doubt of it.

The Master. But what of that priest with his hands tied behind his back? And all the other people? And the revenue officers or the mounted police? And the return of the procession to the city? Your captain is alive; on that score I have no doubts. But what do you know of his comrade?

Jacques. The story of his comrade makes a fine line of the Great Scroll, or of what is written up yonder.

The Master. I hope . . .

Jacques's horse did not let the master finish. He is off like a flash, deviating neither to right nor to left, straight down the highway. Jacques was no longer to be seen, and his master, convinced that the road ended up at some gallows, held his sides from laughing. And since Jacques and his master are good only when they're together, and are worth no more separated than Don Quixote without Sancho and Richardet without Ferragus (which the continuer of Cervantes and the imitator of Ariosto, Monsignor Forti-Guerra, did not realize),[17] let's just chat together, reader, until they are back together again.

You will take the story of Jacques's captain for a tale of fiction, and you make a mistake. I protest that exactly as the story was told to the master, just so did I hear it told at the Invalides on St. Louis' day, of I know not what year, while sitting at table in the house of a certain M. de Saint-Etienne, commanding officer of the institution; and the storyteller, speaking in the presence of several officers of the house, who knew of the affair, was a serious fellow and not at all a jokester. So I repeat to you, for now and for later, be very careful in this conversation of Jacques and his master if you don't want to take the true for the false, and the false for the true. There now! You've been warned and I wash my hands of the affair.—These are (you will say) two very extraordinary men!—So that's why you distrust the story! In the first place, nature is so diverse, especially in the question of instincts and character, that there is nothing so strange in the mind of a poet that experience and observation of nature cannot offer you a model of it. As I stand here right now speaking to you, I once met the counterpart of a character in *The Doctor in Spite of Himself,* which I had always regarded until then as the maddest and gayest of fictions.—What! the counterpart of the husband whose wife says: "I have three children hanging on my arm," and who replies: "Put them on the ground." "But they're asking for bread." "Give them the whip!"—Precisely. And here's his conversation with my wife:

"Ah, there you are, M. Gousse."

"Yes, madame, I am no other."

"Where have you been?"

"Where I just went."

"What were you doing there?"

"I mended a windmill that was in bad shape."

"Whose windmill?"

"How should I know? I didn't go to mend the miller."

"You are unusually well dressed. But why, under that very clean suit, do you wear such a dirty shirt?"

"Because I have only one."

"And why have you only one?"

"Because I have only one body at a time."

"My husband isn't here now, but that mustn't keep you from eating here."

"Quite so, for I have entrusted him with neither my stomach nor my appetite."

"How is your wife?"

"As she pleases; that's her business."

"And your children?"

"Wonderful!"

"And the husky little one with such pretty eyes and such lovely skin?"

"Much better than the others. He's dead."

"Are you teaching them anything?"

"No, madame."

"What! Neither reading nor writing nor their catechism?"

"Neither reading nor writing nor catechism."

"And why, pray tell?"

"Well, they taught me nothing and I am not the more ignorant for it. If they have a mind, they'll do as I did. If they're stupid, what I should teach them would make them only more stupid."

If you ever run into this character, you don't need to know him to go up and speak to him. Take him into a cabaret, tell him your troubles, ask him to follow you twenty miles, and he'll follow you. After having used him, send him back without a cent; he'll return satisfied.

Have you ever heard of a certain Prémontval,[18] who gave public mathematics lessons in Paris? Gousse was his friend. But perhaps Jacques and his master are back together by now; shall we go to them, or do you want to stay with me? Gousse and Prémontval ran a school together. Among the many students who went there was a young lady named Mlle Pigeon,[19] the daughter of that skilled artist who constructed the two fine planispheres that have been taken from the *Jardin du Roi*[20] to the hall of the Academy of Sciences. Mlle Pigeon went there each morning with her brief-case under her arm and her compass and pencil case stuck in her sleeve. One of the professors, Prémontval, fell in love with his student and somehow through all the propositions about solid figures inscribed on spheres, a baby got itself constructed. Father Pigeon was not a man to accept with understanding the truth of such a corollary. The situation of the lovers becomes embarrassing; they confer together. But having nothing, absolutely nothing, what could possibly be the outcome of their deliberations? They call their friend Gousse to their assistance. And he, without saying a word, sells everything he owns—linen, suits, furniture and books; gets together a sum of money; throws the two lovers into a post chaise, and accompanies them on horse as far as the Alps. There he empties his purse of the little money remaining, gives it to them, embraces them, wishes them a good journey, and comes back on foot, begging alms until he gets to Lyons, where, by painting the walls of a monks' cloister, he was able to earn enough to get back to Paris without begging.—That's very, very fine!—Certainly, it was; and after that heroic deed, I suppose you think Gousse an exceptionally good, moral man. Well, disillusion yourselves; he had no more sense of morality than a fish head.—That's impossible. —It's true. I employed him once. I gave him a check for eighty francs on my constituents. The sum was written in figures, and what does he do? He adds a zero and gets paid eight hundred francs.—Ah! How horrible!—And he's no more dishonest when he robs me than he is honest when he gives up all for a friend. He's a character completely without principles. Those eighty francs weren't enough, so with a pen scratch he got himself the eight hundred he needed. And those rare books he gave me!—What about those books?—But Jacques and his master? And how about Jacques's loves? Ah, reader, the patience with which you listen to me proves the little interest you are taking in my two characters, and I'm tempted to leave them where they are. I needed a rare book; he brings it to me. Sometime later I need another; again he brings it to me. When I try to pay him, he refuses the just price. Then I need a third rare book. "As for this one," he says, "you won't get it for you have spoken too late. My Sorbonne doctor friend is dead."

"And what has your Sorbonne doctor to do with the book I want? Did you take the two others from his library?"

"Why, certainly."

"Without his permission?"

"What need of permission is there in making a fair redistribution? I only changed those books about for the best by transferring them from a spot where they were useless to another spot where someone could make good use of them." After that try to make pronouncements on the conduct of men! It's the story of Gousse with his wife that is really excellent.[21] I hear you; you've had enough, and you're of the opinion that we should go join our two travelers. Reader, you treat me like an automaton, and that's not polite. Tell Jacques's love story. Don't tell Jacques's love story; I'd like to hear the story of Gousse, I've had enough of it. Naturally, sometimes I must follow your fancy, but sometimes I have to follow my own—this without even considering that any listener who allows me to start a story takes it upon himself to hear me to the end.

Thus I've given you an "in the first place." However, an "in the first place" presupposes at least a second place. Secondly, then . . . listen to me or don't listen to me, I'll talk to myself. Jacques's captain and his friend might have been troubled with a violent and secret jealousy. For that's a sentiment friendship does not always obviate. There is nothing so hard to pardon as real merit. Weren't they perhaps apprehensive of some special favor granted to one, which would have offended them both equally? There's no doubt, they were each trying, in advance, to be rid of a dangerous competitor; they were feeling each other out for a future eventuality. But then how can you have such an idea of a man who cedes his place of command so generously to his indigent friend? He did cede it, it is true; but perhaps had he not been granted it initially, he would have demanded it at the point of a sword. With soldiers, if an advancement by favor doesn't honor the one who profits, it does dishonor his rival. But let's leave off all that, and say that it was their own little touch of madness. Doesn't everyone have his touch? The folly of our two officers was for several centuries the folly of all Europe; they called it chivalry. All that shining multitude, armed from head to toe, decorated with varied livery of love, bouncing on their palfreys, lance in hand, visor up or down, watching each other proudly, exchanging wary glances, threatening, overthrowing each other in the dust, spreading the earth with a vast tourney of bits of broken armour—these were only friends jealous for the merit in vogue. These friends, at the moment when they held their lances in couch, each at his end of the field, and when they had pressed their chargers' flanks with their spurs, became the most terrible enemies. They rushed upon each other with the same fury they would have had on a battlefield. Well, our two officers were only two paladins, born in our day, with the customs of our ancestors. Every virtue and every vice comes in and goes out of style. Bodily force had its day, skill in tourney had its day. Bravery is now more, now less, respected. The more common it is, the less it is praised and the less one is vain about it. Trace and study the inclinations of men and you will notice some who seem to have come into the world too late; they belong to another century. And what's to prevent our thinking that these two soldiers engaged in their dangerous daily combats only out of a desire to find the weak side of a rival and thus gain superiority over him? Duels appear again and again in society under all forms—between priests, between lawyers, between writers, between philosophers. Each calling has its lance and its horsemen; and our most respectable and amusing gatherings are only little tournaments where betimes we carry the livery of love at the bottom of our heart if not on our sleeve. The bigger the audience, the livelier the bout. The presence of women pushes our passion and obstinacy to ridiculous proportions. And the shame of having given up in their presence is scarcely ever forgotten.

And Jacques? Jacques had gone through the gates of the city, traversed the streets to the acclamation of the children, and reached the opposite suburb, where, when his horse turned suddenly into a low gate, there occurred betwixt the lintel of the door and Jacques's cranium a terrible crash in which either the lintel had to give or Jacques be thrown back. It was, as you can well imagine, the latter that happened. Jacques fell, his head cracked, and he was unconscious. They pick him up, and call him back to life with spirits; I believe he was even bled by the master of the house.—The man was a doctor, then?—No. Meanwhile his master had arrived and was asking information from everyone he met. "You wouldn't by any chance have seen a tall fellow, riding a piebald horse?"

"He's just gone by. He was going as if the devil had caught him up. He must have gone to his master's."

"And who is his master?"

"The executioner."

"The executioner?"

"Yes, for it was his horse."

"Where does he live?"

"Rather far, but save yourself the trouble, for here come his men carrying the tall fellow of whom you inquire, and whom we took for one of his lackeys."

And who was talking thus to Jacques's master? It was an inn-keeper at whose door he had stopped. There could be no doubt about that; he was short and fat, like a barrel; his shirt sleeves were rolled to the elbow; he had a cotton cap on his head, a kitchen apron about him, and a large knife at his side. "Quickly, quickly! A bed for this poor fellow," Jacques's master said to him, "A surgeon, a doctor, a druggist!" Meanwhile, they had laid Jacques out at the master's feet, his forehead covered with an enormous, thick compress, and his eyes closed. "Jacques? Jacques?"

"Is it you, my master?"

"Yes, it is I; look at me."

"I can't."

"Whatever happened to you?"

"Ah, the horse, that cursed horse! I'll tell you all about it tomorrow, if I don't die during the night."

While they were carrying him up to his room, the master directed the move, crying: "Be careful, go gently, gently, for God's sake, you're going to hurt him. You, there, with his legs, turn to the right; you, with his head, turn to the left." And Jacques kept muttering in a low voice: "It was written up yonder."

Scarcely was Jacques in bed when he fell into a deep sleep. His master passed the night at his bedside, feeling his pulse, and cease-lessly wetting down his compress with curative water. Jacques surprised him at this upon awakening and said: "What are you doing here?"

The Master. I'm watching over you. You are my servant when I'm sick or well; but I'm yours when you are sick.

Jacques. I'm very happy to know you are human; it's not too common a trait of masters with their servants.

The Master. How is your head?

Jacques. As good as the beam with which it had the bout.

The Master. Take the sheet between your teeth and shake hard. What do you feel?

Jacques. Nothing. The jug seems to be without a crack.

The Master. Good. You want to get up, I suppose?

Jacques. What do you want me to do here?

The Master. I want you to rest.

Jacques. Well, my idea is that we should eat and then leave.

The Master. And the horse?

Jacques. I left it with its master, an honest man, an obliging fellow, who took it back for what we paid.

The Master. And this honest, this obliging gentleman, do you know who he is?

Jacques. No.

The Master. I'll tell you once we're on the road.

Jacques. And why not now? What mystery is there to that?

The Master. Mystery or no mystery, what need is there to know it either now or any other time?

Jacques. None.

The Master. But you need a horse.

Jacques. The innkeeper perhaps will ask nothing better than to sell us one of his.

The Master. Sleep another minute or two; I'll go see about it.

The master goes down, orders breakfast, buys a horse, comes back up and finds Jacques dressed. They ate and then were off, Jacques protesting the while that it was impolite to go off without paying a courtesy call on the citizen at whose door he was stricken and who had so obligingly helped him. The master quieted Jacques in the matter of such a delicate thought with the assurance that he himself had very well recompensed the fellow's satellites for carrying Jacques to the inn. Jacques held that money given to servants did not acquit one with the master, and that it was just in this way that one encouraged a regret and distaste for well-doing, and thus gave to others the impression of ingratitude. "My master, I can hear everything that man is saying about me from what I should say of him if our places were reversed."

They were leaving the city, when they met a tall, vigorous fellow, a wide-brimmed hat on his head and wearing a suit adorned with lace on all the edges. He was alone except for the two big dogs walking in front of him. Jacques no sooner saw him than in a matter of seconds he had jumped off his horse crying, "That's the man!" and threw himself about his neck. The man with the dogs seemed very embarrassed at Jacques's caresses, pushed him off gently and said: "Sir, you do me too much honor."

"Not at all, I owe my life to you. I couldn't thank you too much."

"You don't know who I am."

"Aren't you the obliging citizen who aided me, bled me, and bathed me, when my horse . . ."

"That is true."

"Are you not the honest citizen who took back that horse at the same price you sold it?"

"I am." And Jacques started again to kiss him first on one cheek, then the other, his master laughing throughout, while the two dogs stood up as if amazed by a scene they were seeing for the first time. Jacques, after adding to the demonstrations of his gratitude a great many bows that his benefactor did not return, and many good wishes which were coldly received, gets back on his horse and says to his master: "I have the greatest possible respect for that man; you ought to help me know him better."

The Master. And why should he be so venerated in your eyes?

Jacques. Because, not attaching the slightest importance to the services he gives, he must be by nature obliging, and have a long record of kindness.

The Master. And how do you arrive at that?

Jacques. From the cold, indifferent way in which he received my thanks; he doesn't bow to me at all, he says not a word, he seems to ignore me, and perhaps this very minute he is saying to himself, scornfully: "Kindness must be foreign to this traveler, and the exercise of justice must be painful to him since he is so touched." What then is so absurd in what I say to make you laugh so much? However that may be, tell me the name of this man so I can write him down in my books.

The Master. Very glad to. Write . . .

Jacques. Say, then.

The Master. Write: "The man for whom I have such deep respect . . ."

Jacques. "Deep respect" . . . yes?

The Master. "Is . . ."

Jacques. "Is . . ."

The Master. "The executioner of ———."

Jacques. The executioner!!

The Master. Yes, yes, the executioner.

Jacques. Could you please tell me what's the point of that joke?

The Master. I'm not joking at all. Just follow the links of your curb bit. You need a horse, Destiny turns you to a passerby, and this passerby is a hangman. The horse takes you twice to the gallows; the third time he drops you at a hangman's house. There you fall lifeless, and they carry you where? Into an inn, a shelter, a common refuge. Jacques, do you know the story of Socrates' death?

Jacques. No.

The Master. He was the sage of Athens. The role of the wise man has for some time now been dangerous among fools. His fellow citizens condemned him to drink hemlock. Well, Socrates did as you've just done. He treated the executioner who gave him the hemlock as politely as you. Jacques, you're a kind of philosopher, admit it. I know very well that they're a race of men hated by the powerful, before whom they fail to bend the knee; hated also by the lawyers who protect by profession the prejudices they follow; hated by the priests who find them very infrequently at their altars; hated equally by the poets, those unprincipled men who look stupidly upon philosophy as the ax of the fine arts, without realizing that those who are practiced in the hateful art of satire are themselves only flatterers; they are even hated by the people, who from all time have been slaves of the tyrants who oppress them and of the rascals who trick them and of the clowns who amuse them. So, as you can see, I know all the dangers of your profession and the importance of the avowal I am asking of you. I shall not take advantage of your secret. Jacques, my friend, you are a philosopher, and I'm sorry for you. And if it is permitted to read in present events, those things which must one day happen, and if what is written up yonder becomes manifest to men some-time long before the fact, I presume that your death will be philo-sophic, and that you will take the cord with as good faith as Socrates took the cup of hemlock.

Jacques. My master, a prophet could not speak better, but happily . . .

The Master. You don't much believe me—which, in the final analysis only adds strength to my presentiment.

Jacques. And you, sir, do you believe it?

The Master. I believe it; but, even were I not to believe, it could make no difference.

Jacques. And why not?

The Master. It's because there is danger involved only for those who speak. And I keep quiet.

Jacques. And as for the presentiments?

The Master. I laugh at them, but I confess that I tremble the while. There are some that are so striking! We've been rocked on those stories since the cradle. If your dreams had worked out five or six times, and you dreamed your friend had died, you would hurry to his place in the morning to see how things stood. But the presentiments that are impossible to forget are, above all, those which come up at a time when something is going on far away from us, for they have a symbolic air about them.

Jacques. Sometimes you are so subtle and sublime that I don't understand you. Couldn't you clear this up a little, for example?

The Master. Nothing could be easier. A woman was living in the country with her octogenarian husband who suffered from gall-stones. The husband leaves his wife and comes to the city for an operation. The night before the operation he writes to his wife:

"At the very time you get this letter, I shall be under the knife of Brother Cosme. . . ." [22] You know those wedding rings which separate into two parts, with the name of the husband engraved on one part, and the name of the wife on the other, don't you? Well, this woman was wearing one like that when she opened her husband's letter. At that very instant, the two halves of the ring separate, and the part bearing her husband's name falls broken on the opened letter while the section bearing her own name stays on her finger. Tell me, Jacques, do you think any head is strong or solid enough not to be upset at such a time, in such circumstances? And so this woman thought she should die of it. Her terror lasted until the next post when her husband wrote her that the operation had been successful, that he was out of danger, and that he looked forward to embracing her before the end of the month.

Jacques. And did he embrace her?

The Master. Yes.

Jacques. I asked you that because I have many times noticed that Destiny is fickle. You say at first that it has lied, and the next minute you find it was true. Just like you, sir, who believe me to be in a predicament of symbolic presentiment, and yet, in spite of yourself, you think I am in danger of a philosopher's death.

The Master. I cannot hide that thought from you. But to put away such a sad thought, couldn't you . . . ?

Jacques. Take up again the story of my loves?

Jacques continued his love story. We had left him, I think, with the doctor.

The Doctor. I'm afraid there will be work to do on that knee for many a day.

Jacques. There will be exactly as much as for the time written up yonder, but what does it matter?

The Doctor. Well, at so much a day for lodging, food, and care, that will make quite a sum.

Jacques. Doctor, it's not a question of what sum for all that time, but how much it will be per day.

The Doctor. Would twenty-five sous be too much?

Jacques. Much too much. Come now, doctor, I'm a poor devil. So let's reduce that by half, and think of arrangements for transporting me to your house as soon as possible.

The Doctor. Twelve and a half sous; that's hardly anything. You're willing surely to make it thirteen?

Jacques. Twelve and a half. Thirteen. Agreed!

The Doctor. And you'll pay every day?

Jacques. That is my agreement.

The Doctor. It's just that I have a devil of a wife who doesn't stand for nonsense, you know.

Jacques. Come, doctor; have me carried as quickly as possible to your devil of a wife.

The Doctor. One month at thirteen sous a day—that makes nineteen livres, ten sous. You'll make it twenty francs, I suppose.

Jacques. All right, twenty francs.

The Doctor. And you want to be well fed, well cared for, quickly recovered, eh? Beside the food, lodging, and care, there will be medicine, linen, and probably . . .

Jacques. And so?

The Doctor. Well, by heaven, the whole thing should be worth twenty-four francs.

Jacques. All right for the twenty-four francs, but no more strings.

The Doctor. One month at twenty-four; two months, that makes it forty-eight; three months, would be seventy-two. Ah, how happy the wife would be if you pay in advance half of those seventy-two when you arrive!

Jacques. I agree.

The Doctor. And she would be even happier if . . .

Jacques. If I paid for the quarter? All right, I'll pay it.

Jacques added: "The surgeon went to find my peasants, told them of our arrangement, and the next minute the man, the wife and the children assemble about my bed with pleasant faces. There were endless questions on my health and my knee; praises for their neighbor, the doctor and his wife; eternal good wishes, the most touching friendliness—such interest and enthusiasm at the thought of being useful to me! And yet the surgeon had not told them that I had money. But they knew their man; he had agreed to take me home and they knew it! I paid them what I owed and made little presents to the children, which the father and mother didn't leave long in their hands.

"It was morning. The peasant left for the fields; his wife took her basket on her back and left; the children, unhappy and saddened at being robbed of their money, disappeared; and when it was time to pull me from my pallet, dress me, and put me on the stretcher, there was no one to be found except the doctor, who started to shout at the top of his lungs without being heard."

The Master. And Jacques, who likes to talk to himself, very probably said: "Never pay in advance, if you don't want to be badly treated."

Jacques. No, not at all, my master. This was no time for moralizing, but rather for losing temper and cursing. I got angry and I swore; I moralized afterward. And while I was moralizing, the doctor, who had left me, came back with two peasants whom he had hired to transport me at my own expense, a fact he did not fail to make clear to me. These fellows performed all the details preliminary to laying me on the sort of stretcher they had made for me from a blanket and some poles.

The Master. Thank God! So you're finally in the doctor's house and in love with the wife or daughter of the doctor.

Jacques. I believe, sir, that you are mistaken.

The Master. And do you think I'm going to wait three months in that house without hearing the first word of your love life? Ah, Jacques, that's not possible. Spare me, I pray, the description of the house, the character of the doctor, the humors of his wife, and the progress of your recovery. Jump, jump over all that! Let's get to the point. So your knee is almost cured, you're in good health, and you're in love.

Jacques. I'm in love, then, since you're in such a hurry.

The Master. And whom do you love?

Jacques. A big, eighteen-year-old brunette, well constructed: big brown eyes, little red mouth, lovely arms, pretty hands. Ah, my master, those pretty hands! Those hands there . . .

The Master. You look as if you were still holding them.

Jacques. Those hands there—you have taken them and held them more than once on the sly, and it only depended on those same hands whether or not you had your way.

The Master. My word, Jacques, I didn't expect that.

Jacques. Neither did I.

The Master. No matter how I think it over, I can remember neither a big brunette nor pretty hands. Please explain what you mean.

Jacques. I agree, but only on the condition that we retrace our steps and go back to the doctor's house.

The Master. Do you think that's written up yonder?

Jacques. It is you who must tell me that. But it is written down here that *chi va piano va sano.*

The Master. Likewise that *chi va sano va lontano,* and I should like to get there.

Jacques. Well then, what have you decided?

The Master. Whatever you wish.

Jacques. Well, in that case we're again back at the surgeon's, and it was written up yonder that we would come back. The doctor, his wife, and his children so well concerted their efforts to dry up my purse with all sorts of little raids thereon, that they would very soon have succeeded. The cure of my knee seemed very well along without really being so. The wound was practically closed; I could get out and around with a crutch, and I had exactly eighteen francs left. There is no one who likes to talk more than a stutterer; no one who likes to walk more than a limper. One fine day in autumn, after dinner, I planned a long walk. From the village where I lived to the neighboring one was a distance of about two leagues.

The Master. And this village was . . . ?

Jacques. If I named it for you, you would know everything. When I arrived there I went into a cabaret, rested, and had a drink. The day started to draw to a close and I was getting ready to start back home, when, from the spot where I was sitting, I heard a woman shrieking very shrilly. I went out; a crowd was gathered about her. She was on the ground, tearing her hair. She cried, pointing out the remnants of a great jug: "I am ruined, I am ruined for a whole month; and during that time, who will feed my children? That steward whose heart is harder than stone, won't give me the benefit of a single sou. Oh, how miserable I am! Ruined, ruined!" All the bystanders were pitying the woman; I heard on every side only "the poor woman," but nobody put his hand in his pocket. I came up quickly and asked her: "My good woman, what has happened?" "What has happened? Can't you see? They sent me for a jug of oil; I slipped and fell; my jug is broken and there goes the oil it was filled with." At this point the little children of the woman came up; they were almost naked, and the shabby clothing of the mother showed the miserable state of the whole family; the mother and children started to bawl. As I stand here now, it would have taken ten times less to move me; my insides were all roiled with pity; tears started to fill my eyes. I asked the woman in a broken voice how many francs' worth of oil were in the jug. "How much?" she replied, lifting her hands high, "nine francs' worth—more than I could earn in a month." At this point, undoing my wallet, and throwing her two big écus, I said: "Here, my good woman, here are twelve. . . ." And without waiting for her thanks, I took the road back to my village.

The Master. Jacques, you did a wonderful thing there.

Jacques. I did a stupid thing, an' it please you, sir. I was no more than a hundred paces from the village when I said as much to myself; I was halfway home when I said it even more convincingly; and when I got back to my doctor's with empty pockets, I thought of it in a wholly different way.

The Master. Perhaps you are right, in which case my praise would be as out of place as your pity. But no, no, Jacques; I persist in my first judgment. It's the forgetting of your own need which constitutes the principal merit of your action. I can see the effects. You will be laid open to the inhumanity of your doctor and his wife; they will chase you out; but, even were you to die on a dung heap, on that dung heap you would be content with yourself.

Jacques. My master, I have not that force of character. I was traveling along clip-clop, regretting, for I must confess it, my two écus which were nonetheless already given away, and thereby spoiling the good work I had done on my first reaction. I was about midway between the villages, and the day had come completely to a close, when three bandits come out from the thicket that bordered the road, jump on me, knock me to the ground, frisk me, and are surprised to find such a pittance of money on me. They had counted upon a better victim, for, seeing the charity I had manifested in the village, they had imagined that a man who could so easily throw away half a louis must have at least twenty. In their anger at being deceived, and vulnerable to having their bones broken on the rack for a handful of small change in the event they should be taken and I should recognize and denounce them, they hesitated a moment as to whether they ought not kill me. Luckily, they heard some noise; they fled, and I was let off with some contusions incurred in falling while they were robbing me. The bandits gone, I pulled myself together and got back to the village as best I could. I got there at two in the morning, pale, disheveled, the pain in my knee greatly heightened, and suffering in various parts of the anatomy from the blows with which I had been rewarded. The doctor . . . my master, what is the matter? You are gritting your teeth, and you are as excited as if you were face to face with an enemy.

The Master. Indeed, I am that. I have sword in hand, I fly into those thieves and avenge you. Tell me how he who has written on the Great Scroll could have written that such should be the reward of a generous act? Why is it that I, who am only a bundle of faults, go to your defense, while he, who calmly saw you attacked, overturned, mistreated, and kicked, he who, they say, is the combination of all perfection.

Jacques. My master—peace, peace. What you are saying there smells to high heaven of the stake.

The Master. What are you looking at?

Jacques. I am looking to see if there is anybody around to hear us. The doctor felt my pulse and found I had fever. I went to bed without speaking of my adventure, dreaming in my bed of coping with the two of them. And good God! What a pair! Me without a sou, and without the slightest doubt that the next day, upon awakening, they would ask me for the agreed price for the day.

At this point the master threw his arms about the neck of his lackey and cried: "My poor Jacques! What are you to do? What will become of you? Your predicament terrifies me."

Jacques. My master, control yourself; I am here.

The Master. I wasn't thinking of now. I was thinking of tomorrow, I was beside you at the doctor's at the moment when you awake and they come to get their money.

Jacques. My master, in this life we know neither when to rejoice nor when to be sad. The good brings the bad, the bad brings forth good. We walk in the night beneath what is written up yonder, equally senseless in our wishes, in our joys, and in our affliction. When I cry, I often find I am stupid.

The Master. And when you laugh?

Jacques. I find I am still stupid. And yet I cannot keep myself from laughing or crying, and that's what makes me so furious. I have tried a hundred times. I didn't close an eye all night.

The Master. No, no, don't go on; tell me what you tried.

Jacques. To make fun of everything. Ah, if only I had been able to. . . .

The Master. What good would that have done?

Jacques. It would have delivered me from care; I should no longer have needed anything, I should have been perfect master of myself —as happy with my head against a curbstone at the street corner as on a fine pillow. Sometimes I am like that, but the devil of it is that it doesn't last, and, hard and firm like a rock as I am in big things, it often happens that a tiny contradiction, a mere nothing, will undo me. It's enough to make me want to slap myself. I have given up, and decided to be just what I am. I have seen, upon reflecting a bit on it, that it all comes down to about the same thing if you add: "What does it matter how one is?" It's another kind of resignation—easier and more convenient.

The Master. More convenient, that's sure.

Jacques. At dawn the doctor pulled my curtains and said: "My friend, let's see your knee, for I must go quite a distance today."

"Doctor," I replied in a painful tone of voice, "I'm sleepy."

"So much the better; that's a good sign."

"Let me sleep; I can't be bothered with a dressing."

"Well, there's no great trouble about that, sleep on."

Having said that, he closed the curtains, yet I still could not sleep. An hour later the wife drew back my curtains and said: "Come, my friend, sit up and eat your toast."

"Madame," I replied, in a painful voice, "I have no appetite."

"Eat, eat; for you'll pay neither more nor less."

"I don't want to eat."

"Well, too bad, then. The children and I shall eat it."

And having said that, she pulls the curtains, calls her children, and they set about dispatching my sugared toast.

Reader, suppose I were to pause here, and take up again the story of the man with only one shirt because he had only one body at a time. I wonder what you would say? That I have become lost in one of M. Voltaire's impasses, or, to put it in the vernacular, in a *cul-de-sac*,[23] from which I don't know how to escape, and that therefore I'm flying off at will into a story to gain time and find some way out of the one I have already started. Well, my reader, you are wrong all round. I do know how Jacques will get out of his difficulties, and what I am going to say about Gousse, the man with only one shirt because he had only one body at a time, is not at all a story.

It happened one day during Pentecost. In the morning I got a note from Gousse, asking me to visit him in a prison where he was confined. While getting dressed, I tried to figure out his adventure. And I thought that probably his tailor, his baker, his wine merchant, or his landlord had obtained a writ of arrest against him. I arrive and find him sharing a room with other fellows of ominous aspect. I asked him who these others were.

"The old man you see there with his glasses on his nose is a clever fellow who knows all about calculations and is trying to make the records he copies correspond with his own accounts. It's not easy, and we've talked about it, but I have no doubt he will figure it out."

"And that other one?"

"He's stupid."

"But is that all?"

"A stupid fellow who invented a machine for counterfeiting currency—a bad, vicious machine which fails in twenty ways."

"And that third fellow who is dressed in livery and plays the bass viol?"

"He's only here while waiting for transfer; this evening or tomorrow morning he'll be transferred to Bicêtre." [24]

"And how about yourself?"

"Me? Oh, my affair is even less important."

After this reply, he gets up, puts his hat on the bed, and immediately his three cellmates disappear. When I came in, I had found Gousse in a dressing robe, sitting at a small table, tracing out geometrical figures and working as peacefully as if he were at home. We are now alone.

"And you, what are you doing here?"

"Me, I'm working, as you can see."

"And who had you put here?"

"I did."

"How's that? You did?"

"Yes, I did, sir."

"And how did you go about that?"

"Just as I would have gone about putting someone else here. I brought action against myself, I won, and as a result of the judgment I obtained against myself and the subsequent verdict, I have been arrested and brought here."

"Are you crazy?"

"No, sir, I tell you the affair just as it happened."

"Well, couldn't you bring another case against yourself, win it and as a result of another judgment and verdict, get yourself out?"

"No, sir, I could not."

Gousse had a pretty serving girl who served as his better half more often than his wife. This unfair sharing had upset the domestic peace. Although nothing was so hard as bothering this fellow who bothered less than anyone about rumors, he decided to leave his wife and live with his servant. But his whole fortune was tied up in furnishings, in machines, designs, tools, and other movable effects. And he preferred to leave his wife naked rather than to go off empty-handed. So here is the plan he conceived. He would write notes drawn on himself to his servant who would follow through their payment and thus obtain seizure and sale of his effects, which would then be taken from Saint Michael bridge to the house where he hoped to live with his servant. He is completely taken with the idea; he writes notes, signs himself away, gets two lawyers. And there he is, running from one to the other, pursuing himself with all possible ferocity, attacking well, defending badly. And he is finally condemned to pay up under penalty of law. And in his mind he was already laying hands on everything in the house. But it didn't work out quite that way. He was dealing with a very experienced tart, who instead of having the seizure put on his effects, had it transferred to his person, and had him put in prison. So that, however strange his story had sounded in the enigmatic replies he had given me, it was nonetheless true.

While I have been telling you this story, which you will take for fiction. . . . —And how about the man who sawed away on his bass viol?—Reader, I promise on my honor, you shan't lose that story, but please let me get back to Jacques and his master. Jacques and his master had arrived at the inn where they were to spend the night. It was late; the city gates were closed and they were obliged to stay in the suburbs. There I hear a great noise.—You! You hear! You weren't even there! It's not a question of your hearing.—That's true. Well then, Jacques . . . his master . . . one hears a frightening uproar. I see two men.—You don't see anything; it's not up to you; you weren't there.—That's true. There were two men talking quietly at a table near the door of their room; there was a woman, fists on hips, who was vomiting out at them a torrent of insults. And Jacques was trying to pacify that woman, though she paid no more attention to his pacifying remonstrances than the two men paid to the invective she showered on them. "Come, come, my good woman," Jacques said to her, "patience, control yourself. Let's see here; what is this all about? These gentlemen seem honest enough folk."

"Them! Honest folk! They're brutes, without pity, without humanity, without the slightest feeling. Humph! And what did poor little Nicole do to them to be maltreated so badly? She'll probably be crippled the rest of her days."

"Perhaps it's not as bad as you think."

"The blow was terrifying, I tell you; she'll certainly be crippled."

"We must see; you ought to send for the doctor . . ."

"They've already gone for him."

"Ought to put her to bed."

"She's already there, and she's sobbing to break your heart. My poor Nicole!"

Amidst these lamentations someone rang and cried: "Hey there, landlady, some wine!" She replied: "I'm coming." They rang from another quarter and shouted: "Hey there, landlady, some linen up here!" She replied, "Coming." "Some cutlets and a duck!" "Coming." "A wine pot and a chamber pot!" "Coming, coming." And from another part of the establishment a furious gentleman shouted: "Cursed gossip, rabid gossip! What are you getting mixed up in? Are you going to make me wait until tomorrow? Jacques! Jacques!"

The landlady, having gotten over her pain and fury a bit, said to Jacques: "Ah, sir, leave me; you are too kind."

"Jacques, Jacques!"

"Run quickly. Ah, if you but knew all the sorrows of this poor creature."

"Jacques, Jacques!"

"Go along now; I think it's your master calling."

"Jacques! Jacques!"

It was indeed Jacques's master who had undressed by himself and who was dying of hunger and growing impatient at not being served. Jacques went upstairs, and a moment later the landlady arrived. She seemed completely exhausted. "A thousand pardons," she said to Jacques's master. "It's just that there are some things in this life a person can't stomach. What would you like? I've got chicken, squab, an excellent *râble de lièvre,* some rabbit—this is the district for good rabbit, you know. Or maybe you would like a river bird?" Jacques ordered for his master and for himself as was customary. Dinner was served and while they were devouring the food, the master said to Jacques: "What the devil were you doing down there?"

Jacques. Possibly some good, possibly ill; who knows?

The Master. And just what good or what ill were you doing?

Jacques. I prevented that woman from having herself set upon by two men who are down there, and who have at very least broken her serving girl's arm.

The Master. And maybe it would have done her good to be beaten.

Jacques. That for ten reasons each one better than the other. One of the greatest joys of my life, as I stand before you . . .

The Master. Was to get beaten? Wine, wine!

Jacques. Yes, sir, beaten, beaten up on the highway, one night, coming back from the village, just as I told you, after having done by my standards a fool thing; according to you, the fine act of giving my money away.

The Master. Oh yes, I remember. Wine! And what was at the base of that quarrel you quieted down there, and of the maltreatment received by the landlady's servant?

Jacques. Good heavens, I don't know.

The Master. You don't know the wherefore of the thing, and you get mixed up in it! Jacques, that is not in keeping with prudence, justice, or any other principle. Wine!

Jacques. I don't know what your principles are unless rules for one's own benefit laid down for the conduct of others. Every sermon sounds like the preamble of a royal edict; all the preachers want us to practice their lessons because we might be the better for it, but as for themselves—Virtue. . . .

The Master. Virtue, Jacques, is a good thing. The good and the evil alike speak well of it. Wine!

Jacques. That's because they both find it to their advantage.

The Master. And why was it such a joy for you to be beaten?

Jacques. It's late; you've eaten a lot and so have I. We're both tired. Take my advice, let's both go to sleep.

The Master. Not possible, and anyhow the landlady still owes us something. While waiting, take up your story.

Jacques. Where was I? I beg of you, my master, for this time, and for all the others, put me back on the trail.

The Master. I'll take that responsibility, and to start out my role of prompter, you were in your bed, penniless, at your wits' end, while the doctor's wife and her children ate your toast.

Jacques. Then we heard a coach stop at the door of the house. A lackey enters and asks: "Isn't it here that I can find a poor fellow, a soldier with a crutch, who came back last night from the neighboring village?"

"Yes," replied the doctor's wife, "what do you want with him?"

"We want to put him in the coach and take him with us."

"He's in his bed; pull the curtains and talk to him."

Jacques was at just this point when the landlady entered and asked, "What do you want for dessert?"

The Master. Whatever you have.

The landlady, without troubling to go down again, called: "Nanon, bring some fruit, some cakes and jam."

At mention of Nanon, Jacques said in an aside: "Ah, it's her daughter they mistreated; enough to infuriate a man, unless . . ."

And the master said to the landlady, "You were quite angry a little while ago?"

The Landlady. And who wouldn't get angry? The poor creature had done nothing to them. She was scarcely in their room when I heard shouts, but such shouts! God be praised! I feel a little better. The doctor says it will be nothing. However she has two large contusions, one on the head, the other on her shoulder.

The Master. Has she been with you long?

The Landlady. Two weeks at least. She was abandoned at the next stop down.

The Master. What do you mean, abandoned?

The Landlady. Just that, good Lord, abandoned. There are some people who are harder than rocks. She almost drowned while swimming the river that flows nearby. She made it miraculously and I took her in out of charity.

The Master. How old is she?

The Landlady. I think maybe about a year and a half.

At this Jacques bursts out into laughter and cries: "It's a dog!"

The Landlady. The loveliest beast in the world. I wouldn't give up my Nicole for ten louis. My poor Nicole.

The Master. Madame has a good heart.

The Landlady. You're right; I look after my animals and my servants.

The Master. That's a very good thing. And who are these people who mistreated Nicole?

The Landlady. Two merchants from the next town. They have been whispering ceaselessly to each other. They think we don't know what they're saying, and that we don't know their story. They haven't been here three hours yet and already I know all their affairs. It makes an interesting story. If you weren't any more anxious to get to sleep than I am, I should tell it you exactly as their servant told it to my servant, who happened by chance to be from her part of the country. She told it to my husband and he told it to me. The mother-in-law of the younger [25] passed through here not three months ago; she was going off, much against her wishes, to a provincial convent where she didn't linger long; she died there. And that's why our two young men are in mourning. But here, without even wanting to I'm getting into their story. Good evening, gentlemen, and good night. You found the wine good?

The Master. Very good.

The Landlady. And you were satisfied with supper?

The Master. Very happy. Your spinach is a little salty.

The Landlady. Sometimes I lay on with a heavy hand. You'll sleep well and in clean sheets. We never use them twice here.

Having said that, the landlady withdrew and Jacques and his master went to bed laughing at the misunderstanding which had made them take a dog for the daughter or servant of the house, and chuckling at the passion of the landlady for a lost dog which she had had only two weeks. Jacques said to his master as he tied the strings of his nightcap: "I'll bet that of everything that is alive in this inn, she loves only her Nicole." His master replied: "That's possible, but let's sleep."

While Jacques and his master are resting, I'm going to make good my promise with the story of the man in prison who sawed away on his bass, or rather of his comrade, Sir Gousse.

"This third fellow," he said, "is a steward in a large house. He fell in love with a pastryman's wife who lives on the rue de l'Université. The pastrymaker was a good fellow who paid more attention to his oven than to his wife's conduct. Thus it wasn't so much his jealousy, but rather his assiduity that bothered our two lovers. How did they deliver themselves from such a curb? The steward gave to his master a written complaint in which he represented the baker as a man of bad habits, a drunkard who never left the tavern, a brute who beat his wife, the most honest and unhappy of women. On the strength of this petition he obtained a *lettre de cachet*,[26] and this letter, which took care of the husband, was put into the hands of a police officer to be carried out without delay. It happened that by chance this officer was a friend of the baker. They were in the habit of going together to the wineshop from time to time; the baker furnished the little pastries; the police officer, the bottle. The officer, with the *lettre de cachet,* passes by the pastry shop and gives the usual sign. And the two are off, busily eating and wetting down their little pastries. The officer asks his friend how his business is going—

Very well.

Whether he had any troubles—

None.

Whether he had any enemies—

He didn't know of any.

How he was getting along with his relatives, his neighbors, and his wife—

In friendship and in peace.

"From whence does it come, then," asked the officer, "that I have this order to arrest you? If I did my duty I should collar you.

There would be a coach standing ready and I should take you to the place prescribed on this *lettre de cachet*. Look here, read it."

The baker read and grew pale. The officer said to him: "Don't be upset, let's just think together what we can best do for your safety and my own. Who frequents your house?"

"Nobody."

"Even though your wife is pretty and coquettish?"

"I let her do as she pleases."

"Nobody has set his sights on her?"

"Goodness no, unless it's a certain steward who comes from time to time to shake her hand and to spin out a bit of idle chatter. But that's in my shop, right in front of me, and in the presence of my boys, and I don't believe anything goes on between them that isn't completely proper and honorable."

"You're a good man!"

"That may well be, but it's best in any case to believe your wife is honest, and that's what I do."

"And this steward, for whom does he work?"

"For M. de Saint-Florentin." [27]

"And from whose offices do you think the *lettre de cachet* comes?"

"Probably from M. de Saint-Florentin's offices."

"You've guessed it."

"Oh! Eat my pastry, lay my wife, and then have me shut up—that's a little too much, and I can't believe it!"

"You are a good man! How has your wife been these last few days?"

"More sad than gay."

"And the steward? Has it been long since you've seen him?"

"Yesterday, I think; yes, it was yesterday."

"You didn't notice anything?"

"I'm not very observing, but it seemed to me that when they parted they made certain signs with their heads as if one were saying yes and the other no."

"And whose head was it that said yes?"

"The steward's."

"Either they are innocent or they are conspiring. See here, my friend, don't go back home. Escape to some sure spot, to the Temple, in the Abbey,[28] where you will. In any case, leave it to me. Above all, remember . . ."

"Not to be seen and to be quiet."

"Exactly so."

At this very moment the baker's house is surrounded by spies. Informers, in all sorts of attire, call on the pastryman's wife and ask for her husband. She tells one that he is sick; another, that he has gone to a celebration; a third, that he has gone to a wedding. When will he be back? She has no idea.

The third day, about two in the morning, they inform the officer that a man, his face hidden in a cloak, had been seen gently opening the street door and slipping into the baker's house. Immediately the police officer accompanied by a commissioner, a locksmith, a carriage, and several policemen go to the scene. They pick the lock, and the officer and commissioner go quietly upstairs. They knock at the wife's bedroom door. No reply. They knock again. No reply. The third time someone asks from within, "Who is it?"

"Open up."

"Who is it?"

"Open in the name of the King."

"Good," said the steward to the wife, with whom he was sleeping, "there is no danger. It's the police officer coming to carry out his orders. Open up, I shall make myself known, he will withdraw, and everything will be finished."

The baker's wife, in her nightgown, opens up, and gets back in bed.

The Police Officer. Where's your husband?

The Wife. He's not here.

The Police Officer (pulling back the curtain). Then who is that?
The Steward. It is I; I am M. de Saint-Florentin's steward.

The Police Officer. You are lying; you're the baker, because the baker is the man who sleeps with the baker's wife. Get up, get dressed and follow me.

He had to obey, and they brought him here. The minister, informed of the villainy of his steward, approved of the police officer's conduct. The officer is to come tonight to take the steward from this prison to Bicêtre, where, thanks to the economies of the prison administration he will eat his quarter of bad bread, his ounce of cow, and will saw away on his bass fiddle from morning till night.

If I were to lay my head on a pillow, too, while waiting for Jacques and his master to wake up, what would you think?

3

❧ ❧ ❧

THE NEXT DAY JACQUES GOT UP EARLY, PUT HIS HEAD OUT OF THE window to look at the weather, saw that it was a miserable day, went back to bed and let us sleep—his master and myself—as much as we pleased.

Jacques, his master, and the other voyagers who had stopped off at the same inn thought it would clear up about noon. It didn't at all. The rain from the storm had swollen the stream that separated the suburb from the city to the point where passage became dangerous. All those who were going in that direction decided to lose another day and wait. Some spent their time talking, others paced to and fro, sticking their noses out the door, looking out at the weather and coming back cursing and stamping their feet. Several launched into drinking and politics; many played cards. And the rest of them smoked, slept, and did nothing. The master said to Jacques: "I trust that Jacques will take up the story of his loves, and that heaven, which wants me to have the satisfaction of hearing their end, will keep us here by reason of bad weather."

Jacques. Heaven that wants! We don't know what heaven does or does not want, and perhaps heaven itself knows nothing about it. My poor captain, who is no more, repeated that to me a hundred times. And the more I have lived, the more I realize he was right. To your health, my master.

The Master. I agree. You were, I believe, at the part about the coach and the lackey, and the doctor's wife had told him to open your curtains and speak to you.

Jacques. This lackey comes to my bed, and says: "Come, comrade, get up, dress, and let's leave." I reply to him from beneath the sheets and the covers in which my head was enveloped, without seeing him and without being seen: "Comrade, let me sleep and go away." The lackey replies that he has orders from his master and that he must carry them out.

"And this master, who lays down orders to a man he doesn't know—has he the money to pay what I owe here?"

"It's already been taken care of. Hurry, everybody is waiting for you at the castle where, I can assure you, you will be better off, at least if what is to follow corresponds to the anticipation they now feel at seeing you."

I allow myself to be persuaded. I sit up, dress, and they support me under the arms. I had made my adieux to the doctor's wife, and I was about to get into the coach when that woman, coming up to me, takes me by the arm and begs me to come into a corner of the room, for she wanted a word with me. "Now, my good friend," she said, "you have no complaint to make of us, I should think. The doctor saved your leg, and I have cared for you well. I hope you will not forget us up there at the château."

"What could I do for you up there?"

"Request that it be my husband who comes to give you your dressings. There are so many people there! It's the best practice in the district. The lord is a generous man, and pays well. Depending upon you alone, we could make a fortune. My husband has tried several times to get in up there, but without success."

"But, Madame, isn't there already a doctor at the château?"

"Certainly."

"And if he were your husband would you be happy to have them discontinue his services and put him out?"

"Well, that doctor is a man to whom you owe nothing, and I think you do owe my husband something. If you now walk on two feet as you did before, it's thanks to him."

"And so because your husband has done me a good turn, I must do a bad one to another? It would be different if the practice were open."

Jacques was going to continue when the landlady, holding Nicole all wrapped up in her arms, came in, kissing, pitying, caressing, and talking to the dog as to a child: "My poor little Nicole; she cried only once the whole night. And you, gentlemen, did you sleep well?"

The Master. Very well.

The Landlady. The weather is bad all about.

Jacques. Yes, we are rather put out about it.

The Landlady. Are you gentlemen going far?

Jacques. We have no idea.

The Landlady. The gentlemen are following someone then?

Jacques. We're following nobody.

The Landlady. Then you go and stop according to the business you have along the way?

Jacques. But we have no business.

The Landlady. The gentlemen are traveling for their pleasure then?

Jacques. Or for their discomfort.

The Landlady. I trust it is for the former.

Jacques. Your trust isn't worth an iota; it will be according to what's written up yonder.

The Landlady. Oh! it's a marriage then?

Jacques. Perhaps yes, perhaps no.

The Landlady. Gentlemen, be careful. That man who is downstairs and who treated my little Nicole so rudely, made a very strange marriage. Come here, my little animal, come; let me kiss you; I promise it will never happen again. You see how she is quivering all over.

The Master. And what was so strange about the marriage of this fellow?

Upon this question from the master, the landlady said: "I hear noise downstairs; I'll give my orders for the day, then I'll come back up and tell you all about it." Her husband, tired of shouting: "Wife, my wife!" comes up, unaware that he is being followed by his neighbor. The landlord says to his wife: "What the devil are you doing up here?" Then, turning and seeing his neighbor, he says: "Did you bring me some money?"

The Neighbor. No, my friend, you know very well that I have none.

The Landlord. You have none, eh! Well, I know what to do with your plow and horses, your cattle and your bed. What's the meaning of this, good-for-nothing?

The Neighbor. I am not a good-for-nothing.

The Landlord. Well, what are you then? You live in poverty, you don't know which way to turn to get enough to sow your fields. Your landowner, tired of making you advances, will give not one jot more. You come to me, and that woman intercedes for you, that cursed gossip who is the cause of all the mistakes of my life convinces me I should lend you some money. So I do, and you promise to return it. You have failed me ten times. Well, I can assure you, I shan't fail you. Now get out of here!

Jacques and his master were getting ready to plead for the poor devil, but the landlady, putting her finger on her mouth, signaled to them to be quiet.

The Landlord. Get out of here.

The Neighbor. Neighbor, all you are saying is true. It is also true that the sheriff's men are at my house, and that at any minute now we shall be reduced to begging—my daughter, my son, and myself.

The Landlord. It's what you deserve. What's the idea of coming here at this hour of the morning? I leave off filling my wine bottles, I come up from the cellar, and I don't find you here at all. Get out of here, I tell you.

The Neighbor. My friend, I did come earlier. But I was afraid of the reception you would give me. I went back again and I'm going back now.

The Landlord. And you do well.

The Neighbor. And so my poor Marguerite, who is so good and so pretty, will go off to Paris into domestic service.

The Landlord. Into service! In Paris! You want her to become a poor unfortunate?

The Neighbor. It's not I who want it; it's the harsh man to whom I'm speaking.

The Landlord. Me, a harsh man! I am not at all harsh and never have been, and you know it very well.

The Neighbor. I am no longer able to feed my daughter and son; my daughter will go into service, my boy will join up.

The Landlord. And I shall be the cause of it! No, it shall not be. You are a cruel man; as long as I live you will be my cross to bear. Now then, let's see what you need.

The Neighbor. I need nothing. I am grieved at owing you, and I shall never again in my life be in your debt. You do more ill with your insults than good with your services. If I had money, I should throw it in your face; but I have none. My daughter will become whatever it pleases God to make of her; my boy will get himself killed if he must. And I, I shall beg, but not at your door. No more, no more obligations to a man like you. Go to it and pocket the money from my cattle, my horses and my effects—may they be of great use to you! You were born to make ingrates, and I don't want to be one of them. Farewell.

The Landlord. My wife, he is going off. Stop him!

The Landlady. Come now, neighbor. Let's think how we can help you.

The Neighbor. I want no help, not his; it is bought too dearly.

The landlord repeated in a low voice to his wife: "Don't let him go! Stop him, stop him! His daughter in Paris, his boy in the army, and himself begging at the church door! I could never stand that!"

Meanwhile his wife was trying in vain. The peasant, who very definitely had his feelings, wanted no part of it, and needed four men to hold him back. The landlord, tears in his eyes, turned to

Jacques and his master and pleaded: "Gentlemen, try to sway him." Jacques and his master got into the affair; all together they implored the peasant. If I have ever seen . . . —If you have ever seen! But you weren't there. Say rather, if one has ever seen.— All right, so be it. If one has ever seen a man embarrassed by a refusal, and ecstatic that someone should want his money, it was that landlord. He embraced his wife, he embraced his neighbor, he embraced Jacques and his master and he cried: "Go quickly to his house and chase away the sheriff's men."

The Neighbor. Agree also . . .

The Landlord. I agree that I spoil everything. But, neighbor, what do you expect? As you see me, so I am. Nature made me the hardest and yet the tenderest man; I know neither how to refuse nor how to concede.

The Neighbor. Couldn't you be otherwise?

The Landlord. I am at an age when you don't improve or change much. But if the first people who had to deal with me had been a little rough with me as you have been, perhaps I should have been better. Neighbor, I thank you for your lesson, perhaps I shall profit by it. Wife, go quickly, go downstairs and give him what he needs. What the devil, woman, move! By God, come; move now! Are you going? Wife, I beg you, please hurry a bit and don't keep him waiting. You can come back afterward to these gentlemen with whom it would seem you are very happy.

The wife and the neighbor went down; the landlord remained another minute, and when he had gone, Jacques said to his master: "Now there's a strange fellow! Heaven that held us here by way of bad weather so you could hear my love story—what do you think is its pleasure now?"

The master, stretching out in his chair, yawning and tapping his snuffbox, replied: "Jacques, we have more than one day to live together, unless . . ."

Jacques. That is to say that, for today, heaven wants me to be silent and let the landlady do the talking. She's a gossip, who couldn't ask for better. Well, let her speak then.

The Master. Jacques, you're falling into a mood.

Jacques. Well, I like to talk too.

The Master. Your turn will come.

Jacques. Or else it won't.

I understand you, reader. Here, you say, is the true ending of the *Burbero benefico*.[29] I think so too. I should have put into that play, had I been the author, a character that would have seemed episodic and would have turned out not to be. This character would have appeared several times, and his appearances would have been motivated. The first time, he would have come to ask for extension, but the fear of a bad reception would have made him leave before Geronte's arrival. Upset by the arrival of the sheriff in his house, he would have had the courage to wait a second time upon Geronte. But this time Geronte would have refused to see him. Finally I should have brought him in at the end, where he would have played exactly the role that the peasant played with the landlord. He would have had, like the peasant, a daughter whom he was about to place with a millinery merchant, a son whom he would have taken from school to put into apprenticeship, and as for himself, he would have decided to beg until he had had enough of life. You would have seen the *burbero benefico* at the feet of this fellow, you would have heard that beneficent bear scolded as he deserved to be. He would have had to appeal to his whole family, gathered there about him, to sway his debtor and bring him to take additional financial aid. The bear would have been nicely punished; he would have promised at that instant to become a changed man, but at the same instant he would have reverted to his character by growing impatient with the characters on the stage as they argued politely over who should go back first into the house. He would have said brusquely: "To the devil with all this cerem . . ." But he would have stopped short halfway through his sentence, and in a gentle tone, would have said to his nieces: "Come, my nieces,

give me your hands and we shall go in."—And to tie in this character, you would have made him a protégé of Geronte's nephew,
perhaps?—Very good.—And it would have been at the nephew's
insistence that the uncle lends his money?—Marvelous!—And this
moneylending would have been in the way of compensation for
an injury of the uncle to the nephew?—Exactly so.—So that the
end of this play would no longer be a mass remonstrance on the
part of the whole company for the things he had formerly done
to each singly?—You are right.—Well, if I ever meet M. Goldoni,
I'll recite for him the scene of the inn.—And you would do well,
for he is a man much cleverer than he need be to take advantage
of such a scene.

The landlady came back up with Nicole still in her arms and
said: "I hope you will have a good dinner; the poacher has just
come, and the game preserve warden won't be far behind." And
saying that, she took a chair. And once seated, she begins her story.

The Landlady. You must be careful of lackeys; masters have no
worse enemy.

Jacques. Madame, you don't know what you're saying. There
are good ones, and there are bad ones. And you could perhaps
count more good lackeys than good masters.

The Master. Jacques, you are forgetting yourself, and you're
committing the same fault which has just shocked you.

Jacques. Well, it's just that masters . . .

The Master. Just that lackeys . . .

Well now, reader. Why don't I stir up a violent quarrel between
these three characters? Why shouldn't the landlady be taken by
the shoulders and thrown out of the room by Jacques? Or why not
Jacques taken by the shoulders and sent out of the room by his
master, so that one goes one way, the other another way, and then
you would hear neither the landlady's story nor the rest of Jacques's?
Rest easy, I shall do nothing of the sort. So the landlady continued.

"Well, at least you've got to admit that if there are very bad
men, there are also very bad women."

Jacques. And that you don't have to go far to find them.

The Landlady. And why are you butting in? I am a woman and I have a right to say about women anything I please, but I don't need your help.

Jacques. My help is as good as any other's.

The Landlady. Sir, you have there a lackey who likes to act the know-it-all and he fails you therein. I have servants, too, but I like them to know their place.

The Master. Jacques, be quiet, and let Madame tell her story.

The landlady, encouraged by this remark of the master, gets up, torments Jacques, takes at him on both sides with her fists, forgets she is holding Nicole, and drops her. There is Nicole on the floor, disheveled and struggling in her wrappings, and barking furiously, the landlady adding her cries to those of the dog, Jacques joining his guffaws to the barks of Nicole and the shrieks of the landlady, and the master opening his snuffbox, taking his pinch, and unable to keep from laughing. The entire hostelry is in tumult. "Nanon, Nanon, quick! Bring the brandy bottle. My poor Nicole is dead. Unwrap her. How clumsy you are!"

"I'm doing my best."

"Listen to her cry. Get out of the way. Let me do it. Ah, she is dead. Laugh on, big ninny; for it is indeed laughable. My poor Nicole is dead!"

"No, Madame, no; I believe she will come around. There, she's stirring now."

And so Nanon continues to rub the dog's nose with brandy, and makes her swallow some; and the landlady weeps and wails and lashes out against all impertinent lackeys. Nanon says hopefully: "Look, Madame, she is opening her eyes; she is looking at you."

"The poor thing. See how she talks to me! Who would not be touched?"

"Madame, caress her a bit; talk to her a bit."

"Come to me, my poor Nicole; cry, my baby, cry, if that makes you feel better. There is a destiny for animals just as for men. It sends happiness to the surly, noisy, greedy good-for-nothing, unhappiness to another who is the best creature in the world."

"Madame is very right; there is no justice here below."

"Be quiet! Wrap her up again, and carry her over to my pillow, and remember that for the least cry she makes, I'll hold you responsible. Come, my little animal; let me kiss you one more time before they carry you off. Well, bring her here, closer, stupid that you are. Ah, dogs, they are so good. They're worth more than . . ."

Jacques. Than father, mother, brothers, sisters, children, lackeys, and husbands.

The Landlady. Why yes, and don't laugh. They're innocent and do you no wrong. They're faithful to you, whereas the rest . . .

Jacques. Long live dogs! There's nothing more perfect under the heavens.

The Landlady. Well, if there is something more perfect, at least it's not a man. I wish you could know the miller's dog; he's my Nicole's lover. There's not a one of you, whoever you are, that wouldn't blush with shame over him. He comes at daybreak, over a league, plants himself in front of this window, and then there are sighs enough to draw pity from anyone. Whatever the weather, he stays on; rain falls on his little body; it gets buried in the sand; you can scarcely see his ears and the tip of his nose. Would you do as much for the woman you most loved?

The Master. That's very gallant.

Jacques. But at the same time, where is the woman as worthy of such attentions as your Nicole?

The landlady's passion for animals was not, however, her dominant passion, as you can well imagine. That passion was talking. The more you were patient and agreeable in listening, the more you were worth to her. And so she didn't need to be coaxed to take up again the interrupted story of the strange marriage. She attached only one condition—that Jacques should be quiet. The master promised silence on Jacques's part. Jacques stretched out languidly in a corner, eyes closed, his cap pulled down over his ears and his back turned to the landlady. The master coughed, spat, blew his nose, drew out his watch, looked at the time, took his snuffbox, tapped the lid, took his pinch, and the landlady got all set to savor the delicious pleasure of oration.

The landlady was about to start when she heard her dog cry.

The Landlady. Nanon, see to that poor animal. It bothers me so I don't know where I'm at any more.

Jacques. Up to now, you haven't said a thing.

The Landlady. These two men—the ones I got in a quarrel with over my little Nicole, when you arrived, sir . . .

Jacques. Say rather sirs.

The Landlady. And why?

Jacques. Just that up to now people have always treated us with that respect and that I'm used to it. My master calls me Jacques; but the others call me Monsieur Jacques.

The Landlady. I shall call you neither Jacques nor Monsieur Jacques, for I'm not speaking to you. (—Madame?) What is it? (—The bill for number five.) Look on the corner of the chimney. These men are quite proper gentlemen; they come from Paris and are going to the estate of the older man.

Jacques. Who knows that?

The Landlady. They do, for they told me.

Jacques. Now there's a fine reason for you.

The master made a motion to the landlady upon which she understood that Jacques was a little off in the head. The landlady replied to the master with an understanding shrug of the shoulders and added: "At his age! It's very unfortunate."

Jacques. Very unfortunate indeed—not to know where you're going.

The Landlady. The older of the two is the Marquis des Arcis. He was a gay fellow, very likable, and with little faith in the virtue of women.

Jacques. He was right.

The Landlady. Monsieur Jacques, you are interrupting me.

Jacques. Madame Landlady of the Grand-Cerf, I'm not talking to you.

The Landlady. However, the marquis found one who was different enough to hold him in check. She was known as Mme de La Pommeraye. She was a widow of morals, birth, fortune and position. M. des Arcis broke with all his acquaintances and attached himself to Mme de La Pommeraye only, paid her court with the greatest diligence, tried by every imaginable sacrifice to prove to her that he loved her, even proposed to marry her. But this woman had been so unhappy with a first husband that she . . . (—Madame?) What is it? (—The key to the oats.) Look on the nail and if it's not there, look on the box . . . that she would have preferred all sorts of unhappiness to the danger of a second marriage.

Jacques. Ah! If it had been written up yonder! ,

The Landlady. This lady lived quite in retirement. The marquis was an old friend of her husband; she had received him and continued to do so. If you could pardon him his incontinent taste for playing the gallant, he was what you might call a gentleman of honor. This constant courting by the marquis, seconded by his personal qualities, his youth, his appearance, the outward marks of his true passion, his solitude, his leaning toward tenderness— in a word, all which loses us to the seduction of men . . . (—Madame?) What is it? (—It's the mail.) Put it in the green room and deliver it as usual . . . had its effect, and Mme de La Pommeraye, after having struggled against the marquis and against herself for several months, and after having demanded the usual solemn pledges, gave in to the marquis. The marquis would have had the happiest of lives if he had been able to preserve for his mistress the feelings he had sworn to and which she had sworn for him. You see, gentlemen, only women know how to love; men don't understand it at all. (—Madame?) What is it? (—The mendicant brother.) Give him twelve sous for these gentlemen, six for me, and let him go to the other rooms. After several years, the marquis began to find life with Mme de La Pommeraye too even. He suggested that she get back into society; she consented. He proposed receiving several ladies and gentlemen; she consented. He proposed giving a supper; she consented. Little by little, two days would pass without his seeing her. Bit by bit he began to miss the supper they had arranged; bit by bit, he started to shorten his visits—he had business which called him away. When he did arrive, he would say a few words, stretch out in an armchair, take up a recent pamphlet, throw it away, talk to his dog, or fall asleep. In the evening, his health, which had become bad, would require him to retire very early. This was Tronchin's advice. "Tronchin is a great man. My goodness, I have no doubt that he will pull our friend through, though all the others despaired for her." [30] And talking the while, in such manner, he would take his cane and hat and leave, sometimes even forgetting to kiss her. Mme de La Pommeraye . . . (—Madame?) What is it? (—The cooper.) Take him down to the cellar and have him look at the two barrels in the corner. Mme de La Pommeraye felt that she was no longer loved. She had to be sure and this is how she went about it . . . (—Madame?) I'm coming, I'm coming.

The landlady, tired of all these interruptions, went downstairs and apparently took measures to have the interruptions stopped.

The Landlady. One day after dinner she said to the marquis: "My friend, you are dreaming."

"And you, too, madame."

"It is true, and really rather sadly so."

"What's the matter?"

"Nothing."

"That's not true. Come, madame," he said while yawning, "tell me all about it; it will keep us both from getting bored."

"What, you are bored?"

"No, it's just that there are some days . . ."

"When you are bored?"

"No, my dear, you are wrong; I swear you are wrong. But there are days, as a matter of fact—I don't know what causes it."

"My friend, for a long time now I have been tempted to confess to you, but I'm afraid of hurting you."

"Could you hurt me, you?"

"Perhaps. But heaven is witness of my innocence." (—Madame? Madame? Madame?) Whoever and whatever it is, I have forbidden you to call me; call my husband. (—He's not here.) Gentlemen, I beg your pardon; I shall be back in a minute.

And the landlady is down, back up, and continuing her story:

"But all that has happened to me without my consent, without my knowing it, through one of those curses to which all human kind is apparently subject, since, even I have not escaped."

"Oh, it's about yourself, madame. And here I was afraid . . . What is it about?"

"Marquis, it's about . . . I am truly sorry; I shall make you feel bad, and, in the long run I think it better that I should be quiet."

"No, my dear, speak up. Could you keep deep in your heart a secret from me? Wasn't the first of our agreements that we should open ourselves to each other without reserve?"

"That is true and that's what bothers me. For that's the reproach that is the final blow to another reproach I have been making to myself. Do you not notice that I no longer have the same gaiety? That I have lost appetite, and eat and drink only mechanically? And I can't sleep. Our most intimate contacts displease me. At night I ask myself: Is he less lovable? No. Have you any complaints? No. Could you suspect him of secret love affairs? No. Has his tenderness for you diminished? No. Why, then, if your friend is the same, has your heart changed? For it has and you can't deny that. You no longer wait for his arrival with the same impatience, you no longer find the same pleasure in seeing him. That anxiety when he was late in coming, that tender emotion at

the noise of his carriage, when he was announced, when he appeared
—you feel it no longer."

"How is that, madame?"

Here Mme de La Pommeraye covered her eyes with her hands,
bowed her head, and was silent for a moment, after which she
added: "Marquis, I was prepared for all your astonishment, all the
bitter things you would say. Marquis! Spare me! No, no, don't
spare me; say them. I shall listen to them with resignation, because
I deserve it. Yes, my dear Marquis, it is true—yes, I do, but isn't
it a great enough misfortune that the thing has happened, without
adding to it the shame and the scorn of being false in hiding it
from you? You are the same, but your friend has changed. Your
friend respects you, reveres you as much and more than ever, but—
but a woman, as accustomed as she is to examining closely what
happens in the most secret folds of her soul, and used to being surprised at nothing, cannot hide from herself the fact that love has
gone away. The discovery is frightful, but it is nonetheless real.
The Marquise de La Pommeraye, me, me, inconstant! Unfaithful!
Marquis, go into a rage! Seek out the most hateful names; I have
already given them to myself. Call me those names, I am prepared
to suffer all of them. That is, all except the name of a false woman,
which you will spare me, I hope, for, in truth, I am not one."
(—My wife?) What is it? (—Nothing.) You don't have one
minute's rest in this house, even on the days when there are practically no guests and you think there's nothing to do. How a
woman of my condition is to be pitied, especially with a stupid
husband! Having said that, Mme de La Pommeraye fell over on
her chair and started to weep. The marquis threw himself at her
knees and said: "You are a charming woman, an adorable woman,
the like of which exists nowhere. Your frankness and your honesty
confound me and ought to make me die of shame. Ah! What
superiority you have over me in this moment. How big you seem
to me and how small I feel! For you have spoken first and I was
guilty first. My friend, your sincerity draws me on. I should be a

monster if it did not, and I shall confess to you that the history of your heart is word for word the history of my own. Everything you have said to yourself, I have said to myself; but I was silent and I suffered and I do not know when I should ever have had the courage to speak."

"True, my friend?"

"Nothing could be more true, and there remains only to congratulate ourselves at having lost that delicate and deceptive feeling which united us, at precisely the same moment."

"How true, indeed! How unfortunate had my love lasted after yours had stopped!"

"Or if it had been in me that love first stopped!"

"You are right, I feel it."

"Never have you seemed so lovable and so beautiful to me as in this moment, and if the experience of the past had not taught me caution, I should think I loved you more than ever." And the marquis, speaking to her thus, took her hand and kissed it. (—My wife?) What is it? (—The straw merchant.) Look on the register. (—And where is the register? . . . Stay up, stay up, I have it.)

Mme de La Pommeraye, shutting up inside the mortal spite which tore at her, began to speak again and said to the marquis: "But, Marquis, what is to become of us?"

"We have not taken false advantage of each other; you have the right to my full esteem; I don't think I have entirely lost the right I had to yours. We shall continue to see each other, we shall surrender ourselves to the intimacy of the tenderest sort of friendship. We shall have spared ourselves all the worries, all the little deceptions, all those reproaches, all that moodiness which usually accompanies a dying passion. We shall be unique. You shall recover all your freedom; you will give me back mine. We shall go out again into the world; I shall be the confidant of your conquests, and I shall not hide my own—if I should have any, which I doubt very much, for you have made that very difficult. It's going to be wonderful! You will help me with your advice, and I shall not refuse you mine in those perilous circumstances when you think you need it. Who knows what might happen?"

Jacques. Nobody.

The Marquis. "It is very likely that the more I see of things, the more you will gain by comparison, and perhaps I shall come back to you more passionate, more tender, and more convinced than ever that Mme de La Pommeraye was the only woman created for my happiness. And after this return, there is everything to indicate that I shall remain faithful to you to the end of my life."

"And if it should happen that upon your return you didn't find me? For, after all, Marquis, we are not always foolproof, and it's not beyond the realm of possibility that I should find leanings, fancy, even passion for another, who would not be worth yourself."

"I should most certainly be heartbroken, but I should have no complaints. I should blame only the destiny that had separated us when we were together and that would be bringing us close together again when we could no longer stay together."

After this conversation, they set about moralizing on the inconstancy of the human heart, on the fickleness of oaths, on the bonds of marriage . . . (—Madame?) What is it? (—The coach.) "Gentlemen," said the landlady, "I must leave you. This evening when all my work has been done, I shall come back and finish for you this adventure if you are curious about it." (—Madame?— My wife?—Ho-there, Landlady?) Coming, coming.

The landlady having departed, the master said to his lackey: "Jacques, did you notice one thing?"

Jacques. Which one?

The Master. Just that this woman tells a story much better than is natural for the landlady of an inn.

Jacques. That's true. The frequent interruptions of the people in this house upset me many times.

The Master. And me, too.

And you, reader, speak up frankly, for, you see, we are in a fine mood for frankness. Do you want me to leave off here this elegant and verbose gossip of a landlady, and shall we take up again Jacques's love story? As for me, I don't care one way or the other. When that woman comes back up, the loquacious Jacques would like nothing better than to resume his role and to slam the door in her face. He'd be more than satisfied with saying through the keyhole: "Good night, Madame; my master is sleeping and I am going to bed. You'll have to put off the rest until our next stop here."

"The first mutual vow made by two fleshly beings was sworn at the foot of a rock already crumbling into dust. They called as witness to their fidelity a sky that is never for an instant the same. Everything was changing, in them and about them; yet they believed their hearts free from vicissitudes. Oh, children! Ever children!" I don't know whose reflections these are: Jacques's, his master's, or my own. It's certainly one of the three and it's certain that they were preceded or followed by many others which would have taken us—Jacques, his master, and myself—until suppertime, after supper, up to the return of the landlady, that is, if Jacques had not said to his master: "See here, sir, all these grand aphorisms that you have just reeled off for no good reason are not worth one single fable of our get-togethers of an evening in my village."

The Master. And what is your fable?

Jacques. It's the fable of the Sheath and the Dagger. One day the Sheath and the Dagger got into a quarrel. The Dagger said to the Sheath: "Sheath, my darling, you are a tart, for every day you keep receiving new daggers." The Sheath replied to the Dagger: "My friend Dagger, it is you who are the rascal for every day you change Sheaths." "Sheath, this is not at all what you promised me." "Dagger, you deceived me first." This quarrel had come up at the table. The one who was sitting between the sheath and the dagger took the floor and said to them: "You, Sheath, and you, Dagger, you did well to change, for a change pleased you. But you were wrong to promise each other that you wouldn't change. Dagger, can't you see that God made you to fit into several Sheaths; and you, Sheath, to take more than one Dagger? You used to consider as mad certain Daggers who took vows to get along completely without Sheaths, and equally mad certain Sheaths who took vows to be closed to all Daggers. And yet you did not think that you were almost as mad yourselves when you swore: you, Sheath, to limit yourself to one Dagger; you, Dagger, to limit yourself to one Sheath."

. . . If the Master had not said: "Your fable is not very moral, but it's gay. You can't imagine the singular idea that just passed through my head. I'm going to marry you to our landlady and then I'll see what a husband can do, when he loves to talk, with a wife who never stops talking."

Jacques. Just what I did the first twelve years of my life spent with my grandfather and grandmother

The Master. What were their names? And what was their profession?

Jacques. They were dealers in secondhand goods. My grandfather Jason had several children. The whole family was serious. They got up, they dressed, and they would go off to their business; they came back, they dined, and would return to work again without saying a word. In the evening they would throw themselves into chairs; the mother and the daughters spun, sewed, and knitted without saying a word; the boys rested; the father read the Old Testament.

The Master. And you, what did you do?

Jacques. I ran all around the room with a gag in my mouth.

The Master. With a gag!

Jacques. Yes, with a gag, and it's to that cursed gag that I owe my madness for talking. Sometimes a whole week would go by without anyone's opening his mouth in the Jasons' house. Throughout her life, which was long, my grandmother had said only: "Hats for sale," and my grandfather, whom one saw at inventory time, upright, his hands in his greatcoat, had ever said only, "One sou."

There were days where he was tempted not to believe the Bible.

The Master. And why so?

Jacques. Because of the repetition, which he regarded as gossiping unworthy of the Holy Ghost. He used to say that people who repeat are stupid asses who take those who listen to them for stupid asses.

The Master. Jacques, suppose in order to make up for the long silence which you observed during the twelve gagged years at your grandfather's and during the time the landlady talked . . .

Jacques. I were to take up my love story again?

The Master. No, but another on which you left me dangling; I mean the story of your captain's comrade.

Jacques. Oh, my master, what a cruel memory you have!

The Master. My Jacques, my little Jacques!

Jacques. What are you laughing at?

The Master. At what will cause me to laugh more than once; I mean seeing you at your grandfather's with a gag.

Jacques. My grandmother used to take it off me when there was no one else around, and when my grandfather noticed this he was not at all happy. He would say to her: "Go on, just keep it up, and that child will be the most frantic gossip that has ever existed." His forecast has already materialized.

The Master. Come, my Jacques, my little Jacques; let's have the story of your captain's comrade.

Jacques. I shall not refuse, but you won't believe it.

The Master. It must be quite a marvelous story.

Jacques. No, it's just that it had already happened to another man, a French soldier called, I believe, M. de Guerchy.[31]

The Master. Well, I'll say then what a French poet who had made a rather good epigram said to someone who attributed it to himself in the poet's presence. "And why couldn't this gentleman have written it, for I managed to write it myself?" So why couldn't the story of Jacques have happened to his captain's comrade since it had already happened to the French soldier de Guerchy? But

while telling it, you will kill two birds with one stone, for you will
be telling me the adventure of two other people, for I don't know it.

Jacques. All right, all right, but swear to me you won't complain.

The Master. I swear to you.

Reader, I am tempted to ask the same agreement from you, but
I shall content myself with pointing out a singularity in Jacques's
character that he apparently got from his grandfather Jason, the
silent secondhand man. For Jacques, unlike most gossips, however
much he loved to talk, had an aversion to repetition. And so he
would sometimes say to his master: "Sir, you prepare for me the
saddest of futures; for what shall become of me when I no longer
have anything to say?"

"You'll start over again."

"Jacques! Start over! The opposite is written up yonder, and if I
ever had to repeat, I should not be able to keep from crying: 'Ah,
if your grandfather could hear you now.' And I should miss my
gag."

The Master. You mean the one he used to put on you.

Jacques. In the days when they played at games of chance at
the Saint-Germain and Saint-Laurent fairs . . .

The Master. But that's at Paris, and your captain's comrade was
commandant at a frontier post.

Jacques. For God's sake, sir, let me go on. Several officers entered
a shop and found there another officer who was talking with the
mistress of the shop. One of them proposed to this officer that they
play *passe-dix*,[32] for you must know that after the death of my
captain, his comrade, having become rich, had also become a
gambler. And so he, or M. de Guerchy, accepts. Destiny puts the
dice box into the hand of his adversary, who passes, passes, and
keeps passing without end. The game was warming up, and they
had bet the all, the all in all, the little halves, the big halves, the
grand all, and the grand all in all, when one of the audience took
it into his head to say to M. de Guerchy, or to my captain's comrade, that he would do well to stop there and cease play because

they knew more about the game than he. At this remark, which was only a joke, my captain's comrade (or M. de Guerchy) thought he was dealing with a swindler. He slipped his hand artfully into his pocket and pulled out a well-sharpened knife, and when his rival put his hand on the dice to place them in the box, he plants the knife in the player's hand and nails him to the table, saying: "If those dice are fixed, you are a rascal; if they are good, I am wrong." The dice were found to be good. M. de Guerchy said: "I am very sorry and I offer whatever satisfaction you want." This was not the remark of my captain's comrade. He said: "I have lost my money; I have pierced the hand of an honorable man; but on the other hand I have found again the pleasure of dueling whenever I like." The wounded officer withdraws and goes off to have his hand dressed. When he had recovered he comes to search out the nailing officer and demands satisfaction. This latter (or M. de Guerchy) finds the demand quite just. The other, or my captain's comrade, throws his arms about the officer's neck and says: "I have been waiting for you with an impatience which I cannot describe." They go off to the fields. The nailer (M. de Guerchy or my captain's comrade) receives a solid body thrust. The nailed officer lifts him up, has him carried to his house and says to him: "Sir, we shall see each other again." M. de Guerchy replied nothing, but my captain's comrade replies: "Sir, I certainly hope so." They fight a second time, a third time—up to eight or ten times, and it is always the nailer who is left on the field. They were both distinguished officers, men of merit. Their adventure was talked of far and wide; the ministry got into it. They kept one of them at Paris, and restricted the other to his post. M. de Guerchy submitted to the orders; my captain's comrade was heartbroken—such is the difference of two men who are brave by character, but of whom one is wise and the other has a grain of madness.

Up to this point the stories of M. de Guerchy and of my captain's comrade are the same; they're exactly the same and that is why I kept naming the two of them, don't you see, my master?

At this point I am going to separate them, and I shall speak only of my captain's comrade, for the rest of the story belongs only to him. Ah, sir, it is here you will see how little we are masters of our destiny and how many strange things are written on that Great Scroll.

My captain's comrade, or the nailer, asks permission to return to his home country. He gets it. His road lay by Paris. He reserves a place in a public conveyance. At three o'clock in the morning this coach is passing in front of the opera; people were coming out from a ball. Three or four young masked madcaps get the idea of going to supper with the travelers. They get around to the supper at daybreak. They look at each other. And who was the surprised gentleman? It was the nailee, who had recognized his nailer. The latter gives him his hand, embraces him, and tells him how very happy he is at such an unexpected meeting. Immediately, sword in hand, they go behind a barn—one in a greatcoat, the other in domino. The nailer, or the comrade of my captain, is again laid out. His enemy sends for aid, and goes back to the table with his friends and the rest of the coach, and eats and drinks merrily. Some of them were getting ready to pursue their journey, others to return to the capital, masked and on post horses, when the landlady returned and put an end to Jacques's story.

Here she is back upstairs, reader, and I warn you that it's no longer in my power to send her away.—Why not?—Because she came back with two bottles of champagne, one in each hand, and it was written up yonder that any speaker who should appeal to Jacques with such an exordium would be heard of necessity.

She comes in, puts the two bottles on the table, and says: "Come, Monsieur Jacques; let's make peace." The landlady was not in the bloom of youth; she was a big, bulky woman, nimble, of pleasant aspect, quite plump, with a rather large mouth, but with lovely teeth, broad cheeks, prominent eyes, a square forehead, very fine skin, an open face both lively and gay, a bosom ample for two days of lolling about thereon, arms somewhat heavy but with superb hands—hands to be painted or sculpted. Jacques took her about the waist, and squeezed her tightly. His rancor had never held out against good wine and a pretty woman. That was written up yonder, reader, about him, you reader, me and a good many others. "Sir," she said to the master, "are you going to let us drink all alone? Why, see here, were you to go yet another hundred miles, you would not find better to drink all along the way." Speaking thus, she placed one of the bottles between her knees and pulled out the cork. It was with singular skill that she covered the foam with her thumb, not letting a single drop escape. "Come, Jacques, quickly, your glass." Jacques holds his glass; the landlady, moving her thumb a little to the side, lets air into the bottle, and Jacques's face is completely covered with the spray. Jacques lent himself well to this foolery and the landlady laughed as Jacques and his master roared. They drank several bumpers, one after the other, to assure themselves of the bottle's wisdom, then the landlady said: "God be praised; they are all in their beds, and won't interrupt me any more. So I can continue my story." Jacques, regarding her with eyes whose natural vivacity had been accentuated by the champagne, said either to her or to his master: "Our landlady must have been as pretty as an angel; what do you say, my master?"

The Master. Have been! Great heavens, Jacques, she still is.

Jacques. Sir, you are right. I'm not comparing her to another woman, but rather to herself when she was young.

The Landlady. Well, I'm not worth much at present. It's when you could have taken my waist between the two first fingers of each hand that you should have seen me. They went out of their way for four leagues around in order to stay here. But let's leave at that the bad and the good heads I managed to turn, and get back to Mme de La Pommeraye.

Jacques. Suppose first of all we drink one round to the bad heads you turned, or to my health.

The Landlady. Very willingly. There were some that were worth the trouble, taking yours into consideration or not. Do you know that for ten years I was the great resource of all the soldiers? With honorable intentions naturally. I encouraged a great number who would have had difficulty getting through their campaigns without me. They are good fellows, and I have no complaints about any of them, nor they about me. Never any bad checks; they made me wait sometimes, but at the end of two, three, or four years my money always came back to me.

And so she started to make an enumeration of the officers who had done her the honor of digging into her purse—a Monsieur So-and-So, colonel of the regiment of ———, a Monsieur So-and-So, captain of the regiment of ———, and thereupon Jacques lets out a cry: "My captain, my poor captain! You knew him!"

The Landlady. Did I know him? A tall man, well built, a little gaunt, with a noble, severe air about him, a good solid calf, and two little red spots on his right temple. You were in the service?

Jacques. Was I in the service!

The Landlady. I love you the more for it. You must have retained many good qualities from your first profession. Let's drink to your captain's health.

Jacques. If he is still alive.

The Landlady. Dead or alive, what does it matter? Isn't a soldier made to be killed? Wouldn't he be outraged after ten sieges and five or six battles to die amidst the dregs of black humanity? But let's get back to our story, and have another drink.

The Master. By heaven, landlady, you are right.

The Landlady. I am very happy that you should think so.

The Master. For your wine is very good.

The Landlady. Oh! It's my wine you were talking about? Well, you're still right. Do you remember about where we were?

The Master. Yes, at the end of the most deceitful of confessions.

The Landlady. M. des Arcis and Mme de La Pommeraye embraced, delighted one with the other, and parted. Since the lady's pain had been much restrained in his presence, it was only the more violent after he had left. "It is only too true, then," she cried, "that he loves me no longer." I shall not give you in detail all our extravagances when we are deserted; you would become too vain. I told you that this woman was proud, but she was also, in quite another way, revengeful. When the first frenzy had been calmed, and she again enjoyed the tranquillity of her indignation, she thought of avenging herself—but vengeance of a cruel sort, of a sort to terrify all those who in the future might feel tempted to seduce and deceive a lady. She avenged herself and cruelly, but her vengeance exploded and corrected nobody. For we have not since been any less villainously seduced and deceived.

Jacques. That might be so for the others, but you!

The Landlady. Alas! Me, first of all. Oh! how stupid we are. It would be different if those villainous fellows would profit by their experience! But let's drop that. What was she to do? As yet she doesn't know too well herself. She will think about it; she does think about it.

Jacques. Suppose while she's thinking, we . . .

The Landlady. A good idea. But our two bottles are empty. Jean! (—Madame.) Two bottles, those away at the back behind the woodpile. (—All right, I know.) By dint of thinking about it, here's what came to her mind. Mme de La Pommeraye had formerly been acquainted with a provincial woman, called to Paris for a lawsuit along with her daughter, who was young, pretty, and well raised. She had learned that this woman, ruined by the loss of her lawsuit, had been reduced to running a bawdy house. People assembled there, played and supped, and usually one or two of the guests stayed on and spent the night either with the woman or with her daughter, as he chose. She sent one of her domestics in search of these women. They were found and invited to pay a visit to Mme de La Pommeraye, whom they scarcely remembered. These women, who had taken the names of Mme and Mlle d'Aisnon, didn't need to be coaxed. The very next day the mother called on Mme de La Pommeraye. After the customary compliments, Mme de La Pommeraye asked the d'Aisnon woman what she had done and what she was doing since the adverse decision of her case.

"To tell you the truth," replied the d'Aisnon woman, "I have been following a dangerous, infamous, and not very lucrative calling that does not at all please me. But necessity is a harsh master. I had almost decided to put my daughter in the opera, but she has only a small chamber voice, and was never much of a dancer. I took her, during and after my trial, to lawyers, noblemen, prelates, and financiers, who took care of her for a while and then let her drop. It's not that she isn't as pretty as an angel and she has grace and delicacy, but she has no feeling for libertinage, none of those talents aimed at awakening the languor of blasé gentlemen. I offer gaming and supper and in the evening those who care to stay, stay. But what harmed us more than anything is that she fell for a little titled abbé—impious, unbeliever, dissolute, hypocrite, and an anti-philosophe [33] whom I shan't name to you. But he is the last of those who, to get to the bishopric, took the road that is at once the most certain and requires the least talent. I don't know what he told my daughter as he read to her every morning his dinner pamphlets, his supper pamphlets, and his hodgepodge pamphlets. Will he ever be a bishop or not? I couldn't say. Luckily they broke off. My daughter asked him one day if he were acquainted with the people against whom he wrote, and the abbé replied he was not. She asked him if he had any other convictions except those he ridiculed, and the abbé replied he hadn't. She let her quick anger flare up and made clear to him that his position was worthy of only the most wicked and false of men."

Mme de La Pommeraye asked if they were very well known in Paris.

"Much too well, unhappily."

"From what I can see, you are not enthusiastic about staying in your present situation."

"Not at all, and my daughter complains every day that the most miserable plight seems preferable to her present condition. She falls into such a melancholia that she succeeds in driving away from her . . ."

"If, then, I were to take it into my mind to create a most brilliant future for both of you, you might agree?"

"For much less."

"But it's important to know if you will be able to conform to the strictness of the orders I am going to give you."

"Whatever they may be, you can count on us."

"And you will follow my orders at my will and to my liking?"

"We shall await them with impatience."

"Good, that will suit me. Go on back home; my orders will not be long in coming. Meanwhile, get rid of your furnishings, sell everything; don't even keep your dresses if you have any gay ones, for that doesn't fit in with my plans."

Jacques, who began to be interested, said to the landlady: "Suppose we have a drink to the health of Mme de La Pommeraye."

The Landlady. Gladly.

Jacques. And to the health of Mme d'Aisnon.

The Landlady. Right.

Jacques. And you wouldn't refuse one to Mlle d'Aisnon, who has a little chamber voice, very little ability for the dance, and a melancholia that puts her in the unfortunate necessity of having a new lover every night.

The Landlady. Do not laugh! It's the cruellest of fates. If you only knew the torture you feel when you don't love.

Jacques. To Mlle d'Aisnon because of her cross to bear.

The Landlady. Let's go on.

Jacques. Dear landlady, do you love your husband?

The Landlady. Not much.

Jacques. Well then, you are to be pitied for he seems to be a healthy specimen to me.

The Landlady. All that glisters is not gold.

Jacques. To the good health of our landlord.

The Landlady. You can drink that one alone.

The Master. Jacques, Jacques, my friend; you're going rather strong.

The Landlady. Never fear, sir, he is a good fellow; and tomorrow you'll never know it.

Jacques. Well, since we won't know it tomorrow, and since I'm not making great use of my reason tonight, my master, my lovely landlady, one more toast, a toast which really means something to me—to the abbé of Mlle d'Aisnon.

The Landlady. Shame on you, Jacques—a hypocrite, an ambitious, ignorant, and intolerant calumniator. For that's what you must call, it seems to me, people who would gladly slit the throat of anyone who doesn't think as they do.

The Master. What you don't know, Madame Landlady, is that Jacques, there before you, is a sort of philosopher, and he has an infinite esteem for those little imbeciles who dishonor both themselves and the cause they defend so badly. He says that his captain called them the antidote for the Huets, the Nicoles, and the Bossuets.[34] He didn't understand anything in that, and neither do you. Has your husband gone to bed?

The Landlady. Oh, long ago.

The Master. And he allows you to talk like this?

The Landlady. Our husbands are trained. Mme de La Pommeraye gets into her coach, goes house hunting in the suburbs farthest away from the d'Aisnons' present district, rents a little apartment in a respectable house close by a parish church, has it furnished as simply as possible, invites the mother and daughter to dinner and installs them either that day or several days later in their house—leaving for them a complete list of rules as to the conduct they are to follow.

Jacques. My landlady, we forgot the health of Mme de La Pommeraye, and the Marquis des Arcis. Ah! that's not fair.

The Landlady. Come now, Jacques; the cellar is not empty. . . . Here is the list of rules or what I remember of it:

You will not frequent public walks, for your old friends must not discover you.

You will receive nobody, not even your neighbors, for you must affect the most complete withdrawal from the world.

You will wear, starting tomorrow, the attire of religious women, for you must be taken for such.

You will keep only pious books at your place for there must be nothing lying about which could give you away.

You will observe the greatest regularity in the services of the parish, feast days and workdays alike.

You will arrange to gain entrance to the parlor of some convent; the gossip of these recluses will be useful to us.

You will become very closely acquainted with the curate and the priests of your parish, for I shall need their testimony.

As a rule you will receive none of them at home.

You will go to confession and partake of the sacraments at least twice a month.

You will resume your family name, for it's a respectable one, and sooner or later they will be making inquiries in your section of the country.

You will contribute from time to time to small charities, and you will receive none under whatever pretext it may be. You must be thought neither rich nor poor.

You will spin, sew, knit, embroider, and you will give your work to the Sisters of Charity to be sold.

You will live in the greatest sobriety. Two small restaurant portions and that's all.

Your daughter will never go out without you, nor you without her.

Of all the possible easy ways of impressing on others your good reputation, you must forget none.

Above all, and I repeat, may there never be at your house either priests, monks, or religious women.

You will walk in the streets with eyes lowered; at church you will see only God.

"I agree that this life is hard, but it won't last forever, and I promise you the most worthwhile reward. Take thought now, and see if this restraint seems above your strength. Confess frankly to me; I shall be neither offended nor surprised. I forgot to tell you that it would be helpful were you to affect a mystic vocabulary, and equally helpful if the history of the Old and the New Testaments became familiar to you so that you will be taken for pious ladies of long standing. Become Jansenist or Molinist,[35] as you will, but the best would be to adopt the convictions of your curate. Never miss a chance, however you manage it, to lash out against the philosophers. Shout that Voltaire is the Antichrist. Know the writings of your little abbé by heart, carry them about if necessary. . . ."

Mme de La Pommeraye added: "I shall never see you at your place, for I am not worthy of relations with such devout women. But do not worry; you will come here secretly sometimes, and we shall make up for your penitent's regimen in our own little circle. But, while playing completely at devotion, do not become lost in it. As for your household expense, that's my affair. If my plan works, you won't need me any longer. If it fails, and not from any fault of yours, I am rich enough to assure a better future, more respectable than this, your present state, which you have given up for me. But above all, submission, submission, absolute submission to my will, for without that I agree to nothing for the present and promise nothing for the future."

The Master (*rapping on his snuffbox and looking at the time*). Now there is a terrifying piece of woman. God forbid I should meet her like.

The Landlady. Patience, patience, sir; you don't know her yet.

Jacques. Whilst waiting, my lovely, my charming landlady, suppose we said a word or two to the bottle.

The Landlady. Jacques, my champagne beautifies me in your eyes.

The Master. I have been holding back a question, perhaps indiscreet, that I have been wanting to ask you for so long now, that I can't keep it any longer.

The Landlady. Ask your question.

The Master. I am sure that you weren't born in a hostelry.

The Landlady. That is true.

The Master. And that you have ended up there from a higher position through extraordinary circumstances.

The Landlady. You are right.

The Master. Now suppose we were to cut off for a moment the story of Mme de La Pommeraye.

The Landlady. I'm sorry, that's not possible. The adventures of others I tell willingly, but not my own. I'll tell you only that I was brought up at Saint-Cyr, where I read very little of the Gospels and a great many novels. From the royal abbey to the inn I now run is a long story.

The Master. That will suffice; make believe I said nothing.

The Landlady. While our two devout women were building up their reputation, and while the virtuous smell of their piety and the holiness of their morals were reverberating all about, Mme de La Pommeraye carried on with the marquis the outward signs of esteem, friendship, and the most perfect trust. Always welcome, never scolded nor sulked at even after absences, he told her all his good little bits of amorous luck and she seemed to be openly amused. She gave him words of advice in cases where success seemed difficult. From time to time she threw in some talk about marriage but in such a disinterested tone that one could hardly suspect that she spoke for herself. If the marquis did chance to address to her some of those tender and gallant remarks with which a man can hardly dispense when dealing with a woman he has known, either she smiled or she let them pass unnoticed. To hear her talk, her heart was quite peaceful, and although she never would have thought it possible, she felt that such a friend as he was sufficed for happiness in life, and then too, she would say, she was no longer young and her tastes were quite blunted.

"What! You have nothing to confide in me?"

"Nothing."

"But the little count, dear friend, who pursued you so heartily during my reign?"

"I closed my door to him, and I see him no more."

"Now that is very strange! And why did you send him off?"

"Just because I don't like him."

"Ah, madame, I think I have guessed it. You still love me."

"That's possible."

"You are counting upon a return of love?"

"Why not?"

"And you are laying up for yourself all the advantages of spot-less conduct?"

"Something like that."

"And if I had the good fortune or misfortune to love you again, you would at least find for yourself some merit in the silence you would keep about my past indiscretions."

"You believe me very delicate and quite generous."

"My dear friend, after what you have done there is no heroism of which you would not be capable."

"I am not too unhappy that you should think so."

"By heaven, I am taking the greatest risks with you, I am sure of it."

Jacques. And so am I.

The Landlady. For about three months they had been at about this same point when Mme de La Pommeraye thought it time to play her trump cards. One lovely summer day while waiting for the marquis to come to dinner, she had the d'Aisnon woman and her daughter notified that they should come to the *Jardin du Roi*. The marquis arrived and dinner was served early. They dined and dined gaily. After dinner Mme de La Pommeraye suggested a walk to the marquis if he had nothing more interesting to do. This particular day there was neither opera nor theater; it was the marquis himself who remarked on that. And in order to make up for an amusing spectacle by a useful spectacle, chance so had it that it was he who invited the marquise to go see the *Cabinet du*

Roi.[36] She didn't refuse, as you can well imagine. So the horses are called for, they depart, arrive at the *Jardin du Roi,* and there they are, mixing in the crowd, looking at everything and seeing nothing just like all the others.

Reader, I have forgotten to paint for you the positioning of the three characters here in question—Jacques, his master, and the landlady. By reason of this inattention, you have heard them speak, but you haven't seen them at all. Better late than never. The master, to the left, in nightcap and dressing robe, was stretched out lazily in a great upholstered armchair, his handkerchief thrown over the arm of the chair, and his snuffbox in his hand. The landlady was at the back of the scene, opposite the door, near the table, and with her glass in front of her. Jacques, without a hat, sat to her right, his elbows on the table, and his head bent over between two bottles; two others were on the floor next to him.

After they had come out of the *Cabinet,* the marquis and his lady friend went walking in the garden. They were following the first path that is to your right upon entering, near the forestry school, when Mme de La Pommeraye cried out in surprise, saying: "If I'm not mistaken, I believe it is they. Yes, it is indeed they."

Immediately she leaves the marquis and goes ahead to meet our two devout ladies. The d'Aisnon daughter was ravishing in a simple dress which, not attracting attention at all, drew one's complete interest to her person. "Ah, it is you, madame."

"Yes, it is I."

"And how have you been, and what has become of you for this past eternity?"

"You know our troubles. We had to resign ourselves, and live in retirement as was suitable to our small fortune—withdraw from society when we could no longer show ourselves there decently."

"But what about me! After all, to abandon me, a friend who is not in society and who has always had the good sense to find it as ridiculous as it is!"

"One of the inconveniences of misfortune is the distrust it gives rise to. The poor are afraid of being importunate."

"You, unwelcome for me! Why even to consider such a thing is an insult!"

"Madame, I am completely innocent, for I reminded mother of you several times, but she would always say: 'Mme de La Pommeraye? Neither she nor anyone else thinks of us now, my daughter.'"

"What an unjust remark! Let's sit down and talk. This is M. the Marquis des Arcis; he is a friend of mine, and his presence need not bother us. How big mademoiselle has grown! And how pretty she has become since last we saw each other."

"Our present situation has that one advantage for it deprives us of all that is harmful to health. Look at that face, those arms— that's what she owes to a frugal, regulated life—to sleep, work, a good conscience; and that at least is something."

They sat down; they chatted in a friendly manner. The d'Aisnon woman spoke very much; her daughter spoke very little. Piety was the tone for both, but with ease and without prudishness. Long before nightfall our two devout women got up. The others tried to convince the ladies that it was still quite early; mother d'Aisnon whispered rather loudly into Mme de La Pommeraye's ear that they still had a pious duty to carry out, and that it would be impossible for them to stay longer. They were quite a distance away when Mme de La Pommeraye regretted not having asked for their address, and not having given them her own. "It's a slip which I certainly should not have made in times past." The marquis ran to catch them. They accepted the address of Mme de La Pommeraye, but, however much the marquis insisted, he could not get theirs. He did not dare offer them his carriage, although he admitted to Mme de La Pommeraye that he had been sorely tempted.

The marquis was not long in asking Mme de La Pommeraye just who these women were.

"They are two creatures much happier than ourselves. Just look at the good health they are enjoying! The serenity which reigns on their faces! The innocence, the decorum which prompts their remarks! We see very little of that, hear nothing of it in our circles. We pity pious people, and they pity us, but to tell the truth, I think it is they who are right."

"But, Madame, are you tempted perchance to become a devout lady?"

"And why not?"

"Be careful; I shouldn't like our break-up, if it is one, to lead you that far."

"And would you rather I opened my doors again to the little count?"

"Much rather."

"And you advise me to do it?"

"Without hesitation."

Mme de La Pommeraye told the marquis what she knew of the name, native province, former condition, and lawsuit of her two devout friends, and she recounted their story with all the interest and pathos possible. Then she added: "They are two women of rare worth, especially the girl. You can guess that with a face like hers, a woman need lack nothing in this society if she is willing to use it. But they preferred honest modesty to shameful luxury. What they have left is so little that in truth I do not know how they manage to get along. They work night and day. To be able to withstand poverty when one is born into it—that a lot of people know how to do. But to pass from opulence to direst necessity, to be content and find happiness there—that's what I don't understand. There's the value of religion. Our philosophers will say what they will; religion is a fine thing."

"Especially for the unfortunate."

"And who is not more or less unfortunate?"

"I shall die if you turn devout."

"Oh, what a great misfortune! This life is so little when compared to the eternity to come."

"Why, you're talking like a missionary already."

"I am talking like a woman with convictions. Now, Marquis, answer me true. Wouldn't all our riches be but poor rags in our eyes if we were filled with desire for the benefits and with fear of the ills of the afterlife? To corrupt some young lady, or a woman attached to her husband with the feeling that you might fall to sleep in her arms, only to fall suddenly into endless tortures—you must agree that would be the most unbelievable nightmare."

"And yet it happens every day."

"It's because people don't have any faith; they have forgotten themselves."

"It's because our religious opinions have little influence on our morals. But, dear friend, I can assure you that you are already well on your way to the confessional."

"That's exactly what is best for me."

"Come, come, now; you must be mad. You still have some twenty years of pretty little sins to commit. Don't miss them. Afterward you can repent, and you can go boast about it at the feet of your priest if you've a mind to. But we're getting into a very serious conversation. Your imagination is rapidly darkening, and it's the effect of that abominable solitude in which you've kept yourself. Do believe me and call back your little count as soon as possible. You will see no more devils, no hells, and you'll be your own charming self once again, as before. You are afraid I shall cast it up to you should we ever come back together. But, first of all, perhaps we shall never come back together, and through this apprehension, rightly or wrongly inspired, you are depriving yourself of a very sweet pleasure. Believe me, the honor of your being more worthy than myself is not worth that sacrifice."

"You speak the truth, and it is certainly not that which holds me back."

They continued to say still many more things which I can't remember.

Jacques. Landlady, let's have another drink; it freshens the memory.

The Landlady. Here's to you. After several turns about the paths, Mme de La Pommeraye and the marquis got back into the carriage. Mme de La Pommeraye said: "How old I feel! When that little thing came to Paris, she was not much taller than a cabbage."

"Are you speaking of the daughter of that lady we just met on our walk?"

"Yes. It's like a garden where the faded roses make way for the new ones. Did you look at her?"

"I shouldn't have missed such a chance."

"And what did you think of her?"

"It's the head of a Raphael virgin on the body of his Galatea. And what gentleness in her voice!"

"What modesty in her countenance!"

"What propriety in her bearing!"

"And decorum in her speech which has struck me in no other girl as in that one. That's the result of upbringing."

"When prepared by a basic beautiful nature."

The marquis dropped Mme de La Pommeraye at her door, and she felt nothing more urgent than to inform her two women how satisfied she was at the manner in which they had played their roles.

Jacques. If they continue as they have begun, my poor des Arcis, were you the devil himself, you would not get out of this pass.

The Master. I should certainly like to know what their plan is.

Jacques. As for me, I should be quite upset to know; that would spoil everything.

The Landlady. From this day on the marquis became a more regular visitor at the house of Mme de La Pommeraye, who noticed it without asking any questions. She never spoke to him first of the two devout women; she waited for him to broach the subject—which he did always with impatience and ill-feigned indifference.

The Marquis: "Have you seen your friends?"

Mme de La Pommeraye: "No."

The Marquis: "You know that's not very decent, don't you? You're very rich, and they are in straits. And you don't even invite them to an occasional dinner!"

Mme de La Pommeraye: "I hoped M. the Marquis knew me a little better than that. Before, love used to lend me virtues; now friendship finds faults in me. I have invited them at least ten times without succeeding in having them once. They refuse to come to my place for very strange reasons. And when I go to visit them, I have to leave my carriage at the entrance of the street and walk, dressed simply, and without cosmetics and jewels. We mustn't be too surprised at their circumspection; one false report would suffice to alienate the minds of a certain number of charitable folk, and thus deprive them of assistance. Marquis, it apparently costs a lot to do good."

The Marquis: "Especially costly for the pious."

Mme de La Pommeraye. "Yes, for the slightest pretext seems to be enough to justify their giving it up. If they knew that I took an interest, they would soon be saying: 'Mme de La Pommeraye is looking out for them; they need nothing.' And their charities would stop."

The Marquis: "Charity?"

Mme de La Pommeraye: "Yes, charity."

The Marquis: "You know them, and yet they accept charity."

Mme de La Pommeraye: "Once again, Marquis, I see that you no longer love me, and that a great part of your esteem has gone with your affection. And who told you that if these women are in need of parish charity, it is my fault?"

The Marquis: "Your pardon, Madame, a thousand pardons; I was wrong. But what reason have they for refusing the help of a friend?"

Mme de La Pommeraye: "Ah, Marquis, we people of society, we are far from understanding the delicate scruples of timorous souls. They don't feel free to accept help from all persons indiscriminately."

The Marquis: "But that means taking from us the best way of expiating our mad dissipations."

Mme de La Pommeraye: "Not at all. Should I suppose, for example, that the Marquis des Arcis were touched with pity for them—then why doesn't he have his assistance pass through more worthy hands?"

The Marquis: "And less sure ones too."

Mme de La Pommeraye: "That is always possible."

The Marquis: "Tell me, if I were to send them some twenty louis, do you think they would refuse?"

Mme de La Pommeraye: "I am certain they would. And I suppose such a refusal would seem out of place in a mother who has such a charming daughter?"

The Marquis: "Did you know that I tried to go see them?"

Mme de La Pommeraye: "I don't doubt it. Marquis, Marquis, take care. Here is a movement of compassion which seems very sudden and suspicious."

The Marquis: "However that may be, would they have received me?"

Mme de La Pommeraye: "Certainly not! With the glitter of your coach, your clothes, your lackeys, and the charm of your person, they would need nothing more to start up the gossip of their neighbors and thus be undone."

The Marquis: "You trouble me, for this was certainly not my design. We must then give up the hope of seeing and helping them?"

Mme de La Pommeraye: "I'm afraid so."

The Marquis: "But if I were to have my help passed to them through you?"

Mme de La Pommeraye: "I should not consider that help disinterested enough to be responsible for it."

The Marquis: "Now that's cruel!"

Mme de La Pommeraye: "Yes, cruel is exactly the word."

Jacques the Fatalist and His Master

The Marquis: "What foresight, Madame! And yet, you are jesting. A young lady whom I've seen only one time."

Mme de La Pommeraye: "But one of those few whom you don't forget once you've seen her."

The Marquis: "It's true that such faces haunt you."

Mme de La Pommeraye: "Marquis, please be careful, for you are preparing disappointments for yourself. And I prefer to keep you from them rather than to console you afterward. Don't confuse this young lady with those you have known. She is not like them— with ladies like her, you don't tempt and seduce. You don't get near her sort, for they don't listen. You would never succeed in your intentions."

After this conversation the marquis remembered all of a sudden that he had some urgent business. He rose abruptly and left worriedly.

During a rather long period of time the marquis didn't let a day pass without seeing Mme de La Pommeraye. But he would arrive, sit, and keep completely silent. Mme de La Pommeraye talked to herself; at the end of a quarter of an hour he would get up and leave.

Thereafter there was a lapse of about one month, after which he reappeared, but sad, melancholy and defeated. The marquise, upon seeing him in such a state, said: "How dreadful you look! Where have you come from? Have you been spending all your time in a love nest?"

The Marquis: "By heaven, almost. From the despair where I was before, I threw myself into the most unbridled libertinism."

Mme de La Pommeraye: "What do you mean, despair?"

The Marquis: "Yes, despair."

Whereupon he started to prance to and fro without saying a word. He went to the windows, he looked at the sky, he stopped in front of Mme de La Pommeraye, he went to the door, he called his servants to whom he had nothing to say, he sent them away, he came back in, he came up to Mme de La Pommeraye, who was working without noticing him; he wanted to say something but he didn't dare. Finally Mme de La Pommeraye took pity on him and said: "Whatever is the matter with you? For one whole month I haven't seen you; you come back with the face of a corpse, and you stalk about like a soul in pain."

The Marquis: "I can stand it no longer; I must tell you all. I have been much taken with the daughter of your friend. I have done everything, everything, to forget her. And the more I have done, the more I have remembered her. That angelic creature has possessed me. Do me an important service."

Mme de La Pommeraye: "What service?"

The Marquis: "I must absolutely see her again; will you do me that favor? I have put my spies about. Their only coming and going is from their house to the church and from church to their house. Ten times I have planted myself in their way; they didn't even notice me. I have stayed at their door without result. First they made me as dissolute as a monkey, then as pious as an angel. I have not missed mass once in the last two weeks. Ah, dear friend, what a face! How beautiful she is!"

Mme de La Pommeraye knew all this. "That is to say," she replied to the marquis, "that after having done everything to cure yourself, you didn't overlook anything to drive you mad again— and it's the last attempt which has been successful."

The Marquis: "And just how successful I should never be able to tell you. Won't you have pity on me, and may I not owe you a debt of happiness at seeing her again?"

Mme de La Pommeraye: "The thing will be very difficult, but I shall look into it upon one condition. You must leave these poor people alone and stop tormenting them. I shall not hide from you the fact that they have written me of your persecution with bitterness; here is their letter."

The letter she gave the marquis to read had been concocted between them. It was Mlle d'Aisnon who would seem to have written it at her mother's command. Into it they had mixed everything that might turn the marquis' head—for it was honest, tender, touching, elegant, and witty. And so as he read it he accompanied each word with an exclamation. There was not a sentence which he didn't read twice. He was weeping with joy as he said to Mme de La Pommeraye: "You must agree, madame, it would be impossible to write better than that."

Mme de La Pommeraye: "I agree."

The Marquis: "At each line one is filled with admiration and respect for women of such character."

Mme de La Pommeraye: "You cannot help it."

The Marquis: "I shall keep my word to you, but remember, I beg of you, not to forget yours."

Mme de La Pommeraye: "In truth, Marquis, I am as mad as yourself. You must have preserved a terrible influence over me. It frightens me."

The Marquis: "When shall I see her again?"

Mme de La Pommeraye: "I have no idea. I must first take care to arrange things so as to avoid all suspicion. They cannot be unaware of your way of life. You can see how my compliance would look to them, if they thought I were acting in concert with you. But, Marquis, just between the two of us, why should I get embroiled in such an embarrassing situation? What should it matter to me whether you're in love or not in love? Whether you rave on or not? Untangle your own intrigue. The part you are having me play is really too ridiculous."

The Marquis: "My dear friend, if you abandon me, I am lost. I shall not speak for myself because I offend you, but I shall plead for those worthy and interesting beings who are so dear to you. You know me; spare them the folly of which I am capable. I shall go to their house, yes, I warn you, I shall. I shall force the door and go in against their wishes. I shall sit down and I don't know what I shall say or do. What couldn't happen in the violent state where I now am?"

You will have noticed, gentlemen, that from the beginning of this story and up to now, the marquis said not one word which was not a dagger pointed at Mme de La Pommeraye's heart. She was choking with indignation and rage. So she replied to the marquis with a trembling and faltering voice: "Of course you are right. Ah! If I had been loved like that, perhaps . . . but enough of that. It is not for you that I shall act. At least, I should like to think, Marquis, that you will give me some time."

The Marquis: "The least, the least possible."

Jacques. Oh, my landlady! What a devil of a woman! Lucifer is not worse. I am trembling from it, and I need another drink to get a grip on myself. Are you going to let me drink all alone?

The Landlady. Well, you see I'm not quite so shaken. Mme de La Pommeraye was saying within herself: "I am suffering, but not alone. Cruel man! I do not know how long my suffering will last, but I shall make yours eternal." She held the marquis off for about a month waiting for the interview she had promised, which is to say she left him the time to suffer and become well intoxicated with his passion, and under the guise of soothing him for the delay, she allowed him to talk to her of that passion.

The Master. And to make it all the stronger by talking.

Jacques. What a woman! What a devil of a woman! My good lady, my fright redoubles.

The Landlady. And so the marquis would come each day to chat with Mme de La Pommeraye, who managed to grow angered and hardened, and destroy the marquis with her most artificial discourse. He obtained information as to the country, the birth, the upbringing, the fortune, and subsequent ruin of these women. He would come back to the subject endlessly, and never felt well enough informed, never deeply enough touched. The marquise pointed out to him the inordinate intensity of his feelings, and kept warning him as to the outcome under pretext of frightening him off. "Marquis," she would say, "be careful; this thing will take you far. Someday my friendship which you are abusing strangely might no longer excuse me, either in your eyes or my own. Which is not to say that we don't commit greater follies every day. But Marquis, I am afraid that you will get this girl only under conditions which up to now have not been to your liking."

When Mme de La Pommeraye believed the marquis well ripened for the success of her plan, she arranged with the two women that they should come dine with her. Also with the marquis, who, seemingly to fool them, would surprise them in country clothes. Which was done.

They had arrived at the second course when the marquis was announced. The marquis, Mme de La Pommeraye, and the two d'Aisnon women all played a superb role of surprise. "Madame," said he to Mme de La Pommeraye, "I have just come from my country estate; it is too late to go home where I am not expected until tonight, and I was sure you could not refuse me dinner." And while talking thus, he had taken a chair, and sat down at the table. They had laid the table in such a way that he was beside the mother and across from the daughter. He thanked Mme de La Pommeraye with a wink for this delicate forethought. After the embarrassment of the first minutes, our two women regained control of themselves. They chatted, they were even gay. The marquis displayed the greatest attention for the mother, the most reserved politeness for the daughter. It was a very amusing secret for the three women—this scruple on the marquis' part of saying nothing, permitting himself no overt act which might frighten them. They were cruel enough to have him talk about matters of religious piety for three hours in a row. Mme de La Pommeraye remarked to him: "Your conversation is full of praise for your parents; the first lessons one receives are never lost. You understand all the subtlety of divine love as if you had been nourished solely on St. François de Sales. Might not you have been somewhat of a Quietist?" [37]

"I don't remember."

It is not necessary to tell you that our pious women put into their conversation all of the grace, wit, seduction, and finesse that they possessed. They touched, in passing, upon the chapter of passions, and Mlle Duquenoi (for this was her family name) held that there was only one dangerous passion. The marquis agreed with her. Between six and seven, the two women withdrew, and it was impossible to delay them further. Mme de La Pommeraye agreed with Mme Duquenoi that one should be firm in carrying out duties, without which there would be practically no single day's pleasure unspoiled by remorse. And so they left to the great regret of the marquis, and he stayed on in a tête-à-tête with Mme de La Pommeraye.

Mme de La Pommeraye: "Well, Marquis, do you not think I have been truly kind? Find me in Paris one other woman who would have done as much."

Marquis (*throwing himself at her knees*): "I do agree; there is not one like you. Your kindness overcomes me; you are my only true friend in the whole world."

Mme de La Pommeraye: "Are you sure that you still appreciate as you should the price of my services?"

The Marquis: "I should be an ungrateful monster if I should change my opinion."

Mme de La Pommeraye: "Let's change the tone. How goes your heart?"

The Marquis: "Must I tell you frankly? I must have that girl, or I shall perish."

Mme de La Pommeraye: "You will have her without doubt, but it is to be seen just how."

The Marquis: "We shall see."

Mme de La Pommeraye: "Marquis, Marquis, I know you and I know them. Everything is clear."

The marquis was about two months without showing up at Mme de La Pommeraye's, and here are the measures he took during that interval. He made the acquaintance of the confessor of the mother and daughter. It was a friend of the little abbé of whom I've spoken to you. This priest, after having found all the hypocritical objections that could be adduced for a dishonest intrigue, and having sold as dearly as possible the sanctity of his ministry, lent himself to the marquis' every desire.

The first villainy of the man of God was to alienate the esteem of the curate, and to persuade him that these two protégés of Mme de La Pommeraye were receiving charitable aid from the parish at the expense of other poor, more to be pitied than they. His object was to bring them to his way of thinking through misery.

Later, in the confessional, he worked at separating the mother from her daughter. When he heard the mother complain of her daughter, he played up the faults of the daughter and gave rise to resentment in the mother. If it was the daughter who complained of the mother, he insinuated to her that the power of mothers and fathers over their children was limited, and that, if this persecution on the part of her mother were carried to a certain point, it would not be impossible perhaps to free her from such tyrannous authority. Then, for her penance he told her to come back to confession.

Another time he talked to her about her charm, but in a clever way. It was one of the most dangerous presents God could give to a woman, to judge from the impression made by her charm on an honest gentleman whom he did not identify but whose name was not hard to guess. He passed from there to the discussion of heaven's infinite grace and its indulgence for faults that certain circumstances made necessary: the natural weakness for which each of us finds the excuse in himself, the frequency and violence of certain leanings from which even the holiest of men were not exempt. He asked her afterward if she had no desires, if her true temperament didn't speak to her in her dreams, if the presence of men did not trouble her. Then he would come to the question of whether a woman ought to yield to a passionate man or whether she ought to resist him, and thus allow to die and be damned him for whom the blood of Jesus Christ had been spilled. He dared not make the decision for her. Then he would sigh deeply, lift his eyes to heaven, and pray for the peace of troubled souls. The young lady let him go on. Her mother and Mme de La Pommeraye, to whom she gave a faithful accounting of the remarks of her confessor, suggested to her other confidences all of which tended to encourage the confessor.

Jacques. Your Mme de La Pommeraye is a wicked woman.

The Master. That's easily said, Jacques. But where does her wickedness come from? From the Marquis des Arcis. Make him a man such as he had sworn to be and ought to have been, and then find for me any fault in Mme de La Pommeraye. When we shall again be on the road, you can accuse her and I shall defend her. As for that priest, the vile seducer, I leave him to you.

Jacques. He is such an evil man that from this story alone I think I shall never again go to the confessional. How about you, our landlady?

The Landlady. Well, as for me, I shall continue to make my visits to my old curate, who is not curious and who hears only what you tell him.

Jacques. Suppose we drink to the health of your curate?

The Landlady. This time, I shall give in to you, for he is a good man who on Sundays and feast days lets the girls and boys dance, and allows men and women to come to my establishment so long as they don't get drunk. To my curate.

Jacques. To your curate!

The Landlady. The women were fairly sure that any time now the man of God would chance passing on a letter to his penitent. This was done, but with such care! He did not know who had written it, but he had no doubt it was from some kindly and charitable soul who had discovered their straits and was proposing to help them. He delivered more like it quite often. "For the rest, you are discreet and madame, your mother, is prudent, and I demand that you open it only in her presence." Mlle Duquenoi accepted the letter and handed it over to her mother, who immediately passed it on to Mme de La Pommeraye. That lady had the priest come see her and with the letter in her hand poured on him the reproach he deserved, and threatened to disclose him to his superiors, if she heard anything more about him.

In this letter the marquis had exhausted himself in praise of himself and in praise of Mlle Duquenoi; he painted his passion as violent as it was and suggested strong means, even kidnapping.

After having taught the priest his lesson, Mme de La Pommeraye called the marquis. She showed him how unworthy of an honest gentleman his conduct had been, warned him just how far she could be compromised, showed him his letter and protested that, in spite of the tender friendship which united them, she could not but produce it before a law tribunal or show it to Mme Duquenoi if some scandalous adventure were to happen to the daughter. "Ah, Marquis," she said to him, "love has corrupted you. You were ill-born, for the maker of great things inspires in you only base ones. And what have these poor women done to you that you thus add ignominy to their poverty? Just because this girl is beautiful and wants to remain virtuous, must you become her persecutor? Is it your place to make her hate one of heaven's most treasured gifts? And how have I thus deserved to become your accomplice? Come, Marquis, throw yourself at my feet, ask my pardon, and take an oath to leave my poor friends in peace." The marquis promised to undertake nothing else without her permission, but he repeated that he must have that girl at any cost.

He was not in the least faithful to his word. The mother was informed; he did not hesitate to turn to her. He confessed the crime of his plan. He offered a considerable sum, hopes for the future; and a casket of rich gems accompanied his letter.

The three women held council. The mother and her daughter were inclined to accept, but this was not at all the desire of Mme de La Pommeraye. She reminded them of the promise they had given her; she threatened to tell all. And to the great regret of our two women, after the youngest had detached from her ears the diamond sprigs which looked so well on her, the casket and the letter were sent back, along with a reply full of pride and indignation.

Mme de La Pommeraye complained to the marquis of the little faith one could have in his promises. He excused himself for the impossible taste he had shown in making such an indecent proposal. "Marquis, Marquis," Mme de La Pommeraye said to him, "I have already warned you and I repeat, you have not yet come to the point you wish for. But this is no time for preaching; that would be only words wasted. There's nothing more to do."

The marquis confessed that he thought the same and asked her permission to make one last try. This was to settle a considerable amount of money on the two women, to share his fortune with them, and to make them lifetime owners of one of his city houses and one of his country estates. "Do so," said the marquise, "I forbid only violence. But believe me, my friend, honor and virtue, when they are real, have no price in the eyes of those who possess them. Your new offers cannot succeed any more than the others; I know these women and I'll lay a wager on it."

The new proposals are made. And there is another meeting of the three women. The mother and the daughter waited silently for Mme de La Pommeraye's decision. The latter walked about for a moment without speaking. "No, no," she said, "that will not suffice for my wounded heart." And thereupon she pronounced her refusal. Immediately the two women melted into tears, threw themselves at her feet, and tried to show her how horrible it was for them to push aside an immense fortune that they could have accepted with no unhappy consequences. Mme de La Pommeraye replied, drily: "Do you think that what I am doing, I do for you? Who are you? What do I owe you? What keeps me from sending both of you back to your bawdy house? If what he is offering is too much for you, it is much too little for me. Madame, you will write the reply I am going to dictate and it will be sent under my eyes." The women went back home really more frightened than unhappy.

Jacques. That woman is possessed by the devil. What does she want? What! A cooling off in love is not already punished enough by the sacrifice of half a large fortune?

The Master. Jacques, you were never a woman, much less an honorable woman, and you are judging by your own character and not at all by Mme de La Pommeraye's. Do you want me to tell you what I think? I am very much afraid that the marriage of the Marquis des Arcis to a whore was written up yonder.

Jacques. Well, if it's written up yonder, it shall be.

The Landlady. The marquis was not long in reappearing at Mme de La Pommeraye's. "Well," he asked, "how about our new offer?"

The Marquis: "Made and rejected! . . . I am desperate! I should like to tear this unhappy passion from my heart, should like to tear out my very heart, and yet I cannot. Marquise, look at me; don't you find there some resemblance between that girl and myself?"

Mme de La Pommeraye: "I hadn't said anything to you about it, but I have noticed it. However it's not a question of that. What have you decided to do?"

The Marquis: "I can decide nothing. Sometimes I feel like jumping into a post chaise and traveling to the end of the earth. A moment later my strength is gone; I am overwhelmed; my head is all mixed up. I am growing utterly stupid, and I don't know what's to become of me."

Mme de La Pommeraye: "I shouldn't advise you to travel. What's the use of hurrying off to Villejuif only to come back again?"

The next day the marquis wrote to Mme de La Pommeraye that he was leaving for the country, that he would stay there as long as he could, and that he was begging her to talk for him to her friends if the occasion arose. His absence was very short; he came back determined to marry.

Jacques. This poor marquis arouses my pity.

The Master. Not mine.

The Landlady. He arrived at Mme de La Pommeraye's door. She was out. Upon her return she found the marquis stretched out in an armchair, his eyes closed, and absorbed in deep reverie. "Ah, Marquis! You are here? The country didn't have much attraction for you."

"No, nowhere do I feel at ease and I come back determined to do the stupidest thing a man of my condition, age, and character could possibly do. But it is better to marry than to suffer. I shall marry."

Mme de La Pommeraye: "Marquis, this is serious and needs some reflection."

The Marquis: "I have made only one reflection, but it is a good one. It's to the effect that I could never be unhappier than I now am."

Mme de La Pommeraye: "You could be mistaken, you know."

Jacques. The traitress!

The Marquis: "Here then finally, my dear friend, is a negotiation which I may honestly entrust to you, I should think. Go see the mother and the daughter; question the mother and sound out the daughter's heart. Tell them my plans."

Mme de La Pommeraye: "Easy, easy, Marquis. I believed I knew them well enough for what I then had to do with them. But now that it's a question of my friend's happiness, your happiness, you must allow me to look more closely at their background. I shall make inquiries in their section of the country, and I promise to follow them step by step during the whole of their stay at Paris."

The Marquis: "These precautions seem rather superfluous to me. Women in their straits who resist the temptations I have held out to them can only be the very rarest of souls. With what I offered, I could have had my way with a duchess. What's more, didn't you tell me once yourself . . ."

Mme de La Pommeraye: "Yes, I said everything to please you. But even so, allow me to satisfy myself."

Jacques. The bitch! The hussy! The rabid harridan! Why get mixed up with such a woman?

The Master. And why seduce her and then leave her?

The Landlady. Why stop loving her without rhyme or reason?

Jacques (pointing up yonder with his finger). Ah! my master!

The Marquis: "Madame, why don't you get married too?"

Mme de La Pommeraye: "And to whom, if you please?"

The Marquis: "To the little count; he has a mind, family, and fortune."

Mme de La Pommeraye: "And who should assure me of his fidelity? You, perhaps?"

The Marquis: "No, but it seems to me that you can rather easily overlook the problem of a husband's fidelity."

Mme de La Pommeraye: "I agree. But if mine were unfaithful, I should perhaps be just strange enough to take offense, for I am vindictive."

The Marquis: "Well, then you would avenge yourself, that goes without saying. We could take a house together and live, the four of us together, in the most pleasant society."

Mme de La Pommeraye: "All that is very pretty, but I'm not going to get married. The only man I might possibly have been tempted to marry . . ."

The Marquis: "Is myself?"

Mme de La Pommeraye: "Now I can tell you without embarrassment."

The Marquis. "And why didn't you tell me before?"

Mme de La Pommeraye: "As it turned out, I acted wisely. The one you will get suits you much better from every point of view."

The Landlady. Mme de La Pommeraye put into her inquiries all the exactitude and rapidity she wished. She produced for the marquis the most flattering affidavits—both from Paris and from their home province. She asked another two weeks of the marquis to examine things further. Those two weeks seemed an eternity to him. Finally she was forced to accede to his impatience and pleading. The first interview took place at her friends' house. They agree to everything, the banns are published, the contract drawn up, the marquis makes Mme de La Pommeraye a present of a superb diamond, and the marriage is consummated.

Jacques. What a plot and what a vengeance!

The Master. Incomprehensible!

Jacques. If you spare us the first night of the honeymoon, I see no great evil up to now.

The Master. Be quiet, booby.

The Landlady. The wedding night went very well.

Jacques. But I thought . . .

The Landlady. Think about what your master has just told you. (And in speaking thus, she smiled, and in smiling she passed her hand over Jacques's face and tweaked his nose.) But the next day . . .

Jacques. The next day was not like the night before?

The Landlady. Not completely. The next day Mme de La Pommeraye wrote a note to the marquis inviting him to come see her as quickly as possible. The marquis did not tarry.

She received him with the strongest indignation written on her face. Her speech was not long. Here it is: "Marquis, learn to know who I am. If other women esteemed themselves enough to equal my resentment, your likes would be rare. You acquired an honest woman and you didn't know how to keep her. That woman is myself. She has avenged herself in having you marry a woman worthy of you. Leave my house and go to the Hotel de Hambourg, on the rue Traversière; there they will inform you of the filthy trade your wife and your mother-in-law have plied for ten years under the name of d'Aisnon."

The surprise and the consternation of the poor marquis cannot be described. He didn't know what to think. But his uncertainty lasted only as long as it took him to go from one end of the city to the other. He did not return to his house all day; he roamed the streets. His mother-in-law and his wife had some suspicion of what had happened. At the first blow the mother-in-law had fled to her room and locked herself in. His wife waited for him, alone. At her husband's approach she read on his face the fury which possessed him. She threw herself at his feet, her face against the parquet floor, and said nothing. "Get out, shameless woman," he cried, "far from me!" She tried to get up but she fell again on her face, her arms outstretched on the floor between the marquis' feet. "Sir," she said, "trample me under your feet; crush me, for I deserve it; do with me what you will, only spare my mother."

"Get out!" shouted the marquis, "get out! You have covered me with enough disgrace; spare me a crime."

The poor creature stayed in the same position and said not a word. The marquis was sitting in an armchair, his head buried in his arms, and his body half leaning on the foot of the bed, sobbing from time to time without looking at her. "Get out!" The silence and stillness of the unfortunate girl surprised him. He repeated in a louder voice: "Will you get out! Can't you hear me?" Then he leaned down and pushed her roughly, and, realizing that she was senseless and almost lifeless, he took her around the waist and stretched her out on a sofa. He watched her for a moment with a look reflecting alternate pity and fury. Then he rang. His valets came. He called her women and said to them: "Your mistress is not well. Take her to her apartment and take care of her." Very shortly thereafter he sent secretly to find out how she was. They told him that she had come out of her first fainting, but that the swoonings were recurring frequently, and becoming indeed so frequent and so prolonged that they could give him no assurance. An hour or two later he sent again secretly to hear of her condition. They told him that she was choking, and that she had started a kind of hiccough which could be heard as far as the courtyards. Upon the third instance, they told him that she had wept very much, that the hiccough had calmed down, and that she seemed to be resting.

The next day the marquis had his horses harnessed to his post chaise and disappeared for two weeks without anyone's knowing what had become of him. However, before going away he had provided for everything necessary to the mother and daughter, and had given orders that Madame be obeyed as himself.

During this absence the two women stayed always together in almost complete silence, the daughter sobbing, sometimes screaming and pulling her hair, and the mother not daring to come near to console her. One was the very picture of despair; the other, the picture of cynical callousness. The daughter said twenty times to her mother: "Mama, let's leave this place; let's flee." Each time the mother refused and replied: "No, my daughter, we must stay; we must see what will come of this. This man will not kill us." "Would to God he had already done so!" her daughter would answer. To which the mother replied: "You would do better to be quiet than to talk like a fool."

Upon his return the marquis shut himself up in his room and wrote two letters: one to his mother-in-law, one to his wife. The mother left the same day and entered a Carmelite convent in a neighboring city, where she died several days ago. The daughter got dressed and dragged herself to her husband's apartment, where he had apparently summoned her. At the door she threw herself at his knees. "Get up," said the marquis.

Instead of getting up, she crawled to him on her knees. She was trembling all over, she was disheveled; her body was slightly bent, her arms stretched toward him, her head lifted as she fastened her eyes on his; her face was flooded with tears. "It seems to me," she said, a sob separating each word, "that your heart which was justly wrathful has grown calm, and perhaps you will be merciful to me. Oh, sir, have pity, yet be not too hasty to pardon. So many virtuous girls have become shameful women that perhaps I shall be the contrary exception. I am not as yet worthy to be touched; wait then, and but give me the hope of forgiveness. Keep me far from you; you will observe my conduct; you will judge it. Oh, a thousand times too happy should you deign to call me back! Show me the hidden corner of your house where you will allow me to stay;

there I shall stay without a murmur. Ah! if only I could tear away the name and title that they made me usurp, and then die—at that moment you would be satisfied! I let myself be led on through weakness, seduction, authority, and threats, led on to an infamous deed. But do not think, sir, that I am evil; I am not, since I did not hesitate to come before you when you called, nor dare to lift my eyes to you and address you. Ah! could you but read in the depths of my heart and see how many past faults are now far from me, how many immoralities of my likes are foreign to me! Corruption settled upon me, but it did not stay. I know myself, and in all justice I know that by my tastes, my feelings and my character, I was born worthy of the honor of belonging to you. Ah! had I only been free to see you, there was only one little word to say and I think I should have had the courage to say it. Sir, do with me what you will; call in your servants; have them strip me and throw me into the streets by night. I shall agree to all. Whatever the destiny you prepare for me, I submit to it. The far reaches of the countryside, the obscurity of the cloister could take me forever from your eyes. Only speak and I shall go. Your happiness has not been lost without remedy, and you can forget me."

"Rise," said the marquis very tenderly, "I have pardoned you. From the very first moment of my wound, I respected in you my wife. There has never come from this mouth a word to humiliate that wife, or at least I repent of such words, and I assure you that she shall never hear another to humiliate her, as long as she remembers that she cannot make her husband unhappy without becoming so herself. Be virtuous, be happy, and see to it that I am also. Rise, I beg you, rise, my wife, and embrace me. Madame la Marquise, rise, for you are not in your place there; rise, Mme des Arcis. . . ."

While he had been thus talking, she had remained there, her face hidden in her hands, and her head leaning against the marquis' knees. But at the sound of the word "wife," and "Mme des Arcis," she rose abruptly, threw herself on the marquis' neck and, half-suffocated with joy and pain, held him in close embrace. Then she detached herself, fell to the ground, and kissed his feet.

"Ah!" said the marquis, "I have already pardoned you, but I see you do not believe it at all."

"It was natural and necessary," she said, "that it should be so, and that I should never believe it."

The marquis added: "In truth, I think I repent of nothing, and that Pommeraye woman, instead of avenging herself, has done me a great favor. My wife, go and dress while they busy themselves with your trunks. We shall leave for my estate and there we shall stay until such time as we can return here without embarrassment for you and for me."

And so they passed in this way about three years away from the capital.

Jacques. And I wager that those three years passed like one day, and that the Marquis des Arcis was the best of husbands, and had one of the best wives in the whole world.

The Master. I shall concur, but in truth I don't know why, for I was not at all satisfied with that girl throughout the machinations of Mme de La Pommeraye and her mother. Not one minute of fear, not one sign of hesitation, not a single moment of remorse; I saw her lend herself, without repugnance, to that long horror. All that they asked of her, she never hesitated to do it: she goes to confession, she takes Communion, she makes a joke of all religion and its vicars. She seemed to me just as false, as hateful, and as evil as the others. My landlady, you tell a story well, but you are not yet perfected in the art of dramatics. If you wanted that girl to draw sympathy, you should have made her frank, and shown her to be the powerless and innocent victim of her mother and Mme de La Pommeraye. The cruellest treatment should have dragged her, despite herself, to agree to a series of continuing transgressions for a year. In this way you should have prepared us for the reconciliation with her husband. When you create a stage character, his role must be consistent. Now I ask you, charming landlady, if the girl who plots with the other two scoundrels is indeed the same suppliant woman we saw at her husband's feet? You have sinned against the rules of Aristotle, Horace, Vida and Le Bossu, which is to say, literally, The Hunchback.[88]

The Landlady. I know none of them, either hunchback or straight. And I have told the thing to you as it happened, omitting nothing and adding nothing. And who is to know what went on in that girl's heart, and whether in the very moment when she seemed to us to act most cleverly, she was not secretly devoured by remorse?

Jacques. Landlady, this time I shall have to agree with my master, who will forgive me for it, for it happens very rarely. I must agree with this Bossu whom I don't know, and the others whom I don't know any better. If Mlle Duquenoi, heretofore d'Aisnon, had been a good girl, it would have shown.

The Landlady. Good girl or no, she is at least an excellent woman, with whom her husband is as happy as a king and whom he would not change for any other.

The Master. I congratulate him; he has been more happy than wise.

The Landlady. And as for me, I wish you a good night. It is late, and I must be the last one in and the first one out in the morning. What a cursed occupation! Good evening, gentlemen, good evening. I promised you—and I don't know any more on what score— the story of a strange marriage. I think I have kept my word. Monsieur Jacques, I don't think you'll have any trouble getting to sleep, for your eyes are already more than half shut. Good night, Monsieur Jacques.

The Master. How now, landlady, there is absolutely no way to hear your own story?

The Landlady. No.

Jacques. You certainly have a mad taste for stories!

The Master. It's true. They instruct and amuse me. A good storyteller is a rare thing.

Jacques. And that's exactly why I don't like stories, unless I'm telling them myself.

The Master. You like more to talk—even badly—than to be quiet.

Jacques. That's true.

The Master. And as for me, I should rather hear bad talk than nothing at all.

Jacques. That puts us both in a comfortable spot.

I don't know where the landlady, Jacques, and his master had put their heads not to have found a single favorable thing to be said on the score of Mlle Duquenoi. Did this girl understand a single move in the artifices of Mme de La Pommeraye before the end? Wouldn't she have much rather accepted the gifts than the hand of the marquis, and had him rather for lover than husband? Wasn't she continually under the threats and the despotism of Mme de La Pommeraye? Can you blame her for her aversion to her former infamous way of life? And if you decide to admire her for that, can you demand of her very much delicacy and scruple in the choice of methods for getting out of it?

And are you thinking, reader, that the apology for Mme de La Pommeraye is harder to make? Perhaps it would have been more agreeable to you to hear Jacques and his master on this subject, but they apparently had so many other interesting things to talk about that they neglected this one. Allow me, then, to take over for a minute.

You work yourself into a frenzy at the name of Mme de La Pommeraye, and you cry: "Ah! that horrible woman, that hypocrite, that miscreant!" Let's have no exclamations, no wrath, no partiality; let's just reason this thing out. Every day blacker deeds are perpetrated without any talent. You can hate and you can fear Mme de La Pommeraye, but you cannot scorn her. Her vengeance is terrible, but it is soiled with no motive of self-interest. We didn't tell you that she threw the lovely diamond given her by the marquis in his face, but she did. I know this on the surest kind of information. There was no question of augmenting her fortune or acquiring new titles of honor. Why, if this woman had done as much to win her husband just reward for his service, if she had prostituted herself to a minister or even to his deputy for a *cordon* or a first regimental company, to the depositary of the Beneficial List [39] in return for a rich abbey, that would seem natural to you; you are used to it. But when she avenges herself for perfidy, you rise up against her instead of seeing that her resentment makes you indignant only because you are incapable of feeling such deep resentment yourself, or because you don't make such an issue of a woman's virtue. Have you reflected somewhat upon the sacrifices Mme de La Pommeraye had made to the marquis? I shall not insist upon the fact that her purse was always open to him, and that for several years he had no other home or table than hers—that would only make you shrug your shoulders. But she had given in to all his fancies, all his tastes; to please him she had completely upset the plan of her life. She had been enjoying the highest consideration in society because of her purity of conduct, and then she condescended to a common plane. When she fell victim to the attentions of des Arcis, they said: "Finally that miraculous Mme de La Pommeraye has become one of us." She noticed ironic smiles all about her; she could hear the mocking, and often she had lowered her head and blushed at it. She had drained the cup of bitterness prepared for women whose impeccable conduct has for too long been a satire on the morals of all those surrounding her. She had withstood that explosion of scandal with which other women hope to avenge themselves on imprudent prudes who make a great case of virtue. She was proud, and she would have died rather than to parade about in society the ridicule due a jilted woman after the shame of having abandoned virtue. She was getting to the age when the loss of a lover cannot be remedied. Such being her character, this event condemned her to boredom and solitude. A man can stab another for a mere gesture, for a contradiction, and yet it's not permitted to a virtuous woman, lost, dishonored, and betrayed, to throw the traitor into a courtesan's arms? Ah, my reader, you are very flighty in your praise and very severe in your blame! But, you will say, it's not so much the thing itself as the way she did it for which you reproach Mme de La Pommeraye. I can't, you say, reconcile myself to such long resentment—a weaving of lies and deceits which lasts a whole year. Nor can I, nor Jacques, nor the master, nor the landlady. But you will pardon everything on grounds of first impulse; and I say to you that if the first impulse of other people is short, that of Mme de La Pommeraye and women of her character is long. Their souls remain throughout their lives just as in the first moment of their injury. And what is wrong, what is unjust, about that? I can see in it only a less common sort of betrayal, and I should strongly approve a law that would condemn to courtesans any man who has seduced and abandoned an honest woman. To common men, common women!

While I have been preaching, Jacques's master has been snoring as if he had been listening to me, and Jacques, whose leg muscles refused to serve him, has been roaming about the room, barefooted and in his undershirt, bumping into everything he passes, and waking his master who says to him through the curtains: "Jacques, you are drunk."

"Or close to it."

"When do you think you'll go to bed?"

"In a little while, sir. It's just that . . . that there is . . ."

"That there is what?"

"That there's a little left in that bottle which will go flat. I can't stand half-empty bottles; it would keep turning through my head when I'm in bed, and that's all I should need to keep me awake. Our landlady, by heaven, is an excellent woman, and her champagne is excellent wine. It would be a shame to let it go flat. Pretty soon it will be covered—then it can't go flat."

And in the midst of a yawn, barefooted and in his undershirt, Jacques had polished off two or three shots without punctuation, as he put it, which is to say, from bottle to glass to mouth. There are two versions as to what happened after he blew out the lights. Some pretend that he started to feel his way along the wall without finding his bed and that he said: "My word, it's not there any more, or if it is, it's written up yonder that I shall not find it; in both cases I shall have to do without it," and that he decided to stretch out on some chairs. Others hold that it was written up yonder that he should get his feet mixed up in the chairs, fall on the flagging, and stay there. Of these two versions, tomorrow, or the next day, having rested your weary head, you may take your choice of the one you like better.

4

❧　❧　❧

OUR TWO TRAVELERS, WHO HAD RETIRED LATE WITH RATHER WINY
heads, slept very late the next day: Jacques on the floor or on the
chairs, according to the version you preferred, and his master more
comfortably installed in his bed. The landlady came up and told
them that the day was not going to be favorable, and that even
if the weather permitted them to leave, they would risk their lives
or be stopped short because of the swelling of the stream they had
to ford. Several men who hadn't believed as much had been forced
to backtrack. The master said to Jacques: "Jacques, what shall we
do?" Jacques replied: "First of all, we'll eat with the landlady,
which might give us an idea." The landlady swore that this was
wisely said. Luncheon was served. The landlady liked nothing
better than to be gay; the master would have lent himself to her
mood, but Jacques started to suffer—he ate grudgingly, he drank
little, and was quiet. This last symptom was especially upsetting.
It was all the effect of the bad night he had spent and the bad bed
he had slept in. He complained of pains in his joints, his rasping
voice pointed already to a sore throat. His master advised him to
go back to bed; he wanted no part of that. The landlady suggested
some onion soup. He asked them to have a fire built in his room
for he felt shivery; he requested them to prepare him some medicinal tea and bring him a bottle of white wine—all of which was
done immediately. The landlady had gone and Jacques was in
conversation with his master. The master, going to the window,
said, "What nasty weather!" looked at his watch (for it was the
only one he trusted) to see the time, took his pinch of snuff, starting
the whole cycle over again every few minutes, crying each time,

"What nasty weather!" and turning to Jacques to add: "What a fine time to take up again and finish your love story! But it is hard to talk of love or anything when you're not feeling well. Come, see if you're in a condition to continue; if not, drink your tea and go to sleep."

Jacques held that silence was bad for him, that he was a talkative animal, and that the principal advantage of his present condition, the advantage which was closest to him, was the freedom of compensating for the twelve gagged years spent with his grandfather, upon whom may God have mercy.

The Master. Talk then, since it makes both of us happy. You had come to I know not what dishonest proposal on the part of the doctor's wife. It had to do I think with pushing out the doctor who served at the château and settling her husband there.

Jacques. I'm with you. But just a minute, if you please. Let's wet our whistles.

Jacques filled a big goblet with herb tea, poured in a little white wine, and swallowed it. It was a recipe he had gotten from his captain and one which M. Tissot, who got it from Jacques, recommends in his treatise on common illnesses. The white wine, said both Jacques and M. Tissot, causes pissing, is diuretic, makes up for the flatness of the herb tea, and settles the stomach and the intestines. His glass of tea swallowed, Jacques continued: "And so I have left the doctor's house, been put into the coach, arrived at the château and find myself surrounded by all who live there."

The Master. Were you known there?

Jacques. Certainly! You will recall no doubt a certain woman with a jug of oil?

The Master. Very well.

Jacques. Well, this woman was the errand girl of the steward and the servants. Jeanne had spread the word all over the château concerning the act of pity I had performed in her behalf; my good works had come to the attention of the master. They had not forgotten to inform him of the blows with which my act had been rewarded that night on the highway. He had ordered them to search me out and to bring me to his place. And so there I am. They look at me; they question me; they admire me. Jeanne embraced me and thanked me. "Let him be well quartered," said the master to his servants, "for I want him to lack nothing." To the house doctor he said: "You will visit him regularly." All was done quite faithfully. Well then! my master, who knows what is written up yonder? Let them now say that it is either good or bad to give away one's money, or that it's a misfortune to be beaten up. Without those two events, M. Desglands would never have heard of Jacques.

The Master. M. Desglands, the lord of Miremont? It's at Miremont Château that you are? With my old friend M. Desforges' father, the commissioner for the province?

Jacques. Quite right. And the young brunette with the slim waist and black eyes . . .

The Master. Is Denise, Jeanne's daughter?

Jacques. The same.

The Master. You are right! She is one of the loveliest, most virtuous creatures for twenty leagues round about. I, and the majority of those who frequented Desglands' château, had tried everything, but all in vain, to seduce her. And there was not a single one of us who would not have committed the greatest follies for her on the condition that she would commit a little one for him.

Jacques stopped talking at this point and his master asked him: "What are you thinking about? What are you doing?"

Jacques. I'm saying my prayers.

The Master. Do you pray?

Jacques. Sometimes.

The Master. And what do you say?

Jacques. I say: "Oh, you who have made the Great Scroll, whoever you may be, and whose finger has traced out all the writing up yonder, you have known from time immemorial what I needed. May thy will be done. Amen."

The Master. Wouldn't you do just as well to be quiet?

Jacques. Perhaps yes, perhaps no. I pray in any case and whatever happens to me, I should neither rejoice nor complain if I had control over myself. But I am inconsistent and violent, and I forget my principles and my captain's lessons, and I laugh and I cry like a fool.

The Master. Didn't your captain cry at all? Didn't he ever laugh?

Jacques. Very rarely. Jeanne brought her daughter to me one morning and, speaking at first to me, she said: "Sir, here you are in a lovely château where you will be a little better off than with your doctor. Especially at the beginning, oh! you will be cared for to perfection. But I know these servants, I've been one myself for a long time. Bit by bit their fine enthusiasm will cool off. The master won't think of you any more, and if your sickness lasts, you will be forgotten, but so completely forgotten, that if you decided to die of hunger, you could do so very easily." Then turning to her daughter, she said: "See here, Denise; I want you to visit this fine fellow four times a day; in the morning, at dinnertime, about five o'clock, and at suppertime. I want you to obey him as you would me. That's what I have to say and don't fail me."

The Master. Do you know what happened to that poor Desglands?

Jacques. No, sir, but if the wishes I made for his prosperity have not come true, it is not by reason of their insincerity. It is he who gave me to Commander de La Boulaye, who perished at Malta; it's Commander de La Boulaye, who gave me to his elder brother, the Captain, who has perhaps recently died of a fistula; it's this captain who gave me to a younger brother, the Attorney General of Toulouse, who went mad and was put away by his family. It was M. Pascal, the Attorney General of Toulouse, who gave me to the Count of Tourville, who preferred to let his beard grow inside a Capuchin robe rather than imperil his life; it's the Count of Tourville, who gave me to the Marquise du Belloy, who ran off to London with a foreigner; it's the Marquise du Belloy, who gave me to one of her cousins, who ruined himself with women and went off to the islands; it's that cousin who recommended me to a certain M. Herissant, a usurer by profession, who made money for M. de Rusai, a Sorbonne doctor, who had me introduced to Mlle Isselin, whom you were keeping and who placed me with you, to whom I shall owe a crust of bread in my old age, for you have promised me as much if I remained with you. And there's not much likelihood that we shall part. Jacques was made for you, and you were made for Jacques.

The Master. But, Jacques, you have passed through a good many houses in a rather short time.

Jacques. That is true; sometimes I was dismissed.

The Master. Why?

Jacques. Because I was born a gossip and those particular people wanted someone who was quiet. It's not like life with you, who would send me packing tomorrow if I were to be quiet. I have exactly the vice that suits you. But what did happen to M. Desglands? Tell me that while I prepare another glass of tea.

The Master. You mean you stayed in his château and never heard about his plaster?

Jacques. No.

The Master. Well, that will be a story for the road; the other one is short. He made a fortune at gaming. He grew attached to a woman whom you might have seen in his château—witty, but serious minded, taciturn, unpredictable, and strict. This woman said to him one day: "Either you like me better than gambling, and in that case, give me your word of honor that you will never gamble; or you like gambling more than me, in which case speak to me no more of your love, and gamble as much as you please." Desglands gave his word of honor that he would gamble no more. —"Neither for big nor for little stakes?" "For neither big nor little." They had been living together for about ten years in the château that you know, when Desglands, called to the city on some business, had the misfortune to meet at his lawyer's one of his old gambling [40] friends who took him to dinner in a gaming house where he lost in one sitting all he owned. His mistress was inflexible; she was rich. She granted Desglands a modest pension and parted from him forever.

Jacques. I am sorry about that, for he was a gentleman.

The Master. How's your throat?

Jacques. Bad.

The Master. That's because you talk too much and don't drink enough.

Jacques. And that's because I don't like herb tea and I do like to talk.

The Master. And so, Jacques, there you are at Desglands', near Denise, and with Denise authorized by her mother to pay you at least four visits a day. The young hussy! Prefer a Jacques to me!

Jacques. A Jacques! A Jacques, sir, is a man like any other.

The Master. You are wrong, Jacques; a Jacques is not at all a man like any other.

Jacques. No, he's sometimes better than another.

The Master. Jacques, you are forgetting yourself. Continue the story of your loves, and remember that you are and will ever be only a Jacques.

Jacques. If, in that thatched inn where we found the renegades, Jacques hadn't been worth a little more than his master . . .

The Master. Jacques, you are insolent. You take advantage of my kindness. If I have committed the folly of pulling you out of your place, I shall know very well how to put you back in your place. Jacques, take your bottle and your kettle and go downstairs.

Jacques. It might please you so to command, sir, but I like it here and I shall not go down.

The Master. I tell you you will go down.

Jacques. I'm quite sure you're not telling the truth. What, sir, after having accustomed me to living with you like a companion these ten years . . .

The Master. It pleases me to make an end to that.

Jacques. What? After having suffered all my impertinences . . .

The Master. I choose to suffer them no longer.

Jacques. After having seated me next to you at the table, called me your friend . . .

The Master. You don't even know what the name friend means when given by a superior to his subordinate.

Jacques. When everyone knows that all of your orders are but hot air until ratified by Jacques; after having so well joined your name to mine that one does not go without the other, and everybody says Jacques and his master—suddenly it pleases you to separate them! No, sir, that will never be. It is written up yonder that as long as Jacques lives, and as long as his master lives, and even after they are both dead, people will say Jacques and his master.

The Master. And I'm telling you, Jacques, to go downstairs and to go immediately because I order you to.

Jacques. Sir, order me to do any other thing if you want me to obey.

At this point Jacques's master got up, took him by the lapel, and said to him very gravely: "Go downstairs."

Jacques replied coldly: "I am not going down."

The master, shaking him violently, said: "Go down, rascal! Obey me."

Jacques replied coldly once again: "Rascal as much as you please, but the rascal is not going down. Look you, sir, what I have in the head, as they say, I have not in the heel. You are exciting yourself uselessly. Jacques will stay where he is and will not go downstairs."

And then Jacques and his master, having been moderate up to now, both let loose at the same time and start to cry at the top of their voices:

"You will go down."

"I shall not go down."

"You shall go down."

"I will not go down."

At this noise the landlady came up to find out what was going on. But nobody answered her for a while; they continued to shout: "You will go down"; "I shall not go down." Afterward the master, his heart heavy, pacing about the room, grumbled: "Have you ever seen anything the like of that?" The landlady, standing there astounded, asked: "Well, gentlemen, what's it all about?"

Jacques, without becoming excited, said to the landlady: "It's my master, who's off his head; he's mad."

The Master. He's stupid, you mean.

Jacques. As you will.

The Master (to the landlady). Did you hear him?

The Landlady. He is wrong. But peace, peace! Speak, one or the other of you, and let me know what's going on.

The Master (to Jacques). Speak, good-for-nothing.

Jacques (to his master). Speak yourself.

The Landlady (to Jacques). Come now, Monsieur Jacques, speak; your master orders you to. After all, a master is a master.

Jacques explained the affair to the landlady. The landlady, after having heard the story, said to them: "Gentlemen, would you like me to act as arbiter?"

Jacques and his Master (in unison). Very gladly, very gladly, our landlady.

The Landlady. And you give me your word of honor to carry out my decision?

Jacques and his Master. Word of honor, word of honor.

Then the landlady, seating herself at a table and assuming the tone and the bearing of a very serious magistrate announced: "Having heard the deposition of Monsieur Jacques and upon facts tending to prove that his master is a good, a very good, a too good master, and that Jacques is not at all a bad servant, albeit a little subject to confusing absolute and immovable possession with temporary and gratuitous concession, I abolish the equality which has become established between them over a period of time, and I immediately re-establish it. Jacques will go down and when he has gone down, he will come back up. He will come back into possession of all the prerogatives he has enjoyed up to now. His master will offer him his hand and will say to him in a friendly voice: 'Good day, Jacques, I am very happy to see you again.' Jacques will reply: 'And I, sir, am extremely happy to see you again.' I further forbid that this affair ever come up between them again, and that the prerogative of either master or servant should ever again be disturbed. Let us hope that the one shall order and the other obey, each to the best of his ability, and that there be left, between what the one can do and what the other ought to do, the same obscurity as heretofore obtained."

Upon finishing this pronouncement, which she had lifted from some contemporary work published on the occasion of a similar quarrel, and in which one heard a master cry to his servant from one extremity of the kingdom to the other, "You will go down," and the servant cry from his side, "I shall not go down," she said to Jacques: "Come, now, give me your arm without further parley."

Jacques cried out mournfully: "It was written, then, up yonder, that I should go down."

The Landlady (to Jacques). It was written up yonder that from the minute man takes a master he will go down, go up, go forward, go backward, or stay, and all that without his feet being free to countermand the head's orders. Give me your arm, and let my order be carried out.

Jacques gave his arm to the landlady, but scarcely had they passed the threshold of the room when the master threw himself upon Jacques's neck and embraced him, left Jacques and embraced the landlady, and while embracing them both said: "It was written up yonder that I should never be rid of that character, and that as long as I live he would be my master and I, his servant." The landlady added: "And that in all probability neither of you would be the worse off."

The landlady, after having settled this quarrel, which she took for the first and which was far more than the hundredth quarrel of this same sort, and after having reinstated Jacques in his position, went about her business. The master said to Jacques: "Now that we are cooled off and in a position to judge sensibly, don't you agree with me?"

Jacques. I agree that when you have given your word of honor you must hold to it, and that since we have promised our judge on our word of honor not to return to this matter, we ought not speak any more about it.

The Master. You are right.

Jacques. But without coming back to this affair, couldn't we pre-arrange a hundred others by some reasonable agreement?

The Master. I consent to that.

Jacques. Let us stipulate, then, that First: since it is written up yonder that I'm essential to you, and since I feel and know that you cannot get along without me, therefore I shall abuse these advantages at any and all times that the occasion permits.

The Master. But, Jacques, no one has ever stipulated any such thing.

Jacques. Stipulated or not stipulated, that has always happened, happens today, and will happen as long as the world stands. Don't you think that others, like yourself, have attempted to escape that decree? And do you think you will be cleverer than they? Get rid of that idea and submit to the law of necessity, from which it is not in your power to free yourself.

Let us also stipulate that Second: since it is as impossible for Jacques not to realize his influence and power over his master, as it is for his master to be unaware of his own weakness and cancel his indulgence, therefore Jacques must of necessity be insolent and, for the general peace, his master must not take notice. All that has been arranged without our knowledge; all that was sealed up yonder the moment nature made Jacques and his master. It was decreed that you would have the title and I should have the stuff. If you tried to oppose the will of nature, you would pass but clear water.

The Master. But at that rate your lot is better than mine.

Jacques. And who's disputing that?

The Master. But under those circumstances I have only to take your place and put you in mine.

Jacques. Do you know what would happen? You would lose the title and you wouldn't have the stuff. Let's stay as we are; we're both well off. And may the rest of our life be passed in making a proverb.

The Master. What proverb?

Jacques. Jacques leads his master. We shall be the first of whom they've said it, but they shall repeat it about thousands of others who are worth more than you and me.

The Master. It seems rather hard to swallow, very hard.

Jacques. My master, my dear master, you are going to kick against a prick that will but prick you the more painfully. And so that's what has been agreed between us.

The Master. And what makes us consent to a necessary law?

Jacques. A lot of things. Do you think it's not useful to know once and for all, clearly and plainly, how to act? All our quarrels up to now have come only from the fact that we had not yet clearly said to ourselves that you would be called my master and that it is I who would be yours. But now that's understood, we have only to continue on our way with that in mind.

The Master. But where the devil did you learn all this?

Jacques. In the Great Book. Ah, my master, you may reflect, meditate, and study as much as you like in all the books in the world but you are only a petty scholar until you have read the Great Book.

After dinner the sun came out. Several travelers assured them that the stream could be forded. Jacques went down; his master paid the landlady very handsomely. There are gathered about the door of the inn a rather large number of travelers who had been held back by the bad weather and who are now preparing to continue their journeys. Among these are Jacques and his master, the man who had made the strange marriage and his companion. The pedestrians have taken their sticks and their wallets; the others are settling themselves in their carriages and wagons; the horsemen are mounted and drinking the stirrup cup of wine. The affable landlady is holding a bottle in her hand, passing out glasses, and filling them, without forgetting her own. They are saying obliging things to her to which she replies politely and gaily. They spur their horses, wave farewell, and disappear.

It so happened that Jacques and his master, the Marquis des Arcis and his traveling companion, had the same road to follow. Of these four characters, it is only the last who is unknown to you. He was scarcely twenty-two or twenty-three years old. He was of a timid nature and it showed on his face; he held his head a little bent toward the left shoulder. He was silent and without much knowledge of society. If he bowed, he bent the upper part of his body without moving his legs. While sitting, he had the habit of taking the tails of his coat and crossing them over his thighs, the while holding his hand in the gaps. He listened to those who were talking with his eyes almost shut. From his unusual appearance Jacques figured him out, and coming close to his master's ear, he said: "I'll bet that young fellow has worn monastic robes."

"And why so, Jacques?"

"You will see."

Our four travelers went along together, making much small talk, about the landlady, the landlord, and the quarrel of the Marquis des Arcis over Nicole. That starved and unkempt dog would continually come and rub against his stockings. After having chased her away several times uselessly with his napkin, out of patience, he had let fly a rather violent kick. And so immediately the conversation turned to the strange attachment of women for animals. Each one had his say. Jacques's master, turning to Jacques, asked: "And what do you think of the matter, Jacques?"

Jacques asked his master if he hadn't noticed that however poor common people were, and without bread even for themselves, they nevertheless always had dogs. He asked if he had not noticed that these dogs, having been instructed to do tricks—walk on two feet, dance, retrieve, jump for the king, jump for the queen, play dead— were the most unhappy beasts in the world by reason of just such education. From which he concluded that all men wanted to give orders to someone else, and that since the animal was of that society immediately beneath the last class of citizens who were ordered about by all the other classes, they wanted an animal so that they, too, could order someone about. "And so," said Jacques, "everyone has his dog. The minister is the king's dog, the head deputy is the minister's dog, the wife is the husband's dog, or the husband the wife's dog. Favori is this woman's dog, whereas Thibaud is the dog of that man on the corner. When my master makes me speak at times when I should prefer to be quiet (which in truth happens but rarely); when he makes me keep silent at times when I should like to speak (which is very difficult); when he asks me for my love story and I had rather talk of other things; when I have started my love story and he interrupts me—what else am I but his dog? Weak men are strong men's dogs."

The Master. But, Jacques, I don't notice this attachment to animals solely in the lower classes. I know some high ladies surrounded by throngs of dogs, not to mention cats, parrots, and other birds.

Jacques. It is their satire and a satire on what surrounds them. They love nobody and nobody loves them, and they throw to the dogs feelings for which they have no other use.

The Marquis. To love animals and throw one's heart to the dogs —now that's a strange view of things.

The Master. What they give to those animals would suffice for the nourishment of two or three unfortunates.

Jacques. As things are nowadays, are you surprised?

The Master. No.

The Marquis des Arcis turned his eyes on Jacques, smiled at his ideas. Then turning to his master, he said: "You have there an uncommon servant."

The Master. A servant? You are very kind. It is I who am the servant and only this morning he came close to proving it to me formally.

As they thus talked among themselves, nightfall arrived and they all stayed at the same inn. Jacques's master and the Marquis des Arcis ate together. Jacques and the young man were served separately. The master sketched for the marquis in four words the whole story of Jacques and his fatalistic turn of mind. The marquis spoke of the young man who accompanied him. The young man had been a Premonstratensian monk. He had left his monastery through a strange adventure; friends had recommended him to the marquis, and he had made the lad his secretary while the fellow waited for something better. Jacques's master said: "That's very amusing."

The Marquis. And what do you find amusing about that?

The Master. I am talking about Jacques. Scarcely had we come into the inn we have just left [41] when Jacques whispered to me: "Sir, look at that young man over there; I'll wager he was a monk."

The Marquis. Well, he guessed exactly right, though I don't know how. Do you go to bed early?

The Master. Not as a rule, and this evening I have less reason than ever to hurry off for we have made only a half day.

The Marquis. If you have nothing better or more agreeable to do, I shall tell you the story of my secretary. It's not a usual story.

The Master. I shall hear it gladly.

I hear you, reader. You say to me: "And what about Jacques's love story?" Don't you think I'm as curious as you are about it? Have you forgotten that Jacques liked to talk and particularly about himself—a usual mania with people of his class, which pulls them out of their abjection and puts them on the tribunal, transforming them instantly into interesting people? What, to your way of thinking, is the motive that attracts people to public executions? Inhumanity? You are wrong; the masses are not inhuman. That unfortunate wretch about whose gallows they gather—they would snatch him from the hands of justice if they could. They go to the

Grève [42] rather to find a scene which they can retell upon their return to their district. This scene or the other, it matters not, so long as the people can play a role, gather their neighbors about them, and make themselves heard. Give an amusing gala on the boulevards, and you will see that the execution square will be empty. The people are mad for spectacle, and they rush to spectacles because they are amused by watching them, and still more amused by the retelling they do upon their return. The mob is terrible in its fury, but that doesn't last long. Its own misery makes it sympathetic. The mob turns its eyes away from the spectacle of horror it went looking for; it grows tender and returns with tears in its eyes. Everything I'm handing to you now, reader, I have had from Jacques, I confess, for I don't like to take credit for the thinking of another. Jacques did not know the name of vice and virtue; he held that we are happily or unhappily born. When he heard the words recompense and punishment, he shrugged his shoulders. For him recompense was encouraging the virtuous; punishment, terrifying the wicked. "How can it be otherwise," he would say, "if there is no freedom and if our destiny is written up yonder?" He believed that a man wended his way just as necessarily toward glory or ignominy as a ball, being conscious of its existence, would follow the slope of a mountain; and that, if the chain of causes and effects which form the life of a man from the first instant of his birth up to his last sigh could be known to us, we would remain convinced that he had done only what it was necessary to do. I have many times contradicted him, but to no avail and without changing him. As a matter of fact, what is there to reply to the man who tells you: "Whatever the sum total of elements which make up me, I am one—a whole. Now, a cause has but one effect; I have always been a single, unique cause. Thus I have never had but one single effect to produce. My existence in time, therefore, is but a series of necessary effects." Just thus did Jacques reason, following his captain's lead. Distinguishing a physical world from a moral world seemed to him void of sense. His captain had filled Jacques's head with all these ideas drained out of his Spinoza, which he knew by heart. According to such a system, one might imagine that Jacques rejoiced and was sorrowed about nothing. Such, however, was not the case. He behaved very much as you and I. He thanked his benefactor so that he would continue to be good to him. He grew angry at the unjust man and when it was then pointed out to him that he was thereby like the dog that bites the stone which strikes him: "Not at all," he would say. "The stone bitten by the dog does not change; the unjust man is modified by the stick." Often he was inconsistent, like you and me, and subject to forgetting his principles, save in those few circumstances where his philosophy clearly dominated him. It was then he would say: "That had to be, for that was written up yonder." He tried to prevent evil; he was prudent, yet all the while he had the greatest scorn for prudence. When the inevitable accident happened, he reverted to his old refrain, and was consoled by it. For the rest, he was a good fellow, frank, honest, brave, affectionate, faithful, strong-headed, but more than all these, talkative, and he was vexed, as are you and I, to have started his love story with practically no hope of ever finishing it. And so, reader, I advise you to reconcile yourself, and in place of Jacques's love story, to take the adventures of the Marquis des Arcis' secretary. Moreover I can see him, our poor Jacques, his neck wrapped in a great kerchief, his gourd, up to now filled with good wine, at present filled with herb tea, coughing, cursing the landlady they had left and her champagne—all of which he would not have done if he had remembered that all is written up yonder, even his cold.

And then, too, reader; always, always love stories! One, two, three, four love stories I have already spun out for you—three or four other love stories which are still due you; that's a lot of love stories! It is true, on the one hand, that since I am writing for you, I must either give up your applause or cater to your taste, and this taste you have already quite clearly indicated as being for love stories. All your short stories, whether in prose or verse, are love stories; almost all your poems, elegies, eclogues, idyls, songs, *epîtres,* comedies, tragedies, and operas are love stories. Practically all your sculpture and paintings are but love stories. You have been nourished on nothing but love stories since you have existed and you have not yet grown tired of them. They have been holding you to this diet and they will hold you to it for a long while, men and women, big and little children, before you tire of it. In truth, 'tis miraculous. I should very much like the story of des Arcis' secretary to be another love story. But I'm afraid it's not one at all, and that you will be bored. Well, too bad for the Marquis des Arcis, for Jacques's master, for you, reader, and for myself.

"There comes a moment when nearly all young men and women fall into melancholy; they are tormented by a vague unrest which meets them at every turn, which nothing can calm. They seek solitude; they weep; the silence of the cloisters touches them; the image of that peace which seems to reign in religious retreats seduces them. They take for the voice of God calling them to him, the first voice of their own true temperament which is developing. And it is at precisely this moment when nature is calling them, that they embrace a sort of life contrary to the wishes of nature. The error does not last long; nature's expression becomes clear. They recognize it for what it is, and the recluse falls into regrets, languor, the vapors, madness or despair." Such was the preamble of the Marquis des Arcis. Disgusted with the world at seventeen years, Richard (that was the secretary's name) fled his paternal home and took the robe of a Premonstratensian.

The Master. A Premonstratensian? I am happy for him. They are white like swans and St. Norbert, who founded them, omitted only one thing from his regulations.

The Marquis. To assign a vis-à-vis to each of his brothers.

The Master. If it were not the habit of cupids to go about naked, they would dress as Premonstratensians.[43] There reigns in that order a very strange policy. They allow you to have a duchess, a marquessa, a countess, a president's wife, a counselor's wife, even a financier's wife, but not a shopkeeper's wife. However pretty the merchant lady, you will rarely see a Premonstratensian in a shop.

The Marquis. That's what Richard told me. Richard would have taken his vows after two years of novitiate if his parents had not opposed such a move. His father demanded that he come back home, and that there he be permitted to feel out his calling by observing all the rules of the monastic life during a year. This agreement was faithfully carried out by both parties. This year of testing having rolled by under his family's eyes, Richard asked permission to take his vows. His father replied: "I granted you a year to make a last decision, I trust you will not refuse me one for the same reason. I ask only that you go spend it wherever you will." While waiting for the end of this second year, the abbé of the order attached Richard to himself. It was during this time that he became involved in one of those adventures which could happen only in a monastery. There was at that time, at the head of one of the houses of the order, a superior of an extraordinary character. His name was Father Hudson.[44] He had the most interesting face— broad forehead, oval face, aquiline nose, big blue eyes, handsome broad cheeks, a fine mouth, pretty teeth, a very subtle smile, and a head covered with a forest of white hair, which added dignity to the interest of the face. He had wit, knowledge, and bearing; he was gay, of honest design, with a love of order and hard work, but with the most lively passions, the most unbridled taste for pleasures and women, a talent for intrigue carried to extremes, and the most dissolute morals; yet he was the most absolute despot in his chapter house. When they charged him with the chapter's administration, the place was infected with ill-informed Jansenism. Studies were done badly, temporal affairs were in disorder, religious duties had fallen into neglect, the holy services were celebrated with indecency, extra quarters were occupied by dissolute boarders. Father Hudson either converted or got rid of the Jansenists, took charge of the studies himself, re-established order in temporal things, put the rules in strict practice, expelled the scandalous boarders, brought regularity and decorum to the celebration of holy services, and made his little community one of the most edifying then existing. But the austerity to which he subjected the others, he dispensed with for himself. The yoke of iron under which he held his subordinates, he was not stupid enough to impose upon himself. And so they were aroused against Father Hudson with a pent-up fury that was the more violent and dangerous. Every man was his enemy and a spy; each tried in secret to pierce the shadows surrounding his personal conduct; each kept an account of his hidden debauchery; each was fully resolved to ruin him. He took no step unobserved; his plans were hardly cast before they were known to all.

The abbot of the order always occupied the house connecting with the monastery. This house had two doors, one opening on the street, the other into the monastery. Hudson had forced the locks; the abbatial house had become the den of his nocturnal scenes, and the abbot's bed his pleasure couch. It was through the street door, late in the night, that he himself introduced into the superior's apartments women of all classes; it was there they held their exquisite suppers. Hudson heard confessions and had corrupted all those among his women penitents who were worth the trouble. Among these penitents was a little confectioner who had a reputation in the district for her coquetry and her charms. Hudson, who could not go to her, shut her up in his seraglio. This sort of rape was not accomplished without arousing the suspicions of her family and her husband. They paid him a visit. Hudson received them with an air of consternation. As these good folk were in the midst of explaining their trouble, the clock struck; it was six o'clock in the evening. Hudson commands silence, takes off his hat, rises, makes a great sign of the cross, and intones with a tender and affected voice: *"Angelus Domini nuntiavit Mariae."* And the father of the little confectioner and her brothers, ashamed of their suspicions, said to the husband while going down the stairs: "My son, you are stupid." "Brother, aren't you ashamed? A man who says the Angelus, a saint!"

One winter evening as he returned to the monastery he was set upon by one of those creatures that solicit trade among the passers-by. She seemed pretty to him. He follows her, and scarcely has he entered her place when the Watch appears. That adventure would have ruined any other. But Father Hudson was a man with a mind, and the accident gained him the good will and protection of the police magistrate. Conducted before that officer, here is what he said: "My name is Hudson, I am the superior of my house. When I came here all was in disorder; there was neither learning, discipline, nor morals; the spiritual side of things was neglected scandalously; the damage in temporal things threatened the chapter with imminent ruin. I have brought order to all, but I am a man, and I prefer to turn to a corrupted woman rather than to a virtuous one. You can now do with me what you will." The magistrate recommended that he be a bit more circumspect in the future, promised to keep the present adventure a secret, and evinced the desire to know him better personally.

Meanwhile the enemies who surrounded him had each, on his own, sent memoranda to the general of the order, in which what they knew of Hudson's bad conduct was exposed. The very number of the memoranda strengthened their effect. The general was a Jansenist, and, as a result, much disposed toward exacting vengeance on Hudson for the persecution he had exercised against adherents of the general's own ideas. He would have been only too happy to extend to the whole sect the charge of corrupted conduct leveled against one single defender of "The Bull" [45] and relaxed morality. And so he put the different memoranda of the deeds of Hudson in the hands of two commissioners whom he sent secretly with orders to proceed to the verification and legal deposition of complaints, enjoining them above all to put the greatest circumspection in their management of the affair. This was the only way to overwhelm the culprit suddenly, and take from him the protection of the court and of Mirepoix, the bishop in whose eyes Jansenism was the greatest of all crimes, and submission to the *Unigenitus*

Bull, the foremost of virtues. Richard, my secretary, was one of those commissioners.

And so these two men, having left their novitiate, are settled in the house of Hudson, and advancing silently in their inquiries. They would very soon have collected a list of grave sins that would have sufficed to put fifty monks in the *in pace*. Their stay had been long, but their procedure so clever that nothing had been discovered. Hudson, clever as he was, was skirting his own ruin, and had not the slightest suspicion of it. However, the little attention these two newcomers had shown in paying him court, the secret of their coming, their excursions, sometimes together and sometimes separately, their frequent conferences with other brothers, the sort of people they visited and by whom they were visited, caused him some anxiety. He spied on them, had them spied on, and soon the object of their mission became evident to him. He was not at all upset. He took much thought not as to how to escape the threatening storm, but how to draw it onto the heads of the commissioners. And here is the very extraordinary course of action he followed.

He had seduced a girl whom he held hidden in a little house in the *faubourg* Saint-Medard. He runs to her and holds the following conversation: "My child, all has been discovered; we are lost. In a week you will be shut up and I don't know what will happen to me. Do not despair—no weeping; control yourself. Listen to me, and do as I say. Do it well, and I shall take care of the rest. Tomorrow I shall leave for the country. During my absence, go find the two commissioners (and he mentioned their names). Ask to speak to them in private. Once alone with them, throw yourself at their feet, ask for their help, ask for their justice, ask them to intercede for you with the general on whose mind you know they have much influence. Weep, sob, tear your hair, and while weeping and sobbing and tearing your hair tell them our whole story, and tell it in the way best calculated to awaken pity for yourself and revulsion for me."

"What, sir, I shall tell them . . . ?"

"Yes, you must tell them who you are, to whom you belong, that I seduced you in the confessional, tore you from your parents' arms, and closed you up in the house where you are. Say that after I stole your honor and drew you into crime, I abandoned you to misery. Say you don't know what's to become of you."

"But, Father . . ."

"Do what I have outlined, and what I shall add in a minute, or rest assured of your ruin and my own. Those two monks will not fail to pledge you their assistance. They will ask you for a second meeting, which you will grant them. They will make inquiries about you and your family, and since you will have said nothing that isn't true, you cannot be suspected by them. After this first and second interview, I shall lay down what you have to do in a third. Only remember to play your part well."

Everything happened as Father Hudson had foreseen. He took a second trip. The two commissioners informed the girl of it; she came back to the monastery. They asked her again for the story of her unfortunate adventure. While she told it to one of them, the other took down notes on a tablet. They sighed over her destiny, told her of the desolation of her parents, which was only too true, and promised her surety for her own person and revenge against her seducer, but on the condition that she would sign a confession. This proposal seemed at first to revolt her. They insisted and she complied. It was now only a question of the hour and place at which this document would be drawn up for they needed time and proper accommodations. "Where we now are it is not possible, for if the prior came back and noticed . . . I shouldn't dare to suggest my quarters." The girl and the commissioners separated, having agreed on a time to take care of their difficulties.

That very day Hudson was informed of what had happened. He was at the height of joy; he was nearing his triumph. Soon he would teach those innocent babies with whom they were playing. "Take this pen," he said to the girl, "and grant them rendezvous in the place I shall indicate. This meeting will suit them I am sure.

The house is respectable and the woman who lives there enjoys the best reputation in the neighborhood and among the other tenants."

The woman was, however, one of those clandestine adventuresses who play at religion, worm their way into the best houses, are sweet, affectionate, and wheedling in tone, and deceive the confidence of mothers and daughters only to lead them to debauch. That was the use Father Hudson made of her; she was his procuress. Had he let the woman in on the secret or not, that I don't know.

The two commissioners of the general did indeed accept the rendezvous. And there they are with the girl. The older woman withdraws. They start to draw up the paper, when there is a great noise in the house.

"Gentlemen, whom do you want?" "We are looking for Dame Simion." (This was the adventuress' name.) "You are at her door."

They knock loudly on the door. "Gentlemen," asked the girl, "shall I reply?"

"Reply."

"Shall I open?"

"Open."

The man who did the talking was an officer with whom Hudson was closely acquainted. Whom didn't he know? He had disclosed his peril to the officer and laid down the role he was to play. "Aha!" said the officer as he entered, "two monks in a tête-à-tête with a woman! And she's not a bad specimen!" The girl was so indecently dressed, that it was impossible to make a mistake about her vocation and what she could possibly have to do with two monks, the older under thirty. The monks protested their innocence. The officer chuckled, the while passing his hand under the chin of the girl, who had thrown herself at his feet and was begging for mercy. "We are in a respectable house," said the monks.

"Oh, yes, yes, a respectable house," said the officer.

"We are here on important business."

"Yes, we know what sort of important business goes on here. Speak up, mademoiselle."

"Officer, what these gentlemen are telling you is the truth."

However the officer did some drawing up of statements himself, and since there was nothing in the statement except pure and simple explanation of fact, the monks were obliged to sign. As they left, they found all the tenants on the landings of their apartments; at the door of the house they found a great crowd, a coach and officers who put them into the coach to the accompaniment of invective and catcalls. They had covered their faces with their robes; they were sorely afflicted. The deceitful officer cried: "And why, my fathers, must you frequent these places and creatures of the sort? However, you are safe; I have the order of the police to place you in the hands of your superior, who is a fair man and indulgent. He will not see more importance in this adventure than it merits. I don't believe they behave in your order as do those cruel Capuchins. If you were mixed up with the Capuchins, by heaven, I should pity you."

While the officer spoke thus to them, the coach started out toward the monastery. The mob thickened; they surrounded, preceded, and followed with hurried step. One could hear on all sides: "What is it? Over there?" "It's monks." "What did they do?" "They were caught with whores." "The Premonstratensians with whores!" "Why certainly! They're following in the steps of the Carmelites and Franciscans." Finally they arrive. The officer gets down and knocks at the door, knocks again, and again and again. Finally it is opened. They notify Father Hudson, who makes them wait at least a half hour, in order to give the scandal its proper uproar. Finally he appears. The officer whispers in his ear, seems to be acting as intercessor. Hudson rudely rejects his proposal. Finally, with severe face and firm tone he says: "I have no dissolutes in my establishment; these two are strangers unknown to me, perhaps two disguised rascals, with whom you may do as you please."

On these words the door is closed; the officer gets back into the coach and tells our two poor devils, more dead than alive: "I did all I could; I should have never believed Father Hudson so harsh. But then, why the devil go off with whores?"

"If the one with whom you found us is one, it is certainly not debauchery which took us there."

"Oh ho! gentlemen. And it's to an old officer that you tell that! Who are you?"

"We are monks, and the robes we wear are our own."

"Just remember that your case will have to be cleared up tomorrow; tell me the truth, and perhaps I'll be able to help you."

"We have told you the truth. But where are we going?"

"To the little Châtelet." [46]

"To the little Châtelet! To prison!"

"I am indeed very sorry."

In effect, it was there that Richard and his companion were left; but Hudson's plan was not to leave them there long. He had taken a post chaise and had arrived at Versailles. He was speaking to the minister and interpreting the affair as best suited his own interests. "That's what one is exposed to, monsignor, when he brings reform to a dissolute house and chases out the heretics. In another short while I should have been ruined, dishonored. Persecution will not stop with that; you will hear of all the horrors on my score with which it is possible to blacken a virtuous man. But I trust, monsignor, that you will recall that our General . . ."

"I know, I know, and I pity you. The services you have rendered the Church and your order will not be forgotten. The Lord's elected have from time immemorial been exposed to disgrace. They were able to withstand it; you must imitate them in courage. Count upon the good will and protection of the king. Monks, monks! I was one once, and I know from experience of what they are capable."

"If the happiness of both Church and State could only obtain that your Eminence survive me, I should persevere fearlessly."

"I shall not be long in getting you out of this. Come now."

"No, monsignor, I shall not leave without a special order."

"Freeing those two evil monks? I can see that the honor of your religion and of your robe touches you to the point of forgetting personal injury. That is very Christian and I am impressed without being surprised to find such charity in a man like yourself. This adventure will cause no scandal."

"Ah, sir, you fill my soul with joy! For at this moment that is all I dreaded."

"I shall work on your request."

That very evening Hudson had the order to free the monks, and the next day Richard and his companion, at dawn, were twenty miles from Paris, under surveillance of an officer who was conducting them back to their mother house. He also carried a letter begging the General to cease such methods and to impose monastic punishment upon the two young men.

This adventure threw consternation among Hudson's enemies. There was not a single monk in his house that did not tremble at Hudson's every glance. Several months later he was granted a rich abbey. The General was mortally spited. He was old, and there was every reason for fearing that Hudson would succeed him. He loved Richard tenderly. "My poor friend," he said to him one day, "what is to become of you if you fall under the authority of this rascal Hudson? It frightens me. You have not taken final vows. If you listen to me, you will leave the order." Richard followed his advice and returned to his father's house, which was not far from Hudson's abbey.

Hudson and Richard frequented the same houses; it was impossible that they should not sooner or later meet. In effect, they did meet. Richard was one day visiting the mistress of a château between Châlons and Saint-Dizier, nearer Saint-Dizier than Châlons, and just a stone's throw from Hudson's abbey. The lady told him: "We have here your former prior. He is very pleasant. But what sort of man is he really?"

"The best of friends and the worst of enemies."

"Wouldn't you like to see him?"

"Not at all."

Scarcely had he made this reply, when they heard the noise of a cabriolet entering the driveway. They saw Father Hudson get down, accompanied by one of the prettiest ladies in the district. "You will see him despite your feelings," said the mistress of the château, "for there he is."

The lady and Richard go to meet Father Hudson and his lady friend. The women embrace; Hudson, coming up to Richard and recognizing him, cries out: "Oh, it is you, my dear Richard? You tried to ruin me, but I forgive you. Do you but pardon me your visit to the Châtelet and we'll think no more of the matter."

"You must agree, sir, that you were the greatest sort of rascal."

"That is possible."

"And that if justice had been done, not I, but you would have made that visit to the little Châtelet."

"That also is possible. It is to the peril I was then in, I believe, that I owe my changed way of life. Oh! my dear Richard, all that has caused me to think, and how I have changed!"

"That woman with whom you arrived is charming."

"I have eyes no longer for that sort of charm."

"What a waist!"

"All that has become indifferent to me."

"And how nicely plump!"

"One breaks off sooner or later from a pleasure which can be had only on the pinnacle of a roof, in imminent danger each moment of falling and breaking one's neck."

"She has the prettiest hands I ever saw."

"I have given up the habit of such hands. A wise head returns to the consciousness of his position, which is the only happiness."

"And those eyes with which she stealthily watches you. You must agree, as the connoisseur that you are, that you have scarcely attracted any eyes more scintillating, more tender. What grace, lightness, and nobility in her step, in her bearing!"

"I think no more of such vanities; I read the Scriptures and ponder the holy fathers."

"And from time to time, the perfections of that woman, no doubt. Does she live far from Montcetz? And is her husband young?"

Hudson, growing impatient at all these questions, and convinced that Richard was not going to take him for a saint, said abruptly: "My dear Richard, you are making a f——ing fool out of me, and you are right."

My dear reader, pardon the exactness of my expression, and admit that here, as in so many other good stories, the polite word would ruin everything. For example, that story of the conversation between Piron and the late abbé Vatri. . . .[47] —What about that conversation?—Go ask his publisher, who did not dare write it but who does not need to be coaxed to tell it.

Our four characters came together again at the château; they dined well and gaily, and toward evening parted with promises to see each other again. But while the Marquis des Arcis was chatting with Jacques's master, Jacques was not silent on his side with the secretary, Richard, whom he found a likeable character. This would happen more often among men if, first of all, education and, secondly, the experience of society did not wear them down like coins that, as a result of circulation, lose their stamp.[48] It was late; the pendulum clock advised the masters and their servants that it was time to retire, and they followed its advice.

Jacques, while undressing his master, said: "Sir, do you like painting?"

The Master. Yes, but in words. For in color and on canvas, although I have my definite amateur likings, I confess that I don't understand any part of it. I should be embarrassed to have to distinguish one school from another, and they could give me a Boucher for a Rubens or for a Raphael. I could take a bad copy for a sublime original; I could value a six-franc horror at a thousand écus, and a thousand-écu masterpiece at six francs. I confess that I have never bought anything except at a certain Tremblin's place on Notre-Dame bridge; in my time he was the sole resource of poverty and debauchery, and the ruination of the talent of Vanloo's young students.[49]

Jacques. And how is that?

The Master. What does it matter? Relate to me your picture and be brief, for I am falling with sleep!

Jacques. Put yourself in front of the Fountain of the Innocents, or near the Saint-Denis Gate; these are two accessories that will enrich the composition.

The Master. I'm there.

Jacques. Now see in the middle of the street a fiacre, with suspension straps broken and lying on its side.

The Master. I have it.

Jacques. A monk and two tarts have gotten out. The monk is fleeing as fast as he can. The coachman scurries from his seat. A poodle dog has set out in pursuit of the monk, and has seized him by his coat. The monk does everything he can to rid himself of the dog. One of the tarts, disheveled, her breast uncovered, is holding her sides from laughing. The other one, who bumped her head, is leaning against the coach door, and pressing her temples in her hands. Meanwhile the populace troops to the scene; little urchins arrive screaming; shopkeepers and their wives form a border along the sills of their shops while other spectators hang out their windows.[50]

The Master. Devil take me, Jacques! Your composition is well ordered, rich, amusing, varied, and full of action. Upon our return to Paris take that subject to Fragonard,[51] and you will see what he'll be able to do with it.

Jacques. After what you have confessed to me about your critical acumen, I can accept your praises without lowering my eyes.

The Master. I'll wager that was one of Father Hudson's adventures.

Jacques. You are right.

Reader, while these good people are sleeping, I should like to propose a little question for you to turn over on your pillow. What would the child born of Father Hudson and Mme de La Pommeraye be like? Perhaps a decent fellow. Perhaps a wonderful rascal. You can tell me about that tomorrow.

5

AND THAT MORROW HAS COME AND OUR CHARACTERS HAVE SEPA-
rated, for the Marquis des Arcis no longer followed the same road
as Jacques and his master.—Then we shall resume Jacques's love
story?—I hope so, but what is more certain is that the master
knows the time, has taken his pinch of snuff, and is saying to
Jacques: "Well, Jacques, how about your love story?"

Jacques, instead of replying to that question, said: "Isn't it the
very devil! From morning to night men curse life, yet they can
never decide to leave it. Is it because, when all is said and done,
life as it is, is really not so bad, or because they fear a worse one
to come?"

The Master. It's both. Apropos, Jacques, do you believe in the
life to come?

Jacques. I neither believe nor disbelieve. I don't even think about
it. I am enjoying as best I can the life that has been granted me
in advance inheritance.

The Master. As for me, I think of myself as a cocoon. And I
like to think that the butterfly, or my soul, managing one day to
break the shell, will fly off to divine justice.

Jacques. Your imagery is charming.

The Master. It's not mine. I read it, I believe, in some Italian
poet named Dante, who wrote a work entitled: *The Comedy of
Hell, Purgatory, and Paradise.*[52]

Jacques. Now there's a strange subject for a comedy!

The Master. There are, by heaven, some good things in it—especially in his hell. He shuts up heretics in tombs of fire from which
the flames escape and cause widespread destruction. He puts the

ungrateful into niches where they pour forth tears that freeze on their faces; the lazy in still other niches, and of these last he says that their blood escapes from their veins and is gathered up by disdainful worms. But what brought on your tirade against our scorn for a life we are afraid of losing?

Jacques. It was what the secretary of the marquis told me about the husband of the pretty lady in the cabriolet.

The Master. She's a widow!

Jacques. She lost her husband during a trip she made to Paris, and that devil of a fellow didn't want to hear any talk about sacraments. It was the lady of the château where Richard met Father Hudson who was asked to help get such a bee out of this fellow's heretic bonnet and bring him back to piety.

The Master. What are you trying to say with your bonnet?

Jacques. The bonnet is the headdress they pull over newborn babes.

The Master. I see your point. But how did she set about pulling her [53] bonnet over this fellow?

Jacques. They were all gathered about the fire. The doctor, after having felt his patient's pulse, which he found very weak, came to sit down with the others. The lady in question went up to the bed, and asked him several questions, but without raising her voice any more than was necessary for the fellow to grasp what they were trying to make him understand. After this a conversation started between the lady, the doctor, and several of the people present, which I shall reproduce for you.

The Lady: "Well, doctor, give us the news of Mme de Parme."

The Doctor: "I have just left a house where I was assured she was so low that there was very little hope."

The Lady: "That princess has always showed signs of piety. As soon as she felt herself in danger she asked to be shriven and given the last sacraments."

The Doctor: "The curate of St. Roch is bringing her a relic from Versailles today, but it will arrive too late."

The Lady: "The princess is not the only one to give such an example. The Duke of Chevreuse, who was very ill, did not wait for his family to propose the sacraments; he called for them himself —which gave his family great pleasure."

The Doctor: "He's much better now."

One of the Group: "It's certain that it does no harm; on the contrary."

The Lady: "Truly, as soon as a person feels in danger, he ought to carry out those last obligations. Sick people apparently don't realize how hard it is for those about them, and yet how necessary it is to propose the sacraments to them."

The Doctor. "I have just come from a patient who asked me two days ago: 'Doctor, how am I?'

" 'Sir, your fever is high, and there are frequent paroxysms.'

" 'Do you think another will come soon?'

" 'No, I fear only for tonight.

" 'That being so, I want to send for a man with whom I have some private business, so I may finish it while I am still in my right mind.' He confessed, received the sacraments. I came back in the evening—no paroxysm. Yesterday he was better, and today he is completely out of danger. Many times during my years of practice I have seen that effect from the sacraments."

The Patient (*to his servant*): "Bring me my chicken."

Jacques. They bring it to him. He tries to cut and hasn't the strength. They cut up a wing into little pieces for him. He asks for bread, snatches it, and makes a great effort to chew a mouthful, which he is incapable of swallowing and spits up in his napkin. He calls for wine; wets the corners of his mouth with it, and announces: "I feel fine." Ah, yes, but half an hour later he was no more.

The Master. That lady nevertheless did her best. And now your loves?

Jacques. With the condition in mind that you accepted?

The Master. Yes, I remember. You were settled in Desglands' château, and the old servant Jeanne had ordered her daughter Denise to visit you four times a day and take care of you. But before going any further, tell me: was Denise still a virgin?

Jacques (coughing). I think so.

The Master. And yourself?

Jacques. As for my virginity, it had been roaming the fields for a long time.

The Master. This was not, then, your first love affair?

Jacques. Why do you ask that?

The Master. It's just that you love the woman to whom you give your virginity, just as you are loved by her from whom you take it.

Jacques. Sometimes yes, sometimes no.

The Master. And how did you lose it?

Jacques. I didn't lose it; I gave it in good, fair exchange.

The Master. Tell me a little of that exchange.

Jacques. That would be like the first chapter of St. Luke—a litany of endless begats from the beginning right up to Denise.

The Master. Who believed she had her virginity and didn't at all.

Jacques. And before Denise, the two neighbor women at home.

The Master. Who thought they had theirs and didn't.

Jacques. Exactly so.

The Master. To miss a virgin twice in a row—that's not very clever.

Jacques. See here, sir, I can guess from the slight lifting of the corner of your right lip, and your left nostril which is dilating, that I might as well go through the thing voluntarily without being begged to. All the more so, since I feel my sore throat getting worse. The rest of my whole love story is long, and I have the courage to take on only one or two short anecdotes.

The Master. If Jacques really wanted to make me happy . . .

Jacques. What would he do?

The Master. He would start off with the loss of his virginity.

Shall I confess it? I have always been keen on stories of that first great event.

Jacques. And why, may I ask?

The Master. It's just that of all stories in the same class, it's the only type that is really interesting. The rest are but insipid and common repetitions. Out of all the sins of a pretty lady penitent, I'm sure the confessor is most attentive to that one.

Jacques. My master, my master, I see you have a corrupted mind, and in your agony the devil could very well appear to you in the same form of digression as that in which he appeared to Ferragus.[54]

The Master. That is possible. But you had your eyes opened, I'll wager, by some shameless old thing from your village. No?

Jacques. Don't bet, for you would lose.

The Master. Then it was by the serving woman of your curate.

Jacques. Don't bet, for you would still lose.

The Master. Then it was by his niece.

Jacques. His niece was stifling with passion and religious piety—two qualities that go quite well together but do not suit me.

The Master. This time, I think I have it.

Jacques. I'm not at all sure.

The Master. One market day or one day at the fair . . .

Jacques. It was neither market day, nor fair.

The Master. You went to the city . . .

Jacques. I went not at all to the city.

The Master. And it was written up yonder that you should, in some tavern, meet up with one of those obliging creatures, that you would get drunk . . .

Jacques. I had neither eaten nor drunk, and what is written up yonder is that at about this time you would wear yourself out in false conjecturing, and that you would take on a vice against which you've been warning me—that is, the fury of guessing, and always wrong. As I stand here before you, sir, I was once baptized. . . .

The Master. If you are planning to start the story of the loss of your virginity at the baptismal font, we're going to be quite a while.

Jacques. And so I had a godfather and a godmother. Master Bogger, the best-known wheelwright in the village had a son. The senior Bogger was my godfather, and his son Bogger was my friend. At the age of about eighteen or nineteen we both went overboard at the same time for a little seamstress named Justine. Otherwise she was not thought of as particularly cruel, but she did consider it fashionable to become known for an initial show of scorn, and so her choice for such scorn, fell on me.

The Master. Just one of those strange whims of women, impossible to understand.

Jacques. The entire quarters of the wheelwright Master Bogger; my godfather, consisted of a shop with a loft above. His bed was in the back of the shop. Bogger, my friend, slept in the loft, to which he climbed by means of a little ladder situated about equidistant from his father's bed and the shop door

When my godfather Bogger was fast asleep, my friend Bogger would open the door gently and Justine would climb up to the loft on the ladder. The next day, at the break of dawn, before the old Bogger was awake, this son of a Bogger would come down from the loft, open the door, and Justine would escape as she had entered.

The Master. To go visit some other loft thereafter, either her own or another.

Jacques. Why not? The relations between Bogger and Justine were fairly pleasant, but they were doomed to trouble. It was written up yonder and so it came to pass.

The Master. Trouble from the father?

Jacques. No.

The Master. From the mother?

Jacques. No, she was dead.

The Master. From a rival?

Jacques. No, no, no! By all the devils in hell, no! My master, it is written up yonder that for as long as you live you will guess, and I repeat, always guess wrong.

One morning my friend Bogger, wearier than usual either from the work of the day before or from the night's pleasure, was resting peacefully in Justine's arms, when a terrifying voice was heard at the foot of the ladder. "Bogger, Bogger, you lazy Bogger! The Angelus has rung; it's almost five-thirty and there you are still in the loft. Are you going to stay there until noon? Must I come up and get you and bring you down here faster than you like? Bogger, Bogger!"

"Yes, father?"

"And how about the axle that old crab of a farmer is waiting for? Do you want him to come back again with his fuming?"

"The axle is ready, and he'll have it in another quarter of an hour."

I let you judge of the terror felt by Justine and Bogger.

The Master. I am sure Justine promised herself she would never again be found in that loft, and that she was back again that night. But how did she get out that morning?

Jacques. If you're going to set about guessing it, I'll be quiet. Meanwhile, Bogger, son, had leaped out of bed, barelegged, his trousers in his hand, and his jacket over his arm. While he was dressing, his father grumbled: "Ever since he met that little baggage, everything goes wrong. That's got to stop; it can't go on, for I'm beginning to grow sick of it. If it were a girl who was worth the trouble, but what a creature! God only knows what sort! Ah! if his poor dead mother, who was honorable to her finger tips, could have seen that, she would have long since beat the one and torn the other's eyes out on the church porch after mass in front of everybody. For nothing stopped that one. But if I've been too soft up to now, and if they think I'm going to continue that way, they're in for a surprise."

The Master. And Justine heard these remarks up in the loft?

Jacques. No doubt. Meanwhile Bogger had gone off to the

farmer with his wheel on his shoulder and the old Bogger got down to his work. After several blows with the adze, his nose calls for a pinch of snuff. He looks for his snuffbox in his pockets, at the head of his bed, and finds it nowhere. "It's that rascal who has taken it as usual; let's see if it isn't up there." And up the ladder he comes to the loft. A minute or two later, he notices that his pipe and knife are missing and goes back up again.

The Master. And Justine?

Jacques. She had hurriedly gathered her clothes together and slid under the bed where she was stretched out flat, more dead than alive.

The Master. And how about your friend Bogger?

Jacques. After the wheel had been returned to the farm, replaced, and paid for, he had run to my house and had outlined the terrible situation he was in. After having my share of amusement, I said to Bogger: "Listen, Bogger; go walking in the village, where you will, and I shall get you out of this. I ask only one thing—give me plenty of time." You are smiling, sir, what's the matter?

The Master. Nothing.

Jacques. My friend Bogger leaves. I dress, for I had not yet gotten up. I go to his father's house and he no sooner sees me than, crying with surprise and joy, he shouts: "Hey there, godson. Where are you coming from and what are you doing here so early in the morning?" My godfather Bogger really liked me and so I reply frankly: "It's not so much a question of where I come from as how I shall ever get back home."

"Ah! godson; you are becoming a roué. I'm afraid you and Bogger make a pair. You slept out, eh?"

"And my father will stand for no nonsense on that score."

"Your father is right, godson, to feel that way. But let's start things with a bite to eat; the bottle will give us an idea."

The Master. Jacques, that man had good principles.

Jacques. I replied to him that I wanted and needed neither food nor drink, but that I was dead tired and sleepy. Old Bogger, who in his day never came out second, added laughingly: "Godson, she was pretty and you tuckered yourself out. Look here, Bogger is out. Go up to the loft and stretch out on his bed. But one word before he comes back. He's your friend. And when you have a talk together, tell him I'm very disappointed, very. It's about a little Justine whom you must know (for what lad in the village doesn't?) who has debauched him for me. You would do me a great service if you got him away from that girl. He used to be what you would call a good boy, but since he made that unfortunate acquaintance . . . you're not listening; your eyes are closing; go up there and rest."

I go up, undress, lift the covers and the sheets, feel all about— no Justine. Meanwhile old Bogger was saying: "Oh! these children! these cursed children; there's another one who's breaking his father's heart." Since Justine wasn't in the bed, I suspected she was under it. The little hole of a room was completely blind and black. I kneel down, feel about with my hands. I bump into one of her arms, grab it and pull it toward me. She comes out from under the bed, quivering. I embrace her, reassure her, and motion her to get in bed. She wrings her hands, throws herself at my feet, grasps my knees. I should perhaps not have resisted such a mute scene, if day had lighted up that place. But when shadows don't frighten you, they make you daring. Moreover, I had her former scorn for me weighing on my heart. In reply to her scene, I pushed her toward the stairway which led to the shop. She let out a cry of terror. Bogger, who heard it, mused out loud: "He must be dreaming." Justine fainted away; her legs gave way under her, and in her delirium she said in a stifled voice: "He's coming, he's coming, I hear him coming up—I am lost!" "No, no," I replied in a low voice. "Control yourself, be quiet and get into bed." She persists in her refusal; I remain firm; she resigns herself, and there we are next to each other.

The Master. Traitor! Criminal! Do you know what crime you are about to commit? You are going to violate that girl, if not by force, at least by terror. Were the thing to come to court, you would feel all the rigor meted out to rapists.

Jacques. I don't know whether or not I violated her, but I do know I didn't hurt her any and she didn't hurt me. At first, turning her mouth aside from my kisses, she found my ear and whispered: "No, Jacques, no. . . ." At this I pretended to get out of bed and go down the ladder. She holds me back and says again in my ear: "I should never have thought you so wicked. I can see I should not expect pity from you. But at least promise me, swear to me . . ."

"What?"

"That Bogger will hear nothing about it."

The Master. You promised, you swore, and all went well.

Jacques. And went well again.

The Master. And then went well yet again?

Jacques. It's exactly as if you had been there. Meanwhile, my friend Bogger, impatient and worried, tired of walking all about town without meeting me comes back to his father, who snaps at him sullenly: "You were away a long time for nothing." Bogger, son, replies still more sullenly: "Well, didn't I have to plane down that devilish axle at each end? It was too big."

"I warned you about it, but you must always have your way."

"Well, it's easier to take it off than to put it back on."

"Take this rim and go finish it there by the door."

"Why at the door?"

"Because the noise of your tools would awaken your friend, Jacques."

"Jacques!"

"Yes, Jacques. He is up there in the loft resting. Ah! how unfortunate to be a father! If it's not one thing it's something else. Well, are you going to move? While you're standing there like an imbecile with your head bent, your mouth open, and your arms swinging, the work is not getting done."

My friend Bogger, furious, flies toward the ladder. Old Bogger holds him back, saying: 'Where are you going? Let that poor devil sleep, overcome as he is with fatigue. If you were in his place, would you want to be awakened?"

The Master. And Justine heard all that too?

Jacques. As clearly as you hear me.

The Master. What did you do?

Jacques. I laughed.

The Master. And Justine?

Jacques. She had torn her headdress apart, she pulled at her hair, raised her eyes to heaven I should presume, and twisted her arms.

The Master. Jacques, you are a savage; you have a heart of iron.

Jacques. No sir, I have sensitivity, but I save it for better occasions. The dissipaters of that rich commodity have been so generous with it when they should have been sparing, that they find no more left when they need to be generous with it. Meanwhile, I get dressed and go down. Old Bogger says: "You needed that rest; it did you good. When you arrived you looked like a corpse, and here you are red and fresh like a babe just suckled. Sleep is a good thing. Bogger, go down to the cellar and bring up a bottle so we can have lunch. Now, godson, you will eat, won't you?" "Very gladly." The bottle arrives and is placed on the bench about which we are standing. Bogger, father, fills his glass and mine; Bogger, son, pushing his glass away, growls in a nasty tone: "As for me I don't get thirsty so early in the morning."

"You don't want anything to drink?"

"No."

"Aha! I know what's wrong, godson; there's some Justine in this, you'll see. He probably passed by her place and didn't find her in, or surprised her with somebody else. This pouting against the bottle is not natural, I'll tell you that."

I: "Why, you just might have guessed right."

Bogger, son: "Jacques, that's enough of your jokes, in order or out of order; I don't like them."

Old Bogger: "Just because he doesn't want to drink, that mustn't stop us. To your health, godson."

I: "To yours, godfather. Bogger, my friend, drink with us. You upset yourself for too little."

Bogger, son: "I have already told you I'm not drinking."

I: "O come now, see here. If your father guessed it, what the devil, you'll see her again and you'll explain things and admit you were wrong."

Old Bogger: "Oh, let him alone. Isn't it proper that the little hussy should punish him for the trouble he's been giving me? Now then, one more drink, and let's get down to business. I can see I'll have to take you to your father, but what do you want me to tell him?"

I: "Whatever you like, all you have heard a hundred times when he brings back your son."

Old Bogger: "Come then; let's be on our way."

He goes out, I follow, and we come to my front door. I let him go in alone. Curious to know the conversation of father Bogger and my father, I hide in a corner, behind some paneling, where I can hear every word.

Old Bogger: "Come, friend and neighbor, you'll have to forgive him this one more time."

"Forgive him? For what?"

"You act as if you didn't know."

"Well, I'm not acting; I don't know."

"You are angry and you're perfectly right."

"But I'm not at all angry."

"You are, I say."

"If you want me to be, all right then; I shan't argue with you. But let me find out first of all what stupid thing he's done now."

"Agreed. Three times, four times—that's still not habitual. They get with a crowd of young fellows and girls; they drink and dance and the hours fly and meantime the house door is locked."

Bogger, lowering his voice, added: "They can't hear us, but now really, were we any better at their age? Do you know what sort of fellows make bad fathers? Those who have forgotten the faults of their own youth. Tell me true now: didn't we ever sleep out?"

"And you tell me, Bogger: didn't we ever have affairs that didn't please our parents?"

"And so I'm crying louder than I'm hurt. Do as much."

"But Jacques did not sleep out this night; I'm sure of that."

"Well, if it wasn't last night, it was another one. What matters is that you're not angry with your boy, are you?"

"No."

"And after I've gone you won't treat him badly?"

"Not at all."

"You give me your word?"

"I do."

"Word of honor?"

"Word of honor."

"Then all's taken care of; I'm going back."

As my godfather Bogger was standing on the doorstep, my father tapped him gently on the shoulder and said: "Bogger, my friend, there's a fly in the ointment somewhere here. Your boy and mine are two damned clever toms, and I'm afraid they've played us for the fool this time. But we shall see in time. Good-by, neighbor."

The Master. And how did the adventure end between Justine and your friend Bogger?

Jacques. As it should. He got angry, she got angrier. She cried, he grew tender. She swore to him that I was the best friend he had. I swore she was the most virtuous girl in town. He believed us, asked our forgiveness, and loved and esteemed us the more for all of it. And so there is the beginning, the middle, and the end of how I lost my virginity. And now, sir, I should like you to teach me the moral of this impertinent story.

The Master. To know women better.

Jacques. And did you need that lesson?

The Master. And to get to know your friends better.

Jacques. And did you ever think there was a single one who could hold off your wife or your daughter if they once proposed his downfall?

The Master. Then it must be to know your parents and children better.

Jacques. Come now, sir. They have always been, and will always be, the reciprocal dupes one of the other.

The Master. The things you are saying to me are indeed eternal truths but truths upon which one cannot too much insist. Whatever is the story you proposed to tell me next, rest assured that it will be devoid of instruction only for a dolt, and continue.

Reader, I begin to have some scruples of honoring Jacques and his master with reflections that really belong to you. If this is so, you may take them back without hurting their feelings. I thought I felt that you were hurt by the word Bogger. I should like to know why. For it's the real name of my wheelwright's family—the baptismal records, the death notices, and the marriage contracts are all signed Bogger. The descendants who hold the shop today are called Boggers. When their children, who are pretty, go through the streets, people say: "Look at those cute little Boggers." When you pronounce the word Balls, you are calling to mind the greatest cabinetmaker there has ever been. In Bogger country, even today, you can't pronounce the word Bogger without remembering the greatest wheelwright of memory. The Bogger, whose name you read at the end of all the books for religious offices at the beginning of this century, was one of the family. If ever a descendant of Bogger becomes famous through some great deed, the personal name of Bogger will become no less imposing to you than that of Caesar or Condé. For there are Boggers and Boggers, just as there are Williams and Williams. If I were to say simply William, it would be neither the Conqueror of Great Britain, nor the cloth merchant in *Pathelin;* the name of William, all alone, is neither heroic nor bourgeois. And so it is with Boggers. Bogger alone is neither the famous wheelwright, nor any of his common antecedents, nor any of his common descendants. Can a family name ever be in good or bad taste? The streets are full of alley cats called Pompey. Get rid of your false delicacy or I shall treat you as Lord Chatham once treated the members of Parliament. "Sugar, sugar, sugar," said he, "what's ridiculous about that?" [55] And so I say to you: "Bogger, Bogger, Bogger; why shouldn't a man be called Bogger? As the officer said once to his general, the great Condé, 'There are proud Boggers, like Bogger the wheelwright; there are nice Boggers like you and me; and then there are dirty Boggers like an infinity of others.'"

Jacques. It was a wedding celebration; Brother Jean had married off the daughter of one of our neighbors. I was ring boy. They had put me at the table between the two jokesters of the village. I seemed to be a great booby, although I wasn't as stupid as they thought. They asked me some questions on the subject of wedding nights. I replied rather stupidly and they burst out laughing, and their two wives shouted from the other end of the table: "What's going on up there? You are certainly very gay." "Oh! it's too funny," said one to his wife, "I'll tell you tonight." The other woman who was no less curious asked her husband the same question and got the same answer. The dinner continues with the same questions, my same stupid answers, and the guffaws of the husbands and their wives. After dinner, dancing; after dancing, the bedding of the couple and the gift of the garter. [56] Then me in my bed, and the jokesters in theirs telling their wives the amazing, the unbelievable fact that at twenty-two, big and strong as I was, rather good-looking, alert and not stupid, I was still innocent, just as innocent as the day I had left my mother's womb. The two women were as amazed as their husbands. But the very next day, Suzanne made motion to me and said: "Jacques, haven't you anything to do right now?"

"No, neighbor. What can I do for you?"

"I should like, I should like . . ." she said, and in saying, she squeezed my hand and looked at me strangely. "I should like you to take our scythe and come down on the common with me to cut two or three faggots of brush. It's such a hard job for me alone."

"Very gladly, Madame Suzanne."

I take the scythe and we set out. On the way, Suzanne let her head fall on my shoulder, took me by the chin, pulled my ears, and pinched my sides. We arrive. The place was on a slope. Suzanne lies down, completely stretched out, at the very highest spot, her legs stretched far apart, and her hands under her head. I was below her, swinging my scythe on the thicket. Suzanne folded her legs back, pulling her heels up to her thighs. Her raised knees made her skirt very short, and I kept swinging my scythe on the brush, scarcely looking, as I struck and struck often to the side. Finally Suzanne says: "Jacques, are you soon finished?"

"Whenever you like, Mme Suzanne."

"Can't you see," she said in a soft voice, "that I want you to finish."

And so I finished, then caught my breath, and finished again, and Suzanne . . .

The Master. Took from you the virginity you no longer had?

Jacques. True. But Suzanne made no mistake on that score. And she smiled as she said: "You've played a good one on my husband, and you're a rascal."

"What do you mean, Mme Suzanne?"

"Nothing, nothing; you understand only too well. Deceive me a couple more times the same way, and I'll forgive you. . . ." I tied up the faggots, put them on my back, and we came back home; she to hers, and I to mine.

The Master. Without stopping along the way?

Jacques. No.

The Master. It must not have been very far then, from the common to the village.

Jacques. Not any farther than from the village to the common.

The Master. Was that all she was worth?

Jacques. Perhaps for another she was worth more, or for some other day; each moment has its price.

Some time thereafter, Dame Marguerite, the wife of the other jokester, had some grain to be ground and didn't have the time to go to the mill. She came to ask my father for one of the boys to go for her. Since I was the biggest she had no doubt that my father would choose me—which didn't fail to happen. Dame Marguerite leaves and I follow; I put the sack of grain on my donkey and take it to the mill alone. The grain was ground and we were on our way home, the donkey and I, and I was rather sad for I thought I should get nothing out of it but the work. I was wrong. There was a little patch of woods to pass through between the mill and the village. It was there I found Marguerite sitting along the road. Night started to fall. "Jacques," she said, "finally you are here. Do you know I have been waiting a whole eternal hour for you?"

Reader, you are really too exacting! You are right, the eternal hour is more for city women, the solid hour would better fit Dame Marguerite.

I: "Well, the water was low and the mill turned slowly; then, too, the miller was drunk. However hard I tried, I couldn't come back any sooner."

Marguerite: "Sit down there, and let's chat a bit."

I: "Dame Marguerite, I should like to very much . . ."

So there I am seated next to her to chat and still we were both silent. And so I said to her: "Dame Marguerite, you're not saying a word and we're not chatting."

Marguerite: "Oh, I was thinking of what my husband said about you."

I: "Don't believe a word he says; he's always jesting."

Marguerite: "He assured me you have never had a love affair."

I: "Well, as for that, he was right."

Marguerite: "What! never in your whole life?"

I: "Never in my life."

Marguerite: "How can that be? At your age you don't even know what a woman is?"

I: "I beg your pardon, Dame Marguerite."

Marguerite: "Tell me: what is a woman?"

I: "A woman?"

Marguerite: "Yes, a woman."

I: "Let's see—it's a man with a skirt, a headdress, and big breasts."

The Master. You scoundrel!

Jacques. Well, the other one hadn't been fooled and I wanted this one to be fooled. Upon my reply, Marguerite burst out laughing, and laughed without stopping. Completely ashamed, I asked what she was laughing at. She said she was laughing at my innocence. "How is it possible as big as you are? Can it be true you don't know any more than that?"

"It's true, Dame Marguerite."

Whereupon, Dame Marguerite was silent and I too. "But, Dame Marguerite," I said to her again, "we sat down here to talk and you're not saying a word, and we're not talking at all. Dame Marguerite, what's the matter? You are dreaming."

Marguerite: "Yes, yes, I am dreaming, I am dreaming."

As she said these "dreamings," her breasts rose, her voice grew weak, her limbs trembled, her eyes closed, and her mouth fell half open. She sighed deeply, fainted away, and I acted as if I thought she had died. I started to shout with fright. "Dame Marguerite, Marguerite, speak to me! Dame Marguerite, are you ill?"

"No, my child; let me rest a minute. I don't know what's come over me—it came on so suddenly."

The Master. She was lying.

Jacques. Yes, of course, she was lying.

Marguerite: "I was just dreaming . . ."

I: "Do you dream like that sometimes at night with your husband?"

Marguerite: "Sometimes."

I: "That must frighten him."

Marguerite: "He's used to it."

Marguerite recovered bit by bit from her fainting and said: "I was thinking of the wedding party a week ago. My husband and Suzanne's made fun of you. That made me sad, and I felt all funny inside."

I: "You are too kind."

Marguerite: "I don't like them to make fun. I was just thinking that at the very first occasion, they'll start in again and I shall feel bad all over again."

I: "But it's entirely up to you to stop all that."

Marguerite: "How could that be?"

I: "By teaching me . . ."

Marguerite: "What?"

I: "What I don't know, and what made your husband and Suzanne's husband laugh so much. They wouldn't laugh again, if . . ."

Marguerite: "Oh! no, no. I know very well that you're a good boy, and that you wouldn't tell anybody, but I shouldn't dare."

I: "And why not?"

Marguerite: "I just wouldn't dare."

I: "Ah! Dame Marguerite, teach me, I beg you, and I shall have the deepest gratitude, only teach me." Begging her in this manner, I squeezed her hand and she squeezed mine too. I kissed her eyes and she kissed my mouth. Meanwhile it had become completely dark. I said again to her: "I can see, Dame Marguerite, that you don't think enough of me to teach me; I feel very sad about it Come, let's get up and go back." Dame Marguerite was silent; she took back one of my hands, and I don't know exactly where she put it, but the fact is that I suddenly cried out: "There is nothing! There is nothing!"

The Master. Rascal, double rascal.

Jacques. The fact is that she was very much undressed, and I was too. The fact is that I still had my hand where there was nothing on her, and that she had put hers where the same was not true on me. The fact is that I found myself under her, and, as a result, her on top of me. The fact is that, not being able to calm it for all her fatiguing, she had to take it all. The fact is that she lent herself so well to my instruction, that there came a moment when I thought she should die of it. The fact is that as upset as she was, and not knowing what I was saying, I cried out: "Ah, Dame Suzanne; how happy you make me!"

The Master. You mean Dame Marguerite.

Jacques. No, no. The fact is I took one name for the other and instead of saying Dame Marguerite, I said Dame Suzanne. The fact is that I confessed to Dame Marguerite that all she had thought she was teaching me that day, I had already learned from Suzanne, a little differently, it is true, three or four days before. The fact is that she cried: "What! Suzanne and not I!" The fact is that I replied: "It was neither one nor the other." The fact is that all the while she was laughing at herself, at Suzanne, at the two husbands, and handing me slight insults, I found myself on her and as a consequence her under me, and that as she admitted to me that this was enjoyable but not as much so as the other, she was on me and I again as a result under her. The fact is that after a little rest and silence, I found neither myself nor her above nor yet myself nor her below, for we were both on our sides, and she had her head bent forward and her two buttocks tightly pressed against my thighs. The fact is that, if I had been less learned, I should have learned all there is to learn. The fact is that we had trouble getting back to the village. The fact is that my sore throat is much worse, and I don't think there's much hope I shall be able to speak again for two weeks.

The Master. And didn't you see these women again?

Jacques. Oh, I beg your pardon—more than once.

The Master. Both of them?

Jacques. Both of them.

The Master. They didn't quarrel?

Jacques. Being useful one to the other, they were only the closer friends for it all.

The Master. I suppose my kind would surely have done as much, but more likely each one with her own. You are laughing.

Jacques. Every time I think of that little man, shouting, cursing, foaming, shaking his head, feet and hands, his whole body, and all set to throw himself from the top of the hayloft, at the risk of killing himself, I can't stop laughing.

The Master. And who is this little man? Suzanne's husband?

Jacques. No.

The Master. Marguerite's husband?

Jacques. No. Always the same; the same as long as he lives!

The Master. Well, then, who is he?

Jacques didn't reply to this question and the master repeated. "Only tell me who the little man was."

Jacques. One day a child seated at the foot of a goods counter was crying with all his might. The worried shopgirl asked him: "Little friend, why are you crying?"

"Because they want me to say 'A.'"

"And why don't you want to say 'A'?"

"Because no sooner have I said 'A' than they'll want me to say 'B.'" Which is to say I shall no sooner have told who the little man was than I shall have to tell all the rest.

The Master. Perhaps.

Jacques. That is sure.

The Master. Come, now, my friend Jacques; tell me who this little man is. You're dying to tell it, aren't you? Satisfy yourself.

Jacques. He was a sort of dwarf; hunchbacked, crooked, stammering, blind in one eye, jealous, lecherous, in love with, and maybe loved by, Suzanne. He was the village vicar.

Jacques resembled the little boy in the clothing shop like two peas in a pod, with this difference; that since he had his sore throat, it was hard to get him to say 'A,' but once on the way, he went on all by himself to the end of the alphabet: "I was in Suzanne's barn, all alone with her."

The Master. And you weren't there for nothing.

Jacques. No. When the vicar arrives, he takes offense; he growls and asks imperiously of Suzanne what she was doing thus in tête-à-tête with the most debauched of the village lads, in the most out-lying part of the farm.

The Master. From what I gather, you already had a reputation.

Jacques. And fairly well deserved. He was really angry. On this same subject he added a few other remarks even less complimentary. Then I get angry. From insult to insult, we finally arrive to blows. I grab a pitchfork, put it between his legs—one tine on each side—and throw him up on the hayloft, like no more nor less than a bale of hay.

The Master. And was the hayloft high?

Jacques. Ten feet at least, and the little fellow could not have gotten down without breaking his neck.

The Master. And so?

Jacques. And so then I pull back Suzanne's dickey, take her bosom in my hands and caress it. She defends herself halfheartedly. There was there a donkey's packsaddle whose accommodating use-fulness was known to us; I push her onto this saddle.

The Master. And you lift up her skirts?

Jacques. I lift up her skirts.

The Master. And the vicar saw that?

Jacques. As clearly as I'm seeing you.

The Master. And he said nothing?

Jacques. Oh no, not at all. Unable to hold in his rage, he started to cry out: "Mm—mmm-murr—ddd—er! Ffff—iyuh—yer! Sssst—op th—th . . . ief!" And there is the husband who we thought was far off, running up.

The Master. That makes me angry; I don't like priests.

Jacques. And it would have delighted you, I suppose, if under his very eyes . . .

The Master. I admit it would.

Jacques. Suzanne had had time to get up. I pull myself together and flee, and it was Suzanne who told me what follows. The husband seeing the vicar perched on the hayloft starts to laugh. The vicar says to him: "Lllll—augh hard sttttt—upid fffff—oooool th—th—aat you are." And the husband followed his advice and laughed all the more, asking him who had nested him there. The vicar replies: "Ggggg—et mmmmm—eee ddddd—own from here." The husband still laughs on and asks him how he should go about it. The vicar replies: "Th—the wwwww—ay I ggggg—ot up; wwww—ith the ppppp—itch fff—orrrk." "Now by heaven, you are right; that's what it is to have studied." The husband takes the fork, pushes it toward the vicar. He straddles it just as I had straddled him with it. The husband gives him two or three turns all about the barn on the barnyard implement, accompanying the ride with a sort of atonal chant. The vicar was crying: "Lllll—et mmmmm—e ddddd—own, sccccc—ounnnnn-drel!" The husband asked him: "And why shouldn't I parade you this way through all the village streets? People would never have seen a lovelier procession." However, the vicar had suffered nothing more serious than terror, and the husband put him on the ground. I don't know what he said to the husband for Suzanne had fled. But I did hear: "Wrrrr—etch! You are sttttr—i-king a ppppr-eeee-st; I'llllll ex—cccommmm-unnn-icccc-ate you; you'llll bbbbb-eee ddd-amned!" It was the little man shrieking as the husband chased him with the pitchfork. I arrive on the scene with several others. As soon as the husband recognized me in the distance, putting his fork at rest, he called: "Come here, come here."

The Master. And Suzanne?

Jacques. She got out of it.

The Master. Badly?

Jacques. No; women always get off easily when you don't catch them *in delicto flagrante.* What are you laughing at?

The Master. At what will make me laugh, like yourself, every time I remember the little priest riding on the end of the husband's pitchfork.

Jacques. It was shortly after this adventure, which came to the ears of my father and made him laugh too, that I joined up as I have already told you.

After several moments of silence or coughing on Jacques's part— so some say; or after having continued to laugh, say others—the master, turning to Jacques, said: "And how about the story of your loves?" Jacques shook his head and said nothing.

How can a sensible man, a man of morals, who pretends to know philosophy, amuse himself at spinning out tales of such obscenity?—First of all, reader, these are not tales, this is history. And I feel no more guilty, perhaps less, when I write of these tricks of Jacques, than did Suetonius when he transmitted to us the debauchery of Tiberius. And yet you read Suetonius and find no reproach for him. Why don't you lift your eyebrows at Catullus, Martial, Horace, Juvenal, Petronius, La Fontaine, and a host of others? Why don't you say to the Stoic Seneca: "What need have we for the vulgarity of your slave with the concave mirrors?" [57] Why have you indulgence only for the dead? If you reflect just a bit on this partiality, you will see that it rises from some vicious principle. If you are innocent, you won't be reading me; if you are already corrupted, you will read me without disastrous results. And if what I say here doesn't satisfy you, open the preface of Jean-Baptiste Rousseau, [58] and you will find there my apology. Who is there among you that would dare to blame Voltaire for having written *la Pucelle?* [59] Not a one of you. You have, then, a double standard for men's actions?—But, you will say, *la Pucelle* is a masterpiece!—So much the worse, for it will be read all the more. —And your *Jacques* is only an insipid agglomeration of facts, some real, some imagined, written without grace and distributed about with no order.—Why, then, so much the better, my *Jacques* will be less read. Whichever way you turn, you are wrong. If my work is good, it will amuse you; if it is bad, it will do you no harm.

There is no book more innocent than a bad book. I am amusing myself at writing under borrowed names all the stupid things you do; your stupidity makes me laugh, my writing makes you angry. Reader, to be frank with you, I find that the more wicked of us is not myself. How happy I should be if it were as easy to protect myself from your malice as it is for you to protect yourself from the boredom or dangers in my work. Nasty hypocrites, leave me in peace. Go on and f—— like mad donkeys, but at least permit me to say f——; I offer you the action, grant me the word. You pronounce quite brazenly: kill, steal, and betray, and yet the other, you dare not permit between your teeth! Is it because the less you exhale these so-called impurities in words, the more there remains of them in your mind? And what has the genital action done to you—an action so natural, so necessary, and so right— that you thus exclude its word symbol from your conversations, that you imagine your eyes, ears, and mouth to be soiled by it? It is a good thing that the least-used terms, the least-written, the most-silenced should be the most generally known and recognized. And that's how it works out in fact. Thus, the word *futuo* [60] is no less familiar than the word bread. No age has ignored it; no idiom is without it; it has a thousand synonyms in every language; it is stamped upon each language without being expressed, without voicing, without a symbol. Yet the sex which does the most of it is accustomed to hushing it up the most. I hear you still object- ing: "Shame, shame, cynic! Shame, impudent man! Shame, sophist!" Take courage, and insult an esteemed author whom you have always in your hands, and of whom I am but the translator here. The license of his style is practically a guarantee to me of the purity of his habits. He is Montaigne—*Lasciva est nobis pagina, vita proba.* [61]

Jacques and his master passed the rest of the day without open- ing their mouths. Jacques coughed and his master remarked: "That's a serious cough!" looked at his watch for the time, opened his snuffbox without knowing it, and took his pinch of snuff without feeling it. What makes me sure is that he did all this three or four times in a row in exactly the same sequence. A moment later Jacques coughed again, and his master said: "What a devil of a cough! Yet you sopped up that landlady's wine right up to the knot in your throat! And yesterday with that secretary you were no more sparing. When you got up, you were staggering; you didn't know what you were saying; and today you have made at least ten halts. I'll bet there's not a drop of wine left in your gourd, is there?" Then he grumbled, looked at his watch, and gave his nostrils another treat.

I forgot to tell you that Jacques never traveled without a wine jug filled with the best. It was suspended from the horn of his saddle. Each time his master would interrupt his story with a somewhat lengthy question, he would loosen his gourd, pour one down mariner style, and put the gourd back in its place only when his master had stopped talking. I have also forgotten to tell you that in a case which demanded reflection, his first movement was to question his gourd. Whenever it was necessary to solve a problem of morals, discuss a fact, prefer this road to that one, embark upon, follow or abandon an affair, weigh the advantages or disadvantages of some political operation, of speculation on finance or commerce, on the wisdom or folly of a law, the outcome of a war, the choice of an inn, and in the inn the choice of a suite, and in the suite the choice of a bed—in all these cases, his first words would be: "Let's consult the bottle." His last would be: "Such is the bottle's opinion and my own." When destiny became mute in his head, he took counsel by the gourd; it was a sort of portable Pythia, which was silenced the instant it was empty. At Delphi, the Pythia, with skirts pulled up, and seated barebottomed on her tripod, received her inspiration from the bottom up; Jacques, on his horse, his head turned up toward heaven, his gourd uncorked and the mouth of the vessel near his own, received his inspiration from the top down. When the Pythia and Jacques pronounced their oracles, both were drunk. He held that the Holy Ghost had come down to the disciples in a bottle; he called Pentecost the feast day of gourds. He has left a little treatise on all sorts of divination—a profound treatise in which he shows preference for the divination by Bacbuc [62] or by the gourd. He had to protest, however great the veneration he felt for him, against the curate of Meudon who consulted the divine Bacbuc by the shake-of-the-belly method. "I love Rabelais," he would say, "but I love truth even more than Rabelais." He calls the word *Engastrimyth* heretical; and he proves by a hundred reasons, each better than the other, that the true oracles of Bacbuc or the gourd, could be heard only through the neck of the bottle. He places in the ranks of distinguished adherents to Bacbuc the true gourd-inspired of these last centuries: Rabelais, La Fare, Chapelle, Chaulieu, La Fontaine, Molière, Panard, Gallet, Vadé. [63] Plato and Jean-Jacques Rousseau, who extolled good wine without drinking it, are, to his way of thinking, two false brothers of the gourd. Formerly the gourd had several celebrated temples: the Pomme-de-Pin, the Temple, and the Guinguette, [64] whose history he wrote up separately. He made a magnificent picture of the enthusiasm, the passion, and the fire with which the Bacbutians and the Peri-gourdians were (and still are) taken when, at the end of a meal, their elbows resting on the table, the divine Bacbuc would appear to them, place himself in their midst, hiss, throw off his mantle, and cover his worshipers with prophetic spray. His manuscript is illustrated with two portraits, beneath which can be read: "Anacreon and Rabelais—one among the Ancients, the other among the Moderns—Sovereign Pontiffs of the Gourd."

And Jacques really used the word *engastrimyth?*—Why not, reader? Jacques's captain was a Bacbutian; he might have known that expression; and Jacques, who picked up everything he said, might have remembered it. However, the truth is that *engastrimyth* is mine, and that in the original text, the reading is *ventriloquist*.

All that is very well, you will rejoin, but how about Jacques's loves?—As for Jacques's loves, Jacques is the only one who knows about them, and here he is suffering from a sore throat, thus reducing his master to his watch and snuffbox—a deprivation that hurts him as much as it does you.—What is to happen to us then?—My goodness, I have no idea. This would be a good time to interrogate the divine Bacbuc or the sacred gourd. But its cult is falling, its temples deserted. Just as at the birth of Our Lord, the oracles of the pagans stopped, so at the death of Gallet,[65] the oracles of Bacbuc were silenced. And so no more great poems, no more of those pieces of sublime eloquence, no more of those productions bearing the imprint of intoxication and genius! All is reasoned, formal, stiff, academic, and flat. Oh, divine Bacbuc! Oh, sacred gourd! Oh, divinity of Jacques! Come back to our midst! I have a sudden desire, reader, to talk to you about the birth of the divine Bacbuc, the miracles that accompanied and followed it, the marvels of his reign and the disasters of his retreat. And if Jacques's sore throat continues, and his master persists in his silence, you may very well have to be contented with this episode, which I shall try to stretch out until Jacques is better and can continue his love story.

6

❧ ❧ ❧

THERE IS AT THIS POINT A TRULY LAMENTABLE LACUNA IN THE
conversation of Jacques and his master. Some fine day a descendant
of Nodot, or the Président de Brosses, or Freinshémius, or Father
Brottier [66] will fill it up perhaps, and the descendants of Jacques
or his master, owners of this manuscript, will have a good laugh.

It seems that Jacques, reduced to silence by his sore throat, suspended the history of his loves, and that his master started the
story of his own loves. This is only a conjecture and I give it to
you for what it's worth. After several lines of punctuation that
mark the lacuna, we read: "There is nothing sadder in this world
than to be a dolt." Is it Jacques who offers that apothegm? Is it
his master? All that would be the subject of a long and thorny
dissertation. If Jacques was insolent enough to address those words
to his master, the master was certainly frank enough to have
addressed them to himself. However that may be, it is evident,
it is even very evident that it is the master who continues.

The Master. It was the eve of her birthday and I had not a bit
of money. The Chevalier de Saint-Ouin, my intimate friend, was
never stopped by anything. "So you have no money?" he said
to me.

"No."

"Well, then, we've only to make some."

"And you know how that's done?"

"Certainly." He gets dressed, we go out, and he takes me
through several winding streets into an obscure little house, where
we mount a dirty narrow staircase to the fourth floor. I enter an
apartment which is rather spacious and singularly furnished.

· 210 ·

Among other things, there were three chests of drawers, all of them of different shapes. Behind the one in the middle, there was a large mirror with a crest too high for the ceiling, so that a good half foot of this mirror was hidden by the chest of drawers. On these chests there was merchandise of every sort; there were two *trictrac* boards, and about the apartment there were some rather pretty chairs, not any single one like the other. At the foot of a bed without curtains was a superb chaise longue. Against one of the windows was a bird cage without birds, but brand new. Against the other window a chandelier was hanging on a broom handle; the two ends of the broom handle were resting on the backs of two ugly straw chairs. Then, in addition, to right and to left, pictures, some hanging on the walls, the rest stacked in a pile.

Jacques. That smells of the secondhand merchant for a mile around.

The Master. You have guessed it. And there were the chevalier and M. Le Brun (that's the name of our secondhand dealer and loan-broker) throwing themselves into each other's arms. "Ah! it is you, chevalier?"

"Why, yes, it is I, my dear Le Brun."

"But what has become of you? It's an eternity since I've seen you. Times are really bad, aren't they?"

"Very bad, my dear Le Brun. But it's not a question of that now. Listen, I would have a word with you."

I sit down. The chevalier and Le Brun withdraw to a corner and talk. Of their whole conversation I can give you but a few words that I caught by chance.

"Is he a good risk?"

"Excellent."

"Of age?"

"Very much so."

"And it's the son?"

"The son."

"Do you know that our last two arrangements . . ."

"Speak lower."

"The father?"

"Rich."

"Old?"

"And in his dotage."

Le Brun then said in a loud voice: "See here, chevalier, I don't want to get mixed up in anything again. There are always unhappy consequences. It's your friend and that's all very fine. The gentleman looks like an honest man, but . . ."

"My dear Le Brun!"

"I have no money at all."

"But you know people!"

"They are rascals, confounded cheats. Sire, my chevalier, aren't you tired of passing through their hands?"

"Necessity knows no law."

"The necessity that presses you is a pleasant one, a game of *bouillotte,* or a hand of *la belle,*[87] or some woman."

"Dear friend . . . !"

"Yes, I am always the one. I'm weak as a child, and as for you, I don't know if there's anyone whose resolutions you wouldn't weaken. All right then; ring, so I'll know if Fourgeot is at home. No, don't ring; Fourgeot will take you to Merval's."

"Why not you?"

"I have sworn that that abominable Merval would never work again either for me or for my friends. You must take full responsibility for the gentleman, who is perhaps, who is without doubt, an honest fellow. Let me answer to you for Fourgeot only, and Fourgeot will be responsible to me for Merval."

Meanwhile the serving woman came in and asked: "Is it to M. Fourgeot's place?"

Le Brun said to her: "No, it's not to any place. Chevalier, I cannot . . . I absolutely cannot. . . ."

The chevalier embraces him, caresses him: "My dear Le Brun,

my dear friend." I come up and join my pleas to those of the chevalier: "M. Le Brun! My dear sir."

Le Brun lets us convince him.

The servant, smiling at this foolery, leaves, and in a blink of an eye comes back with a little limping man, dressed in black, cane in his hand, with a gaunt and wrinkled face, a quick eye—and a stutterer. The chevalier turns to him and says: "Come now, M. Mathieu de Fourgeot, we have not a minute to lose; take us quickly."

Fourgeot, without seeming to hear, was untying a little chamois purse.

"You are jesting; that's our business," the chevalier said to Fourgeot. I come up, pull a small écu out, which I slip to the chevalier, who gives it to the servant, the while chucking her under the chin. Meanwhile Le Brun was saying to Fourgeot: "I forbid it; do not take these gentlemen."

Fourgeot: "But, M. Le Brun, why not?"

Le Brun: "He is a rascal and a no-good."

Fourgeot: "I know very well that M. de Merval . . . but pardon for every sin; and then, I know of nobody except him that has any money right now."

Le Brun: "Fourgeot, do as you please; gentlemen, I am washing my hands of the affair."

Fourgeot (*to Le Brun*): "Sir, aren't you coming with us?"

Le Brun: "Me! God preserve us! He's an infamous scamp whom I shall never see again as long as I live."

Fourgeot: "But without you we won't be able to arrange anything."

The Chevalier: "That's true. Come along, my dear Le Brun. The point is that you're helping me; you're obliging a gentleman who is in a spot. You can't refuse me; you will come."

Le Brun: "Go to a Merval's house! Me! Me! Go there!"

The Chevalier: "Yes, you will come, for my sake."

By dint of persuasion Le Brun let himself be dragged along, and there we all are, Le Brun, the chevalier, Mathieu de Fourgeot, and myself; on the way, the chevalier amicably patting Le Brun's hand is saying to me: "He's the best man, the most generous man in the world, the very best acquaintance."

Le Brun: "I fear my good chevalier would be capable of bringing me to counterfeit for him."

Finally we arrive at Merval's.

Jacques. Mathieu de Fourgeot . . .

The Master. Yes, what are you trying to say?

Jacques. Mathieu de Fourgeot . . . what I was thinking was that Sire, the Chevalier of Saint-Ouin knows all those people by last name and first name, and that he is a rascal, and in league with the whole crowd.

The Master. You might very well be right. It would be impossible to meet a man more gentle, better mannered, more honest, more polite, more human, more sympathetic, more charitable than M. de Merval. Once he had assured himself that I was of age and solvent financially, M. de Merval took on a sad and affectionate manner and told us with great compunction that he was truly embarrassed, and that he had been obliged, that very morning, to help out one of his friends who was in very urgent need, and that he was at present completely drained of funds. Then, turning to me, he said: "Sir, do not chide yourself for not having come earlier; I should have been very upset to refuse you, but I should have refused you. Friendship comes before all else."

And so there we are again desperately confused: the chevalier, Fourgeot, and even Le Brun himself are on their knees before M. de Merval as he says to them: "Gentlemen, you all know me; I like to serve you and I always try not to spoil that service by making you beg for it. But, my word of honor, sirs, there are not four louis in all the house."

As for me, in the midst of all those people there, I looked like a culprit who has heard his sentence. I found myself saying to the chevalier: "Come, Chevalier, let us go away, since these gentlemen cannot help us." At which, the chevalier drew me aside, and said: "Don't even think of it; tomorrow is her birthday. I have talked to her about it, I can warn you. And she's expecting some gallant gesture from you. You know how she is; it's not that she thinks of herself, but she's like all the others, and she doesn't like to be deceived in her expectations. She has probably already boasted about it to her father, her mother, her aunts, and her friends. And after all that, if she has nothing to show them, it will be mortifying for the poor thing." And so back he goes to Merval, pleading with him all the more sincerely. After letting himself be put upon for some time, Merval said: "I am the stupidest soul in this world; I cannot stand to see people in difficulties. I have just been thinking, and an idea comes to me."

The Chevalier: "What idea?"

Merval: "Why couldn't you take some merchandise?"

The Chevalier: "You have some?"

Merval: "No. But I know a woman who can give you some, a fine woman, a sincere woman."

Le Brun: "Yes, but she'll give us rags and sell them at their weight in gold and we'll end up with nothing."

Merval: "Not at all. There will be fine materials, silver or gold jewelry, all sorts of silks, pearls, some precious stones. There will be very little lost on those things. She's a good soul and contented with very little as long as she has assurance of payment. These are things picked up in business deals which she gets at a good price. In any case, you can go look at them; it won't cost you anything to look."

I tried to point out to Merval and the chevalier that I was not in a position to sell, and that even if such an occupation were not distasteful to me, my way of life would hardly give me the time to handle it. The obliging Le Brun and Mathieu de Fourgeot said almost in unison: "Don't you worry yourself about that. We'll do the selling for you; it's a simple half-day's job." And so the meeting was put off until that afternoon at M. de Merval's, and that gentleman, patting me gently on the shoulder, said in an unctuous and fatherly tone: "Sir, I am only too delighted to help you; but, please believe me, you must not do this sort of thing very often. It always ends up in ruin. It's no small miracle that in this country you can still do business with such honest folk as MM. Le Brun and Mathieu de Fourgeot."

Le Brun and Fourgeot de Mathieu or Mathieu de Fourgeot, thanked him with a deep bow, insisting that he was very kind, that they had always tried to conduct their affairs conscientiously up to the present time, and that they really deserved no praise.

Merval: "There you are wrong, gentlemen, for who nowadays possesses a conscience? Ask the Chevalier de Saint-Ouin, who must surely know something about that."

And so we file out of Merval's. He is asking us from the top of his staircase if he can depend on us should he get in touch with his woman merchant. We all assure him on that score and the four of us go off to dine in a neighboring inn, while waiting for the time of the meeting.

It was Mathieu de Fourgeot who ordered the dinner, and he did it well. At dessert, two tarts came over to our table with their lutes. Le Brun begged them to sit down. They were wined, they joked and talked, and they played. While my three companions amused themselves toying with one of them, her friend, who was next to me, whispered: "Sir, you are in very bad company there; there's not a one of these fellows whose name isn't on the police register."

We left the inn at the proper time and went to Merval's. I forgot to tell you that this dinner emptied the wallets of both the chevalier and myself, and that on the way over, Le Brun said to the chevalier, who repeated it to me, that Mathieu de Fourgeot demanded ten louis as his commission, and that it was really the least you could give him, and continued to explain that if he was satisfied with us, we would get a better price on the merchandise, and that we could easily make up his commission on the sale prices.

And so we are back again at Merval's where the woman had already arrived with her merchandise. Mademoiselle Bridoie (for that was her name) overwhelmed us with courtesy and curtsies, and laid out her goods for us: fabrics, laces, rings, diamonds, and gold boxes. We took a little of everything. It was Le Brun, Mathieu de Fourgeot, and the chevalier who set the price for things, and it was Merval who added up. The total came to nineteen thousand seven hundred and seventy-five livres, for which I was to give my note when Mlle Bridoie curtsied to me and said (for she never addressed anyone without curtsying): "Sir, do you plan to pay your note when it falls due?"

"Certainly," I replied.

"In that case," she said, "I suppose it doesn't matter to you whether you make a note or a bill of exchange."

The mention of a bill of exchange made me grow pale. The chevalier noticed it and said to Mlle Bridoie: "A bill of exchange, Mademoiselle! But bills of exchange circulate and you never know into whose hands they might fall."

"You are jesting, sir; we know, after all, the consideration which we owe to people of your rank." And thereupon another curtsy. "We hold such papers in our wallets and bring them out only on the date due. You see? Look here." And with another curtsy she pulls her wallet from her pocket and reads a great list of names of all classes and ranks. The chevalier had come up to me and was saying: "Bills of exchange! That can be damnably serious! Think soberly what you want to do. This woman seems honest enough to me and then, too, before the due date you'll either have funds or I'll be there."

Jacques. And so you signed the bill of exchange?

The Master. I did.

Jacques. It's the usual thing for fathers, when their children leave for the capital, to preach a little sermon to them: don't frequent bad company; be respectful to your superiors by diligently carrying out your duties; hold to your religion; avoid questionable

women and chevaliers in business, and above all never sign bills
of exchange.

The Master. What do you expect? I did as all the others. The
first thing I forgot was my father's lesson. And so here I am
weighted down with merchandise to sell when it's really money I
need. There were several pairs of lace cuffs, very pretty ones. The
chevalier grabbed up some at cost, telling me: "There is already
a part of your purchases on which you'll lose nothing." Mathieu de
Fourgeot took a watch and two gold boxes and went off to bring
me their cost price. Le Brun put the rest in trust at his house.
I put into my pocket superb trimming along with some ruffles;
it was but one of the blooms of the bouquet I was to present.
Mathieu de Fourgeot came back in a flash with sixty louis; of these
sixty louis, he kept out ten for himself and I got the other fifty.
He told me he had sold neither the watch nor the two boxes but
that he had pawned them.

Jacques. Pawned them?

The Master. Yes.

Jacques. And I know where.

The Master. Where?

Jacques. The lady with the curtsy, la Bridoie.

The Master. You are right. Along with the pair of ruffles and
the trim which enhanced them, I took also a pretty ring and a
tiny little rouge box lined with gold. I had fifty louis in my pocket
and the chevalier and I were in the highest of spirits.

Jacques. That's all very well. There's only one thing in all of
this which intrigues me. And that's the seeming disinterestedness
of Sire Le Brun. Didn't he get any part of the spoils?

The Master. Come now, Jacques, you must be jesting. You don't
know M. Le Brun. I proposed some mark of appreciation for his
kind services. He grew angry and he replied that I apparently
took him for a Mathieu de Fourgeot and that he had never stretched
out a hand. "That's my dear Le Brun for you," cried the chevalier,
"he's always like that, but we should be embarrassed if he were

more honest than ourselves." And therewith he took from our merchandise two dozen handkerchiefs and a length of muslin that he pressed on Le Brun for his wife and daughter. Le Brun began to look over the handkerchiefs and they seemed so handsome to him, and began to examine the muslin and he found it so fine: it had been offered him with such good grace; he had after all such an opportune chance to deceive us by selling the effects which remained in his hands, that he let himself be persuaded. And so we left and were hurrying in our fiacre to the house of my love to whom the cuffs and the ring were destined. The gifts succeeded beautifully. The lady was charming to us. She tried on the cuffs and the trim immediately; the ring seemed to have been made for her finger. We dined, and that gaily, as you can well imagine.

Jacques. And you slept there?

The Master. No.

Jacques. It was the chevalier who did?

The Master. I think so.

Jacques. At the rate they were proceeding with you, your fifty louis didn't last long.

The Master. No, at the end of a week we went back to Le Brun's to see what the rest of our affairs had brought.

Jacques. Nothing, or very little. Le Brun was sad; he lashed out at Merval and the lady with the curtsy, called them rascals, cheats, scamps, swore to have nothing to do with them henceforward, and handed over to you seven or eight hundred francs.

The Master. Just about—eight hundred seventy livres, to be exact.

Jacques. And so, if I can calculate at all, eight hundred seventy livres from Le Brun, fifty louis from Merval or de Fourgeot, the trim, the cuffs, and the ring—oh, let's say fifty more louis and that's what came back to you from your nineteen thousand seven hundred seventy-five livres in merchandise. By God, that's honesty for you. Merval was right; it isn't every day one negotiates with such very worthy people.

The Master. You are forgetting the cuffs which the chevalier took at cost.

Jacques. Only because the chevalier never spoke to you of them again.

The Master. I must confess you are right. And how about the two gold boxes and the watch that were pawned by Mathieu; you didn't say anything about them.

Jacques. It's because I wouldn't know what to say.

The Master. Meanwhile the due date of the bill of exchange arrived.

Jacques. And neither your funds nor those of the chevalier did arrive.

The Master. I was obliged to go into hiding. My parents were notified; one of my uncles came to Paris. He pressed charges against all those rascals with the police. The complaint was sent on to a process server. This fellow was in the pay of Merval. They replied that since the business had been carried out strictly according to law, the police had nothing to do with it. The pawnbroker with whom Mathieu had left the two boxes took out a writ against Mathieu. I intervened in the case. The costs of justice were so enormous that after the sale of the watch and the boxes we still lacked five or six hundred francs to pay off everything.

So you won't believe this, reader? Suppose I tell you of the man who ran a café and who died a little while ago in my neighborhood leaving two orphans of a tender age. The commissioner comes to the dead man's house and attaches the property. They release the property, make an inventory, and have a sale. The sale brings eight to nine hundred francs. Of those nine hundred francs, after the costs of justice have been deducted, there remain exactly two sous for each orphan and so they put two sous each in their hands and send them off to the asylum.

The Master. That's horrible.

Jacques. And it goes on all the time.

The Master. Meanwhile my father died. I settled the bills of exchange, and came out of my hiding place, where, to be quite fair to the chevalier and my sweetheart, I must admit that they had kept me good company.

Jacques. And so here you are just as stupidly taken as before with the chevalier and your beauty. Except that now she makes you pay more dearly than ever.

The Master. And why so, Jacques?

Jacques. Why? It's because you are master of your own actions and possess a goodly fortune. And under those circumstances they can't but make a complete fool of you, that is to say, a husband.

The Master. By heaven, I believe that was their plan, but they didn't succeed.

Jacques. Either you are very lucky, or they were very clumsy.

The Master. But it seems to me, Jacques, that your throat is better and that you speak more easily now.

Jacques. It might seem so to you, but it's not so.

The Master. You couldn't perhaps take up again the story of your loves?

Jacques. No.

The Master. And so you're of the opinion that I should continue mine?

Jacques. I'm of the opinion that I should pause a bit and lift the gourd.

The Master. What! You mean that with a sore throat you still had your flask filled?

Jacques. Yes, but devil take it, it happens to be medicine. Which explains why I'm out of ideas and stupid. And just so long as there's nothing but medicinal tea in the gourd, I'll go on being stupid.

The Master. What are you doing?

Jacques. I'm pouring out the tea; I'm afraid it'll bring us bad luck.

The Master. You're mad.

Jacques. Wise or mad, there's not going to be a teardrop of it left in this gourd.

While Jacques is emptying his gourd on the ground, his master looks at his watch, opens his snuffbox, and prepares to go on with his story. And I, reader, am very much tempted to shut him up by showing somewhere in the distance either an old soldier coming at a gallop all bent over on his horse, or a young peasant lass with a little straw hat and red petticoats, coming along afoot or on a donkey. And why couldn't the old soldier be Jacques's captain or the captain's comrade?—But he is dead!—You think so, do you?— Why couldn't the young lass be Dame Suzanne or Dame Marguerite, or the landlady of the Grand Cerf, or mother Jeanne or even her daughter Denise? A fabricator of novels wouldn't miss the chance; but I don't like novels unless indeed they are Richardson's. I am making up this story and it's going to interest you or not interest you, and that's the least of my worries. My plan is to say what is true, and I have carried it out. And so I shall not have Brother Jean come back from Lisbon; that fat priest coming toward us in a cabriolet, seated next to a pretty, young woman will not be the abbé Hudson.—The abbé Hudson is dead, then?—Do you think so? Were you at his services?—No.—You didn't see him buried?—No.—And so he's either dead or alive just as it pleases you. It depends only on me whether or not I shall stop the cabriolet, or have the prior and his companion step out and with them a chain of events with the result that you would never know further of Jacques's loves nor yet of his master's. But I feel only disdain for all such recourses and I can see only too clearly that with a little imagination and style, nothing is easier to spin out than a novel. Let's stay in the realm of the true, and while waiting for Jacques's sore throat to go away, let's allow the master to talk.

The Master. One morning the chevalier seemed very sad indeed. It was the day after the one we had all spent in the country: the chevalier, his lady or mine (or maybe both), her father, her mother, the aunts, the cousins, and myself. He asked me if I had not let

slip some indiscretion that had given away my passion to the
parents. Then he told me that the father and mother, alarmed
by my assiduity, had questioned their daughter. He added that
if I had honest intentions nothing would be simpler than to confess
them, and they would be honored to receive me under such conditions. He warned that if I did not clarify my position within two
weeks, they would beg me to leave off visits that were being
noticed, about which people talked, and that were unfair to their
daughter since they frightened off advantageous suitors who otherwise would come around without fear of being refused.

Jacques. Well, my master, did Jacques guess it or not?

The Master. The chevalier added: "In two weeks! That's rather
a short time. You are in love and you are loved; in two weeks what
will you do?" I replied frankly to the chevalier that I would retire.

"You will retire from the lists! Aren't you in love?"

"Yes, I'm in love and seriously. But I have parents, a name,
position, certain aspirations, and I should never be able to resign
myself to burying all those advantages in the shop of a little middle-
class female."

"And shall I tell them that?"

"If you want to. But, Chevalier, the sudden and scrupulous
delicacy of these people astonishes me. They allowed their daughter
to accept my presents; they have left me twenty times or more
in tête-à-tête with her; she goes to all the balls, the social gatherings, the theaters, takes excursions in the country and in the city
with the first one who has a good carriage to offer; they sleep
tranquilly while visitors make music and conversation in her quarters; you frequent the house as much as you please, and, just
between you and me, Chevalier, when they admit you to the
house they can very well afford to admit any other. Their daughter
is notorious. I shan't believe nor shall I deny all that people say
about her, but you must agree that those parents could have decided
a little before now to become concerned about their daughter's
honor. Do you want me to tell you the truth? They've been taking

me for a kind of booby whom they've been hoping to lead by the nose right up to the feet of the parish priest. Well, they're mistaken. I find Mlle Agathe charming; she turns my head; and I think that's rather clear from the tremendous expenditures I've made for her. I'm not refusing to continue, but it will have to be with some certainty of finding her a little less adamant in the future.

My plan is not to be eternally losing at her feet my time, a fortune, and sighs that I could very well put to more useful service elsewhere. You can tell that last part to Mlle Agathe, and all the rest to her parents. Either our affair must stop or I must be received on another basis. Mlle Agathe will have to do something better for me than she's done up to now. When you first introduced me into her house, Chevalier, you must admit that you gave me to hope for easier satisfaction than I've found. Chevalier, you have been imposing somewhat upon me.

The Chevalier: My word, I have been imposing on myself first of all. Who the devil would ever have thought that with that flippant air, the gay, free manner of the little wench, she would turn out to be a little dragon of virtue?

Jacques. What the devil, sir! That's pretty strong. So for once in your life you were brave?

The Master. I have days like that. I kept remembering the adventure of the moneylenders, my retreat to St. John Lateran fleeing before Dame Bridoie, and above all the frigidity of Mlle Agathe. I was becoming a bit tired of being made the fool.

Jacques. And so after that courageous speech to your dear friend, the Chevalier of Saint-Ouin, what did you do?

The Master. I stuck to my word and stopped my visits.

Jacques. Bravo! Bravo! Mio caro maestro!

The Master. Two weeks went by without my hearing anything from them; however, the chevalier was faithfully instructing me as to the effects of my absence on the family. He encouraged me to be firm. He would say to me: "They're beginning to wonder, they look at each other, they talk about you, keep asking each other what could possibly be the source of your discontent with them. The young lady is playing dignified; she says with a very artificial indifference through which you can easily see that she's upset: 'We never see that gentleman any more. Apparently he doesn't want to be seen. Oh well, that's his business.' And then she makes a pirouette, starts to hum, goes to the window, comes back, but with red eyes. Everybody notices that she's been crying."

"Been crying?"

"Then she sits down; she takes up her work; she wants to work but she doesn't. The others talk; she is silent. They try to cheer her up and she falls into a mood. They suggest a game, a walk, a play. She accepts, and when everything is in readiness, it's something else she fancies, and ceases to fancy the next minute. Oh, but here you are becoming all distraught. I'll say not a word more."

"But, Chevalier, you think, then, that if I were to reappear . . ."

"I think you would be stupid. You've got to hold out; you must have courage. If you come back without being called, you're lost. You've got to teach that little baggage a lesson."

"But what if they don't call me back?"

"They'll call you back."

"But what if they wait a long time to call me back?"

"They'll call you and very soon. What the devil! A fellow like you isn't easily replaced. If you come back on your own, they'll sulk, they'll make you pay dearly for your breakaway, and they'll lay down the law as it suits them. And you'll have to submit, you'll have to bend to them. Do you want to be master or slave, and a most miserable slave at that? You must choose. To be frank with you, your strategy has been a little flippant; they can hardly think you're a man who's really in love. But what's done is done, and if it's still possible to turn things to your advantage, you mustn't miss the chance."

"She cried!"

"Of course she cried! Better that she should cry than yourself."

"But what if they don't call me back?"

"They'll call you back, I tell you. When I go there, I speak no more of you than if you had never existed. They hint about you and I let them go on. Finally they ask me if I have seen you. I reply quite indifferently—sometimes yes, sometimes no. Then we talk of other matters, but it isn't long before we're back to your absence. The first word can come either from the father, the mother, the aunt or Agathe, and they say: 'And after all the consideration we had for him! The interest we took in his last undertaking! The friendly gestures my niece made to him! The hospitality I showered on him! And so many assurances of affection we received from him! And then you're still supposed to trust men, still supposed to keep your house open to them! And after that people can still believe in friends!' "

"And how about Agathe?"

"Consternation reigns, I can tell you."

"And how about Agathe?"

"Agathe will draw me aside and say: 'Chevalier, can you possibly comprehend your friend? You assured me so often that he loved me; you believed it yourself probably, and why wouldn't you? I certainly believed it.' And then she breaks off, her voice falters, and her eyes become moist. . . . Well, by heaven, old boy, if you're not doing the same thing! I'll say not another word, that is final. I see what you would like, but you'll not get it, not at all. Since you were stupid enough to withdraw without rhyme or reason, I'm not going to let you double your stupidity by throwing yourself at them. You must play this thing to your own advantage in getting ahead with Mlle Agathe. She's got to see that she doesn't hold you so well that she couldn't lose you, unless she sets about a little better toward keeping you. After what you've done for her, and still be at the kissing-the-hand stage! But on that score, friend, come, tell me frankly between friends. You can confess to me without indiscretion. Is it true you never got anything?"

"Yes."

"You're lying; you're playing the modest gentleman."

"I should play modest perhaps if I had any reason to. But I swear that I'm not fortunate enough to be lying."

"That's absolutely unbelievable, for, after all, you're not completely inexperienced. What! There was never even the slightest moment of weakness?"

"No."

"Maybe it came along and you didn't notice it and missed your chance. I'm afraid you've been a little naïve. People such as you who are honest, and decent, and kind tend to be that way."

"But you, Chevalier; what goes on there with you?"

"Nothing."

"You never had any aspirations?"

"If you can but pardon me for it, such aspirations went on for quite a time. But then you came, and saw, and conquered. I realized that it was you they looked at very often, and that they scarcely ever noticed me. So I decided it was all settled. We've remained good friends. You both confide your little secrets in me, follow my advice sometimes, and, because there was nothing else to do, I accepted the role of subaltern to which you reduce me."

Jacques. Sir, two things impress me. One is that I have never been able to follow through on my story without some devil or other interrupting me, and yet yours goes off right away. That's life for you. One fellow runs over thorns without getting stuck; the other can look as carefully as you please where he puts his foot, yet he finds thorns in the best path and arrives home skinned alive.

The Master. Have you forgotten your refrain, and the Great Scroll, and the writing up yonder?

Jacques. The other thing is that I persist in thinking that your Chevalier de Saint-Ouin is a great rascal, and that after having shared your money with Le Brun, Merval, Mathieu de Fourgeot or Fourgeot de Mathieu, and la Bridoie, he's trying to saddle you with his mistress, quite honorably, properly, and naturally, in front of notary and priest, so as to be able to go right on sharing your wife— Owoo! My throat!

The Master. Do you know what you're doing there? Something very common and impertinent.

Jacques. Of that I'm quite capable.

The Master. You're complaining of being interrupted and here you are interrupting.

Jacques. It's all the effect of the bad example you've been giving me. A mother wants to be a gay thing and wants her daughter to be careful. A father wants to be a profligate and expects his son to be economical. A master wants . . .

The Master. To interrupt his lackey, interrupts him as much as he pleases, and is not interrupted by him.

Reader, aren't you afraid to see starting all over again the scene at the inn when they cried: "You will go down" and "I won't go down"? Why don't I give you: "I shall interrupt," "You will not interrupt"? It's fairly certain that however little I push Jacques and his master, the quarrel will be on us. And if I once get started, who knows how it might finish? Well, the truth happens to be that Jacques replied humbly to his master: "Sir, I am not interrupting you; I'm chatting with you, as you've given me permission to do."

The Master. Agreed, but that isn't all.

Jacques. What other offense could I have committed?

The Master. You are anticipating on the storyteller, and you're taking away from him the expression of your surprise on which he's been counting. And thus, since you have by a very misplaced show of wisdom on your part guessed what he had to tell you, he has only to be quiet, and so I shall be quiet.

Jacques. Oh, my master!

The Master. To the devil with clever people.

Jacques. I agree, but you wouldn't certainly be so cruel as to . . .

The Master. Well, you must agree, at least, that you would deserve it.

Jacques. Agreed, but even with all that, you will still look at your watch, take a pinch of snuff, get over your pet and continue your story.

The Master. That character does as he very well pleases with me. . . . Several days after this conversation with the chevalier, he reappeared at my place. He wore an air of triumph. "Well, my friend," he said to me, "maybe the next time you'll believe in my prognostications; I told you we held the upper hand, didn't I, and here's a letter—yes, a letter from her." That letter was very gentle: tender reproaches, complaints, and so forth; and soon I am back in the house.

Reader, you leave off reading; what's the matter? Ah, I think I understand now; you would like to see that letter. Madame Riccoboni [68] wouldn't have missed the chance to show it to you. And how about the letter Mme de La Pommeraye dictated to her two religious friends? I'm sure you missed that one. Although writing that one would have been difficult in a different way from Agathe's letter, and even though I don't presume too much on my talent, I think I could have pulled it off, but it wouldn't have been original. It would have been like those sublime haranguings of Titus Livius in his *History of Rome,* or of Cardinal Bentivoglio in his *Flemish Wars.* One reads them with pleasure but they destroy all illusion. For a historian who imagines conversations his characters did not have, can also conjure up actions which they did not perform. And so I beg of you to get along without these two letters and to continue your reading.

The Master. They asked me the reason for my disappearance, and I told them whatever came to mind. They were satisfied with this and everything resumed its usual routine.

Jacques. Which is to say that you continued to spend money and that your love affair did not get along much further at all.

The Master. The chevalier kept asking for reports and seemed to be losing his patience.

Jacques. And perhaps for good reasons he was really impatient.
The Master. Why so?
Jacques. Why? Why because he . .
The Master. Well, go on.
Jacques. Oh no; not on your life. You've got to let the story-teller . . .
The Master. Ah! My lessons have done some good and I am overjoyed. One day the chevalier proposed a little outing just for the two of us. We went to spend the day in the country. We left early, dined at an inn, and had supper there. The wine was excellent; we drank a lot of it, the while chatting of government, religion, and love. Never had the chevalier shown me such confidence, such friendship. With incredible frankness he had recounted to me all his life's adventures, hiding neither the good nor the bad. He drank, he embraced me, he wept, overcome by tenderness; I drank, I embraced him, and cried my turn. There was in all his past only one event for which he reproached himself. For that he would feel remorse to the death.

"Chevalier, confess to your old friend; you will feel better. What was it all about? What trifle have you exaggerated into importance only out of your extreme delicacy?"

"No, no," cried the chevalier, dropping his head on his hands and covering his face in shame, "it was a foul deed, an unforgivable, foul deed. Could you believe it? I, the Chevalier of Saint-Ouin, once betrayed, yes betrayed, a friend?"

"And how did that happen?"

"Alas! We were both frequent visitors in the same house, just like you and me. There was a young lady like Mlle Agathe. He was in love with her, and I was loved by her. He was ruining himself buying things for her, and I was enjoying all her favors. I never had the courage to confess to him, but if ever we see each other again, I shall tell him. That horrible secret which I carry deep in my heart overpowers me; I must absolutely rid myself of such a burden."

Jacques the Fatalist and His Master

"Chevalier, that would be a good idea."

"You advise me to do so then?"

"I most certainly do."

"And how do you think my friend will take the thing?"

"If he is your friend, if he is fair, he will find your pardon within himself; he will be touched by your frankness and your repentance; he will throw his arms about you; he will do exactly as I should do in his place."

"You think so?"

"I do."

"And that's how you would handle it?"

"I shouldn't hesitate for an inst . . ."

At that moment the chevalier gets up, comes toward me with open arms and with tears in his eyes, and says: "My friend, gather me in your arms."

"What! Chevalier," I said. "It's yourself? And me? And that hussy of an Agathe?"

"Yes, my friend. I give you the right to take back your word; you can deal with me as you like. If, like me, you think that my offense is inexcusable, don't forgive me. Rise and leave me, and never look upon me again without disgust. Leave me to my pain and shame. Oh, my friend, if only you knew the ascendancy that little rascal had taken in my heart! I was born an honest man. Just think how much I had to suffer in this unworthy role to which I lowered myself. How many times have I turned my eyes from her to look at you, the while sighing at her betrayal and my own. It seems impossible that you never noticed it."

Meanwhile I was as rigid as a petrified Terminus; scarcely did I hear the chevalier's words. I cried: "Oh, unworthy, unworthy man! You, Chevalier, you, you . . . my friend!"

"Yes, I was, and I still am, for I have set about freeing you from the bonds of that creature, freeing you from a secret which is more hers than mine. What upsets me is that you have managed to

231

obtain nothing that might in some way pay you back for what you have done for her."

(*Here Jacques begins to laugh and whistle.*)

Why, that's exactly like Collé's *La vérité dans le vin* [69] —Reader, you don't know what you're saying; by trying to be witty, you're only being very stupid. It is so little truth in the wine that quite to the contrary, it's falsehood in the wine. But now I have been crude and I feel badly about it and ask your pardon.

The Master. Bit by bit I got over my anger. I embraced the chevalier; he sat down again and, leaning on the table with his elbows, he pressed his fists to his eyes and dared not look at me.

Jacques. My, my, he was as distressed as all that! And you were kind enough to console him?

(*Here Jacques starts to whistle again.*)

The Master. The best thing to do, it seemed to me, was to turn it all into a joke. With every lighthearted remark, the chevalier would say, completely nonplussed: "There is not another man like you; you are unique. You are worth a hundred of me. I doubt that I had had the generosity and the strength to pardon you for a similar affront. And yet you joke about it; it's absolutely unbelievable. My friend, what can I ever do to repay you? But how could anyone repay such a deed! Never, no never shall I forget my crime and your indulgence; the two are eternally engraved here. I shall recall the first in order to hate myself, and the other to admire you and redouble the links which attach me to you."

"Come now, Chevalier; think no more of it. You are overdoing both your actions and my own. Let's drink to your health. All right, Chevalier, to my own, since you don't seem to want to drink to yours."

Bit by bit the chevalier's spirit was renewed. He told all the details of his betrayal, assailing himself with the harshest epithets. He tore apart daughter, mother, father, aunts—the whole family, which he painted for me as a collection of blackguards unworthy of me, but quite worthy of himself. Those were his very words.

Jacques. And that's exactly why I always counsel women never to sleep with fellows who get drunk. I hate your chevalier as much for his indiscretion in secrets of love as for his perfidious friendship. What the devil! He should have been an honest fellow and spoken to you before. But see here, sir, I persist in thinking that he's a rascal, a downright rascal. I don't know how this thing is going to end, but I'm certainly afraid he's going to betray you again in the very act of unbetraying you. Get me, I beg you, get yourself out of that inn and leave the company of that man.

At this point Jacques took up his gourd, forgetting that there was neither tea nor wine left in it. His master started to laugh. Jacques coughed thereafter for a quarter of an hour without stopping. His master took out his watch and his snuffbox, and continued his story, which I shall break off, if it please you, were it only to make Jacques furious by proving to him that, contrary to what he thinks, it was not written up yonder that he would always be interrupted and his master never interrupted.

The Master (to the chevalier). "After what you've just told me, I trust you won't be seeing them any more."

"I? See that crowd again! But what is really maddening is to go away without avenging ourselves. They will have betrayed, tricked, fooled, and drained an honorable man; they will have taken every advantage of the passion and weakness of another man of honor (for I dare think of myself as such) the better to involve him in a series of horrors; they will have exposed two friends to hating each other, perhaps to killing each other—for you must admit, dear fellow, that if you had fallen upon my unworthy machination, you, who are brave, might very well have conceived such a feeling of resentment that . . ."

"No, things would not have gone as far as that. Why should they? And for whose sake? For a fault that nobody can be absolutely sure he might not commit? Is she my wife? And even if she were? Is she my daughter? No, she's a little baggage, and do you think that for a little slut . . . Come, come, my friend;

let's leave off all this and drink. Agathe is young, lively, fair, plump, and fleshy. She has the nicest, firmest flesh, doesn't she? And the tenderest skin? It must be delicious to have her, and I'll wager you were happy enough in her arms to forget your friends."

"Certainly if the charm of the person and the pleasure of possession could pardon the fault in any way, then surely there is nobody under heaven less guilty than I."

"As for that, Chevalier, I take back what I said; I withdraw my indulgence and I should like to put one condition on my forgetting your betrayal."

"Speak, my friend. Say, order; must I throw myself from the window, hang myself, drown myself, bury this knife in my chest?"

And at this point the chevalier suddenly seizes a knife that was on the table, pulls down his collar, tears open his shirt, and, with wild eyes, raises the point of the knife with his right hand to the cavity of the left collarbone, and seems to await but my order to dispatch himself in the ancient manner.

"It's not a question of that, Chevalier; put down that nasty knife."

"I shall not drop it; it's what I deserve. Only say the word."

"Drop that nasty knife I tell you; not so high a price do I attach to your atonement." Meanwhile the point of the knife was still hovering over the cavity of his left collarbone. I seized his hand, I tore away his knife, and threw it far from us. Then, tilting the bottle over his glass and filling it full, I said to him: "Let's drink first and afterward you will learn to what terrible condition I join my pardon. Agathe, now, is she really very succulent and voluptuous?"

"Oh, my friend, would you could know it as well as I."

"But wait a bit; we must have a bottle of champagne, and then you will tell me the story of one of your nights. Charming traitor, your absolution will come at the end of that story. Come now, start in. Aren't you listening to me?"

"I hear you."

"Does my sentence seem too harsh?"

"No."

"Your mind is wandering?"

"Yes, it is wandering."

"What did I ask you for?"

"The story of one of my nights with Agathe."

"Exactly."

The chevalier, however, was taking me in from head to foot, and was saying to himself: "The same height, about the same age, and even if there were a difference, what with no light, and imagining in advance that it's I, she'll suspect nothing."

"But, Chevalier, whatever are you thinking? Your glass remains full and you aren't starting your story."

"I am thinking, my friend, I have thought, and all is arranged. Embrace me; we shall have revenge, yes, we shall have revenge. It is a low scheme on my part, but if it's unworthy of me, it's not unworthy of that little baggage. You ask me for the story of one of my nights?"

"Yes, is that asking too much?"

"No, but suppose that in place of the story, I should manage to get you the night?"

"That would be worth a little more."

(*Jacques starts to whistle.*)

Thereupon the chevalier pulls two keys from his pocket, one small and the other large. "The little one," he says to me, "is the master key for the street doors; the big one is to Agathe's antechamber. There they are; completely at your service. For about six months now, here is my nightly schedule which you will duplicate. Her windows are on the front of the house, as you know. I walk about in the street as long as I see lights. A pot of basil put outside is the agreed signal. Then I approach the street door, open it, go in, close it, go upstairs as quietly as possible, and turn into the little corridor to the right. The first door to the left in this corridor is hers, as you know. I open that door with this big key, I go into the dressing room on the right, and there I find a little candle by the light of which I can easily undress myself. Agathe leaves the door of her bedroom ajar; I pass through it and go to join her in her bed. Do you understand all that?"

"Very well!"

"Since we are surrounded by family, we are very quiet."

"And then, too, I believe you have better things to do than chat."

"In case of an accident, I could jump out of her bed and shut myself in the closet. However, that's never happened. As a rule we separate about four in the morning. When either pleasure or rest takes us past that hour, we get out of bed together. She goes downstairs and I remain in the anteroom. I dress, I read, I repose, and wait until it's time to appear. I go downstairs, I greet everyone and embrace them as if I had just arrived."

"And tonight? Are you expected?"

"I'm expected every night."

"And you would cede me your place?"

"With all my heart. That you should prefer the night itself to it's recountal doesn't upset me at all, but what I should like is that . . ."

"Finish your sentence. There is very little I don't feel up to undertaking to oblige you."

"It's that I'd like you to remain in her arms until daylight so that I could arrive and surprise you."

"Oh no, Chevalier, that would be too vicious."

"Too vicious? I'm not as vicious as you think. Before that I should have undressed myself in the retiring closet."

"Come, Chevalier, you have the very devil in you. But anyhow, that's not feasible. If you give me the keys you won't have them any more."

"Oh, my friend, how stupid you are!"

"Not too stupid, it seems to me."

"And why shouldn't we go in together? You would go to find

Agathe; I should remain in the closet until you gave me a pre-arranged signal."

"By heaven, that is so amusing and so mad that I'm within an ace of agreeing. But all things considered, Chevalier, I should prefer to reserve that little joke for one of the following nights."

"Oh, I understand; your plan is to take vengeance more than once."

"That is, if it's all right with you."

"Oh quite."

Jacques. Your chevalier is upsetting all my ideas. I kept imagining . . .

The Master. You were imagining . . . ?

Jacques. No, sir; you may continue.

The Master. We drank, we said a hundred stupid things, both as to the night which approached and as to the following nights, and about the night when Agathe would find herself between the chevalier and myself. The chevalier had recovered his charming gaiety, and the tone of our conversation was no longer sad. He prescribed for me certain points of nocturnal conduct that were not all so easy to carry out. But after a long series of nights advantageously employed I could hold up the honor of the chevalier during my first night, however miraculous he pretended to be. There were endless details on the talents, perfections and accommodations of Agathe. The chevalier, with unbelievable art, added the intoxication of passion to the intoxication of the wine. The moment of adventure, the moment of our vengeance seemed to arrive all too slowly. We left the table; the chevalier paid and it was the first time that had happened. We got into our carriage; we were drunk; our coachman and lackeys were even drunker.

Reader, who is there to prevent me from throwing the coachman, the horses, the carriage, the masters, and the lackeys into a ditch? If the ditch has frightened you, who is there to prevent my taking them safely and soundly into the city where I should ram their carriage into another in which I should have enclosed other drunken young men? Then there would be insulting words, a quarrel, swords drawn, a proper scuffle. Who is there to prevent me, if you don't like fights, from substituting for those young drunks Mlle Agathe with one of her aunts? But none of that happened. The chevalier and Jacques's master arrived in Paris. The latter took the chevalier's clothes. It is midnight, they are under Agathe's windows; the light goes out, and the pot of basil appears. They take one more stroll from one end of the street to the other while the chevalier gives his friend a last-minute rehearsal of instructions. They come up to the door. The chevalier opens it, shows Jacques's master in, keeps the passkey, gives him the corridor key; closes the street door, disappears, and after that little detail (furnished so laconically) Jacques's master takes up the story and says: "The place was familiar to me. I go upstairs on tiptoe, I open the corridor door, I close it, I go into the dressing room where I find the little night lamp. I undress. The door of the bedroom was ajar, I go in. I go to the bed alcove where Agathe was not yet asleep. I open the curtains and at that instant I feel two bare arms thrown around my neck, pulling me in. I let myself be pulled, get into bed, am overwhelmed with caresses and return them. There I am, the happiest mortal in the world, and I still am when . . ."

When Jacques's master saw that Jacques was sleeping or pretending to sleep, he said to him: "You are sleeping, you are sleeping, good-for-nothing, at exactly the most interesting point of my story!" It was that very moment which Jacques had been waiting for. "Will you wake up?"

"I don't think so."

"And why not?"

"Well, because if I awake, my sore throat might awake too, and anyhow I think it's better that we both rest."

And thereupon Jacques lets his head fall forward on his chest. "You're going to break your neck."

"Most certainly, if it's written up yonder. Aren't you still in Mlle Agathe's arms?"

"Yes."

"Aren't you happy there?"

"Very."

"Well, stay there then."

"So, it's your pleasure to tell me to stay there?"

"At least until I've heard the story of Desglands' plaster."

The Master. You are seeking vengeance, you traitor.

Jacques. And even if that were true, my master, after your having cut off my love story by a thousand questions, by as many little whims without the least complaint from me, couldn't I implore you to interrupt your story long enough to tell me about the plaster of that good Desglands to whom I owe so much, who rescued me from the surgeon's house at the very moment when, from lack of funds, I didn't know what was to become of me, and in whose house I met Denise—Denise, without whom I should not have spoken a word to you during this whole trip? My master, my dear master, I beg of you the story of Desglands' plaster. You may be as short and to the point as you like. Meanwhile this grogginess which overtakes and overpowers me will be dissipated, and you will be able to count on my full attention thereafter.

The Master (shrugging his shoulders). There was, in Desglands' neighborhood, a charming widow who had several qualities in common with a courtesan of the past century. Wise by her intellect and a libertine by temperament, regretting painfully the next day her stupidity of the night before, she passed her entire life going from pleasure to remorse, and from remorse to pleasure, without the habit of pleasure stifling the remorse or the habit of remorse stifling the taste for pleasure. I knew her in her old age; she used to say that she was finally escaping two great enemies. Her husband, tolerant concerning the only fault he had to reproach her for, pitied her while she lived and missed her painfully for a long time after her death. He held that it would have been as ridiculous to try to keep her from loving as to keep her from drinking. He pardoned her the great multitude of her conquests because of the delicate taste shown in her choice. She never accepted the homage of a stupid or malicious man; her favors were always rewards for talent or honesty. To say of any man that he had been or was her lover was to underwrite him as a gentleman of merit. Since she realized her fickleness, she never pretended to be faithful. "I have never made," she used to say, "but one single false vow in all my life; it was my first." And whether a man lost the feeling he had for her, or whether she lost the feeling he had inspired in her, he remained nevertheless her friend. Never has there been a more striking example of the difference between basic honesty and morals. You couldn't very well say that she had sound morals, yet you had to confess it would be difficult to find a more honest individual. Her curate found her very infrequently before his altar, but at all times he found her purse opened to his poor. She used to say jokingly that religion and laws were like a pair of crutches that you shouldn't take from people with weak legs. The women who feared her society for their husbands were eager to have it for their children.[70]

Jacques (After having mumbled: "I'll get back at you for that damned portrait sketch"). You were mad for that woman?

The Master. I should have become so if Desglands hadn't beaten me to it. Desglands fell in love with her.

Jacques. Sir, are then the story of Desglands' plaster and the story of his love life so closely bound together that you can't separate them?

The Master. Oh, they can be separated. The plaster is only one incident; the other story is everything that happened while they were in love.

Jacques. And did much happen?

The Master. A great deal.

Jacques. In that case, if you give as much time to all of that great deal as you gave to the portrait of the heroine, we'll never get out of it between now and Pentecost, and there's an end to your love story and my own.

The Master. Well then, Jacques, why did you throw me off the track? Didn't you ever notice a small child at Desglands'?

Jacques. Nasty, strong-headed, insolent, and sickly? Yes, I remember him.

The Master. He was a bastard son of Desglands by the beautiful widow.

Jacques. That child is going to give him plenty of worry. It's an only child, which is reason enough to make him a wastrel. Then too, he knows he'll be rich one day, another very good reason for being a wastrel.

The Master. And since he is sickly, they don't teach him a thing. They mustn't upset him, they don't discipline him about anything, which is a third good reason why he'll be a wastrel.

Jacques. One night, that little fool started to scream like no human being. The house is immediately all alarmed; they run to see what goes on. He wants his papa to get up.

"Your papa is sleeping."

"That makes no difference; I want him to get up. I want him to, I want him to."

"He is sick."

"No difference; he has to get up; I want him to, I want him to."

They waken Desglands, who throws his dressing gown over his shoulders and comes on the scene.

"Well, little fellow; here I am. What do you want?"

"I want you to have them come, too."

"Who?"

"Everybody in the château."

So they have everybody gather together: masters, lackeys, strangers, houseguests, Jeanne, Denise, me with my game leg—everybody except one feeble old servant, to whom they had granted a pensioned retreat in a cottage at about a quarter league from the château. He wants them to get her.

"But, my child, it is midnight!"

"I want her, I want her."

"You know she lives rather far away?"

"I want what I want."

"That she is aged and couldn't possibly walk here?"

"I want her to, I want her to."

The poor old thing had to come; they had to carry her for she could have sooner eaten the road than walked it. When we are all finally foregathered, he wants them to get him up and dress him. Up he is and dressed. Then he wants us all to pass into the great ballroom where he is to be installed in the middle of his father's chair. Once installed there, he wants us all to join hands, which is done, and dance round and round, and so we all start to dance round and round. But it's what follows that is unbelievable.

The Master. I trust you will spare the rest?

Jacques. No, no, my master; the rest, you shall certainly hear.

(So he thinks he can spin out with impunity a portrait of the mother a yard long, does he?)

The Master. Jacques, I spoil you.

Jacques. All the worse for you.

The Master. You are irked by the long, boring portrait of the widow, but I think you have paid me back well enough with the long and bothersome story of her child's whimsy.

Jacques. If you think so, then continue with the story of the father. But no more portraits, master; I hate and despise portraits.[71]

The Master. And why do you hate portraits so much?

Jacques. Because there is so little resemblance in them, that if one were to meet, perchance, the real models, he would not recognize them. Relate the facts to me, transcribe faithfully a man's remarks and I shall soon know with what sort of fellow I am dealing. One word, one gesture have sometimes taught me more than the gossiping of a whole city.

The Master. One day Desglands . . .

Jacques. When you are away I go into your library sometimes and take a book—ordinarily a book of history.

The Master. One day Desglands . . .

Jacques. I peruse all the portraits.

The Master. One day Desglands . . .

Jacques. I'm sorry, sir; the machine was wound up and I had to let it go on till it was run down.

The Master. Well, is it run down now?

Jacques. It is.

The Master. One day Desglands invited the lovely widow to dinner, along with some gentlemen of the neighborhood. Desglands' reign was coming to a close, and among the guests there was one fellow toward whom her inconstant heart was beginning to lean. They were at the table, Desglands and rival sitting next to each other and just across from the widow. Desglands was calling on all his wit to animate the conversation; he addressed the most gallant remarks to the widow. But she, distraught, heard none of it and kept her eyes fixed on the rival. Desglands had a raw egg in his hand; a convulsive movement brought on by his jealousy seizes him, he squeezes his hand, with the result that the egg breaks out of its shell and splatters all over his neighbor's face. The rival makes a vague gesture with his hand. Desglands grabs his wrist, stops him, and whispers in his ears: "I shall consider it said and agreed." There is a deep silence; the widow is taken ill. The dinner was short and sad. As they left the table, she called Desglands and his rival into an adjoining suite. All that a woman could decently do to bring about reconciliation, she did. She begged, she cried, she fainted—and in all sincerity. She clutched Desglands' hand, turned her tear-filled eyes up to the other. To the latter she said: "And to think that you love me!" And to Desglands: "And to think you have loved me!" To both she said: "And so you would like to ruin me; you want to make me the fable, the object of scorn and hate for the whole province! Whichever of you takes the life of his rival, him I shall never see again; he can be neither my friend nor my lover. I swear against him an eternal hate which will last until I die." Then she fell back again in a faint, and in her faint she said: "Oh, cruel men, draw your swords and bury them in my breast, and if, as I am dying, I see you embracing one another, I shall die with no regrets." Desglands and his rival either remained silent or helped her, and several tears escaped their eyes. Meanwhile they had to go their separate ways. The poor lady was carried to her rooms more dead than alive.

Jacques. Well now, master. What need had I of the portrait you painted for me of that lady? Wouldn't I know equally well at present all you had said?

The Master. The next day Desglands paid a visit to his charming and faithless lady and found his rival there. Who was the astonished one? Well, they both were to see Desglands' right cheek covered with a large round plaster of black taffeta. "What is that?" asked the widow.

Desglands: "It is nothing."

His Rival: "A little inflammation?"

Desglands: "It will go away."

After a bit of conversation, Desglands went out. In so doing, he made to his rival a sign, which was very well understood. The rival went downstairs. They walked along, one on one side of the street, the other on the other side. They met behind the beautiful widow's garden, dueled, and Desglands' rival remained behind stretched out on the grass, seriously but not mortally wounded. While they are carrying him back to his house, Desglands comes back to his widow, sits down, and they chat again about the accident of the night before. She asks him what is the meaning of the enormous and ridiculous patch that covers his cheek. He gets up, looks at himself in the mirror: "As a matter of fact," he says to her, "I do find it a bit too large." He takes the lady's scissors, pulls off his taffeta patch, trims about the edges a half inch or so, puts it back on and says to the widow: "And how do you like it now?"

"Less ridiculous than before by a half inch or so."

"Well, at least that's something."

Desglands' rival recovered. And so a second duel ended in victory for Desglands, and in the same way five or six in a row. And with each duel Desglands trimmed his taffeta patch a bit around the edge and put the rest on his cheek.

Jacques. What was the end of that adventure? When they carried me to Desglands' château I don't remember any black patch.

The Master. No, the end of that adventure was also the end of the lovely widow. The long grief which it occasioned her finished by ruining her feeble and tottering health.

Jacques. And how about Desglands?

The Master. One day while we were walking together, he receives a note. He opens it and says: "He was a very fine man but I could in no way be upset by his death." And thereupon he tears from his cheek the remainder of his black patch, reduced by dint of his frequent cuttings to the size of an ordinary fly. And so that's the story of Desglands. Is Jacques satisfied, and might I hope that he will now listen to my love story or take up his own?

Jacques. Neither one nor the other.

The Master. And why?

Jacques. Because it's warm and I'm tired and this spot is charming, and then, too, we shall be better off under the shade of these trees where we can rest awhile and breathe the fresh air on the banks of this little stream.

The Master. I agree, but what about your cold?

Jacques. Its attribute is heat and doctors say that contraries are cured by contraries.

The Master. Which is as true from the moral point of view as the physical. I have noticed a very extraordinary thing, which is that there is scarcely any moral maxim that you cannot turn into a medical aphorism, and conversely, few medical aphorisms of which one cannot make moral maxims.

Jacques. That's as it should be.

They dismount and stretch out on the grass. Jacques says to his master: "Are you going to stay awake or are you going to sleep? If you stay awake, I'll sleep; if you sleep, I'll stay awake."

His master replied: "Sleep, sleep."

"I can count on you to stay awake then? Because this time we could lose two horses." The master pulled out his watch and his snuffbox. Jacques set about going to sleep, but every other minute he kept sitting up with a start and clapping his hands together. His master asked him: "What the devil is bothering you?"

Jacques. I am sick and tired of the flies and the gnats. I should certainly like someone to tell me what good those bothersome beasts are.

The Master. And just because you don't know, you think they're good for nothing? Nature made nothing that is useless or superfluous.

Jacques. I believe you, since because a thing exists, it must exist.

The Master. When you have too much blood, or bad blood, what do you do? Why, you call a surgeon, who will drain off two or three pans. Well, these gnats you are complaining about are a great cloud of little winged surgeons that come down with their tiny lances to puncture you and draw off blood, drop by drop.

Jacques. Yes, but completely at random and without knowing whether I have too much or too little. Bring me an emaciated fellow and you'll see if those little winged surgeons won't puncture him just as readily. They're only thinking of themselves and all of nature thinks of itself and only of itself. What does it matter if it's bad for the others as long as it's good for you?

And thereupon he clapped his hands together in the air again and said: "The devil take your little winged surgeons."

The Master. Jacques, do you know the fable of Garo?

Jacques. Yes.

The Master. How do you like it?

Jacques. I think it's bad.

The Master. That's easily said.

Jacques. And very easily proved. If, in place of acorns, the oak had grown pumpkins, would that stupid Garo have gone to sleep under an oak tree? And if he hadn't gone to sleep under an oak tree, what difference for his nose's sake whether pumpkins or acorns fell? Give that to your children to read.

The Master. A philosopher with your name doesn't want to.

Jacques. Well, everyone to his taste and Jean-Jacques [72] is not Jacques.

The Master. And so much the worse for Jacques.

Jacques. And who could know that before reading the last word of the last line of the page we fill out in the Great Scroll?

The Master. What are you thinking about?

Jacques. I was thinking that while you were talking to me and while I was answering, you were talking to me without willing it, and I was replying to you without willing it.

The Master. And so?

Jacques. So? So we were two veritable living, thinking machines. [73]

The Master. And now what are you getting at?

Jacques. By heaven it's still the same thing. There is in the two machines only one more force involved.

The Master. And what additional force is that?

Jacques. May the devil take me if I can conceive how that force can act without cause. My captain used to say: "Postulate a cause and an effect will follow: from a weak cause, a weak effect; from a momentary cause, a momentary effect; from an intermittent cause, an intermittent effect; from a restrained cause, a slow effect; from a vanishing cause, no effect at all."

The Master. But it seems to me that I feel deep down within myself that I am free, just as I feel that I think.

Jacques. My captain used to say: "Yes, now that you don't wish anything; but can you *will* to throw yourself from your horse?"

The Master. That's simple, I'll throw myself.

Jacques. Gaily, without compunction, without effort, just as when it pleases you to dismount before the door of an inn?

The Master. Well, not completely; but what does it matter so long as I do throw myself off and prove that I am free?

Jacques. My captain used to say: "What! You can't even see that without my challenge you would never have taken it into your head to break your neck? So that it is I who take you by the foot and throw you out of your saddle. If your fall proves anything, it's not that you are free, but that you are mad." My captain continued to say that the enjoying of a liberty which could be produced without motive would be the true characteristic of a maniac.

The Master. It's a little too much for me, but in spite of you and your captain, I shall believe that I wish when I wish.

Jacques. But if you are and have always been the master of your willing, why don't you this moment wish to love a little baggage, or why didn't you stop loving Agathe every time you wanted to? Oh, my master, we pass three quarters of our lives at willing without doing.

The Master. That is true.

Jacques. And at doing without willing.

The Master. That point you will perhaps prove to me?

Jacques. If you consent.

The Master. I do consent.

Jacques. Well, it shall be proved, and now let's talk of other things.

After this nonsense and other remarks of equal importance, they were quiet. Jacques put on his enormous hat, umbrella in bad weather, parasol in hot weather, head covering in all weather, the shady sanctuary under which one of the best brains that ever existed used to consult Destiny in major crises. The flaps of this hat, when lifted, put his face at about the middle of his body; when not lifted, he scarcely saw ten paces in front of him—all of which had accustomed him to carrying his nose in the air, and it is then that you could have said of his hat:

> Os illi sublime dedit, coelumque tueri
> Jussit, et erectos ad sidera tollere vultus. . . .[74]

Jacques then, lifting up his enormous hat and gazing about in the distance, perceived a farmer who was uselessly beating one of the two horses he had harnessed to his plow. This horse, young and strong, had lain down along a furrow and the peasant could shake him by the bridle, beg him, caress him, threaten him, swear, beat as much as he liked, still the animal remained motionless and very definitely refused to get up.

Jacques, having meditated some time on this scene, said to his master, whose attention had already been drawn thereto: "Do you know, sir, what's going on over there?"

The Master. And why should anything else be going on except what I see?

Jacques. You can't even guess?

The Master. No. And what are you guessing at?

Jacques. I'm guessing that that stupid, proud, lazy animal is a city horse, who, very proud of his former state of saddle horse, scorns the plow. To tell you all in a word, I think it's your horse, the symbol of Jacques himself and of so many other cowardly rascals like him who have left the country to come wear livery in the capital and who would prefer begging bread in the streets or starving to death to returning to agriculture, that most useful and honorable of occupations.

The master started to laugh and Jacques, speaking to the peasant, who didn't hear him, said: "You poor devil, lay on, lay on as much as you like; he has made up his mind, and you will wear out more than one thong on your whip before you will inspire a little real dignity and taste for work in that rascal there." The master kept on laughing. Jacques, half from impatience and half from pity, gets up, goes toward the peasant, and had not gone two hundred paces when, turning around to his master, he cries: "Sir, come on, come quickly, it is your horse, it is your horse."

As a matter of fact it was. Scarcely had the animal recognized Jacques and his master, than he got up by himself, shook his mane, whinnied, kicked, and tenderly nudged his comrade's muzzle with his own. Meanwhile Jacques, indignant, was muttering: "Scoundrel, good-for-nothing, loafer, what keeps me from giving you twenty kicks with these boots?" His master on the contrary was kissing him, rubbing one hand over his flank, gently patting him on the rump with the other, and, almost crying with joy, was stammering: "My horse, my poor horse, at last I find you."

The peasant understood absolutely nothing of all this. "I can see, gentlemen," he said to them, "that this horse once belonged to you. But nonetheless, I own him quite legally for I bought him at the last fair. If you would like to take him back for two-thirds of what he cost me you would be doing me a great favor, for I can do nothing with him. When I have to pull him out of a stable it's the very devil, and when I harness him it's worse yet. And when it comes to the field work, he just lies down and would much rather take a beating than yield to the yoke or allow a sack on his back. Sirs, will you have the kindness to deliver me from that accursed animal? He is handsome but he is good for nothing but to strut under some horseman, and that's not in my line." They proposed changing the horse against the one of the two others they had which he liked better. To this he agreed and our two travelers returned to the spot where they had rested, from which they were satisfied to see that the horse they had left with the peasant gave himself over to his new condition with no repugnance.

Jacques. Well, sir?

The Master. Well, nothing can be more sure than that you are inspired. Is it of God or of the Devil? That's what I don't know. Jacques, my dear friend, I fear strongly that you have the Devil in you.

Jacques. And why the Devil?

The Master. Because you accomplish prodigious things and your doctrine is very suspect.

Jacques. And what connection is there between the doctrine one professes and the prodigious things one accomplishes?

The Master. I see that you have not read Dom la Taste.

Jacques. And what does he say, this Dom la Taste whom I haven't read?

The Master. He says that both God and the Devil perform miracles.

Jacques. And how does he distinguish between God's miracles and those of the Devil?

The Master. By means of the doctrine. If the doctrine is good, the miracles are God's. If it is bad, the miracles belong to the Devil.[75]

(*Here Jacques started to whistle. Then he added:*) And who's going to teach me, poor ignorant fellow that I am, whether the doctrine of the doer of miracles is good or bad? Come, sir, let's remount. What does it matter to you whether it's by way of God or Beelzebub that we found your horse again? Will he ride less well for it?

The Master. No. However, Jacques, if you were to be possessed . . .

Jacques. What remedy would there be for that?

The Master. What remedy? It would be, while awaiting exorcism, naturally, it would be to put yourself on a strict diet of holy water.

Jacques. Me, sir, on water! Jacques on holy water! I should much rather have a thousand legions of devils in my body than drink a single drop of it, holy or otherwise. Haven't you noticed that I'm hydrophobic?

—Oh, come now, hydrophobic? Jacques said hydrophobic?—No, reader, no; I confess that the word is not his. But with such severity of criticism, I defy you to read one single scene of comedy or tragedy, one single dialogue however well made, without catching the author's word in the mouth of his creation. Jacques really said: "Sir, haven't you ever noticed that at the very sight of water I froth at the mouth?" Well, by saying something other than that I have been less true but much quicker about it.

They got back on their horses, and Jacques said to his master: "You were at the point in your love story where, having been happy twice, you were preparing to be happy again, perhaps, a third time."

The Master. When all of a sudden the corridor door was thrown open. And there is the bedroom crowded with a mob of people running noisily. I notice lights and I hear men's voices and women's voices all talking at once. The curtains are violently pulled aside, and I recognize the father, the mother, the aunts, all the cousins, and a police officer who is seriously pronouncing: "Ladies and gentlemen, no noise. The *delicto* is *flagrante.* Monsieur is an honorable gentleman; there is only one way to repair the evil done; and monsieur would certainly prefer to agree thereto of his own accord rather than be forced by the law."

At each word he was interrupted by the father and the mother who were heaping reproach upon me; by the aunts and cousins who were directing the most unsubtle epithets at Agathe as she tried to cover her head with the sheets. I was stupefied and didn't know what to say. The officer, addressing me, said ironically: "Sir, everything will be all right; would you, however, be so kind as to get up and dress?" This I did, but with my own clothes which had been substituted for those of the chevalier. They pulled up a table and the officer started to draw up a statement. During this time the mother had to be held back forcibly from beating her daughter, and the father was saying to her: "Easy, my wife, go easy; even after you've beaten your daughter the thing is nonetheless done. All will work out for the best." The other people had distributed themselves about on chairs in varying attitudes of pain, indignation, and anger. The father, chiding his wife from time to time, would say to her: "And that's what happens when a woman doesn't properly see to her daughter's conduct." And the mother would reply to him: "With such a good, honest appearance, who would ever have believed that this gentleman . . ." The others were silent. When the statement had been drawn up, they read it to me; and since it contained nothing but the truth, I signed it and went down with the officer who very obligingly asked me to get into a carriage waiting at the door. And so, with a rather large following, they took me straight to For-l'Evêque."[76]

Jacques. To For-l'Evêque! To prison!

The Master. Yes, to prison, and there followed an abominable trial. It was a question of nothing less than marrying Mlle Agathe; her parents would hear of no other arrangement. Early the very next morning the chevalier appeared in my cell. He knew everything. Agathe was very upset; her parents were furious; he himself had undergone the cruellest sort of reproach for the perfidious acquaintance he had introduced to them; it was he who was the first cause of their sorrow and their daughter's dishonor; those poor folks merited one's pity. He had asked to speak to Agathe alone and had not obtained such permission without difficulty. Agathe had thought of tearing his eyes out; she called him the most odious names. He expected it and he let her fury run its course, after which he had tried to bring her around to being a little reasonable. "But that young lady kept saying one thing to which," added the chevalier, "I know of no answer." "My father and mother surprised me with your friend. Should I tell them that I was lying with him only because I thought I was lying with you?" He replied to her: "But can you in good faith believe my friend will marry you?" "No," she said, "it is you, wretch, it is you, scoundrel, who should be condemned to that."

"But," I said to the chevalier, "upon you alone depends my getting out of this thing."

"How's that?"

"How? Why, by telling the story as it is."

"I threatened Agathe with doing that, but most certainly I shall not do it. It is questionable if such a step would be useful, and it's very certain that it would cover us both with shame. It's your fault too."

"My fault?"

"Yes, your fault. If you had approved of the little joke I proposed, Agathe would have been surprised by her family between two men and all of this would have finished in derision. But such is not the case and the question now is how to get out of a bad spot."

"But, Chevalier, could you explain to me one tiny incident? About the clothes I was wearing delivered and yours put back in the closet? By heaven, however much I ponder on it, that remains a confounded mystery. That made Agathe seem somewhat open to suspicion in my eyes, for there came to me the thought that she knew about this trickery and that there was between herself and her parents some sort of connivance."

"Maybe they saw you come up. What is sure is that scarcely were you undressed when they sent back my clothes and asked for yours."

"All of that will perhaps become clearer with time."

As we were thus involved in torturing and consoling ourselves, accusing each other, insulting each other and then asking pardon, the police officer entered. The chevalier grew pale and left hurriedly. This officer was a good man—there are some from time to time— who, having read over the statement, remembered that formerly he had studied with a young man of my name. And there came to him the idea that I might very likely be a relative or even the son of his old collegemate—which turned out to be true. His first question was to ask me the name of the man who had escaped as he came in.

"He didn't escape at all," I said to him, "he just left. That was my intimate friend, the Chevalier de Saint-Ouin."

"Your friend! Well, you've got some friend there. Did you know, sir, it was he who came to get me? And he was accompanied by the father and another relative."

"Saint-Ouin?"

"Himself."

"Are you quite sure of that?"

"Very sure. But what did you say his name was?"

"The Chevalier de Saint-Ouin."

"Oh! The Chevalier de Saint-Ouin; now we're getting somewhere. And do you know what your friend is, your very close friend, the Chevalier de Saint-Ouin? A scoundrel, a man well known for a hundred or more clever tricks. The police give such people the liberty of walking around only because of the services they can draw from them sometimes as informers. They are swindlers and informers on swindlers, and the police apparently find them more useful for the evil they prevent or disclose, than dangerous for the evil they do." [77]

I recounted to the officer my sad adventure just as it had happened. He could not see things in a much more favorable light afterwards, for everything that might have absolved me could neither be pleaded nor proved before a court of law. However, he promised to call on the father and mother, to frighten the daughter a bit, to enlighten the magistrate, and to leave nothing unturned that might serve to justify me, warning me the while that if those people retained good legal counsel, the authorities could do very little for me.

"What, officer; I could be forced to marry her?"

"Marry her! That would be quite harsh and I hardly expect that. But there will be damages and in this case they'll be considerable."

But, Jacques, it seems you have something to say to me.

Jacques. Yes, I wanted to tell you that you were actually more unhappy than myself, who paid and never laid. As for the rest I think I should have heard everything if Agathe had turned out to be pregnant.

The Master. Well, don't get too far away from your conjecturing, for that's precisely what the officer came to tell me several days after my detention. She had come to him to make a declaration of pregnancy.

Jacques. And so there you are father of a child . . .

The Master. Whom I didn't harm at all.

Jacques. But whom you didn't make either.

The Master. Neither the protection of the magistrate, nor all of the steps taken by the officer could prevent the affair from following the course of justice. But since the daughter and her parents were in ill repute there was no prison wedding. They sentenced me to a considerable fine, the expenses of childbirth, and the subsistence and education of a child sprung from the deeds and *gesta* of my friend the Chevalier de Saint-Ouin, of whom the child was a miniature portrait. A big bouncing boy was born very happily to Mlle Agathe between the seventh and eighth months; a good nurse was provided, for whom I have paid every month up to this very day.

Jacques. And about how old might Monsieur your son be?

The Master. He'll soon be ten years old. All this time I have left him in the country where the schoolmaster has taught him to read, to write, and to count. It's not far from the place where we are going, and I shall profit by the coincidence in order to pay those people what I owe them, take the boy away, and put him to some trade.

7

❧ ❧ ❧

JACQUES AND HIS MASTER SLEPT ONE MORE TIME ALONG THE ROAD.
They were too near the end of their journey for Jacques to take
up his love story. Moreover his sore throat was far from cured.
The next day they arrived . . . —Where?—Word of honor I
don't know.—And what business did they have to do where they
were going?—Whatever you please. Did Jacques's master tell his
business to everybody? Whatever it was, they didn't need to spend
more than two weeks. Will those two weeks end well or badly?
I don't know anything about that either. Jacques's sore throat
passed away by means of two remedies that went very much
against his grain: to wit, diet and rest.

One morning the master said to his lackey: "Jacques, harness
and saddle the horses and fill your gourd. We've got to go you
know where." Which was no sooner said than done. And so there
they are riding along toward the spot where some country folk
had for ten years been bringing up the son of the Chevalier de
Saint-Ouin at the expense of Jacques's master. At some distance
from the shelter they had just left, the master addressed Jacques
in these terms: "Jacques, what have you to say about my loves?"

Jacques. Only that there are many strange things written up
yonder. Here is a child made God knows how! Who knows the
role that little bastard will play in the world? Who knows if he is
not born for the glory or for the upheaval of an empire?

The Master. I can tell you that he's not. I'll make a good watchmaker or lathe turner out of him. He'll get married and he'll have
children who will turn out chair spindles in this world to all
eternity.

Jacques. Yes, if it's written up yonder. But then why couldn't a Cromwell come out of a lathe-turner's shop? The one who had his king's head cut off, didn't he come out of a brewer's shop and aren't they saying nowadays that . . . ? [78]

The Master. That's enough of that. You're in good health, you know about my loves, and in all conscience you can hardly excuse yourself from continuing the story of your own.

Jacques. Everything points the other way. First of all, the slim stint of journey that remains to be made; second, the fact that I forgot where I was in the story; and third, some sort of devilish premonition I have that my story is not to be finished, that its telling would bring us bad luck, and that I should have no sooner started it again than it would be interrupted by some catastrophe, be it happy or unhappy.

The Master. Well, if the catastrophe is happy, so much the better!

Jacques. I quite agree, but somehow I have the feeling here that it will be unhappy.

The Master. Unhappy! So be it! But whether you talk or not, will it be any the less apt to happen?

Jacques. And who could know that?

The Master. You were born two or three centuries too late.

Jacques. No, sir, I was born just in time like everybody else.

The Master. You would have been a great augur.

Jacques. I don't know precisely what an augur is and I'm not very worried about knowing.

The Master. Why, it's one of the important chapters in your treatise on divinations.

Jacques. It's true but it's such a long time since I wrote it that I can't remember a word. Look here, sir, here's what knows more than all the augurs, fatidic geese, and holy chickens of the republic, and that's the gourd. Let's interrogate the gourd.

Jacques took up his gourd and consulted it at great length. His master pulled out his watch and his snuffbox, looked at the time, took his pinch, and Jacques said: "It seems to me that I now see Destiny a little less black. Tell me where I was."

The Master. At Desglands' château with your knee a little better and with Denise instructed by her mother to look after you.

Jacques. Denise was obedient. The wound on my knee was almost closed; I had even been able to dance in a circle the night of Desglands' child's whim. However, from time to time I suffered indescribable pains there. The idea came to the château surgeon, who knew a little more than his colleague, that such recurring pains could be caused only by some foreign body that had remained embedded in my flesh after the extraction of the bullet. Consequently he arrived early one morning in my bedroom, pushed a table close to my bed, and when my curtains were drawn back, I saw that table covered with cutting instruments, Denise seated by my side shedding warm tears, her mother standing with crossed arms looking rather sad, and the surgeon, without his frock coat, the sleeves of his shirt rolled up, and his right hand armed with a lancet.

The Master. You frighten me.

Jacques. I was frightened too. "My friend," the surgeon said to me, "are you tired of suffering?"

"Very tired."

"Do you want it to be over and still keep your leg?"

"Most assuredly."

"Then put your leg out of the bed and let me work at my ease."

I put out my leg. The surgeon puts the handle of his lancet between his teeth, hoists my leg under his left arm and balances it there firmly, retrieves his lancet, shoves the point into the opening of my wound and makes a wide and deep incision. I didn't bat an eyelash, but Jeanne turned her head away, and Denise cried out shrilly and became ill.

Here Jacques made a halt in his story and made a new attack on his gourd. The attacks were as frequent as the distances concerned were short or as the geometers would say, in inverse proportion to the distance. He was so precise in his measurement that, however full the gourd upon leaving, it was always just exactly empty upon arrival. The gentlemen of the engineering department would have made an excellent odometer out of him. Each attack on the gourd usually had its own sufficient reason. This one was to make Denise come out of her fainting and also to get over the pain of the incision which the surgeon had made on his knee. So that Denise having been brought around, and feeling somewhat better himself, he continued.

Jacques. This large incision uncovered the very bottom of the wound from which the surgeon drew with his tweezers a tiny shred of material from my trousers which had remained and which was causing all my pain and preventing the complete scarring-over. After the operation my health kept improving, thanks to the attention of Denise: no more pain, no more fever, good appetite, sleep and strength. Denise dressed my wound with care and with infinite delicacy. You should have seen the circumspection and lightness of touch with which she lifted my dressing; you should have seen the fear she had of giving me the least pain, the manner in which she bathed my wound. I was seated on the edge of my bed; she had one knee on the floor, my leg was placed on her thigh against which I would sometimes press a little bit. I had one hand on her shoulder and I watched her do it with a tenderness that I believe she shared. When my dressing was finished, I would take her hands in mine; I would thank her, but I didn't know what to say or how to show her my gratitude. She would stand there with lowered eyes and listen to me without saying a word. Not a single peddler ever passed by the château without my buying her something; one time it was a neckerchief, another time several yards of muslin or printed calico, a gold cross, cotton stockings, a ring, or a garnet necklace. Once my little purchase was made, my embarrassment was to offer it to her and hers to accept it. First I would show her the thing and if she liked it I would say: "Denise, it's for you I bought it." If she accepted it, my hand would tremble as I gave it to her and hers would quiver as she took it. One day, not knowing what to buy her any more, I purchased a pair of garters; they were made of silk, bedecked with white, red, and blue, and with a little motto. That morning before she arrived, I put them on the back of a chair which was beside my bed. As soon as Denise spotted them, she cried: "Oh, what lovely garters."

"They're for my loved one," I replied.

"Oh, you have a sweetheart, Monsieur Jacques?"

"Certainly, haven't I told you about it yet?"

"No. She is doubtless very lovable."

"Very."

"And you love her very much?"

"With all my heart."

"And does she love you in the same way?"

"I have no idea. These garters are for her and she promised me a favor which will drive me mad, I believe, if she grants it me."

"And what is the favor?"

"That of these two garters I shall put on one with my own hands."

Denise blushed, misunderstood my conversation, and thought that the garters were for somebody else. She became sad, fumbled everything, looked for everything she needed for my dressing, had it right under her nose and could not find it. She upset the wine she had warmed, came up to my bed to dress me, took my leg in a trembling hand, undid my bandages all backward, and when it came to cauterizing my wound, she had forgotten everything she needed. She went off to look for it, bathed me, and as she did I saw that she was crying.

"Denise, you seem to be crying. What's the matter?"

"Nothing."

"Has somebody bothered you?"

"Yes."

"And who is the rogue?"

"It's you."

"Me?"

"Yes."

"And how could that have happened?"

Instead of replying she turned her eyes toward the garters.

"What!" I said. "That's what made you cry?"

"Yes."

"Come, Denise, stop crying; I bought them for you."

"Monsieur Jacques, are you really telling the truth?"

"Of course I am; so true, that here they are." And thereupon I gave them both to her but I held onto one and immediately a smile escaped amidst all her tears. I took her by the arm, I pulled her close to the bed, I took one of her feet and put it on the edge of the bed, I lifted her skirts to her knees where she held them tightly clasped with both hands, I kissed her leg and attached the garter that I had kept. Scarcely was it attached when Jeanne, her mother, entered.

The Master. Now there's an ill-timed visit.

Jacques. Perhaps yes, perhaps no. Instead of noticing our embarrassment, she noticed only the garter in her daughter's hand. "Now there's a pretty garter," she said. "But where's the other one?"

"On my leg," Denise replied. "He told me he bought them for his sweetheart, and I thought he meant for me. Isn't it true, mamma, that since I've put one on, I ought to keep the other?"

"Oh, Monsieur Jacques, Denise is right. One garter cannot go without the other and you wouldn't want to take back what she already has."

"And why not?"

"Because Denise wouldn't want you to and neither would I."

"All right then, but prepare yourself, for I shall attach the other right here in your presence."

"No, no, you can't do that."

"Then let her give them both back to me."

"No, you can't do that either."

But Jacques and his master are already on the outskirts of the village where they were going to see Saint-Ouin's child and its foster parents. Jacques was silent; his master said to him: "Let's dismount and take a short rest here."

"Why?"

"Because from all appearances you are coming to the end of your love story."

"Not completely."

"Well, when you've gotten to the knee there is very little road left to make." [70]

"But, my master, Denise had a longer thigh than most."

"Well, let's get down anyhow."

They got off their horses, Jacques first. Jacques ran quickly to the side of his master, who had no sooner put his foot in his stirrup than the cinch straps broke and our horseman, thrown down from his saddle, would have landed flat on the ground had his lackey not caught him in his arms.

The Master. So, Jacques, that's how you look after me! A little more and I would have cracked a rib, broken an arm, smashed my head, or maybe even have killed myself.

Jacques. What a shame!

The Master. What did you say, you wretch? Just wait, just wait, I'll teach you how to speak.

And the master, after having wound the cord of his whip twice around his wrist, went off in pursuit of Jacques, who was running around the horse in gales of laughter. His master cursed and swore and foamed with rage and ran around the horse, too, vomiting out a torrent of insults on Jacques. This race lasted until both of them, dripping with sweat and completely worn out, came to a stop, one on one side of the horse, and the other on the opposite side, Jacques puffing and continuing to laugh, and his master puffing and leering at him furiously. They were beginning to catch their breath when

Jacques said to his master: "And will my master agree with me now?"

The Master. And what do you want me to agree with, you dog, you scoundrel, you wretch, if it is not indeed that you are the most wicked of all lackeys and I, the most unfortunate of masters?

Jacques. Has it not been clearly demonstrated that we act most of the time without willing? Come now, put your hand on your heart and frankly tell me, of all you have said or done this last half hour, have you willed any of it? Haven't you been my marionette and wouldn't you continue to be my puppet for a month if I so decided?

The Master. What! This was all a game?

Jacques. A game.

The Master. And you were expecting the cinch straps to break?

Jacques. I prepared it.

The Master. And your impertinent reply was also premeditated?

Jacques. Completely premeditated.

The Master. And so that was the puppet string you attached over my head so as to lead me about at your fancy?

Jacques. Perfect!

The Master. You are a dangerous good-for-nothing.

Jacques. Say, rather, that thanks to my captain who one day played the same trick at my expense, I am a subtle reasoner.

The Master. But suppose I had been wounded?

Jacques. It was written up yonder and in my foresight that that wouldn't happen.

The Master. Come, let's sit down, we need a rest.

They sit down as Jacques says: "The devil take the stupid ass."

The Master. Speaking of yourself apparently?

Jacques. Yes, of myself, for not saving one more drink in my gourd.

The Master. Have no regrets for I should have drunk it. I'm dying of thirst.

Jacques. The devil still take the stupid ass that I am for not having kept two drinks.

The master begs him to continue his story so as to make them forget their fatigue and their thirst; Jacques refuses; his master sulks; Jacques lets himself be sulked at. Finally Jacques, having protested against the misery which will come of it, takes up again the story of his loves and says:

"One holiday when the lord of the château was hunting." After these words he stopped short and said: "I can't go on, it's impossible. It seems to me that henceforth I have the hand of Destiny on my throat and I can feel it squeezing. For God's own sake, sir, allow me to be quiet."

"Well, then, be quiet, and go ask at the first peasant's house over there where we can find the foster parents."

It was at a door farther down the road, and there they go, each of them holding his horse by the bridle. In a flash the door of the foster parents' house opens and a man comes out; Jacques's master shouts and puts his hand on his sword; the gentleman in question does the same. The two horses are frightened by the clank of arms; Jacques's horse breaks his halter and escapes and at that very moment the chevalier with whom the master was fighting is stretched out stone dead on the ground. The peasants run from the village. Jacques's master jumps to saddle with agile leg and rides off at top speed. They take hold of Jacques, tie his hands behind his back, and take him before the judge of the place who in turn sends him to prison. The dead man was the Chevalier de Saint-Ouin, who that very day had chanced to come along with Agathe to see their child. Agathe tears her hair over the corpse of her lover. Jacques's master is already so far away as to be out of sight. Jacques proceeded from the judge's house to prison mumbling over and over again: "It had to be, for it was written up yonder."

And as for myself, here's where I stop, for I have told you all I know about these two characters.—And how about Jacques's love story?—Jacques said at least a hundred times that it was written up yonder that he wouldn't finish the story, and I see that Jacques was right. I also see, reader, that this upsets you. Well, then, take up the story where he left off and finish it however you've a mind to; or else, pay a visit to Mlle Agathe, find out the name of the village where Jacques is imprisoned, go see Jacques, and ask him. You won't need to urge him; it will keep him from getting bored. According to some memoirs which I have good reason to distrust, I could perhaps supply what is missing, but whatever good would that be? One can be interested only in the truth. However, since it would be a bit rash to say the final word, without a careful examination, on these conversations of Jacques the Fatalist and his master—the most important work to have appeared since the *Pantagruel* of Master François Rabelais, and the life and adventures of the *Compère Mathieu* [80]—I shall reread those memoirs with all the broadness of mind and all the impartiality of which I am capable. And in a week I shall give you a judgment which will be definitive, except that I reserve the right to retract should someone more intelligent than myself prove to me that I was wrong.

The publisher adds: The week has gone by. I have read the memoirs in question. Of the three paragraphs that I find not an integral part of the manuscript in my possession, the first and the last seem original, but the middle one is, to my way of thinking, obviously interpolated. Here is the first paragraph which would presuppose a second lacuna in the conversation of Jacques and his master:

"One feast day when the lord of the château was off hunting, and the rest of his guests had gone to the parish mass at some quarter league's distance, Jacques had gotten up and Denise was at his side. They were very quiet, they seemed sulky, and, in effect, they were sulky. Jacques had done everything to convince Denise that she should make him happy, and Denise had been firm. After this long silence, Jacques, weeping warm tears, says in a harsh and bitter tone of voice: 'It's just that you don't love me.'

Denise, highly vexed, gets up, takes him by the arm, leads him bluntly to the side of the bed, sits down and says: 'So, Monsieur Jacques, you think I don't love you? Well, then, Monsieur Jacques, do with this miserable Denise whatever you will.' And so saying, she melts into tears and suffocates in her own sobbing."

Tell me, reader, what would you have done in Jacques's place? Nothing? Well, that's exactly what he did. He led Denise back to her chair, threw himself at her feet, wiped dry the tears that flowed from her eyes, kissed her hands, consoled her, reassured her, felt that he was tenderly loved by her, and depended henceforth on her tenderness, waiting for the moment when it might please her to reward his own. All this had visibly touched Denise.

You might perhaps object that Jacques, being at Denise's feet, could scarcely dry her eyes—that is not unless the chair were exceedingly low. The manuscript gives us no indication, but it would seem to be taken for granted.

Here is the second paragraph, copied from the *Life of Tristram Shandy,* unless, of course, the discourses of Jacques the Fatalist and his master prove to be anterior to that work, and Rev. Sterne be himself the plagiarist—which I don't believe, but only out of a particular esteem for Mr. Sterne, whom I distinguish from most of his country's writers, so used to robbing us and then insulting us: [81]

"Another time, in the morning, Denise had come to bathe Jacques. Everything in the château was asleep. Denise came toward his room all atremble. Having come to Jacques's door, she stopped dead, uncertain as to whether she would go in or no. She went in all atremble and stayed rather a long time beside Jacques's bed without daring to open the curtains. She opened them gently and said good day to Jacques, still all atremble. All atremble she asked about his health and how he had spent the night. Jacques replied that he had not slept a wink, that he had suffered, and was still suffering from a terrible itching on his knee. Denise offered to give him relief. She took a bit of flannel, Jacques put his leg out of the bed, and Denise started to rub with her flannel below the wound—first with one finger, then with two, then three, then four, then with her whole hand. Jacques watched her at work and grew intoxicated with love. Then Denise started to rub with her flannel on the wound itself, on the still red scar, first with one finger, then with two fingers, then with three, with four, and then with the whole hand. But it wasn't enough to have rubbed below the knee and on the knee, the itching had to be stopped above too, up above where it began to be felt all the more acutely. Denise laid her flannel above the knee and started rubbing there rather vigorously, first with one finger, then with two, with three, with four and with the whole hand. The passion within Jacques, who had not ceased for a moment to watch the operation, swelled to such a point that, no longer able to resist its fury, he swooped upon the pretty hand of Denise—*et la baisa.*" [82]

But what follows leaves absolutely no doubt about the plagiarism. The plagiarist adds: If you are not satisfied with what I reveal to you about Jacques's loves, reader, do better yourself; it's quite all right with me. However you go about it, I'm rather sure you will finish up just where I did.—Ah, there you are wrong, you notorious slanderer. I should not finish as you did, for Denise is a good girl.—And who says the opposite? Jacques swooped forward upon her hand, and *kissed it*—her hand. You are the one with the corrupt mind who sees what isn't said.—You mean, he kissed only her hand?—Why of course; Jacques had much too much sense to take advantage of the woman he wanted to make his wife; too much sense thus to encourage a mistrust which could have poisoned the rest of their existence.—But it says in the preceding paragraph that Jacques had done everything to convince Denise that she should make him happy.—Well, apparently he just wasn't quite ready to make her his wife.

The third paragraph shows us Jacques, our own poor fatalist, with chains on hands and feet, stretched out on the straw at the bottom of a deep dungeon, trying to recall all he had retained

of his captain's philosophic principles and not far from being convinced that he would one day perhaps come to miss that dank,
dark, smelly hole where he was fed with black bread and water,
and where he had at least hands and feet to ward off the attacks
of the mice and rats. We learn that in the very middle of his
meditations, the doors of his prison and dungeon are broken down,
he is liberated along with a dozen brigands, and he finds himself
all of a sudden a member of Mandrin's gang.[83] Meanwhile, the
constabulary, on the trail of the master, had caught up with him,
seized him and sentenced him to another prison. He had gotten
out thanks to the help of the same officer who had served him so
well in a former adventure, and he had been living some three or
four months in Desglands' château, when Destiny returned to him
a servant almost as indispensable to him as his watch and snuffbox.
He never took his pinch, he never looked at the time, but he would
say with a sigh: "Oh, my poor Jacques! What has happened to
you?" One night, Desglands' château is attacked by the Mandrin
gang; Jacques recognizes the establishment of his benefactor and
his mistress; he intercedes with the brigands and saves the château
from pillage. Thereafter can be read the pathetic little detail of
the unexpected meeting of Jacques, his master, Desglands, Denise,
and Jeanne:

"It is you, my dear friend!"

"It is you, my dear master!"

"How is it you are with those people there?"

"And yourself? How is it I find you here?"

"Is that you, Denise?"

"Is that you, Monsieur Jacques? How you have made me cry!"

Meanwhile Desglands was shouting: "Bring on some wine and
glasses; quickly, quickly. For it is he who has saved all our lives."

Several days later the old caretaker of the château died; Jacques
obtains his place and marries Denise with whom he has busied
himself producing little disciples of Zeno and Spinoza.[84] Here he

is loved by Desglands, cherished by his master, and adored by his wife, for just thus was it all written up yonder.

They have tried to convince me that his master and Desglands have fallen in love with Jacques's wife. I don't pretend to know anything about it. But I am quite sure that in the evening he would say to himself: "If it's written up yonder, Jacques, that you'll be a cuckold, you may do what you will, my boy, you will be a cuckold. If, on the other hand, it is written up yonder that you won't be, they may do all they like, you will never be a cuckold. Sleep, then, my friend, sleep. . . ."

And he would go to sleep.

Notes

Sources referred to in these notes are abbreviated as follows:

A-T. *Oeuvres complètes.* 20 vols. Ed. Assézat and Tourneux. Paris: Garnier, 1875–1877.

B. *Oeuvres de Denis Diderot.* 20 vols. Paris: J. L. J. Briere, 1821–1823.

Bel. *Jacques le fataliste et son maître.* Ed. Yvon Belaval. Paris: Club français du livre, 1953.

Corr. *Correspondance de Diderot.* Ed. Georges Roth and Jean Varloot. Paris: Minuit, 1955–1970. 16 vols.

L. Leningrad manuscript (copy) of *Jacques le fataliste.*

L.L. *Jacques le fataliste et son maître.* Edition critique par Simone Lecointre et Jean Le Galliot. Paris, Droz, 1976.

FV. Fonds Vandeul (described fully in Herbert Dieckmann, *Inventaire du Fonds Vandeul* [Genève: Droz, 1951]). This translation is based on a composite of three texts of the work: the text in Vol. VI of *A-T.*, the text of the work found in *FV.* (deposited by Herbert Dieckmann in the Bibliothèque Nationale in Paris), and a microfilm copy of the Leningrad manuscript. For the privilege of examining the latter I am deeply grateful to Richard Arndt of Columbia University, who very kindly put his copy at my disposal. In general, the translation follows the *A-T.* text, except where *L.* and *FV.* agree in a variant. In a few cases the translator has used what seems the best reading regardless of variation among the other sources. An interesting variant throughout *L.* is the spelling of Jaques for Jacques, Madame de la Pommeraye for Madame de La Pommeraye.

1. The battle of Fontenoy was fought between the English and the French on May 11, 1745. The French general was the famous Maréchal de Saxe. From this battle comes

the polite phrase "After you, Messieurs Englishmen." This *politesse* from the past cost the French great losses.

2. Much of these first pages of *Jacques the Fatalist* has been consciously borrowed by Diderot from Laurence Sterne. The following passages from Sterne have already appeared in *Jacques,* sometimes in their entirety:

King William was of an opinion . . . that everything was predestined for us in this world; insomuch, that he would often say to his soldiers that every bullet had its billet.

"Besides," said the corporal, resuming the discourse—but in a gayer accent—"if it had not been for that single shot, I had never, an' please your honor, been in love—."

"So thou wast in love, Trim!" said my Uncle Toby, smiling . . . "I have never heard a word of it before," quoth my Uncle Toby.

"I dare say," answered Trim, "that every drummer sergeant's son in the regiment knew of it."

As the number of wounded was prodigious, and no one had time to think of anything but his own safety. . . . But I was left upon the field, said the corporal. . . . So that it was noon the next day, continued the corporal, before I was exchanged, and put into a cart with thirteen of fourteen more, in order to be conveyed to our hospital.

There is no part of the body, an' please your honour, where a wound occasions more intolerable anguish than upon the knee—

Except the groin; quoth my Uncle Toby. An' please your honour, replied the corporal, the knee, in my opinion, must certainly be called the most acute, there being so many tendons and what-d'ye-call-'ems all about it.

The anguish of my knee, continued the corporal, was excessive in itself; and the uneasiness of the cart, with the roughness of the roads, which were terribly cut up—making bad still worse—every step was death to me; so that with the loss of blood, and the want of care-taking of me, and a fever I felt coming on besides . . . all together, an' please your honour, was more than I could sustain.

I was telling my sufferings to a young woman at a peasant's house, where our cart, which was the last of the line, had halted; they had helped me in, and the young woman had taken a cordial out of her pocket and dropped it upon some sugar, and seeing it had cheered me, she had given it me a second and a third time—So I was telling her, an' please your honour, the anguish that I was in, and was saying it was so intolerable to me, that I had much rather lie down upon the bed turning my face towards one which was in the corner of the room— and die, than go on—when upon her attempting to lead me to it, I fainted away in her arms. . . . By the permission of the young woman, continued the corporal, the cart with the wounded men set off without me: she had assured them that I should expire immediately if I was put in the cart. So when I came to myself I found myself in a still quiet cottage, with no one but the young woman, the peasant and his wife. I was laid across the bed in the corner of the room, with my wounded leg upon a chair, and a young woman beside me holding the corner of her handkerchief dipped in vinegar to my nose with one hand, and rubbing my temples with the other.

The Life and Opinions of Tristram Shandy
Book VIII, p. 516 ff. New York: Modern Library, n.d.

Diderot will close *Jacques* with the rest of this episode retold by Corporal Trim, using it thus as a sort of frame for his novel. These passages constitute the most substantial borrowing from Sterne and lie at the base of most accusations of plagiarism leveled at Diderot. Other passages of *Tristram Shandy* echoed in Diderot will be pointed out in the notes at the appropriate points in the text of *Jacques*.

3. *Bergen-op-Zoom and Port-Mahon:* The first was a fortified city taken by Maurice de Saxe in 1747. Port-Mahon (Mahón), the capital of Minorca, was taken from the English in 1756 by the Duc de Richelieu; so opened the Seven Years War.

4. *St. Roch for hats:* This French expression denotes a superfluity of possessions and has its source in the fact that St. Roch had three hats and is often depicted thus.

5. *Surgeons Dufouart and Louis:* First as the son of a master cutler who made surgical instruments of exceptional quality (the trademark is

known among surgeons as late as the twentieth century), then as philosopher of science and editor of the *Encyclopédie,* Denis Diderot maintained a very lively interest in medical progress, especially surgery. Pierre Dufouart (d. 1813) was a famous surgeon and author of a treatise on wounds made by firearms. Antoine Louis (d. 1792), a surgeon and secretary of the *Académie de Paris,* was responsible for the surgery articles of the *Encyclopédie.* Diderot obviously knew them and their works.

6. *Harpagon:* Diderot slipped here; he meant Géronte in Molière's *Fourberies de Scapin.* This is doubly surprising since Molière was one of his favorite authors, and, as is clear here, one he despaired of equaling. It is a slip of overfamiliarity rather than ignorance.

7. The usual allowance referred to by Diderot was the annual sum paid by the absent holder of a church benefice to the curate who did the actual work of the parish. This annual payment was fixed at 500 *livres* (or francs) until 1786 (*L.L.*). When Diderot mentions the Bernardins in the next lines, he is calling attention to another of the flagrant abuses within the church. The Bernardins (originally an austere sect of the Benedictines founded by St. Bernard) are now luxuriating in the good life while the parish priest must scrounge for a living.

8. *Julien Le Roi:* Master watchmaker well known in Europe. In 1720 he presented to the Paris Academy of Sciences a carefully calibrated pendulum that measured true time. His son Pierre is credited with valuable innovations in creating a marine chronometer, *c.* 1760. The passage is a reflection of Diderot's (and the *Encyclopédie*'s) admiration for the professional artisan. From Diderot's correspondence we know that the watchmaker's son was one of Diderot's companions during his Bohemian years in Paris before 1740. "Once I was invited to supper in a somewhat suspect establishment which I didn't know for such. One of the sons of Julien Le Roi was there. There were other men and women. . . . We were gay. I was young and foolish." (*Letters to Sophie Volland.*)

9. *Cleveland:* A novel of Abbé Prévost, a favorite author of Diderot and creator of the well-known *Manon Lescaut.* The full title is *Histoire de Cleveland, fils naturel de Cromwell, ou le philosophe anglais* (1732).

10. . . . *Sedaine:* These are again favorite authors of Diderot. Molière was followed by Regnard (1665–1709), who, if he did not equal the comic master, left behind several plays of lasting reputation: *Le Joueur, Le Légataire universel.* It was of Richardson that Diderot said in his *Eloge*

de Richardson: "The genius of Richardson has stifled what I had of sensibility. . . . When I start to write . . . the shade of Clarissa appears, I see Grandison . . . and the pen drops from my hands." Sedaine, a friend of the encyclopedic philosophers, wrote in 1765 *Le Philosophe sans le savoir,* a "new" drama in the vein of Diderot's own examples and theorizing. The warm scene of Diderot's congratulation of Sedaine after the performance is preserved in Diderot's correspondence and in *Paradoxe sur le comédien.* For the actual "Pondichéry" poet, see *Correspondance Littéraire,* IX, 350.

11. *Horace:* Diderot refers to a passage from Horace in *Ars poetica,* v. 373. He uses the same quotation in the *Salon of 1765 (A-T, X, 236)*

> . . . Mediocribus esse poetis,
> Non homines, non Di, non concessere columnae.
> (But that poets be of middling rank
> Neither men, nor gods, nor booksellers ever brooked. . . .)
>
> Trans. Fairclough

12. All the information—memoirs, letters, etc.—on Diderot's life tends to prove the frequency of just such visits and demands on his time as those here described. For example, his daughter, Mme de Vandeul (in memoirs on the life of her father), tells, among other incidents including Diderot's having written an early commercial about hair pomade for an untalented promotion man, the story of a certain M. Rivière who, after imposing to the limit upon Diderot's good will and easy heart, took leave of him with the following words: "Do you know about the *formica-leo?* . . . It is a very industrious little insect; he digs a funnel-shaped hole in the earth and covers the surface of the hole with fine, light sand; he draws unwary insects to the spot, seizes them, sucks them dry, then says to them: 'Monsieur Diderot, I have the honor of wishing you a good day.' "

13. *Lisbon:* Reference to the famous earthquake of Lisbon in 1755, which gave rise to much philosophic reflection on divine providence and "the best of all possible worlds." To the incident we owe Voltaire's "Poem on the Disaster at Lisbon" and later *Candide* (in reply to Rousseau's reaction).

14. *discalced Carmelite:* A branch of the order of mendicant friars originally founded in 1156 on Mt. Carmel overlooking the Bay of Acre. This branch of the unshod or barefoot was founded by St. Teresa in Spain in the sixteenth century for both monks and nuns.

15. *Father Angel:* In many respects this character in *Jacques* can be identified with an actual person of that name, a distant relative of the Diderots in Paris. During his Bohemian years Diderot used a feigned interest in a religious (and Carmelite) vocation to extort necessary funds for quite other purposes from Father Angel. Diderot's father finally paid for his son's notion of clever banking.

16. Diderot recounts a similar amusing event to Sophie (*Corr.* VII, 126) where a horse out of force of habit betrays a lover.

17. *continuers of Cervantes and the imitator of Ariosto:* Alonso Fernández de Avellaneda had published a continuation of *Don Quixote* in 1614 at Tarragon. However inferior to its model, this continuation was nonetheless translated into French by Le Sage in 1704 and thus known in the eighteenth century. (*B.*) Forti-Guerra (or Forte-Guerri) (d. 1735) wrote in a very short time an imitation of Ariosto's *Orlando furioso* called *Ricciardetto*. He wrote the first canto in a single day to prove how easy it was to carry off Ariosto-like heroic epics. Originally published in 1738, *Ricciardetto* was translated or rather imitated in French verse by Dumourier in 1766. Mention here of these imitations, which Diderot had read at least in translation, reflect his informed interest in the novel as a literary genre as he composes his "a-novel" *Jacques.*

18. *Prémontval:* Pierre Le Guay de Prémontval taught mathematics around 1740, the end of Diderot's Bohemian years in Paris. After eloping with Mlle Pigeon, he went to Switzerland, then to Berlin, where, although a member of the Academy, he led a rather miserable existence until his death in 1764. (*A-T.*)

19. *Pigeon:* Marie-Anne-Victoire Pigeon (afterwards Mme Prémontval) died in Berlin in 1767. She published in 1750 an obscure work on the ideas of her father, *le Mécaniste philosophe*. In her last years she was *lectrice* to the wife of Henry of Prussia. Years later it was from this German prince that the first copy of *Jacques le fataliste* was procured (1794; published 1796) by the Institut de France. Henry's copy was very probably one sent along with Grimm's *Correspondance littéraire.* But it is interesting to conjecture that the prince's interest in Diderot and in *Jacques le fataliste* owes something to his having known one of the (probably) unwitting characters of the book.

20. *Jardin du Roi:* The important botanical garden of Paris known now

as the *Jardin des Plantes.* Diderot's contemporary, the great natural scientist Buffon, brought the gardens to their present state in 1739, after they had had over a century of precarious existence.

21. *Gousse:* The personality of Gousse (to Diderot an "original"; in modern parlance a "character"), like Rameau's Nephew and so many other similar characters in his writing, at once charms and frightens Diderot: charms, because such characters dare to be themselves despite dull conformism; frightens, since they endanger any rational approach to social morality.

22. *Cosme:* Diderot is very probably thinking here of an actual Brother Cosme of whom he writes to Sophie Volland. Needing a cadaver for experiment, Cosme asked for one from the director of a poorhouse. The director filled a dying man with an overdose of medicine and sent along the cadaver, which regained consciousness at a critical moment to the surprise of all. "Well, well," remarked the good Cosme, "no harm done. We'll wait for another occasion." *Corr.* V, 197. The ring incident is also in *Corr.* IV, 161.

23. *Cul-de-sac:* Voltaire disapproved highly of the word *cul-de-sac* for an impasse. He very probably played at disliking it even more when it became grounds for another easy attack on Fréron. Among other examples of his sensitivity about the word, we read in an introductory letter to *l'Ecossaise,* Voltaire's play against Fréron: "J'appelle impasse, messieurs, ce que vous appelez cul-de-sac. Je trouve qu'une rue ne ressemble ni à un cul ni à un sac. Je vous prie de vous servir du mot impasse . . . en dépit du sieur Fréron, ci-devant jésuite." Another time he attacks one of Diderot's printers, Le Breton, for using the word in his *Almanach royal* as a street address: "Comment peut-on dire qu'un grave président demeure dans un cul? Passe encore pour Fréron: on peut habiter le lieu de sa naissance: mais un président, un conseiller! Fi! monsieur Le Breton; corrigez-vous, servez-vous du mot *impasse,* qui est le mot propre. . . ." (*A-T.*)

24. *Bicêtre:* A public building, built near Paris by Louis XIII in 1632 for veterans and used later as a prison for the insane. Conditions were particularly grim here.

25. One of the rare spots where Diderot has slipped up in this otherwise seemingly disorganized work. Here he clearly means older not younger, for later we learn that the Marquis des Arcis has a younger

man, Richard, as secretary.

26. *lettre de cachet:* It was shockingly easy in the eighteenth century to obtain an envelope bearing the king's seal and enclosing an arbitrary sentence to exile or imprisonment; abuse of this device reached the proportions of a veritable business.

27. *Saint-Florentin:* Phelipeaux de la Vrillière, Comte de Saint-Florentin, minister of state in 1761, had a reputation for overusing *lettres de cachet.* (*L.L.*)

28. *Temple:* Original Knights Templar sanctuary in Paris, at the time still outside normal police jurisdiction. Asylum for debtors and litigants.

29. *Burbero benefico:* A well-known play by Goldoni, presented in Paris for the first time November 4, 1771. Diderot had already been accused of stealing the plot of his own play, *Le Père de famille,* from an earlier Goldoni play, *Il Vero amico.* Thus he is now having his sport at pretending to borrow again from Goldoni, but only to let Signor Goldoni know how he ought to have written his play.

30. *Tronchin:* Théodore Tronchin (1709–1781) was one of a famous family of Geneva Tronchins in the eighteenth century. He was a Geneva doctor with a wide reputation. To consult him, Mme d'Epinay planned a trip from her home in France when the great quarrel broke out between Jean-Jacques Rousseau and all his former friends because he refused to accompany his hostess, Mme d'Epinay, to Geneva. There may be a good reason for Diderot's writing *her* as he remembers these hectic events of 1758.

31. *Guerchy:* Claude-Louis de Regnier, Comte de Guerchy (1715–1767), from 1730 to 1760 a soldier reputed for his courage. Then named ambassador to London, he had equivocal encounters with the equally equivocal Chevalier d'Eon, of which Diderot is doubtless aware as he traces the bizarre story of dueling for the second time. (*Bel.*)

32. *passe-dix:* Game of chance using three dice, in which one of the players bets he can roll more than ten.

33. *anti-philosophe:* Clearly the worst accusation that can be leveled at a man by Diderot and his group. The ideal man of the century is the *philosophe* just as the *honnête-homme* had been the ideal for the preceding century. There is even more contempt here than meets the eye, for Diderot and his friends had seen just such abbés (whose freedom was great during the century) join their group only to betray the philosophic movement

eventually.

34. . . . *Bossuet:* Bossuet (1627–1704) was the great classical writer of religious sermons and funeral orations; his works remain the model of the genre. Pierre Nicole (1628–1695) was a moralist and inmate of famous Jansenist Port-Royal. With Arnauld he collaborated on *La Logique de Port-Royal*. Pierre-Daniel Huet (1630–1721) was a French prelate and scholar, who also wrote a treatise on the origin of the novel.

35. *Jansenist or Molinist:* Jansenism was the movement within the Roman Catholic Church that rivaled the Jesuits during the seventeenth and eighteenth centuries. Its fundamental purpose was to reform the Church by a return to greater personal holiness, and by insisting on the Augustinian necessity of divine grace before salvation. Molinism (Luis de Molina, 1535–1600) was a rather wishful attempt to reconcile divine grace with the notion of human freedom. The Jesuits more or less defended this theory of one of their own members. The group Diderot does not mention here is the Jesuits, for the Jesuits had been outlawed in France in 1762 to the accompaniment of but few tears from Diderot and the *philosophes*.

36. *Cabinet du Roi:* Collection and exhibition of prints established by Louis XIV in 1667. (*Bel.*)

37. *St. François de Sales . . . Quietist:* St. François de Sales (1567–1622), French priest, later Bishop of Geneva, who converted many Protestants. He is famous for his sermons and was a favorite of seventeenth-century devout for his books of devotion: *Introduction to the Devout Life* and *Treatise on the Love of God*. Quietism, originally an extreme mystic position of Miguel de Molinos, in its insistence that the unity of the individual soul with God would be facilitated if the soul remained inert, was taken up again at the end of the seventeenth century, particularly by Fénelon, against whom the more orthodox Bossuet struggled valiantly and successfully. These two names, in some respects incompatible (since quietism could presumably dispense with meditative reading), come together naturally to Diderot's mind, for from the end of the seventeenth century until his day in France, the quietist approach to devotion went along with the vogue of solitary meditation and reading of devotional texts. Quietism (Molinos) is not to be confused with Molinism (Molina) of n. 35.

38. . . . *Le Bossu:* The famous treatises on poetics (as Diderot would

agree) are those by Aristotle, Horace, and Vida (1480–1556). Diderot does not mention his own compatriot Boileau (1636–1711), whose treatise on poetic art has become an accepted, significant work on the subject; why he does not is a matter of conjecture. But he does mention Le Bossu, whose *Traité du poème épique* (1675) appeared in a 1771 edition by Abbé Batteux that must have been familiar to him. Everything—Diderot's feelings about Batteux, the descending order from Aristotle to The Hunchback (literally), and the landlady's subsequent remark—leads one to believe that this whole comment is introduced at the expense of Le Bossu.

39. *Beneficial List:* The list containing the unassigned church benefices and announcing new assignments. The holder of the list naturally enjoyed a great social and political prestige; in Diderot's time this was the Bishop of Mirepoix, an anti-Jansenist, whose name will appear later (p. 171).

40. *gambling:* The game mentioned by name here in the original is *brelan,* a game very much like poker, dating from the eighteenth century. It was so popular and widespread under Louis XIV that players were prosecuted, at which point they replaced *brelan* by a similar game, *bouillotte.* (*Bel.*)

41. This would seem to be another slip by Diderot. At least it is unclear, for Jacques first speaks to his Master of Richard after they have left the Grand Cerf at noon, and they are now stopping for the first time and for the night after making only a half day.

42. *Grève:* Since 1806 the square of the Hôtel-de-Ville in Paris. Before that date, and in *Jacques,* the official execution square.

43. *Premonstratensians:* These monks wore a white woolen habit with nothing underneath; thus the playful suggestion of the Master. The vis-a-vis was a carriage for *two,* ideal for amorous trysts.

44. *Father Hudson:* Like many other characters in *Jacques,* this one is inspired by an actual person. Venturi (*Jeunesse de Diderot*) calls attention to the Abbé of Moncetz (where we shall see Hudson at the end of the episode), of whom Diderot writes to Sophie: "Two girls absent! And no abbé de Moncetz with them! What are you doing these days, abbé Moncetz?" "Your abbé de Moncetz . . . is a man without any sort of religion. He laughs at virtue inside himself. He views the rest of us people of good will as suckers." See also F. Pruner in bibliography.

45. *The Bull:* The famous papal bull of 1713, whose first word is "Unigenitus," condemned 101 propositions of a book by Jansenist Father Ques-

nel. This was fuel for the continuation of the rather vapid theological quarrel (its political implications were not always so vapid) between Jansenists and Jesuits (Molinists). It marks the beginning, after a fashion, of the comeback staged by the Jansenists. In 1709 under Louis XIV they had been chased from Port-Royal (the building itself was destroyed in 1712) as the result of pressure by the Jesuits; in 1762 under Louis XV it will be the turn of the Jesuits to be chased from France.

46. *Châtelet:* There were two fortresses of medieval Paris with this name: the Great and the Little Châtelets. The first, demolished in 1802, and situated on the Right Bank opposite the Pont-au-Change, was the seat of criminal jurisdiction for the general area of Paris. The second, on the Left Bank opposite the Petit-Pont, was used as a prison.

47. *Piron . . . Vatri:* Alexis Piron (1689–1773), minor poet of satires, songs, and generally witty and licentious verse; no great friend of the *philosophes,* ridiculed by Diderot in *Rameau's Nephew.* No information is available as to the conversation between Abbé Vatri and Piron, but see *Corr.* x, 165.

48. *lose their stamp:* This passage can be readily compared with a similar passage in Sterne, *A Sentimental Journey* (Character-Versailles): "I had a few of King William's shillings as smooth as glass in my pocket; and foreseeing that they would be of use in the illustration of my hypothesis, I had got them into my hand, when I had proceeded so far. . . . See, Mons. le Count, said I, rising up, and laying them before him upon the table—by jingling and rubbing one against another for seventy years together in one body's pocket or another's, they are become so much alike, you can scarce distinguish one shilling from another." Diderot himself came back again and again to this simile, as in an interview given around 1779 to the journalist Garat: "On sera tenté de me prendre pour une espèce d'original; mais qu'est-ce que cela fait? Est-ce donc un si grand défaut que d'avoir pu conserver, en s'agitant sans cesse dans la société, quelques vestiges de la nature, et de se distinguer par quelques côtés anguleux de la multitude de ces uniformes et plats galets qui foisonnent sur toutes les plages?" (*A-T.,* I, xxii) Diderot uses much the same figure again in his *Réfutation de l'ouvrage d'Helvétius intitulé "l'Homme."*

49. There are several Vanloo painters: Jean-Baptiste, his brother Carle, and their sons (and nephews) Michel, Charles-Amedee, and Cesar. Diderot's favorite (who did his portrait) is Carle (1703–1765), who became first painter of the King and director of the School of Painting. His studio was a meeting-place for artists. Diderot writes Cath-

erine II about the trash sold on Notre Dame Bridge (*Bel*).

50. This word painting of Jacques reminds the reader in spirit and form of the many paintings described by Diderot in his *Salons*. Indeed, it suggests in many of its details an imagination of Diderot's in the *Salon* of *1765* (*A-T.*, X, 337). Diderot uses this same scene in two other places: a letter to Sophie Volland (*Corr.* V, 95) and one to Grimm (*Corr.* V, 156).

51. *Fragonard:* Jean-Honoré Fragonard (1732–1806), one of the enduring French painters of the eighteenth century, was generally appreciated by Diderot in his *Salons*. His fame rests more and more on voluptuous charm. Grimm, in a note to Diderot (from the same *Salon of 1765* mentioned above), reflects that Diderot was right to give Fragonard serious attention but only because he and Diderot needed to find a successor to Vanloo. He continues: "When we think of the great group of young men returned from Rome . . . we cannot forecast a brilliant future for French painting. . . . We have only a Fragonard who shows promise, against that other crowd . . . who will certainly never amount to anything." (*A-T.*, X, 407)

52. . . . *Paradise:* Dante's passage to which the Master refers is from Canto X of *Purgatorio:* v. 123–126.

> Non v'acorgete voi che noi siam vermi
> Nati a formar l'angelica farfalla
> Che vola alla giustizia senza schermi?

53. This whole passage built around a series of plays on a word (*béguin*) is rather difficult to translate into English. Sterne, it will be remembered, had used the word *Beguine* (*Tristram Shandy*) in precisely the passage (Trim's love affair in Flanders) that Diderot imitates at the end of *Jacques*. Here Sterne (Trim) uses the term in one of its true meanings ("They differ from nuns in this, that they can quit their cloister if they choose to marry," says Trim). Diderot uses the word: (1) in the sense of the headdress worn in the religious order; (2) in the sense of a baby's hat; and (3) rather equivocally in the sense of the verb *embéguiner* or *avoir le béguin* for someone, meaning to infatuate, usually with a momentary but passionate love.

54. *Ferragus:* This is again the Ferragus (Ferrau) of Forti-Guerra's *Ricciardetto,* not the Ferragus from Ariosto's *Orlando furioso*. Ferrau, a

hypocrite become hermit, is somewhat drastically mutilated by the hand of Rinaldo. Says Ferrau:

> . . . padre, il tristo in una macchia
> Castrommi con un ferro di beccai;

(Canto 10, CXVIII)

To add to his agony, the devil, finding him an easy mark, appears before him to show him the remains of his virility. (*A-T.*)

55. The Ball referred to is André-Charles Boule (1642–1732) who became famous for his distinctive furniture (marquetry with brass and tortoise shell), still collectors' items today. The story of William Pitt is told in John Henlage Jesse, *Memoirs of the Life and Reign of King George III,* vol. I, 216. Diderot is not unaware of the suggestiveness of the initial sibilant in English. Pitt began his speech (about sugar) by saying, "Sugar, Mr. Speaker." Seeing the leering smiles of the House, he then repeated the word three times in stentorian tones. "Who will laugh now?" he concluded.

56. *gift of the garter:* This description of a typical provincial wedding feast, the *veillées* (or storytelling) mentioned before, all the details of Jacques's lively recounting of his loss of innocence are (as Venturi, in *Jeunesse de Diderot,* has suggested) reflections of eighteenth-century country or small-town life, very probably of Langres. Some of the incidents are very likely culled from Diderot's own adolescence. For a highly readable account of how much of this tradition persists in France see Laurence Wylie's excellent study *Village in the Vaucluse* (Harvard University Press, 1957). *Veillées* recall B. Despérier's contes (*c.* 1540).

57. *mirrors:* An obvious reference to Seneca's Hostius Quadra, *Questiones Naturales* tr. John Clarke, *Physical Science in the Time of Nero* (London: Macmillan, 1910), p. 41 ff.

58. *Jean-Baptiste Rousseau:* (1671–1741) French lyric poet who, accused of writing obscene verses, was exiled.

59. *la Pucelle:* Reference to Voltaire's famous work about Joan of Arc, a satirical treatment that, despite Diderot's assurance, offended many.

60. Throughout this passage, and despite Diderot's insistence (backed up by Montaigne) on the *mot juste,* either he or his relatives found it difficult to face up squarely to that word. Unlike *A-T.* and *FV.,* L. had (cf. p. 179) *foutez;* in this passage L. reads as follows after the visible crossing-out of all forms of the objectionable verb: "*Aimez* comme des

ânes débâtés; mais permettez-moi que je dise *j'aime, nous aimons, vous aimez, ils aiment.*" ". . . . aussi le mot *sacramental, le mot propre.* . . ." The changes here are not in Diderot's hand (the final paragraph in *L.* is in his hand) and were almost certainly made by his family after his death.

61. *vita proba:* As Diderot points out clearly, all of this passage is freely copied from Montaigne's *Essais,* Book III, chap. v.

62. *Bacbuc:* Brière advises: "In Hebrew *bachbouch,* a bottle, thus named from the noise made when it is emptied. Consult *Pantagruel* (Rabelais) rather than the Bible." (*A-T.*) Rabelais, *Quart Livre.*

63. . . . *Vadé:* Rabelais, of course, needs no explanation in this, or any other, context. La Fare (1644–1713) was known for his memoirs and some agreeable verse, says Voltaire. Chapelle (1626–1686) was a friend of Molière, La Fontaine, and others in their favorite cabarets, and was the author of *Voyage to Languedoc,* in which his treatment of preciosity inspired Molière. Chaulieu (1639–1720), says Voltaire, "lived in delight and died with intrepidity in 1720." His works are usually published with those of La Fare. Panard was a lyricist for contemporary fairs where much interesting vaudeville was given, eventually affecting the formation of comic opera in France. Gallet (1700?–1757) was another fair writer and a heavy drinker. Vadé (1720–1757) was another fair lyricist and dramatic author.

64. . . . *Guinguette:* These are names of famous historical drinking oases. The first was sanctified by Francois Villon, the second was the refuge of Gallet, mentioned in nn. 63, 65.

65. *Gallet:* Gallet, because of the special position granted him here by Diderot, deserves particular attention. "On his death, Panard, his friend and companion of . . . theatre and cabaret, upon meeting Marmontel, cried out in tears: 'I have lost him, I shall no more sing nor drink with him! He is dead, . . . I am alone in the world. . . . You know he died in the Temple? I went there to weep and wail on his tomb. And what a tomb! Ah, sir, they have put him under a gutter, he who since reaching the age of reason has drunk no glass of water.'" (*A-T.*) To the priest giving him extreme unction, he said, "I see you're greasing my boots: no need—I'm departing by water." By force of drinking, he was a victim of dropsy.

66. . . . *Brottier:* These are all authentic although somewhat obscure scholars. Nodot discovered pretended fragments of Petronius. The Prési-

dent de Brosses attempted to restore the text of Sallust. Freinshémius (a name with the familiar ring of Sterne's Slawkenbergius) added supplements to Quintus-Curtius. Brottier was the translator of Tacitus and author of *Memoirs* on several little-known points of Roman customs. (*A-T.*)

67. . . . *La belle:* Bouillotte was a game of chance much like *brelan,* described in n. 40. *La belle* was another game of chance (of which there were many in the eighteenth century), played by drawing numbers corresponding to numbers on a board.

68. *Mme Riccoboni:* Louis Riccoboni (1675–1753), born at Modena, brought Italian comedy to Paris in 1716. His equally talented wife was an actress and novelist (*Lettres de Mistress Fanny Butler* . . .) and corresponded with Diderot.

69. *Collé:* Charles Collé (1709–1783) was one of the best-known *chansonniers* and a dramatic author of note, who wrote a valuable *Journal et Mémoires* of his period. *La Vérité dans le vin,* his first comedy (1747), paints for us, says Sainte-Beuve, "the vices of the times, the effrontery of women in law, the stupidity of husbands, the impudence of abbés . . . which make it one of the historical and moral documents of the eighteenth century."

70. The whole passage is a very clear portrait of the famous intellect, wit, and courtesan, Ninon de Lenclos, who knew Voltaire in his childhood, and who epitomizes the *honnête-femme* of the seventeenth century turned *libertine,* or freethinker. That Diderot lapses into thinking of Ninon to the exclusion of his fictional "widow" is apparent from the fact that he has the "widow's" husband regret her death.

71. Jacques's contempt for portraits invites comparison with Sterne's portrait of Widow Wadman in *Tristram Shandy* (Book VI, chap. xxxviii). Diderot clearly shares most of Jacques's feelings.

72. *Jean-Jacques:* Obvious reference to Jean-Jacques Rousseau, who in *Emile* disapproved of La Fontaine's *Fables.* (The fable mentioned here is "The Acorn and the Pumpkin," Book IX, chap. iv.) This is one of Diderot's later comments on Rousseau, long after the split between the latter and the *philosophes,* and would seem to reflect little of what is many times construed as Diderot's hatred and malice toward the unhappy Genevan.

73. . . . *thinking machines:* The reader of eighteenth-century miscellanies will think immediately of the many crude materialistic works of

the century with which materialist Diderot could not agree, and, above all, of the works of La Mettrie, such as *l'Homme machine* and *Histoire naturelle de l'âme*. As Jacques remarks at this crucial philosophic moment in the work: ". . . there is only one more force to be considered."

74. . . . *vultus:* The original text of Ovid's *Metamorphoses* (a favorite citation of Diderot) reads (Lib. I, v. 85):

> Os homini sublime dedit, coelumque tueri
> Jussit, et erectos ad sidera tollere vultus.

> (He [It] made man [this fellow] stand erect, bidding him look up
> to heaven, and lift his head to the stars.) *Trans. Mary Innes*

75. Dom Louis La Taste (d. 1754) held, in his *Lettres théologiques,* published 1733, at the time of the *convulsionnaires* and other miracles, that devils can produce good miracles and miraculous cures only thereby to authorize error and vice. (*A-T.*)

76. *For-l'Evêque:* Prison for debtors and others, destroyed in 1780, formerly the original seat of temporal jurisdiction of the Archbishop of Paris.

77. These feelings about informers are reflected in a conversation of Diderot with the police chief, M. Sartine, about a certain person whom Diderot received freely, not knowing that he was a police spy: " 'You need such people as that. You use them, you remunerate them, but it is not possible that they be more than mud in your sight.' M. de Sartine began to laugh and we broke off conversation at that point." *Letters to Sophie Volland.* (*Bel.*) (Corr. IV, 158)

78. It would be interesting to know what is being said "nowadays." Belaval's suggestion that this may be guarded allusion to Mme du Barry, born Jeanne Bécu and shopgirl in origin, has some merit, particularly since she had just been influential in sending away the First Minister, Choiseul.

79. This erotic literary use of the garter and placing it high on the leg is general in "boudoir" literature of the eighteenth century. Surely, Diderot is satirizing this tritism as, in general, the taste for stylized "suggestive" lubricity. Even the Germans took to the garter, as in August von Thummel's *Wilhelmine* where, when the heroine shows a dainty knee with a garter embroidered with a verse from Voltaire, the author remarks, "To what remote places a French poet can sneak!" (H. Hatzfeld, *Rococo,* p. 186).

80. *Compère Mathieu:* This novel by Abbé Henri-Joseph Dulaurens (published from 1766 to 1773), was long attributed to Voltaire, who,

in his usual fashion, had used Dulaurens' name for his own *Relation du bannissement des Jésuites de la Chine*. Dulaurens, an overenlightened abbé, led a rather harried existence because of the open daring of his writings. He spent a month in the Bastille, and, on fleeing to Germany, was denounced and lived the last thirty years of his life under surveillance near Mainz. Otis Fellows and Alice Green have written an interesting article on the connections between *Compère Mathieu* and *Jacques le fataliste* in *Diderot Studies I* (Ed., Fellows and Torrey; Syracuse University Press, 1949).

81. The following passage, stated with playful limitation and sincere esteem for Sterne by Diderot, is the end of the *Tristram Shandy* frame in *Jacques* and the conclusion of Trim's story of his adventure with the Beguine in Flanders. Sterne's text follows from Book VIII, chap. xxii.

It was on a Sunday in the afternoon, as I told your honour.

The old man and his wife had walked out—

There was not much as a duck or a duckling about the yard—

—When the fair Beguine came in to see me.

My wound was then in a fair way of doing well—the inflammation had been gone off for some time, but it was succeeded with an itching both above and below my knee, so insufferable, that I had not shut my eyes the whole night for it.

Let me see it, said she, kneeling down upon the ground parallel to my knee, and laying her hand upon the part below it—it only wants rubbing a little, said the Beguine; so covering it with the bed-clothes, she began with the forefinger of her right hand to rub under my knee, guiding her fore-finger backwards and forwards by the edge of the flannel which kept on the dressing.

In five or six minutes I felt slightly the end of her second finger—and presently it was laid flat with the other, and she continued rubbing in that way round and round for a good while; it then came into my head, that I should fall in love—I blushed when I saw how white a hand she had—I shall never, an' please your honour, behold another hand so white whilst I live—

—Not in that place; said my Uncle Toby—

Though it was the most serious despair in nature to the corporal—he could not forbear smiling.

The young Beguine, continued the corporal, perceiving it was of great service to me—from rubbing for some time, with two fingers—proceeded to rub at length, with three—till by little and little she brought down the fourth, and then rubbed with her whole hand: I will never say another word, an' please your honour, upon hands again—but it was softer than satin—

—Prithee, Trim, commend it as much as thou wilt, said my uncle Toby; I shall hear thy story with the more delight— The corporal thanked his master most unfeignedly; but having nothing to say upon the Beguine's hand but the same over again—he proceeded to the effects of it.

The fair Beguine, said the corporal, continued rubbing with her whole hand under my knee—till I feared her zeal would worry her—"I would do a thousand times more," said she, "for the love of Christ"— In saying which, she passed her hand across the flannel, to the part above my knee, which I had equally complained of, and rubbed it also.

I perceived, then, I was beginning to be in love—

As she continued rub-rub-rubbing—I felt it spread from under her hand, an' please your honour, to every part of my frame—

The more she rubbed, and the longer strokes she took—the more the fire kindled in my veins—till at length, by two or three strokes longer than the rest—my passion rose to the highest pitch—I seized her hand—

—And then thou clapped'st it to thy lips, Trim, said my uncle Toby—and madest a speech.

Whether the corporal's amour terminated precisely in the way my uncle Toby described it, is not material; it is enough that it contained in it the essence of all the love romances which ever had been wrote since the beginning of the world.

82. . . . . *et la baisa:* A basic difference between the French and English languages forbids translation here. The translation might be either "and kissed it" (as seen later) or "and kissed her," or something somewhat more involved. Although the change in the meaning of the verb *baiser* is assumed to come later, in the nineteenth century, it seems clear to me that this is an example of an incipient change, perhaps of popular language at the time. This is all the more evident in the light of changes in the *FV*.

text made by Diderot's puritanical son-in-law. Throughout the *FV.* text all passages of an offensive and ambiguous nature are either deleted or changed to innocuous wording. In one case, however, such a change would seem to prove our point. In the story of the pastry-man (p. 86), the word *baiser* has been changed in *FV.* to *coucher avec,* probably with the idea that the sense of the passage is unavoidable but that the second term is less offensive than the first. Cf. also the much earlier (*c.* 1670) popular song "Laissez baiser vos filles" in *Histoire de France par les chansons* (Paris: Gallimard, 1956). In this later passage the family censor must have been napping, or felt helpless to improve the difficult *double-entendre.*

83. *Mandrin:* As Belaval points out, there is a clash in the skeletal time plan already seen in *Jacques* if the reader is to assume that this gang is still led by Mandrin. Mandrin (1724–1755) recruited forces from 1754 on and laid siege to Languedoc, Forez, Bresse, Lyonnais, Bourgogne, Franche-Comté, and Auvergne. Betrayed by his mistress, he was taken by a governmental regiment and executed in 1755. The presence of such bands of outlaws in France is a reflection of continuing bad times suggested throughout *Jacques.*

84. *Zeno and Spinoza:* If it had not been clear before, the presence of Spinoza here in the conclusion shows that Jacques's strange doctrine is inspired (rightly or wrongly) by Spinoza, a philosopher for whom Diderot had much, although certainly not uncritical, admiration. The case of Zeno is even clearer, for throughout the novel Diderot has put into Jacques's mouth many of the key words of Zeno's philosophy used by Diderot himself elsewhere, either in his work on Claude and Nero (in reality, on Seneca), which comes after *Jacques,* or in the article "Stoicism" in the *Encyclopédie.* There can be no doubt that Diderot refers here to Zeno of Citium, founder of the Stoic school. Despite a certain confusion of Zenos on the part of the editors of the *Oeuvres complètes,* Diderot knew his Zenos well; it is for the Stoic Zeno, as later for the Stoic Seneca, that he shows the greater sympathy. Zeno of Elea is always referred to by Diderot as the Eleatic; see article "Eleatic" in the *Encyclopédie.*